RED LIGHTNING
BLACK THUNDER

COLONEL JIMMIE H. BUTLER, USAF (RET.)

RED LIGHTNING

BLACK THUNDER

A DUTTON BOOK

DUTTON
Published by the Penguin Group
Penguin Books USA Inc., 375 Hudson Street, New York, New York 10014, U.S.A.
Penguin Books Ltd, 27 Wrights Lane, London W8 5TZ, England
Penguin Books Australia Ltd, Ringwood, Victoria, Australia
Penguin Books Canada Ltd, Ontario, Canada 10 Alcorn Avenue, Toronto, M4V 3B2
Penguin Books (N.Z.) Ltd, 182–190 Wairau Road, Auckland 10, New Zealand

Penguin Books Ltd, Registered Offices: Harmondsworth, Middlesex, England

First published by Dutton, an imprint of New American Library, a division of Penguin
Books USA Inc.
Distributed in Canada by McClelland & Stewart Inc.

First Printing, November, 1991
10 9 8 7 6 5 4 3 2 1

 REGISTERED TRADEMARK—MARCA REGISTRADA

LIBRARY OF CONGRESS CATALOGING IN PUBLICATION DATA:
Butler, Jimmie H.
Red lightning-black thunder / Jimmie H. Butler.
p.   cm.
ISBN 0-525-93377-8
I. Title.
PS3552.U82618R43   1991
813′.54 — dc20   91-4634
                                                                        CIP

PRINTED IN THE UNITED STATES OF AMERICA
Set in New Caledonia
Designed by Leonard Telesca

PUBLISHER'S NOTE
This is a work of fiction. Names, characters, places, and incidents either are the products of
the author's imagination or are used fictitiously, and any resemblance to actual persons, living or dead, events, or locales is entirely coincidental.

To
Camala Diane Butler
Recipient of the Los Angeles Area Chamber of Commerce
1987 Sands of Time Youth Award for being an outstanding young
lady in aviation.

At twenty-four years of age, my daughter Kami is already closing
on the five thousand hours of pilot time I logged in twenty-four years
of U.S. Air Force service. She has helped me better understand that
women pilots can be as dedicated and determined as were the men
I have flown with in peace and war. That perspective contributed to
the writing of *Red Lightning—Black Thunder*.

Thanks once again to Mr. Paul Gillette (*Carmela* and *Play Misty for Me*) for his friendship. Paul continues to be an indispensable mentor. His encouragement and counsel were extremely useful in the development of *Red Lightning—Black Thunder*.

Thanks to Mrs. Diane Nadson, who, as an accomplished artist, understands the creative process much better than I do. Her comments and critiques were always most helpful.

1

Two hundred fifty miles south of the Arctic Circle, *General-Mayor* (Brigadier General) Petr L. Novikov of the Soviet Strategic Rocket Forces stood near a windswept launchpad. In one gloved hand he held a stopwatch. His other hand held a teak and ivory cane. He wore black boots, a fur-collared greatcoat, and a traditional astrakhan cap, which looked like an eight-inch-tall, cylindrical crown of fur. Except for the insignia—a red star enclosed in gold—on the front of the cap, Novikov's appearance was more suggestive of his Cossack ancestors than of what he was: a high-tech genius of the late twentieth century.

A dozen military officers and civilian technicians stood with Novikov. Most of them preferred to watch from the warmth of a launch-control center instead of being outside in the subzero cold. But since the general had chosen to brave the frigid temperatures, the others could do no less.

Novikov was studying the activities on the launchpad. A locomotive and two large railroad cars were parked on rails that terminated on the pad. The two specially constructed cars, known collectively as a transporter-erector, were used to deliver satellites and their booster rockets from an assembly building two miles away. On this particular afternoon the cars carried an operational booster. The payload was a dummy—a conglomeration of spare parts combined to match the mass, size, and shape of the actual satellites. Novikov demanded realistic simulations for his launch crews, but he would not risk damaging one of his expensive satellites.

The booster's length of nearly 140 feet made it larger than those normally used to launch satellites from the Northern Cosmodrome. It had been horizontal on the two cars as it traveled to the pad. Now powerful hydraulic cylinders on the transporter-erector were raising the nose, rotating the booster to point it toward snow-filled skies. The movement was controlled from behind the reinforced walls of the launch-control center, which was more than a mile away.

Although the most difficult task was being controlled remotely, there was plenty of manual work to be done. More than a dozen men scrambled around, moving quickly but deliberately. These men, members of Novikov's blue team, wore matched sets of blue cold-weather gear. Most of the men were extending hoses from pumping stations in two concrete bunkers near the launchpad. One bunker was connected by pipes to distant tanks of liquid fuel. Pipes from the other led to tanks filled with the oxidizer needed to burn the fuel in the combustion chambers.

Novikov commented when he noticed something that could be done more efficiently, but he was pleased with the progress. His blue team was cutting several minutes off the record set a day earlier by his green team.

He had been pushing his people hard, and they were responding well in spite of the repetitiveness of the rehearsals. He too was tiring of the practices, but the simulations were almost over. Minutes earlier, a messenger had told Novikov that Marshal of the Soviet Union Vadim Murashev wanted to discuss an important briefing. Now as Novikov felt the sting of wind-driven snow on his cheeks, he sensed that Murashev's call signaled the beginning of the real operation. Perhaps the next time his launch teams raced the clock, they would be raising boosters that had real satellites mounted on top.

In a few moments the booster was vertical, with the tip of its nose higher than a thirteen-story building. Four supporting arms—the launchpad's long, girderlike braces—rotated up against the rocket like petals of a flower closing for the night. As the weight of the rocket was transferred to the structure of the launchpad, the transporter-erector's main role was completed. A tower, which permitted access to the payload, clanked into place along the full length of the booster.

Like teams of blue firemen, the men pulled the fuel and oxidizer hoses to fittings near a cluster of exhaust nozzles beneath the booster. Only seconds were necessary to connect each hose, then the men moved toward Novikov and the others. Less than a minute later a small man wearing blue coveralls and a fur-trimmed parka scrambled from beneath the jumble of piping and nozzles. He clasped his hands above his head. This signal indicated that he had attached the umbilical cable, which connected the electronics of the booster to the launch-control center. When Novikov's chief engineer saw the signal, he sounded a blast on a whistle.

Novikov clicked his watch as all faces looked toward him. "Seven minutes better than the record," he shouted enthusiastically.

He shifted his weight and raised his cane, which had relieved some of the pressure on his stiff right leg. Like a Cossack general using his sword to signal a cavalry charge, Novikov whipped his cane skyward, then roared like a bear. His widely recognized growl of enthusiasm dated back to when he had been a high-scoring center on the national hockey team. The workers on the launchpad growled back like a cheering section.

Novikov smiled broadly. His appearance brought to mind a professional athlete a few pounds beyond his prime. When he smiled, he looked as if he could be on a poster extolling the supremacy of Soviet cosmonauts. And indeed he had been. His achievements as a cosmonaut had earned admiration and glory, but his exploits in space had not been without cost—a shattered right knee and a scar that left a slight gap in the hairline behind his right temple. These were permanent reminders of the period of his life he had spent living on the edge. Seven years ago he had been injured during a crash landing that ended his third mission in space—and his career as a cosmonaut.

He was a favorite of Soviet President Grigoriev, and Novikov's standing with the Soviet people was barely less than that bestowed upon Colonel Yuri Gagarin—the man who first carried the Soviet banner into space. The young general's popularity was even greater with the men and women who worked for him here at the Northern Cosmodrome near Plesetsk. His willingness to forsake warmth and comfort to share the hardships facing his crews was just one of his leadership qualities that inspired loyalty.

The muted light of the March day was fading to the darker grays of evening, and Novikov checked the time. An American reconnaissance satellite would pass overhead in about an hour and a half. So far, the enemy satellites had not seen his practices or preparations—other than the modifications done to the two launchpads a few months earlier. He was determined to maintain the secrecy until his teams were cleared to give a performance the Americans in the Pentagon would not forget.

Turning to his chief engineer, Novikov said, "You have eighty-five minutes to get under cover, Dimitri."

"Yes, Comrade General."

In less than an hour, the booster would be in the assembly building.

Meanwhile, Marshal Murashev's telephone call had to be returned. Novikov used his cane as he walked briskly to his black limousine. A few minutes later he reached his complex of offices in the Military Research and Development Center at Kochmas. After telling his secretary to get Marshal Murashev's secretary on the line, Novikov went into the private office he had used for more than three years. An aide brought in a cup of hot tea as Novikov removed the heavy clothing that had permitted him to stay so long on the launchpad.

Sipping his tea, he had mixed feelings about the upcoming conversation. He was eager for orders but was concerned about the role that Marshal Murashev might want to take. Murashev was the commander-in-chief of the Strategic Rocket Forces, arguably the most powerful single military force in the world. Like most of the older generation of marshals and generals, he had little expertise, experience, or interest in satellites and space vehicles. Novikov often repeated Murashev's boasts about entering Berlin as a seventeen-year-old tank commander in 1945. While Novikov's words sounded like praise and admiration, there was always an unsaid message: Murashev had a tank commander's mentality, afraid or unable to comprehend the worth of military spacecraft orbiting high above a worldwide battlefield.

Novikov felt again his resentment for the system that put mediocre men in charge. Murashev had never been a cosmonaut or even assigned at one of the cosmodromes. He had put in years of undistinguished service with the Soviets' fleet of intercontinental ballistic missiles (ICBMs). That experience—and years of personal loyalty to the minister of defense—had elevated Murashev to his powerful position. Thus, the marshal concentrated on the ICBMs and generally ignored space systems. In many respects Novikov preferred it that way, since Murashev seldom meddled—except at critical times such as this.

Novikov was starting to feel warm again when his secretary said that Marshal Murashev was about to come onto the line.

Murashev got right to the point. "Petr, come to Moscow in the morning. We have to prepare a presentation of *Krasnaya Molniya* [Red Lightning]."

Despite the short notice, Novikov was pleased. At last the sequence of events was starting and might advance quickly. "Yes, Comrade Marshal," Novikov said. "When should I expect to brief?"

"You won't," Murashev said firmly. "I will. You must prepare the materials and the script."

Good and bad, Novikov thought as a look of cautious enthusiasm crossed his face. Murashev would not take so much interest unless the briefing was for the president. In a way that pleased Novikov. With one signature, President Grigoriev could order *Krasnaya Molniya* into motion. Unfortunately, preparing Murashev would be much harder for Novikov than giving the briefing himself.

There was little time for contemplation before Murashev added, "Also, bring material on *Cherniy Grom* [Black Thunder]. I don't expect to brief it, but there might be questions."

Novikov winced. *Cherniy Grom* should not have been mentioned on a telephone, even on a secure line. Murashev's carelessness about the Soviet space program was one of the things Novikov resented but never expressed.

"I'll bring what's needed, Comrade Marshal," Novikov said, then asked when to report. He wanted to divert Murashev from additional discussions of the two highly classified operations.

After finishing the conversation and ordering his aide to arrange for an airplane, Novikov took four thick folders from his safe. All were marked with the double red lightning bolts he had adopted as the symbol of *Krasnaya Molniya*.

Four years earlier in developing concepts for ballistic missile defense, American researchers had solved one major problem: their breakthrough in laser technology had increased greatly the effective range of space-based laser weapons. The Americans had not, however, solved the financial problem: how to afford to put enough satellites into orbit to defeat a mass attack of hundreds of ballistic missiles launched within a few minutes.

Novikov had immediately recognized the value of the American discovery and had proposed *Krasnaya Molniya*, a bold plan to get such weapons into orbit first. His proposal was not aimed at defending against ballistic missiles, however. Even with the infusions of capital from the West that had come in the last few years, the Soviet economy also could not afford that many satellite-borne lasers. But, Novikov had argued successfully, the Soviets could afford a few, and those few could achieve an objective that far outweighed their costs. With less than a dozen armed satellites placed in carefully selected orbits, he could control *access to space*.

As he selected items from the folders, his mind raced ahead. He could only speculate about how soon he might be ordered to implement the plan. Once he received the go-ahead, there would be little time to address details overlooked during preparation.

He picked up a two-page summary of the communications required to support the launches of the satellites of *Krasnaya Molniya*, paused for a moment, then pressed a button on his intercom panel. A few seconds later, *Polkovnik* (Colonel) Vitali Bobylev, Novikov's chief of staff, entered through a side door.

"Implement Operation Distant Seas," Novikov said, "at priority-level two."

"Yes, Comrade General," Bobylev said, then left to carry out the order.

Distant Seas called for the Soviet's two largest Space Event Support Ships to sail to operational areas. Priority-level two instructed the captains to put to sea within thirty hours of receiving their orders. He was starting the race a little early, Novikov thought, but waiting for Marshal Murashev to make the decision would start the ships too late. Novikov preferred to have the ships in place waiting on the rockets instead of having the rockets waiting on the ships.

Silently cursing the old marshal, Novikov was determined to keep his contempt for Murashev to himself and continue to be a good soldier. Novikov had put his sweat and soul into *Krasnaya Molniya*. In spite of Murashev's bumbling intervention, Novikov expected to succeed, and he was planning to claim the additional rank and status he deserved.

In Washington, D.C., on the afternoon of the same day, reporters gathered in the White House briefing room. Jeff Marsh, the president's press secretary, stepped to the podium.

"As you all know," he said in a friendly manner, "last October President Anderson ordered a blue-ribbon panel of distinguished Americans to review our Defender satellite program. Today I am pleased to announce the president's decision, which was made with benefit of the panel's meticulous study. The following is the president's statement:

" 'Fellow Americans, today I am determined to take a step that will make the future safer for us and our children. I have carefully considered the Kirkpatrick report submitted to me late last month. Naturally, in our great nation of diverse opinions, there are strongly held feelings on both sides of the question of putting armed satellites into space. I have sided with those who believe that if there are to be superpower confrontations—intended or accidental—the farther away they occur from our fragile earth, the better.

" 'Our Defender satellites have a defensive mission. They do not threaten the balance of power that has maintained peace between the United States and the Soviet Union for half a century. They are not designed to provide a comprehensive defense against intercontinental ballistic missiles. The full constellation of four Defender satellites and an on-orbit spare would make little difference against a full-scale attack.

" 'What the Defenders can do is even more important. As president, I am convinced that these defensive satellites could prevent tragedy in the event of an accidental missile launch—by either side. And as we approach the twenty-first century, there's the increasing possibility of nuclear blackmail. Clearly, we need insurance against terrorists or third world countries that might gain access to a nuclear-tipped ballistic missile.

" 'Therefore, I have this day ordered the secretary of defense to take all necessary actions to launch the Defender I satellite as soon as that reasonably can be done.' "

Marsh folded the copy, indicating that he was finished with the official statement. "President Anderson's words are clear, but I'll be glad to address any questions."

Numerous hands shot up, and Marsh selected the first questioner.

"When and where will the first satellite be launched?"

"We expect to see Defender I in orbit in about a month," Marsh said. "The Air Force will launch the satellite from Cape Canaveral in Florida."

The next questioner asked, "Is there a particular reason that the president didn't make this announcement personally?"

Marsh smiled and did not disguise that his answer was somewhat facetious. "Fred, you know he's a busy man. His words are clear enough that he didn't feel the need to be here for additional interpretation."

The questioner was not deterred by the vague answer. "Wouldn't it be more accurate to say he's choosing a low profile, since the decision to launch Defender I will upset many people here and in Russia?"

"Defender's not a low-profile program in any way," Marsh said, maintaining the calm professionalism that characterized all his dealings with the press. "Certainly, the Soviets have made a determined effort on many fronts to get the president to cancel Defender. President Anderson is just as determined to act, but he sees no reason to be openly confrontational."

Another questioner said, "President Grigoriev has claimed that the Soviet people will consider our placing armed satellites in orbit to be a serious provocation. How can President Anderson ignore the concerns of the Soviet president?"

"Need I remind everyone," Marsh said, "that the first armed satellites were tested in orbit a quarter of a century ago—and those antisatellite weapons, or ASATs, belonged to the Soviet Union?"

"But you're talking about a crude ASAT with only a one-shot capability. That's—"

"But," Marsh interrupted, "it's an operational capability with enough interceptors and launch vehicles at Tyuratam to take several shots a day."

"It's still old technology, nothing compared to the high-tech Defender with laser weaponry."

"True," Marsh said, seeming to enjoy the questions, "but just remember that the North Vietnamese shot down hundreds of American aircraft with old technology. Nevertheless, the Soviet ASATs make the arguments about protecting the 'sanctity of space' seem a bit insincere."

A new questioner asked, "Can you review the Defender's capabilities for us?"

"Nothing's changed from the design we were ready to launch last year. The satellites will orbit about twenty-two thousand miles above the earth. Their sensors can detect rocket launches, and there's some on-board ability to track the potential target. The Defenders' lasers can then fire down on a selected target. Fact sheets on the Defender are available at the exits, along with the president's statement. Since many of you would like to file your stories, I'll take one more question."

"President Grigoriev has made several statements that characterize

Defender as much more ominous than you do. Could such a misconception lead to some form of retaliation by the Soviets?"

"We have to hope that common sense and good reason will prevail in the Kremlin," Marsh said. "The Soviets fully understand the Defenders' capabilities—and their limitations. If President Grigoriev is confused about the defensive nature of the Defender, perhaps some of his generals need to explain that to him."

2

Near Patrick Air Force Base, Florida
Saturday, 6 March, 0920 local (1420 GMT)

U.S. Air Force Colonel Mike Chisholm was one of four passengers on a C-21 jet that was approaching the main runway at Patrick for landing. Although he preferred piloting to riding in the back, he was always glad to get out of Washington, D.C., even if only for a few hours. His real love was flying airplanes, and he had spent much of his career piloting C-141 jet transports throughout the free world. Now in his early forties, he had begrudgingly accepted the bitter lesson that most pilots learned: Air Force flying was primarily a younger man's—or woman's—game. The only colonels who flew with any regularity were those lucky few in senior positions in the operational flying units of the Air Force.

When the time had come to enter a specialty other than flying, Chisholm had chosen to stay at the leading edge of the Air Force of the future. For the last five years he had worked on American military space systems and closely followed Soviet space operations, trying to interpret their potential threat to the land, sea, air, and space forces of the United States. He often could surmise what the mission might be—communications, reconnaissance, strategic warning, navigation, electronic intelligence (ELINT), weather—just by knowing a Soviet satellite's altitude, the shape of its orbit, and how the orbit was oriented in relation to the equator. Now his insights into space warfare far outstripped those of most of his contemporaries and the generals above them.

While becoming deeply impressed with space systems, Chisholm had recognized that the Air Force he belonged to was still guided by lifelong students of air warfare, who had a much more limited knowledge of space. Three years ago he had written a paper that compared the U.S. Air Force in the 1990s to the U.S. Army of the 1930s, when few leaders understood the potential of aircraft—until airpower was demonstrated in German blitzkriegs and Japanese air attacks. Most of his friends had predicted that his controversial treatise had effectively capped his career at the rank of lieutenant colonel. Instead he had been assigned immediately to the Pentagon as the primary adviser on space systems for General Frank Ramsey, the U.S.A.F. vice chief of staff.

Since being promoted to colonel the following year, Chisholm had become the Air Force's unofficial spokesman for Defender. Every time there had been a technical problem or someone had decided it was time to slash Defender's budget, he had been sent to Capitol Hill. Fighting the endless budget battle was a wearisome task Chisholm had little enthusiasm for. Yet his vast knowledge of space issues and the integrity he projected had been very effective, even with senators, congressmen, and staffers eager to build reputations as DoD watchdogs. Occasional visits such as this, where he could see the hardware and talk to people working with it, were one way he made sure he had all the right answers, all the time.

The president's decision to launch Defender I had set many actions into motion. Two of the most important were taking place at Cape Canaveral on this sunny Saturday morning, less than seventy-two hours after the White House press conference. A C-5 Galaxy had landed at Cape Canaveral less than an hour before Chisholm was scheduled to arrive at nearby Patrick Air Force Base. During the night the giant aircraft had flown the Defender I from an aerospace manufacturing plant on the west coast. Delivery of the satellite to the launch base was a significant milestone. Another was the movement of the booster rocket from its assembly building to the launchpad. The huge booster was being moved even as Chisholm's C-21 crossed the perimeter fence and landed smoothly on the runway at Patrick.

Those two events and a couple of questions had brought Chisholm to Florida. When he stepped off the aircraft, he was greeted by Colonel Ken Davis, a friend of many years. Davis was the commander of the Eastern Space and Missile Center at Patrick. He was responsible for all military space launches from Air Force pads at Cape Canaveral.

After the initial exchange of greetings, Davis smiled and said, "Mike, my lieutenants have about five hundred slides ready to dazzle you with."

With an exaggerated frown, Chisholm said, "I suppose the briefing begins with 'And the earth was without form and void.'"

"We don't go back quite that far, but you've been a Washington wizard so long that I was afraid you wouldn't recognize the hardware anymore."

"I haven't had the lobotomy yet," Chisholm said. He and Davis had often complained about how people—military and civilians alike—seemed to lose their perspective of the real world once they started working within the beltway surrounding the nation's capital.

"In that case," Davis said, gesturing toward a helicopter that was parked nearby, "you'd probably prefer an aerial review to the briefing."

"I prefer flying to briefings, any time and any place," Chisholm said as he picked up his briefcase and started toward the helicopter.

In a few minutes the helicopter lifted off, crossed above the morning traffic on Highway A1A, and passed over the white sand beach separating the base from the Atlantic Ocean. The pilot turned north toward Cape Canaveral Air Force Station, which was on the coast between Patrick Air Force Base and NASA's Kennedy Space Center.

"If I'd known you had a personal helicopter," Chisholm said, "I'd have tried to steal your job long ago."

"The chopper's temporary. It's part of the security package we've worked out with the Army and National Guard. When we're moving the hardware like today, we bring in the air cover."

"General Ramsey wanted me to get an update on your security plans," Chisholm said.

"He's not worried about our being able to handle Defender, is he?"

"His concern's pretty much my fault," Chisholm said. "I've convinced him that the Soviets must react to Defender in some way. We're hoping sabotage isn't their answer."

Davis looked uneasy. "Do you have any intelligence reports that I'm not privy to?"

"Not threatening sabotage. That seems like their low-probability option. Personally, I'm more curious about how General Novikov's been spending all his rubles for the last few years."

"After the stops and starts we've experienced," Davis said, referring to the funding uncertainties that had plagued the American program, "he should've had a whole Star Wars constellation in orbit before we were ready to fly."

Chisholm nodded. If the cold war had not given way to detente and Perestroika, both nations would have invested more money to drive the technology to its limits. Even during these years Chisholm had remained suspicious that it was a lack of money, and not a lack of ambition, that had brought a retreat from Lenin's goal of world domination.

"I have one special request. I'd like to get a good look at a launchpad that we modified for our old Titan Twos."

The Titan II had been the nation's "heavy" intercontinental ballistic missile (ICBM) for many years, until those liquid-fueled ICBMs were considered too dangerous to maintain in their underground silos. In the mid-1980s more than fifty were removed from strategic alert and some had been modified to become boosters for American satellites.

"Sure," Davis said, "but here's something you may want to see first."

The helicopter had flown north of Cocoa Beach and reached the military complex at Cape Canaveral. The pilot banked the helicopter, and Davis pointed toward a crowd gathered where a road entered the complex.

"We've got about two hundred fifty demonstrators at the south gate this morning. Everything's peaceful, and I expect it'll stay that way."

"I suppose," Chisholm said, "that when the White House publicizes our operational schedule, we can't expect any privacy." He had been surprised the previous day when a presidential spokesman had announced both the transfer of the satellite and the movement of the booster to the pad. Chisholm's security instincts preferred that such announcements come after the event. However, he had spent enough time defending Defender I on Capitol Hill to know that the political aspects usually overshadowed military considerations.

"That was fine with us," Davis said. "We get an opportunity to test our security procedures with a smaller crowd than the one we expect the day we launch."

Chisholm agreed. He was certain that the launch of Defender I would draw thousands of protestors.

Davis pointed at the first crossroad inside the gate. "We've got two companies of Army troops at the next intersection."

"Army?" Chisholm saw numerous vehicles and troops in an area beyond the view of the demonstrators.

"For close-in security at the launch sites, we rely on our own Emergency Response Teams. However, using the Army makes sure we don't get drawn too thin handling perimeter security if demonstrators show up by the thousands."

The helicopter continued north toward the launchpads.

Whenever Chisholm visited this high-tech gateway to the future, he always experienced the same feeling of irony. The man-made satellites that routinely rocketed from these sandy shores were governed by laws of motion postulated when men could only dream of reaching out into the heavens. The seventeenth-century works of Sir Isaac Newton and the German astronomer Johannes Kepler had explained why planets followed elliptical orbits around the sun. Three centuries later, scientists finally proved that man-made satellites would follow similar orbits around the earth.

The consequence that interested Chisholm the most was that the immutable laws of physics restricted the movements of spacecraft. Therefore satellites moved much more predictably than aircraft, ships, and tanks. That was one thing he loved about the space business: learn a few basics—including what could be ignored, and what couldn't—and much of the mystery disappeared.

Ahead he saw launch towers—past and present—standing like silent sentinels guarding the sacred ground from which man had left the earth for the moon. Farther away he identified the launchpads that had served the space shuttle in triumph and in tragedy. He was stirred by the sense of modern history represented in the few miles of coastline stretched out before him.

At times like this he also felt a twinge of regret that he had decided against becoming an astronaut. Early in his career he had declined an opportunity to enter training. Then, his driving ambition had been to become an Air Force general. As an astronaut spending years away from the operational Air Force, he would have had almost no chance of achieving that goal. Nearly twenty years later he had gotten close, but he had not served in the command assignments given those being groomed for a star. Perhaps, he thought, the sense of failure that occasionally welled up inside of him would have been easier to rationalize if he'd had a couple of space flights to his credit.

In a couple of minutes the helicopter was over the vertical integration building, where the giant boosters for the Defender satellites were assembled. Two parallel sets of rails led from the assembly building onto a level roadbed nearly two miles long. As Chisholm followed the rails with his eyes, he saw the booster for Defender I just a few hundred yards short of the launchpad. Unlike Soviet launch vehicles that were transported horizontally, American boosters stood vertical as their transporters moved them to the pads.

From more than a mile away the booster did not look particularly intimidating. As the helicopter moved closer, Chisholm became more impressed. One of the new Advance Launch System (ALS) design, the booster stood nearly 150 feet tall and was capable of placing up to 160,000 pounds into orbit. The booster would be even taller when the upper stage and satellite were added.

The booster was on a large transporter that was inching along so slowly the movement was hardly noticeable from the air. Chisholm studied the booster and the transporter, which also was a mobile launch platform. The area beneath the booster was open, so that the exhaust could pass through into the flame-deflector pit. An umbilical mast, which was about 10 percent taller than the booster, was part of the platform. The mast helped support the vertical booster and also included the cabling that would power the electronics until seconds before lift-off. During launch the platform and the mast would be subjected to the boosters' powerful exhaust and therefore go through a lengthy and costly refurbishment procedure before being used with another booster.

After circling a couple of times, the helicopter followed the tracks to the launchpad that would be used by Defender I. Just beyond the booster, the tracks climbed a long slope. Because Cape Canaveral was only a few feet higher than sea level, the launchpad was on a mound of earth that had been built up thirty feet above the surrounding sand, scrub brush, and marshes.

As the helicopter banked overhead, Chisholm could see into a concrete pit designed to deflect the flaming exhaust into a horizontal tunnel 150 feet long. The tunnel—an exhaust duct made of concrete—provided an escape route not only for the exhaust plume but for the thunderous roar that shook the earth and the sky in the few seconds after the powerful rockets ignited. Otherwise, the sonic vibrations might damage the satellite during lift-off.

Standing next to the flame pit, the umbilical tower also would be subjected to the scorching heat and fury of the exhaust plumes. The tower, which was two hundred feet tall, had roll-out platforms at fifteen levels that would be used for maintenance and servicing the booster. Refurbishment of the tower was one of the time-consuming jobs that had to be completed before the launchpad could be used again.

Within the next few hours the transporter would come to a stop next to the tower, positioning the ALS directly over the pit. Then a mobile service tower, the most imposing structure of the entire complex, would move into position, fitting snugly around both the booster and the umbilical tower.

As Chisholm studied the mobile tower, he was reminded again of the immense scale of equipment needed to make space operations possible. Built on rails, the tower stood thirty stories tall and weighed five million pounds.

Among other things, the mobile tower provided elevators and an environmentally controlled room over the top of the booster. Then, protected within the room from the thunderstorms, wind, and humidity of the Florida coast, workers could mate the upper-stage booster and the satellite on top of the main booster. The stack would be complete when a fairing was installed on top to protect the spacecraft as the booster rocketed through the atmosphere. After fuel and oxidizer were loaded into the booster's tanks, the mobile service tower would be moved and parked six hundred feet away to minimize damage during the launch.

As the helicopter circled, Davis pointed out the perimeter security posts and the roads used by roving teams. He was mainly concerned with periods of time when the booster was exposed. While encased in the mobile service tower, the booster would be protected in the tower's web of steel. Davis planned to increase his security patrols in the last few hours before launch, when the booster would stand unprotected beside the umbilical tower.

Chisholm was pleased with the security plan and assured Davis that it would satisfy General Ramsey.

There was no reason to land, so Davis directed the pilot to fly to a launchpad used for the modified Titan IIs. A few minutes later the helicopter circled, and Chisholm studied the launchpad. The umbilical tower, mobile service tower, flame-deflector pit, and rest of the hardware were similar to those on the pad for Defender I. The major difference was in scale. The equipment he could see below was sized for the Titan II, which was about 30 percent smaller than the ALS.

"I've had my eyes on a pair of launchpads at Plesetsk," Chisholm said. "Novikov seems to be sizing the pads for the SS-18s the Soviets have been pulling out of their silos."

During the fall and winter Chisholm had studied pictures showing the progress of Soviet construction crews. Since 10 percent of the facilities at Plesetsk were always undergoing some kind of modernization, most other American analysts had taken a "so-what?" attitude.

Davis looked curious. "I haven't heard of them using the SS-18 for a space booster, but that wouldn't surprise me."

Hundreds of Soviet satellites had been launched on boosters that had served as intercontinental ballistic missiles. As the Soviets replaced older ICBMs with modern versions, the retired missiles were shipped to one of the cosmodromes. The American space program had benefited from similar conversions, but in much smaller numbers than the Soviets, who updated their ICBMs continually. Chisholm's current interest was the SS-18 Satan. Capable of sending ten nuclear warheads nearly seven thousand miles, the Satan had been the Soviets' most powerful ICBM for years. He thus expected the Satans to carry heavier satellites than those launched on earlier ICBMs.

"General Novikov's got me confused," Chisholm said. "From last summer to about Christmas, his crews worked like beavers ripping apart a couple of old pads. His troops installed the basics for a pair of new pads, then seemed to quit."

"Maybe they're finished," Davis said.

Chisholm scanned the intricate support equipment on the pad below. "The Soviet pads sure don't look like this one. They have the normal supporting arms above a flame pit and a couple of fueling bunkers, but there's almost no external wiring or plumbing that might be damaged during a launch."

Davis smiled. "Plesetsk's average temp's about seventy degrees colder than here. Maybe Novikov's waiting for spring to finish."

"Could be," Chisholm said, "but he's had people on both pads since the construction stopped."

"Really?" Davis looked more interested.

"I've seen marks in the fresh snow. Several times there's been new ice along the railroad tracks."

"A train's melting some of his snow?"

Chisholm nodded. "But we never see a soul on those pads in any of the pictures."

"They routinely refurbish launchpads much faster than we do. We could bury our plumbing and cabling if your green-eyeshade folks in the Pentagon wanted to shovel money our way for a rapid-reload capability."

"Sorry, Ken," Chisholm said, waving his hands above his head in a time-out signal, "but I'm here for advice, not for a copy of your wish list."

"Okay. Get me some pictures, but your description sounds like very clean pads designed for rapid relaunch."

"I was afraid you were going to say that," Chisholm said with a wary smile. He had already reached the same conclusion. If the pads at Plesetsk were finished, and if they were for the Satans, Chisholm wondered why General Novikov was being so secretive about his preparations.

Davis directed the pilot to land at the runway that was used to bring satellites to Cape Canaveral.

Well before the helicopter reached the airstrip, Chisholm saw a C-5 Galaxy. One of the largest airplanes in the world, the C-5 carried cargo such as Defender I that would not fit into any other American aircraft. Green and brown camouflage paint helped the transport blend into the surroundings but seemed incongruous on such a large aircraft. After all, he thought, even with the C-5 parked at sea level, the top of the sixty-five-foot-tall tail was higher than much of Florida.

The helicopter circled the C-5, then landed nearby. As Chisholm and Davis stepped to the parking ramp, an AC-130 flew across the airfield at a thousand feet. The left side of the aircraft bristled with a 105-millimeter howitzer, rapid-fire cannons, and targeting sensors. Chisholm was surprised to see the heavily-armed gunship, which had been nicknamed Spectre during the Vietnam War.

Chisholm said, "Spectre? You *are* taking security seriously."

"If the KGB were to mount a commando attack," Davis said, "Spectre would even the odds. However, we're mainly taking advantage of the sensors the gunships carry."

As the helicopter lifted off, Davis went on to explain that it was almost impossible to seal off the more than thirty miles of boundaries around the launch base. In addition, much of Cape Canaveral was covered with scrub brush and scattered stands of pine trees that offered abundant cover for infiltrators. So Davis was concentrating most of his security forces around the actual launch facilities, which occupied a small portion of the base. The sensors on the AC-130 would search surrounding areas and warn of intruders.

Chisholm assumed that the Soviets would like to see the Defender launch fail, even though he doubted they would risk a commando attack on American soil. "Do your local sources suggest any particular threat?"

"The Communist party circulates lots of leaflets," Davis said. "They try to turn out a crowd to picket at the gates during some of the missile tests. Most of the demonstrators are college-age kids."

"Just looking to raise a little hell and get an extra day in the sun?"

"Generally," Davis said, then added with a smile, "I suspect that the romantics among them just want to claim they were making it in the woods while rockets thundered in the sky."

"General Ramsey will be pleased to hear your assessment," Chisholm said with a wry smile.

"If the sensors indicate someone's hiding in the brush, we've got security teams with helicopters ready to check it out. At that point, I try our own brand of psywar before I order the troops to start beating the bushes."

"Psychological warfare?" Chisholm knew the term had been used in the Vietnam War when leaflets were dropped or loudspeakers used to try to influence people hiding in the jungles.

"Sure," Davis said with a smile. "I make a broadcast telling them to leave our alligators and water moccasins alone. That convinces most of the intruders to come out of the weeds and welcome a helicopter ride to dry ground."

"You take all the fun out of it, Ken."

"I hope so."

The two colonels were greeted by the project team chief, who reported that the offloading of the Defender I was going smoothly. The chief also provided a short briefing of checkout procedures the satellite would go through in the days that followed.

Following the briefing Davis was called aside to discuss an unrelated problem, so Chisholm walked closer to watch the offloading of the satellite. A large shipping container protected the half-billion dollars' worth of computers, electronics, and other technical gadgetry that made up Defender I. There was little to see other than the container being winched slowly from the cargo deck of the C-5 onto the bed of a specially constructed trailer.

Chisholm recognized a tall, black sergeant on the other side of the trailer. Approaching the sergeant from behind, Chisholm said, "Sergeant Blake, you've got this bird camouflaged so well I almost couldn't find it."

Senior Master Sergeant Anthony Blake turned and smiled broadly when he recognized Chisholm. Gesturing toward the aircraft that towered above them, Blake said, "I told them it wouldn't work, Colonel, unless we painted the tires red and hid it in a strawberry patch."

As Blake spoke, he saluted Chisholm. Military protocol did not require the exchange of salutes on the flight line, so Blake's gesture was one of genuine respect. Chisholm returned the salute with equal regard, then extended his hand. Blake had been one of the youngest men in the Air Force to earn the seven stripes of a senior master sergeant and even now was only in his early thirties.

Years earlier Blake had been a C-141 loadmaster in Chisholm's squadron, and the two men had flown together many times. Chisholm and Blake had once fought their way out of a terrorist ambush just outside Clark Air Base in the Philippines. Since then, they had shared a special bond that transcended the normal separation between officers and enlisted personnel.

After exchanging greetings, Chisholm said, "I never expected to see you with Fat Albert." He used the fliers' nickname for the C-5, which was not as sleek as the smaller C-141.

"Just part time, Colonel," Blake said. He gestured toward the unit patch on the shoulder of his flight suit. "I'm in stan/eval at Twenty-second, so I'm checked out on all the birds."

Blake's assignment to standardization/evaluation at 22nd Air Force confirmed what Chisholm already knew: Blake was one of the most capable loadmasters in the Military Airlift Command. Although often the most junior-ranking members of a C-141 crew, the loadmasters had to ensure the airplane was loaded safely, no matter how heavy, bulky, or dangerous the cargo was. Blake's main responsibility was to administer flight evaluations to other loadmasters, making sure they were qualified to handle the difficult job.

"I was hoping you hadn't taken leave of your senses in your old age," Chisholm said with a smile. Both men had always preferred the C-141.

"This was such a high visibility mission," Blake said, "that the commander wanted me to tag along."

Chisholm nodded mischievously. "Just in case the winch broke and they needed someone to carry the satellite off the plane?"

"Negative," Blake said, smiling at the compliment. Even the unflattering Air Force-issue flight suit did not hide Blake's physique, which could have been that of a tight end on a professional football team. "The general's more interested in my brain than my body. But this crew knows its business, and they don't need any meddling by me."

Chisholm looked around, then gestured toward a water-filled canal off to the side of the parking ramp. "It should be a little quieter over there."

As they started in that direction, Blake asked, "How's Christie? She must be all grown up by now."

Chisholm nodded and an involuntary sigh betrayed his frustration. "She's nineteen and a great kid, but her mother's started her off in school in England this year." Moving around in the Air Force had made it hard enough for Chisholm to see his daughter while she was growing up in Atlanta. "I'm sure it's a great opportunity for Christie, but I wish she were closer to Washington. Speaking of kids that are growing up, how's my godson?"

Blake's son had been born shortly after the incident in the Philippines, and Chisholm had felt honored when he had been asked to sponsor the baby at the baptism.

"Little Tony's a head taller than everyone else in the third grade," Blake said with pride. "I've been getting him ready so that next time you see him, he should be able to handle your fastball."

Chisholm laughed, realizing how happy he was to have run into Blake again. The frequent reassignments of an Air Force career tended to put friendships into suspended animation. Years later an unexpected encounter such as this rekindled the closeness almost as if it took place immediately after the last farewell.

He thought of the happier times in his life, which had included his friendship with Tony and Millie Blake. In those years he had been flying monthly, piloting C-141 Starlifters to the Far East, Australia, or other destinations. His life—personal and professional—

had been full and exciting, especially in comparison to the bureaucratic quagmire that characterized so much of his work in Washington, D.C.

At the canal Chisholm picked up a rock and pitched it at a branch
sticking up from a downed tree trunk near the far side.

When the rock clipped off the top of the branch, Blake nodded
his approval and asked, "You still playing ball, sir?" They had played
together on squadron softball teams.

"Wish I were, Tony," Chisholm said. Years ago he had given up
the promise of a professional baseball career when he had entered
the Air Force Academy. Now he usually arrived at the Pentagon
before sunrise and stayed until after sunset, leaving no time for any
recreational sports. "How about you?"

"Being in the headquarters keeps me too busy for the leagues. I
did play in the annual enlisted versus officers charity game." Blake
paused, then continued with a smile, "Of course none of those officers
can play like you did. They were all doing their Michael Jackson
impersonation—running around with a glove on one hand for no
apparent reason."

Chisholm laughed as he selected another rock. "I'd probably look
that way myself. All my time's taken up trying to protect the money
for that satellite you lugged here from California." Chisholm rifled
the rock across the canal and knocked another piece off the branch.

"That sort of cuts into the love life, I suppose," Blake said.

"It would if I had one," Chisholm said, picking up another rock.

Just as Chisholm was about to release the rock, Blake said, "Had
you heard that Major Turner isn't married anymore, sir?"

The rock missed the log entirely. In those happier years there also
had been a woman—Sandra Turner, a young pilot who had shared
much of his life for more than three years. In the intervening six
years, neither his military assignments nor the women he had met
could match his memories of those special times. There were a million
ways he might have responded, but the only words that came out
were, "That's interesting."

"She'd been instructing in one-forty-ones down at Altus," Blake
said, referring to the Military Airlift Command's training unit at Altus
Air Force Base, Oklahoma, "and got back to Travis a year or so ago."

Chisholm's next rock bounced off the log near the base of the
branch. "I remember hearing she was going to Altus, but I'd lost
track of her in the last couple of years."

As he picked up another rock, Colonel Davis called out that he was finished.

"If you get out California way, Colonel," Blake said as he turned to walk back to the C-5, "please give us a call. Millie and I'd love to have you over for dinner."

"They keep me on a short leash at the Pentagon," Chisholm said, totally preoccupied with thoughts of seeing Sandi again, "but once the Defender gets into orbit, I might break away for a couple of days."

He fired the last rock across the water, shattering the rest of the branch.

3

The Defender I preparations in Florida were going smoother than expected, so Chisholm lost himself in personal thoughts during the commercial flight back to Washington, D.C. First he wrote a letter to his daughter, Christie, a task he tried to complete every couple of weeks, whether he had time to or not. Sometimes the press of his work left little more to write about than to assure Christie that her cat, Charmaine—which Chisholm had been the keeper of for nine years—was still doing fine. This time he was able to fill two pages about the trip to Florida and the visit with Sergeant Blake, whom Christie had met on summer visits.

Seeing Blake and hearing Sandi's name had stirred many pleasant memories, so Chisholm spent the rest of the time debating with himself about Sandi Turner. The affirmative side pressed for going to see her, hoping that both had become six years wiser since drifting apart. The negative reminded him that both were still pursuing careers, which at the moment had them separated by nearly three thousand miles.

Deep in such thoughts, he was looking at clouds obscuring the world beyond the wing of his commercial airliner when he felt a slight change in cabin pressure. Obviously, Chisholm thought without looking at his watch, the time had come for descent. Two minutes later, a flight attendant announced that the captain had started the descent to Dulles International Airport.

Chisholm pushed aside thoughts of Sandi and began concentrating instead on the captain's actions. The habit was left over from the days when Chisholm had flown as a check pilot. Then he had evaluated other Air Force pilots from a jump seat, just behind the radio console between the pilot and copilot.

Whenever Chisholm flew, he wished he were in the cockpit. Yet, while he could not see as well from seat 10A in the passenger cabin, he could tell almost as much from the sounds and feel of the airplane. Although the captain was smooth and the airliner remained within clouds, Chisholm noticed each descent and level-off as an air traffic controller cleared the aircraft down, by steps, toward the wooded hillsides of Virginia.

After a few minutes, the whirring flap motors told him that the aircraft was near enough to the ground to be configured for landing. Looking into the wispy whiteness beyond the window, he watched the flaps slide partway down on the aft edge of the wing. The approach setting for the flaps changed the effective shape of the wing thereby increasing the drag that would slow the aircraft.

The change in flap setting was followed forty-five seconds later by the noisiest step of the procedure. The heavy landing gear lifted off the up-locks, then swung down into the air rushing beneath the wings. Moments later the metallic clunking of the over-center locks told Chisholm that the main gear were safely extended.

Now the flap motors sounded, and the flaps took a more extreme position against the air flowing beneath the wings. The deceleration was more noticeable, and Chisholm felt the nose dip below the unseen horizon as the jetliner intercepted the glide slope toward the runway. An increase in engine noise told him that the captain had added power to hold the final-approach airspeed.

Hoping to catch glimpses of wooded suburbs or the sprawl of parking lots around shopping malls, Chisholm looked toward the ground. Instead he saw only the dull white of clouds that seemed to be moving with the airplane. He decided that the overcast was only a few hundred feet above the ground since the aircraft would have been at about a thousand feet when the captain had called for the final flap setting. Unless the ceiling was lower than three hundred feet, there was no cause for concern. Still, Chisholm preferred to fly in clear weather whenever someone else was at the controls.

Looking around, he saw an older couple sitting across the aisle. Their hands were clasped above the arm rest, and the woman's expression was grim. The man, looking as if he was trying hard to appear calm, gave Chisholm an uneasy smile. Chisholm was wearing his Air Force uniform and sensed that the man was hoping for re-assurance from someone more experienced in the mysteries of flight. Chisholm smiled broadly, gave a thumbs-up signal, then leaned casually against his headrest. A quick glance outside the window told him that the aircraft had broken out of the overcast well above the woods. The man said something to his wife, and she looked nervously across the aisle. Chisholm forced a yawn to signal his lack of concern about the upcoming landing.

Crossing the threshold of the runway, Chisholm was attuned to the signals the airplane was giving him. The throttles were in idle, and he felt the captain raise the nose to break the steady glide toward the concrete. Chisholm got a quick glimpse at a wind sock beside the runway—some crosswind, but not enough to worry him. He could tell that the nose was angled slightly into the wind as the captain held the tires just above the runway.

For a couple of seconds, Chisholm sensed that the landing was going to be very smooth. Nevertheless, the plane continued floating with the airspeed bleeding off as the nose rose almost imperceptibly. The extra couple of seconds in the air convinced Chisholm that while the landing was not going to be dangerous, the captain would never brag about it afterward.

From a few inches above the runway, the airplane dropped with a thud onto the concrete. The nose jerked left as the ground forcibly removed the last bit of crosswind-correction that the captain had overlooked.

About a five-and-a-half on a scale of ten, Chisholm thought as he heard the engines surge into reverse. Looking across the aisle where the couple sat frozen and wide-eyed, he called out, "No sweat." When he had their attention, he added with a wink, "I've made landings a lot worse than that."

The man laughed, and the woman forced a weak smile.

Chisholm had made worse landings, but seldom acknowledged them to anyone who had not been present. One of the few things he had disliked about piloting big airplanes was that you never could hide a bad landing from anyone who had shared the experience.

As the airplane taxied beneath sullen skies, Chisholm noticed a Soviet jetliner parked nearby. Under the watchful eyes of a U.S. Customs agent, workers were unloading luggage from a black limousine and a van. The agent checked the tags before each bag was placed on the conveyer belt leading into the cargo hold.

Obviously, Chisholm thought, the luggage had diplomatic immunity from inspection, and there were a lot of bags. He wondered what group of Soviets might be traveling. In the era of reduced superpower tensions, he no longer paid much attention to the almost routine comings and goings of Soviets. However, the television stations in Washington, D.C., still did, and he could not recall any mention of an upcoming departure of Soviet VIPs.

Saturday afternoon was not a peak time for arrivals or departures, so Chisholm expected the terminal to be nearly deserted. Much to his surprise, the main lobby was overflowing with people. It seemed to him that almost everyone was carrying either a camera or a placard, and the placards had a decidedly anti-American tone. He scanned several and recognized a single focus: the sign carriers did not want Defender I put into orbit.

He felt self-conscious in his uniform—especially knowing how he had spent his time at Cape Canaveral. However, no one was paying any attention to him. Instead, the bright lights and cameras were aimed at someone near a side wall. Chisholm was curious about who was getting the celebrity treatment, but decided against trying to penetrate the crowd. Instead he moved toward baggage-claim. Before reaching the stairs, he noticed a television set on an abandoned ticket counter. The screen was showing a live broadcast of the scene on the other side of the lobby, and Chisholm recognized Yuri G. Galkin, the Soviet ambassador to the United States.

Galkin had been a familiar fixture in Washington for seven years. Initially he had been a chubby figure with the countenance of an academician and a wardrobe that might have been chic in Moscow thirty years earlier. The reforms of Perestroika, however, had benefited Galkin perhaps more than any other person. For him duty in Washington, D.C., had been infinitely more pleasant than for his predecessors during the cold war. Additionally, Galkin had benefited personally from new attitudes resulting from Soviet consultation with an image-making firm in New York. Italian suits and designer eyeglasses had transformed him. Now Chisholm saw Galkin as a chubby figure with the countenance of a diplomat from one of the fashion capitals of Europe.

In the glare of the floodlights Galkin struggled to make his cherubic face look stern and unyielding. Chisholm joined the people gathered around the television set.

Responding to a question Chisholm had not heard, Galkin said,

"To all peoples of common sense, the U.S. administration's head-strong decision to put the so-called Defender satellites into the cosmos can be seen only as a provocation. This is a regrettable affront to the Soviet government and the Soviet people who have tried for so many decades to reduce, not inflame, tensions."

Decades is stretching it a bit, Chisholm thought. He was also reminded of how much he disliked listening to the pedantic, heavily laden pronouncements of Communist spokesmen.

Someone outside camera range shouted, "But President Anderson made it clear that these satellites are defensive in nature. Their—"

"Nothing is new in his words," Galkin interrupted with lines that sounded well rehearsed. "They are strictly inventions that fail to stand against facts. *Defensive* and *humane* and *stabilizing*—merely transparent attempts to mask the president's determination to militarize outer space. It is clear to anyone of normal reasoning that the American 'Star Wars' scheme has always been aimed at deploying space strike weapons, thereby contravening the obvious will of the American people, who strongly oppose such schemes."

As if responding to the nominating speech at a presidential convention, the placard-carrying members of the crowd began chanting and thrusting their signs toward the curved ceiling of the lobby. For the next few seconds Galkin was content to defer to the shouted slogans and general uproar. Then he raised a hand as if trying to hear the next question, and the chanting died away immediately.

Interesting, Chisholm thought, surprised at the apparent coordination between the Soviet ambassador and the American demonstrators. Chisholm had thought that such overt connections were as out of style as the ill-fitting brown suits that Galkin used to wear.

Another reporter shouted, "You implied that Defender I includes strike weapons. The satellite will carry no weapons that can be hurled down against—"

"How do you know?" Galkin bellowed his question, then continued, "Have the conspirers in the Pentagon let you inspect the weapons? These dangerous craft are fraught with calamitous consequences. When the peace-loving peoples of the world are blackmailed by the nuclear weapons over their heads, it will be too late to demand inspections!"

The Russian doth protest too much, methinks, Chisholm thought—with apologies to Shakespeare. For years Chisholm had studied the Soviet protestations and propaganda, especially involving outer space and the overall strategic balance. He had concluded that the most outrageous protests came in one of two circumstances: either the United States had developed a capability that the Soviets were technically incapable of matching or false accusations were being made about something the Soviets were doing themselves.

He was unsure if Galkin's words represented either case. Surely the Soviets did not think Defender I contained nuclear weapons. The intelligence agents of the Soviet's KGB should have confirmed that the Defenders were designed for defense against missiles rising above the atmosphere. More likely, Chisholm thought, Galkin simply was trying to inflame the opposition by linking Defender I with the specter of offensive nuclear weapons.

Galkin's statement had produced a less organized rumble of chants from the demonstrators than those that had come before. When the chants faded, another reporter asked, "How long do you expect to remain in Moscow, Mr. Ambassador?"

"That I cannot predict," Galkin said, forcing a look of serious concern across his pudgy cheeks. "Future developments depend upon the recklessness of your administration. If you could tell me that your president had at this minute canceled the Defender, I would return to the embassy and advise President Grigoriev that common sense has won out over the provocateurs in the Pentagon. Without such a return to sensible policies, my consultations in Moscow will be extensive." Galkin paused with a thoughtful expression, then added, "Your president must be convinced of how strongly the American people oppose his brazen and unjustified attempt to militarize outer space."

With greater intensity than before, chants echoed throughout the cavernous lobby. Galkin gestured toward the protesters and gave an "I told you so" look into the cameras. Then he turned away, and his bodyguards pushed ahead of him as the small cluster of Soviets moved toward a departure gate.

The picture on the television switched to the station's on-scene reporter, who was struggling to hold his position in the ebb and flow of the crowd. With the chanting nearly drowning out his words, he held his microphone close to his lips. "We are witnessing, live, the departure of Soviet Ambassador Galkin from Dulles airport. Less than two hours ago, a stunning announcement came from the Soviet embassy—the ambassador was being recalled to the Kremlin for serious consultations. This diplomatic broadside comes only days after the president's decision to launch the Defender I satellite. Ambassador Galkin's words have a specific message: The Soviet government believes strongly that the president's decision must be reversed."

Deciding he had seen enough, Chisholm hurried toward the lower floor and its exits to the taxi stands. As he stepped on the escalator, he saw half a dozen people carrying placards or handing out leaflets to people at the bottom of the escalator. For an instant he wished he had chosen another route. Decades-old policy required him to avoid confrontations with demonstrators, and he knew his uniform would attract attention. He thought of the small badge just below his pilot wings. Though his Air Force space badge depicted the earth encircled by two orbiting satellites, he doubted that this crowd would connect him and the badge to the Air Force's space program.

As Chisholm stepped from the escalator, a burly man in his midtwenties blocked the way and thrust a leaflet in front of Chisholm's face.

"No, thank you," Chisholm said, starting to step around the man.

"It's something you need to read, Colonel!"

Chisholm stopped but made no attempt to take the piece of paper. Emotions, which had taken root deep within him a quarter of a century earlier, flared with an intensity that he carefully suppressed. He could see that the others with leaflets were watching the encounter, but he focused on the eyes of the man blocking his path. Chisholm growled, "You don't have a thing I need!"

Chisholm shifted his weight to the left, and the man stepped in that direction.

"You people in the Pentagon need educating most of all," the man said, looking above the paper he held between them.

"I'll step aside for any man once," Chisholm said in words that seemed devoid of emotion. Then he added with an edge to his voice, "But only once!" A fierceness in Chisholm's brown eyes punctuated his words. He kept his gaze locked on the eyes of the other man.

The burly man looked uncertain but did not move. His companions stayed out of the way as Chisholm moved left, being careful not to brush his opponent in passing. If there was to be a fight, Chisholm wanted to be able to say afterward that they had touched him first. No one tried.

As Chisholm started up the ramp that led to the street, he noticed the smiles of two porters who had watched the exchange.

One of the porters discreetly offered a thumbs-up gesture and said, "Give 'em hell, Colonel!"

Chisholm smiled and winked, "If you can't be good, be lucky!"

Walking away, he wondered if his words had confused his two admirers. He commonly used that statement when someone had gotten away with something after making what might not have been the smartest choice. Chisholm felt lucky to have avoided a brawling incident. He thought wistfully of his brother, Brett, a fighter pilot who had died years earlier. If Brett had been along—in body as well as spirit—Chisholm was certain they wouldn't have left without a fight.

4

With only minutes to spare, General Petr Novikov entered a
small conference room that was part of the suite of offices of the
Soviet president. Standing beside a podium at the front of the room,
Marshal of the Soviet Union Vadim N. Murashev was rehearsing. He
wore a dress uniform laden with every medal, badge, order, and title
of distinction he had been awarded in five decades in the Soviet
Army. A large pad of flip charts rested on an easel near the podium.
The cover chart, which was decorated with drawings of two bolts of
red lightning, was labeled *Krasnaya Molniya*.

Murashev had been reading from a stack of note cards but looked
up when he heard the young general's cane strike the hardwood floor.
As Novikov had expected, Murashev's expression showed a combination of relief and irritation. The marshal obviously was relieved
that Novikov had arrived, but agitated because the arrival had come
just before the president was scheduled to join them for a briefing.

After offering a curt greeting, Murashev asked questions about
items on two cards. Novikov gave clear, simple answers in the manner
of someone sharing new insights with a respected colleague. However, the answers were not new, and there was little genuine respect.
He had used almost the exact words in explaining the same items to
Murashev several times over the last three days. As Novikov waited
for additional questions, his demeanor remained impeccable in spite
of his unspoken anger at having to coddle the marshal. Murashev
seemed to dismiss Novikov's presence, concentrating instead on a
silent rehearsal of his briefing.

Novikov looked around and was impressed by the elaborate decorations, which seemed more appropriate to Tsarist times than the "classless" society of Lenin and Marx. He also noticed the two other occupants talking quietly on the other side of the large conference table that dominated the room.

The chubby man dressed in a stodgy brown suit was Ambassador Galkin, who had arrived in Moscow after a nonstop flight from Washington, D.C. The other man's urbane appearance suggested someone no more threatening than a retired banker or a doting grandfather. His shaggy brown hair and smooth, round face seemed to inspire trust and confidence. Yet even Novikov felt apprehensive at the sight of Viktor F. Petruk. Petruk was chairman of the Committee for State Security, commonly known as the KGB.

Preferring to avoid contact with Petruk, Novikov turned away. He placed his briefcase in a well-upholstered leather chair at the end of the table near the podium. That chair would put him close at hand if Murashev faltered during the briefing.

Novikov sat on the edge of the table, taking weight off his stiff right leg. He was weary but eager. He had spent all of Thursday and Friday rehearsing Murashev and preparing the note cards and briefing charts. Returning to Plesetsk after another rehearsal on Saturday, Novikov had worked well into the night. He had fallen asleep in the early hours of Sunday morning when the call had come: Galkin had been recalled from Washington, and the president wanted the *Krasnaya Molniya* briefing late on Sunday afternoon.

After three hours of restless sleep, Novikov had awakened and immediately attacked the hundreds of last-minute details that could jeopardize the start of the Soviet Union's most ambitious mission in space. He had studied the weather forecasts and the schedules of the American reconnaissance satellites. He even had delayed his flight to Moscow as late as he dared while his computers had crunched out timing profiles for various launch scenarios.

As Novikov sat in the room that had been a silent witness to some of the most important decisions of the twentieth century, he appeared calm, but inwardly he felt a feverish anticipation. The feeling was similar to that experienced right before being rocketed from Tyuratam into the uncertainty of the cosmos above the steppes of central Russia. He relished a sense of history, and he sensed that this special room was about to host a decision that could rank with—and perhaps overshadow—those that had come before.

A door on the back wall opened, and two men entered. The first was short with piercing blue eyes that quickly surveyed the entire scene. His expression was pleasant but noncommittal. He was President Oleg P. Grigoriev, the most powerful man in the Soviet Union.

Following was a bear of a man who dwarfed the president. Aleksei I. Levchenko was the minister of defense, whose power was second only to that of Grigoriev. Levchenko's smile seemed friendly, perhaps almost mischievous. Sauntering to his chair, Levchenko brought to mind a tavern regular whose good humor—and strength—increased with each shot of vodka that disappeared through eager lips.

Grigoriev exchanged greetings as he took the central chair on the side of the long table. Since he was small—by far the smallest man in the room—his chair was higher than the rest. When everyone but Marshal Murashev was seated, Grigoriev was at the eye level of the others.

Murashev stood at the podium ready to relay the opening remarks on his first note card. However, Grigoriev started a private conversation with Chairman Petruk, who was seated at the president's left. As Murashev waited, his eyes flitted nervously beneath bushy brows, betraying his discomfort.

From the end of the table, Novikov had a good view of everyone. Although he looked quietly supportive—and he was prepared to save the briefing at any point—he found perverse pleasure in his commander's anxiety. As the commander-in-chief of the Strategic Rocket Forces, the preeminent military service in the Soviet Union, Murashev seldom had to show deference to anyone. Below Murashev's chin the sparkle of diamonds glittered from the marshal's star attached to his necktie. His was not a common marshal's star with a single diamond in the middle. His star had five additional diamonds placed between the facet rays, signifying the wearer's attainment of Marshal of the Soviet Union, the highest military rank in the Soviet Union. Nevertheless, Novikov enjoyed the irony that within the select group gathered this afternoon, the marshal was senior in rank only to Novikov.

In a few moments President Grigoriev turned his attention to Murashev and nodded.

"Comrade President," Murashev began in a dry and scratchy voice, "I am here to assure you of the readiness of the Strategic Rocket Forces to proceed with Operation *Krasnaya Molniya*. For the last three years—"

The president interrupted. "Will *Krasnaya Molniya* cause an American counterattack?"

Grigoriev showed no emotion in his tone or his expression. He leaned forward, resting his elbows on the table and his chin on clasped hands. Though he seemed relaxed, his blue eyes fixed Murashev with a gaze that was inescapable.

"Comrade President," Murashev said, hesitantly, "there is every reason to expect that the Americans will feel compelled to make some—"

"Nuclear?" Grigoriev did not allow the marshal to finish. "Will they *feel compelled* to respond with a nuclear strike against the territory of the Soviet Union?"

Before Murashev could respond, Minister of Defense Levchenko answered from beside Grigoriev. "Of course not, Oleg. The Americans often act foolishly—but they are not fools." Levchenko reached with an oversized, fleshy hand and patted the president on his elbow.

Without showing agreement or disagreement, Grigoriev looked at Levchenko, then beyond at Ambassador Galkin.

Hesitating, Galkin removed his designer eyeglasses and seemed to be considering alternatives. "When the politicians learn of *Krasnaya Molniya*, they will bluster and make wild accusations. They will argue among themselves and chastise their military sector for being ill prepared. However, no one has listened to the warnings of the American hawks for years, so a nuclear response is out of the question."

The president nodded without revealing whether the motion represented agreement or simply an acknowledgment. He turned to Chairman Petruk for an additional opinion.

Petruk sat slouched and seemingly relaxed as he carefully twisted a loose thread around a button on his right sleeve. When the button was secure, he looked up and flapped a hand toward the marshal standing nervously at the podium. "How close the Americans come to fighting depends on Marshal Murashev's plan and how effectively Minister Levchenko implements it."

Levchenko's breathing deepened. He looked less friendly but did not respond.

Novikov recognized the unspoken challenge, the subtext of competition the words represented. As head of the KGB, Petruk possessed a power to intimidate that sometimes exceeded that of the president or the minister of defense. Yet Petruk was number three in the inner circle, where power was the overriding currency. Traditionally the influence of the KGB chief increased primarily when the military bungled something badly enough to require a major reorganization or a purge. Less frequently the KGB and the military allied themselves with key members of the Party to topple the leader, as with Khrushchev in the 1960s. Novikov sensed that he was about to see some open sparring that officers of his rank seldom were permitted to witness.

Accepting Petruk's answer without commenting, President Grigoriev resumed his posture with his elbows on the table. He looked toward Marshal Murashev as if there had been no interruption.

After a moment's hesitation, Murashev removed the cover to reveal the first chart. The drawing depicted a view of the earth from high above the north pole. Additionally, there was a single circle with a diameter nearly seven times that of the one representing earth. The title above the drawing was "*Zashchitnik I*," the Russian term for Protector I.

"Operation *Krasnaya Molniya* will place two types of satellites into orbit," Murashev said. "*Zashchitnik I* will be in a geostationary orbit more than twenty-two thousand miles above the equator. Circling the earth once a day, *Zashchitnik I* will appear to remain stationary over a point south of the United States."

Good, Novikov thought. The words matched almost exactly the script he had written.

Murashev looked toward his note cards, then continued, "From that height, the tracking sensors and laser weapons on *Zashchitnik I* will oversee more than forty percent of the earth. The satellite will be able to attack missiles and enemy satellites throughout the majority of the cosmos above those regions. The rate of fire—"

"I leave those details to General Novikov and his technicians," Grigoriev said. "What I want to know is, will one *Zashchitnik* be enough?"

That same question often had been on Novikov's mind as he fell asleep at night. He had great confidence in *Zashchitnik* and its unprecedented design. The Americans would find the satellite to be a formidable weapon. However, Novikov faced a maxim that applied to all space launches, whether American, French, Japanese, Chinese, or Russian. While the success rate for space launches might be 90 or 95 percent, each individual launch faced some possibility of failure.

No matter how detailed the equipment inspections were or how carefully he trained his crews, he could not guarantee the successful launch of any particular payload. He had done everything he could to improve the chances for success, but if the launch of *Zashchitnik I* failed, Novikov could not replace the powerful satellite for at least five months—well after Defender I would be in orbit.

"Naturally," Murashev said, "our preference would be to delay *Krasnaya Molniya* until *Zashchitnik II* also is ready for launch. If the Americans can be convinced to delay their Defenders, we should also delay *Zashchitnik I*."

Grigoriev turned to Ambassador Galkin. "Can we delay the American launch again?"

"I would like to be optimistic," Galkin said as he fidgeted with his glasses.

I bet you would, Novikov thought as a slight smile crossed his lips. *Krasnaya Molniya* would awaken the Americans from the comfortable slumber induced by years of Perestroika. Galkin would become like a lightning rod at the focus of the reactions of hundreds of American politicians. Liberals and conservatives alike would be scrambling to show that they were among those who had remained wary of Soviet intentions. Since Galkin's term as ambassador was over in June, he would escape before the diplomatic firestorm if there was a delay in Defender I and a corresponding delay in *Krasnaya Molniya*.

Galkin continued, "Unfortunately, the Americans are unlikely to delay the launch of Defender I beyond April unless there are technical problems. They would have launched last October if Chairman Petruk had not ensured that Defender became such an issue in the elections. Perhaps Chairman Petruk has a different opinion about being able to cause additional delays."

Petruk's tone was matter-of-fact. "New demonstrations against the Defender start this week in Washington, San Francisco, New York, and Cape Canaveral. Some will turn violent, but the president no longer has to respond to the demands of the people as he did last fall. And the Americans have invested too many dollars to scrap an otherwise viable program. I do not expect delays of more than a few days—unless we sabotage the actual rocket that carries the Defender."

The president's frown suggested Petruk had raised a subject that already had been closed. Novikov agreed with Grigoriev. *Krasnaya Molniya* offered less provocative ways of destroying the Defender than attacking the rocket while it remained on American soil.

"So," Grigoriev said, his voice hardening as his attention moved from Chairman Petruk to Ambassador Galkin to Minister Levchenko, "we *should* delay, but the Americans will not. You've had billions of rubles for *Krasnaya Molniya*, and still the Americans are ready before we are. I do *not* like the choices you place before me."

Grigoriev's comments surprised Novikov. Novikov too would have greater confidence if *Zashchitnik II* were fully assembled. However, everyone in the room knew that *Krasnaya Molniya* had been months behind the Americans. Novikov considered it fortunate that the Soviets now had the opportunity to launch first. He was certain that Grigoriev understood enough about the rest of *Krasnaya Molniya* to know that *Zashchitnik I* was not the only satellite ready for launch.

Levchenko responded, "The second *Zashchitnik* would have been completed last fall if VPK had provided the computers on schedule. In spite of the unjustified difficulties in getting many high-technology parts from VPK, General Novikov has worked miracles."

Petruk reddened, but he did not respond immediately to the indirect finger-pointing.

Novikov moved restlessly in his chair. He wished his name had not been used so prominently in an obvious jab at the KGB, which was accountable for the failure. The VPK was the Military Industrial Commission responsible for acquiring Western technology needed for new Soviet weapons. In this case, advanced computers were essential to meet the complex design of *Zashchitnik I*. The Military Industrial Commission had ordered the KGB to obtain the four sets of computers, which were produced in the United States. So far, Petruk's men had gotten one set out of America.

Grigoriev looked to Petruk.

The KGB chairman opened a black notebook, leafed through a few pages, then said, "Sets two and three will be on the docks in Rotterdam the first week in June. You should have them in Tyuratam by the twenty-fifth." A flush of color that remained in his cheeks was the only sign that Petruk was angry. Otherwise his words were as unemotional as if discussing the delivery schedule for a couple of cases of vodka.

"But," Levchenko said, "June is nine months behind schedule."

Petruk's nostrils flared as he stared at his larger accuser, but his voice concealed the anger that his face betrayed. "If, Comrade Levchenko, you cannot control the Americans with one *Zashchitnik* and a dozen *Borzoi* battle stations, perhaps Comrade Grigoriev needs a new minister of defense." Turning to Grigoriev, Petruk added, "I could offer my driver. He's new, but he learns quickly."

Before President Grigoriev could respond, Levchenko dropped a heavy fist on the table and said to Petruk, "I can handle *Krasnaya Molniya*. Perhaps your driver can be taught to deliver computers on schedule."

Levchenko and Petruk glared at each other. Novikov was embarrassed to witness such an exchange. He was surprised that Grigoriev did not reassert control immediately. Instead Grigoriev seemed satisfied to listen as the heads of the military and the KGB claimed they had done enough to make *Krasnaya Molniya* successful.

Suddenly Novikov realized that Grigoriev had not convened this meeting to hear Murashev's briefing. The president probably had decided to approve *Krasnaya Molniya* even before recalling Ambassador Galkin from Washington. Instead Grigoriev was ensuring that the KGB and the military got their fingerprints all over the decision document, so to speak. Somewhere in a control room beyond the walls, their words of challenge undoubtedly were preserved on an audio recorder. Novikov was more impressed than ever at President Grigoriev's shrewdness.

With the exception of Khrushchev's unsuccessful attempt to put offensive missiles into Cuba in 1962, Novikov thought, nothing had been as bold as *Krasnaya Molniya*. Grigoriev had to be aware that the Cuban fiasco had united the KGB and the military against Khrushchev, sending him into retirement in 1964. Now within a few minutes Grigoriev had gotten the KGB and military declaring that any failure of *Krasnaya Molniya* would be because of the incompetence of the other. If the plan failed, Novikov thought, Grigoriev would not have to fear a united KGB-military front arguing before the Politburo for his ouster. Masterful, Novikov concluded.

"Marshal Murashev," Grigoriev said, breaking the impasse, "do we have enough rockets and satellites now to make *Krasnaya Molniya* succeed?"

"Yes, Comrade President. The next part of the briefing discusses the other satellites."

Grigoriev nodded his willingness to continue, so Murashev displayed the next drawing. The title was *Borzoi*, the term for the

Russian wolfhounds, which were known for their swiftness. The drawing showed a side view of the earth with what appeared to be a Saturnlike ring angled up almost vertical to the equator. The elliptically shaped ring, which represented a satellite's orbit, nearly touched Antarctica. In the northern hemisphere the ring looped well away to a distance almost equal to the diameter of the earth.

"The constellation of eight *Borzoi* satellites will be in highly elliptical orbits such as this one," Murashev said. "The *Borzoi* give continuous coverage of all space-launch bases in the northern hemisphere. All enemy rockets must climb through the field-of-fire of at least one *Borzoi*. The *Borzoi* can find their own targets or receive targeting information from *Zashchitnik*."

Grigoriev stared intently at Murashev. "And you can guarantee a full constellation?"

"General Novikov has nine *Borzoi* configured and mated to their boosters. Other boosters are ready for the backup satellites that will be delivered in April."

Novikov considered commenting, but Minister Levchenko spoke first.

"Comrade President, the Americans would have difficulty lifting their Defender through as few as five *Borzoi*—even if *Zashchitnik I* does not operate perfectly." He leaned his elbows on the table and intertwined the meaty fingers on his massive hands. "We have the power *now* to take complete control of access to outer space."

Novikov agreed. Even five *Borzoi* would guarantee several good shots at Defender I before the American satellite climbed above the orbits of the *Borzoi*.

"If Comrade Levchenko does not destroy Defender I," Chairman Petruk said, still angry over the earlier exchange, "you might as well scrap *Cherniy Grom* [Black Thunder]."

Controlling access to space would clear the way for *Cherniy Grom*, Grigoriev's secret plan to put offensive nuclear weapons on a constellation of Soviet space stations. *Cherniy Grom* would give the president unprecedented power to reassert Lenin's vision of Soviet destiny. For several years the warheads on Soviet ICBMs had been large enough and accurate enough to destroy most American ICBMs in their silos. At last a Soviet leader would be able also to defeat the bombers and submarine-launched ballistic missiles of the triad of American strategic forces.

The Americans' warning system for ballistic missiles, with its massive radars aimed northward, would be useless against nuclear bombs hurled downward from orbiting space stations. The bases of the American bombers could be destroyed with little more warning than that of the lightning that precedes the thunder. At sea the captain of each American missile boat could expect nuclear retaliation to rain down within minutes of launching his first Trident missile.

Novikov knew that *Cherniy Grom* would change forever the balance that Perestroika had seemed to establish. Unfortunately, the space stations and weapons for *Cherniy Grom* were at least a year from completion. During that year the Americans were planning to launch three Defenders. Once in space, those Defenders could attack the Soviet boosters carrying the nuclear-armed satellites into space— if the Americans ever broke through the elaborate security that had kept the program hidden for years.

Grigoriev nodded in response to Petruk's comment about *Cherniy Grom.* "That's why I have no choice but to proceed with *Krasnaya Molniya*—no matter how far behind schedule both of you are."

That was the bottom line, Novikov thought. Perfect or not, *Krasnaya Molniya* had to begin before Defender I reached orbit.

President Grigoriev fixed his gaze on Marshal Murashev. "If *Krasnaya Molniya* fails, you'll envy the fate of Nedelin."

Murashev shifted his weight and looked toward his briefing charts instead of responding. Field Marshal Mitrofan Nedelin had been the first commander-in-chief of the Strategic Rocket Forces. He and hundreds in his command were engulfed in burning fuel when a malfunctioning space booster had ignited on a launchpad in central Russia in 1960.

Novikov stood. He intentionally clattered his cane against his chair, drawing attention away from his embattled commander. Novikov looked at Grigoriev and said confidently, "*Krasnaya Molniya* will succeed, Comrade President. Before daybreak I can be moving two *Borzoi* launchers into position. I only await your command."

Grigoriev's blue eyes flashed for an instant, then a smile spread across his face. On many occasions he had taken advantage of Novikov's popularity to bolster his own standing with the people. "The Soviet Union depends heavily upon you, Petr."

"We have prepared for many years. I am eager to serve, Comrade President."

Grigoriev glanced around at the others in the room, then said, "Let it be done."

"Thank you, sir."

"When you return to Star City, you may want to wear these." Novikov offered the old shoulder boards.

Kalinen looked confused for an instant, then nodded and accepted the boards. "Yes, Comrade General."

"This may not be the time to share your good fortune with anyone—including your wife."

"I understand, sir."

Novikov put an arm around Kalinen's shoulders. "Until Thursday night."

5

The Kremlin, Moscow
Sunday, 7 March, 1905 local (1605 GMT)

Novikov called his command center and passed a code word to verify that *Krasnaya Molniya* had been approved. Before leaving Plesetsk he had put together a tentative schedule that would begin moving *Borzoi I* and *Borzoi II* to the launchpads just before dawn. Novikov's telephone call told his chief of staff to use that schedule.

Before going to the airport Novikov made a personal pilgrimage to spend a few minutes at the Kremlin Wall. Throughout his adult life Novikov had taken special inspiration from the world's first cosmonaut, *Polkovnik* (Colonel) Yuri Gagarin. As a young boy growing up near the Volga River, Novikov had witnessed Gagarin's return to earth on a bright April morning in 1961. Young Novikov had been frightened at first by the blackened sphere and the strangely dressed figure descending below separate parachutes of orange and white. Once he learned that Gagarin was returning from a flight in the cosmos, the ten-year-old decided to become a cosmonaut. Seven years later Novikov, along with much of the adult population in the Soviet Union, had been stunned by Radio Moscow's announcement of Gagarin's untimely death in an airplane crash.

Earlier in the day Novikov had cut a small branch from a pine tree outside his office at the Northern Cosmodrome. Now he had come to place this personal tribute beneath the plaque, which marked the location in the Kremlin Wall where Polkovnik Gagarin's ashes were interred. Novikov put the branch among the shriveled remains of flowers that others had brought. He had considered bringing flowers, but had decided that a cutting from a living pine tree was a more appropriate link between his work at Plesetsk and the man who had been first in space.

As snow started falling, Novikov stood at attention and saluted the plaque before getting into his limousine for the ride to the airport.

After an eight-hundred-mile flight from Moscow, Novikov reached Plesetsk less than an hour before midnight. Stepping from his aircraft, he felt a special sense of history—the important history of his surroundings and the contribution he was about to make.

The spaceport's first launch had occurred more than a quarter of a century earlier. On a cold March day in 1966, Cosmos 112 had rocketed from a hidden launchpad in the nearby forests. The satellite orbited the earth for only eight days, but that had been long enough to betray the existence of a new launch base.

Novikov often enjoyed telling visitors how the secret base had been pinpointed. The discovery had not been made by spies or because of the diligence of American military intelligence. Instead the credit belonged to Professor Geoffrey Perry, who had been using the tracking of satellites to demonstrate the laws of physics at a boys' school near London.

When the professor and his students studied Cosmos 112, they recognized that its orbit was unlike that followed by any previous satellite. This new orbit was incompatible with the more southerly launch bases at Tyuratam and Kapustin Yar. Since orbits of satellites are markedly more predictable than the flight of a maneuvering aircraft, the amateur observers were able to compute the satellite's previous flight path. Perry deduced that Cosmos 112 had been launched from somewhere in northwestern Russia. Later in the year other satellites were launched from the same region. By comparing orbits, Professor Perry and his students deduced that these new satellites had originated in the region of forests and lakes south of the White Sea port of Archangelsk—somewhere near the village of Plesetsk.

Nearly two decades passed before the Soviet government officially confirmed that Plesetsk was a launch base for Soviet satellites. The acknowledgment—in 1983—was not a precursor to the openness of *Glasnost* but was an attempt to quell persistent rumors of unidentified flying objects. The plumes of rockets rising from Plesetsk had caused many reports of eerie lights and other strange atmospheric effects, so the base could not remain an official secret forever.

Although nearly as far north as Fairbanks, Alaska, Plesetsk rapidly became the keystone in the Soviet plan to achieve dominance in space. Despite months of bitter weather each year, the base was well positioned to send spy satellites into polar orbits that would pass over the United States more than a dozen times a day. By the beginning of the 1970s, the spaceport had become the most active in the world. After little more than three years of operations, the new base blasted a payload toward orbit on an average of every six days—for the next ten years.

Plesetsk was the natural launch point for Novikov's *Borzoi* satellites, since their orbits would pass near the north and south poles. Of the hundreds of satellites that had come before, he thought, not one was as important as those his rockets would hurtle skyward.

In the 1970s the base launched more than twice as many satellites as were orbited from American launch bases. In frank discussions away from the ears of eavesdropping political officers, Novikov often acknowledged why Plesetsk´ had been so busy. In the early years Soviet spacecraft did not survive long in the hostile environment of outer space. Frankly, Novikov would say, Soviet satellites had to be replaced more often than the longer lasting American satellites.

On this particular night Novikov was pleased that his predecessors had suffered the burden of being second best. One thing the Soviets had learned—and had learned much better than the Americans— was how to get a booster onto the pad and quickly into the air. In the next few days Novikov planned to give the Americans a demonstration of Soviet mastery that would be remembered in the years ahead.

He sat in back as his driver maneuvered along roads lined and packed with snow. Novikov's mind raced ahead. Like moving through items on a cosmonaut's checklist, he previewed events of the next few hours that would unleash *Krasnaya Molniya*.

Novikov wanted another look at the boosters and satellites. Even with his stiff leg and cane, Novikov was a man who preferred to get his hands on the hardware. He would rather solve problems in a cold maintenance building or on a windswept launchpad than stay isolated in the comfort of the office that his rank and status now justified.

He told his driver to pull into the vehicle shelter at the office in Kochmas. After waiting a few moments to mislead any possible surveillance into thinking he had returned to his office, Novikov had his driver continue toward the launchpads that had been modified for the *Borzoi* boosters. Less than a mile from the *Borzoi* launch zone, the driver left the main road and pulled into a large building in the motor pool. In addition to being a vehicle maintenance shop, the building served as an entry point to the huge complex of tunnels beneath this part of the Northern Cosmodrome.

Novikov left his automobile and rode an elevator down to the main level, which was more than a hundred feet below the frozen forest. There he entered an electrically powered sedan and continued his journey into the *Borzoi* launch zone.

When he had taken over development of *Krasnaya Molniya*, he had ordered a major expansion of the underground facilities to add another layer of secrecy to the operation. The tunnel he was in extended back several miles to where a rail line serviced several warehouses on the surface. Within the warehouses Novikov's men could unload rail cars without being affected by harsh weather or being observed by the American reconnaissance satellites that flew over Plesetsk several times a day.

When Novikov had ridden more than a mile into the *Borzoi* launch zone, the tunnel finally widened into a huge underground assembly area beneath a much smaller building on the surface. The Moscow decision was fresh in his mind, so the first glimpse quickened his pulse even more than usual. Sparkling beneath lights that made the room brighter than noontime on a December day in Plesetsk, seven fully assembled space boosters rested quietly, like reclining warriors awaiting a call to arms.

Novikov stepped from the sedan near one of the boosters, and several technicians and military officers joined him. As he greeted most by name, he assumed that each had the same unspoken question: Why had the general come to check the hardware in the middle of the night? Preferring to let everyone's anticipation build for a few more minutes, he grabbed a metal notebook that covered the maintenance status of the booster and its satellite. Like a doctor checking on a patient, he scanned for items that could delay launch of the booster. There were none.

Novikov said little as he began a ritual walk-around inspection of the booster, which stretched out to the length of a fourteen-story building lying on its side. Months earlier the booster had been an RS-20 ICBM, called the SS-18 Satan by the Americans and other members of NATO. He had decided long ago that most nicknames that NATO assigned to Soviet aircraft and weapons were ridiculous.

The identifiers for fighters all began with an F, producing such meaningless designations as Fishbed, Flogger, Fitter, Flagon, Fulcrum, and Frogfoot. The NATO names for strategic missiles included Sandal, Sego, and Spanker—hardly fitting for rockets that could hurl nuclear weapons between continents.

Nevertheless, Novikov thought that Satan was a fitting name for the RS-20s, since those magnificent rockets could deliver hell in great quantities right to the Americans' doorsteps. The boosters surrounding him had stood for years on combat alert in underground silos at Kartaly, Aleysk, Dombarovskiy, or Imeni Gastello in central Russia. The strategic arms reduction talks, which gained momentum in the late 1980s, had required the Soviets to remove some Satans from the ICBM force. Novikov had been delighted by the lessening of superpower tensions because he had received the first fifteen for use as satellite boosters. His missiles, which represented less than 5 percent of the Soviets' force of Satans, once could have unleashed the destructive power of 300 million tons of TNT. He was proud that he was going to accomplish far more with the missiles than they had achieved in their silos in the missile fields.

As Novikov reached the end with all the exhaust nozzles, it was obvious that his Satans now were much different than they had been as ICBMs. Soviet engineers routinely added more rockets to increase the lifting capability of converted ICBMs, and his Satans were no exception. Four strap-on RD-107 rocket engines, each with four main nozzles, were mounted around the base of the original missile. The net result was an ungainly cluster of nozzles, pipes, and electronics boxes that towered nearly thirty feet above Novikov—even with the missile lying on its side. He took a perfunctory look inside the two nozzles that were close enough to the floor for him to see into. Then he started slowly along the side of the light gray booster.

Extending for nearly half the length of the Satan, the strap-on boosters tapered like feathers on the shaft of an arrow. The middle section had been lengthened to accommodate tanks for more fuel and oxidizer.

At the business end, as Novikov liked to refer to it, another major modification of the Satan was apparent. The bullet-shaped fairing had been replaced by a more massive nose section. Although ten nuclear warheads had fit snugly within the confines of the original fairing, Novikov's large *Borzoi* satellites would not. Even with antennas and solar panels folded closely against its body, the satellite was thirteen feet across, nearly a third larger than the diameter of the Satan. When the booster was pointed toward the sky, the larger nose would look unwieldy, but Novikov did not care about looks— only performance. Unfortunately, the oversized fairings were a clue he could not hide from the Americans, but he had a few tricks in mind that should confuse the analysts until his *Borzoi* were ready to go to work.

After completing his journey around the first booster, Novikov spoke loudly to his chief engineer. "Well, Dimitri, I hope you've had plenty of sleep and vodka in the last few days."

Dimitri, the only nondrinker in the crowd, looked surprised as others laughed at Novikov's comment.

Novikov smiled broadly and added, "Because you will have time for little of either for the next few days."

Novikov's indirect confirmation of the go-ahead produced loud roars of approval.

Moving to the next booster, Novikov asked, "Are there problems on any of the first nine?"

"Only number six," the chief engineer responded. "We have to change a wiring harness. The harness will be available in the morning and should be changed and checked in less than forty-eight hours."

The timing would not be a problem, Novikov thought. He planned to move the *Borzoi* in pairs to the pads. Numbers five and six would not move from the assembly building until Thursday.

He inspected the paperwork on the other boosters. Spending some extra time on the chart for number six, he made a mental note to keep checking on its status. He ended his review beside *Borzoi III* and *Borzoi IV*, which already were mounted on transporters. The elevator would carry these two to the upper level as soon as *Borzoi I* and *Borzoi II* were moved to the launchpads. Then transporters for I and II would be brought down and loaded with *Borzoi V* and *Borzoi VI*. His schedule was ambitious, but his mission had been given the priority and the money he needed.

Novikov and his followers rode a personnel elevator to the surface. The hangarlike structure was colder than the underground facilities. Huge overhead cranes were attached to girders near the ceiling. The transporters carrying *Borzoi I* and *Borzoi II* were on railroad tracks flanking the elevator. A large locomotive was hooked behind each transporter. Beyond the transporters, massive doors held the arctic night at bay.

The upper level was one step closer to making *Krasnaya Molniya* a reality, and Novikov felt a new surge of excitement. He was pleased, certain that the Americans would be astonished by what they observed on the *Borzoi* launchpads in a few hours. There was little above ground to suggest that the two large boosters, which would stand glistening in the morning sun, had been built-up in the small assembly building. Novikov smiled whenever he thought of how mystified the analysts in the Pentagon would be tomorrow—and in the days that followed.

Once satisfied that the hardware was ready, Novikov went to the launch-control center for the *Borzoi* complex. After verifying the timing for the beginning of *Krasnaya Molniya*, he slept a few hours, then was up again well before dawn.

For a few minutes he drank coffee and watched the busy preparations. Workers around consoles in one area wore blue coveralls; those in another wore green. Each team, which had worked together for the last several weeks, would control one launchpad.

Novikov took what seemed like the hundredth look at his watch, then decided it was time to go outside. The next American reconnaissance satellite was not due for ten minutes, but he wanted to let his eyes adjust to the predawn darkness. He pulled on his greatcoat and astrakhan cap, then went out to the snow-covered observation deck adjacent to the launch-control center.

The morning was crisp and clear. A hint of the coming sunrise brightened the southeast horizon. The smell of the forests and peat bogs was invigorating, reminding Novikov of hunting excursions he had shared with other cosmonauts before his accident.

As his eyes adjusted, the stars grew brighter even through the dim shimmering of the northern lights. He leaned against the wall and studied the sky above the horizon north of Plesetsk. He had worked and planned for this day for more than three years. In the calm of this particular morning, Novikov envied no one.

After a few minutes he spotted the American satellite rising above the trees beyond the Yemtsa River. At first the satellite's movement was almost imperceptible. Reflecting the sun that was beyond Novikov's horizon, the satellite was a tiny spot of brightness slowly climbing against the background of dimmer stars. On this orbit the satellite would pass from north to south over a point twenty miles west of Novikov. The satellite would return to northern Russia in less than two hours. During that orbit, however, the rotation of the earth would move Plesetsk more than 700 miles farther east, well toward the edge of the coverage of the sensors on the satellite. Therefore, this satellite would not get another good view of Plesetsk for twelve hours. He would have to disrupt the prelaunch efforts, however, when a second American satellite came over Plesetsk at 1230.

Novikov watched the satellite pass almost overhead. He wondered how good the American sensors were. Would they see the lone figure standing on the observation deck? Would they see the rank of a one-star general in the Strategic Rocket Forces? Novikov fantasized for a moment and raised the cane of polished teak with its ivory inlays. If the Americans could see him, he wanted them to know that General Novikov stood alone on this important morning in history.

As the satellite continued its southward journey, he cradled the cane against the front of his coat. He felt his heart pounding. He had not experienced such excitement since the last few minutes of his final spaceflight. Novikov savored the moment as he watched the shimmering satellite descend toward the southern horizon. Except for intermittent periods of sleep, this could be his last peaceful mo-ment for the next two or three weeks—perhaps the last for the rest of his life. Novikov shook off that thought. He refused to be pes-simistic. No one in the Soviet military—or the American military, for that matter—was better prepared. This was the opportun-ity of a lifetime, and he felt proud to be the man whom fate had blessed.

Mayor (Major) Ganin, Novikov's aide, came outside and said, "Comrade General, the American spy satellite is passing beyond range."

Novikov nodded, then said, "*Poekhali* [Let's go]."

"Yes, Comrade General," Ganin said.

As Ganin started inside to deliver the order, Novikov raised his cane, blocking the door. " '*Poekhali.*' That was what Polkovnik Ga-garin shouted in 1961 just before he rode Vostok I into space."

"Yes, Comrade General," Ganin said, waiting for Novikov to move his cane.

"Remember this moment and the command you are about to pass. We are completing the mission Polkovnik Gagarin began more than thirty years ago."

"Yes, Comrade General."

"Some day, students at the military academies will learn that *Poek-*

hali was General Novikov's command on this fateful March morning at Plesetsk."

"Yes, Comrade General."

He lowered his cane, and Ganin went inside. Novikov leaned against the wall and looked at the assembly building with the railroad tracks that led to the launchpads. He believed in tradition and in the pride it could instill in an organization. That was one of many lessons his experience as a cosmonaut had taught him. He wondered how he could pass on such feelings for military tradition in a world dominated by the political officers who believed only in the traditions of Lenin and Marx.

A crack of light appeared on the front of the assembly building. The light spread slowly as the doors clattered sideways, exposing the transporter loaded with *Borzoi I*. Beyond the building, clumps of darkness were transforming into distinct clusters of trees as sunrise approached the Northern Cosmodrome.

Poekhali, Novikov repeated quietly. Then he turned and hurried inside.

Although he had gotten little sleep in the last four days, he was determined to oversee the procedures necessary to get *Borzoi I* into the cosmos. Now that his creations were moving beyond the cloak of secrecy, he had to get the full constellation of *Borzoi* into orbit as quickly as possible. If there were to be problems that he had not detected during the simulated launches, he wanted to be present when those problems arose.

Before the two boosters had cleared the assembly building, he hurried from the launch-control center to his limousine. Mayor Ganin, slowed by two satchels and a container of coffee, struggled to keep up with his crippled leader.

In a few minutes Novikov was riding alongside the locomotives that slowly were pushing the transporter-erectors that carried the massive boosters. As his car crunched through ruts in the ice, Novikov tried to anticipate problems in the event-filled hours remaining until sunset. He flipped through a notebook on his lap, checking items in contingency plans as various questions passed through his mind. In most cases he knew the answers without bothering to look them up. Besides, there were many blank entries at this point, times that could not be filled in until the first satellite rocketed toward orbit. The launch time for *Borzoi I* was not critical, but it would establish the timing for the other satellites in the constellation.

Novikov wished he could launch both *Borzoi* before the next American reconnaissance satellite passed overhead at 1230, but that was impossible. He expected his green team to take about ten hours to bring the first countdown to zero. The second launch would come at two hours and twenty minutes after the first. Since one of the two American satellites flew above Plesetsk approximately every six hours, he could not keep the boosters hidden. Nevertheless, his strategy included a few tricks to keep the Americans confused.

The pace of events seemed agonizingly slow as the Satans and their expensive payloads were transported the two miles to their widely separated launchpads. Once the boosters reached the pads, the launch teams worked feverishly in the cold of the March morning.

From beside the pad for *Borzoi I*, Novikov watched the booster rise sluggishly from its horizontal position on the transporter-erector. As the morning passed, the exhaustive training and the simulations of the last two months proved themselves. Novikov periodically checked his watch and smiled. His green team was working even faster than the record pace set by the blue team during the last practice. The huge hydraulically powered rods on the transporter-erector moved too slowly to be noticeable from moment to moment, but finally they had the oversized nose of the booster pointed skyward.

Borzoi I was erect over the flame-deflector pit thirty minutes sooner than Novikov's most optimistic predictions. The locomotive inched the transporter-erector away, leaving the rocket sitting on the four stabilizing arms. At the base of the towering booster, men in green cold-weather gear scrambled around the exhaust nozzles, connecting hoses and electrical lines. Finally the team chief signaled—he was ready to have the fuel and the oxidizer pumped into the empty tanks.

Pushing open the door of his limousine, Novikov said to Ganin, "There's enough time for our little ceremony."

He stepped from the car and pulled the collar of his coat up around his neck. His aide followed, carrying a camera, a stencil, and a can of spray paint.

"There's a new step in the procedures list," Novikov called out as the men in green began to assemble. He took the paint can and stencil from Ganin and held them high. "We can't send the first hunter off without being properly christened."

Shouting their approval, everyone moved closer as Novikov walked onto the portable scaffolding around the base of the booster. It was difficult to get in beside the old ICBM at the center of the conglomeration of rocket motors, so he selected a spot on the strap-on booster on the southeast side. The light from the late morning sun was better there, and his markings would not be visible to the American sensors when the next reconnaissance satellite passed almost overhead.

While two men held the stencil against the frigid metal, Novikov sprayed the red paint across the cutouts as Ganin snapped pictures. When the stencil was removed, two bolts of red lightning framed the silhouette of a Russian wolfhound above the number 1.

"The first *Borzoi*," Novikov shouted as he stabbed his cane toward the top of the booster. The men roared noisily in response. "Now let's get it into the cosmos."

The team chief accompanied the general to the limousine. Novikov looked at his watch, then said, "Use the primary deception procedure. Coverage period from twelve-fifteen to twelve-forty-five."

"Yes, Comrade General."

After verifying the accuracy of the man's watch, Novikov got into the car and headed for the other launchpad.

Even before he pulled away, members of the green team began covering exposed hoses and electrical lines. The men used netting and canvas of dirty white, sufficiently discolored to blend in with the snow. The servicing of the booster would continue unabated. However, by 1215 the launchpad would look abandoned—except for the Satan.

When Novikov reached *Borzoi II*, he saw that the blue team had started loading the fuel and oxidizer. He gave the same order about camouflage to the team chief. Finally Novikov was satisfied to return to the launch-control center. Except for removing the hoses when the servicing was complete, the remaining preparations would be controlled from the center.

Eight hours after Novikov had given the command *Poekhali*, he initiated the prelaunch countdown for *Borzoi I*. Preparations for *Borzoi II* were a few minutes behind, but its countdown would be put on hold anyway at T minus thirty minutes.

At T minus fifteen minutes for *Borzoi I*, the launch officer sent commands to rotate the servicing tower away from the booster. For a few seconds the tower remained in place, causing Novikov to think of midwinter launches when the bitter cold seemed to weld metal together. This afternoon, however, there was little wind, and the temperature was near the day's high of minus five degrees Celsius.

He was about to order men onto the pad when all the connectors separated cleanly. The tower moved, then leaned away from the booster. Only the four stabilizing arms remained, holding the booster above the flame pit. Wisps of oxidizer vapor venting from the strap-on boosters were the only sign of activity on the pad.

As was traditional for Novikov, when the count approached T minus one minute, he stepped outside. The hair-raising excitement of each launch seemed muted behind the thick walls of concrete, so he abandoned the safety of a control center whenever possible. Instead he wanted to hear the deafening fury. He loved to feel the vibrations that raced through the air in those first few seconds after the powerful rockets ignited. A headset on a long cord allowed him to monitor—or countermand—prelaunch communications. The cord also kept him close enough to the door to limp—or dive—to safety if the rocket exploded or veered off course.

At T minus ten seconds, the launch controller began counting aloud. "Ten. Nine. Eight."

From behind the waist-high wall along the front of the observation area, Novikov had a good view of *Borzoi I*. He looked at his watch—1612.

"Seven. Six."

He scanned the sky. Clouds that had appeared in the early afternoon were now solid from horizon to horizon. They did not threaten the launch, but they would lessen his enjoyment. Seconds after liftoff, the booster would disappear from view.

"Five. Four. Three."

The controller's countdown and the hum of electronics were the only sounds. In contrast to American launches, zero represented ignition instead of lift-off, so *Borzoi I* remained silent in the last seconds of the countdown.

"Two. One. Zero."

The RS-20 and its strap-on rockets ignited simultaneously.

Reflecting the brilliant yellow-white plumes of fire streaming into the flame-deflector pit, a cloud of deflected exhaust billowed behind the booster. As soon as the thrust buildup exceeded the weight, the Satan rose from the stabilizing arms. Once the four arms were freed of the booster's mass, they rotated outward like petals of a flower—a motion that had earned the stabilizing arms the nickname "tulip."

A deep-throated crackling roar from twenty exhaust nozzles finally reached Novikov. The clouds seemed to magnify the sounds and reflect all the noise and vibration to where he stood. He loved the exhilaration that came whenever he witnessed the sudden release of so much power.

An inexperienced observer might have been overwhelmed by the intensity of the discordant sounds echoing off every surface. However, Novikov listened carefully, perceiving a harmony that assured him all rockets were acting as one.

The steady movement of the supports and the smooth upward acceleration of the booster told Novikov that he had a good lift-off, but the visual spectacle was over almost as soon as it had started. In fewer than twenty seconds, the booster and its tail of flame disappeared into the clouds.

As the roar diminished, Novikov became aware of the enthusiastic shouts of the people who had joined him on the observation deck. He swung his cane toward the clouds in a gesture that under other circumstances might have been interpreted as "Charge!" His traditional growl accompanied the move, followed by smiles, handshakes, and hugs.

With his post-lift-off ritual finished, he hurried inside to await the completion of the first-stage burn. He wanted to follow closely *Borzoi I*'s journey to its initial goal—a circular orbit three hundred nautical miles above the earth.

6

Even before Novikov had lowered his cane, the ascent of *Borzoi
I* was sounding alarms more than five thousand miles away in Colorado. An American warning satellite, orbiting twenty-two thousand miles above the equator south of India, was the first to detect the hot exhaust plume. Within two seconds the satellite transmitted millions of bytes of data. Less than a second later, a communications satellite in geostationary orbit over Brazil relayed that data to the North American Air Defense Command (NORAD) deep within Cheyenne Mountain.

In NORAD's Missile Warning Center, Major Craig Fitzsimmons heard the audible alarm and saw a launch-warning symbol flashing on his console. As he grabbed the handset for the hotline to the command director, he looked at the clock—1212 Greenwich mean time. When the colonel at the other end responded, Fitzsimmons said, "Sir, we have a launch indication from Plesetsk, time twelve-twelve Zulu."

The colonel said, "Standing by for your confirmation."

Even as Fitzsimmons had reached for his telephone, other officers at nearby consoles were placing calls and checking inputs from additional sensors. A second warning satellite already was tracking the launch and sending more millions of bytes of data. Moments later there was confirmation from the Ballistic Missile Early Warning System (BMEWS) radar at Fylingdales Moor, England, followed quickly by a similar report from the BMEWS site at Thule, Greenland.

The reports Fitzsimmons was hearing from the other officers on intercom reinforced what he was seeing on his console. Obviously the initial warning was not due to a glitch in the satellite. He spoke into the hotline, "Sir, the launch is confirmed. A single burner out of the Northern Cosmodrome."

"Roger the single launch," the command director said. "Standing by."

The first thing the director needed to know was that the alarm did not represent a mass attack of Soviet ICBMs. Now Fitzsimmons had to estimate where the rocket's payload was headed. He checked the tiny letters and numbers near the launch symbol on his console. The small AZ had a 03 beside it. A third digit was fluctuating between two and four. The missile had barely started downrange and already the computer was narrowing in on the launch azimuth.

He cross-checked other indicators. They also were converging on the same answer—the rocket was headed north-northeast from Plesetsk. Projecting the ground track forward, Fitzsimmons satisfied himself that the rocket would stay on the Siberian side of the north pole, then start southward toward the equator. The ground track was similar to dozens of space launches he had verified during his two years as a duty officer. After hearing three other votes of "Space launch" over the intercom, he made his next call. "Sir, the event appears to be a space launch. Azimuth estimated at thirty-three degrees."

"Roger, copied. Space. Thirty-three."

Fitzsimmons heard the line go dead as the command director switched to his direct line to General Wade Patterson, the commander-in-chief of NORAD (CINCNORAD) and of the U.S. Space Command.

Fitzsimmons checked the time—forty-two seconds had elapsed. As he hung up the hotline, he noticed the locator information displayed on the front wall. General Patterson was already at his office in the mountain instead of at Space Command Headquarters east of Colorado Springs. Even as the command director was discussing the launch, Patterson would have displays in front of him showing refined information now coming in from seven different sources.

Fitzsimmons began unwrapping a sweet roll that he had set aside less than a minute earlier. By 0515, he thought, General Patterson would have passed his assessment of this event to the National Command Authority in Washington. Then everything in the mountain would return to the peacetime routine of a Monday morning.

Two time zones to the east of Cheyenne Mountain, Chisholm's Monday was off to a more bureaucratic start. He was leaving the staff meeting chaired each morning at 0700 by General Frank A. Ramsey, the vice chief of staff of the Air Force. Ramsey had mentioned Ambassador Galkin's unexpected departure from Washington on Saturday, and there had been a short discussion of the movement of the Defender I satellite to Cape Canaveral. The rest of the meeting had been mundane, as they often were when no new crisis had erupted during the weekend.

Passing through the outer office, Chisholm was hailed by Janice Waters, the senior secretary on Ramsey's staff.

Handing him an envelope, she said, "Here's something you might be interested in, Colonel Chisholm."

Giving her a wary smile as he accepted the envelope, Chisholm said, "Are you playing Ms. Matchmaker again?"

He and Janice had become friends soon after he had arrived at the Pentagon. She had become like an older sister and had taken a special interest in introducing Chisholm to her eligible acquaintances.

"I'm giving you plenty of advance notice this time," she said. "Remember, all work and no play . . ."

He glanced at the envelope and noticed that it was hand-addressed to Colonel O'Chisholm. "Saint Patrick's Day?"

"None other," she said in a simulated Irish brogue. "I'll even tell the general you're on leave that day if that's what it'll take to get you out of the office."

"We'll see," Chisholm said with a friendly smile.

Her telephone rang. Before answering it, she added, "Houlihan's Pub at seventeen thirty. It's hardly out of your way, Colonel."

Chisholm nodded. The pub was only a couple of miles from his apartment, so it would be easy enough to stop by. Walking out into the hallway, he wondered how much more enthusiastic he might be if Blake had not mentioned Sandi Turner on Saturday.

Chisholm's small, cluttered office did not reflect the weight of either his rank or his influence. A well-used chalkboard beside the door displayed dim images of the earth and satellite orbits, dusty remnants of previous brainstorming sessions. Shelves along two walls were piled high with unclassified reports accumulated in the three years he had occupied the office. Four file-cabinetlike safes were crammed with classified documents, mostly on the Defender I. Since the development of the costly satellite was challenged almost weekly by someone, Chisholm liked to keep the data close at hand. Providing quick and consistent answers had proved the most effective way to handle the endless, and often inane, demands of people with various personal political agendas. Thus he had earned the dogged respect of the Defender's most vocal critics, while at the same time becoming somewhat disillusioned with politicians.

The day Chisholm had taken over the office, he had made a pledge to himself: He never would become too comfortable in the Pentagon. Therefore, he had done little to personalize his office. A metal bust of a pilot gazing skyward sat on a bookcase behind his chair. The determined aviator, who was dressed in a World War II-vintage flight jacket, scarf, and goggles, had been a going-away present from Chisholm's people when he had stopped flying six years earlier. The single picture on his desk had been taken near the end of that same assignment. The photograph showed Chisholm in the pilot seat of a C-141 with his then-twelve-year-old daughter, Christie, on his knee. The only other personal item was an empty planter in the form of an early biplane sitting on one corner of his desk. A small flagstaff was attached to the strut on each wing. One flew an American flag; the other, a U.S. Air Force flag. The flags, which had orbited the earth for several days on the space shuttle, were among Chisholm's most prized possessions.

As usual he was scheduled for a string of meetings with few breaks throughout the rest of the day, so now he was trying to clear as much paperwork as possible from his in basket. Like many officers in the Pentagon, he had to waste much of his workday rehashing budget issues. Most of the papers in his in basket reflected the bureaucratic burden of trying to keep funding in place for critical programs such as Defender. He often was angered about how little time was left over to cope with the real challenges to national security.

A copy of a two-page protest leaflet slowed Chisholm's rush through the paperwork. Someone in the administration section had stapled a note on top that said "FYI"—For Your Information. The leaflets were circulated routinely whenever protest demonstrations threatened the normal duty day at the Pentagon.

The front page showed crude drawings of orbiting satellites that were flying the skull-and-crossbones flags. The boldly scrawled headline proclaimed "Defeat Defender Day." In letters almost as big, the next line read, "Shut down the Pentagon—March 12th!"

Great, Chisholm thought sarcastically, while verifying that the demonstration would occur at the end of the current week. He scanned the information scattered across the front page. Above a solicitation for donations he spotted the instructions for where and when to gather: 6:45 A.M. at Arlington National Cemetery, with the march to begin at 7:00. That was the good news among the bad. One benefit of working ten- to fourteen-hour days was that he seldom had to put up with the disruption of demonstrators. They rarely appeared at the Pentagon before 0600; he almost always did.

He studied the second page of the leaflet. One paragraph discussed a nationwide plan for disruptive activities on "Defeat Defender Day." He was not surprised by new demonstrations against the upcoming launch of Defender I. The dramatic departure of the Soviet ambassador was bound to inflame many people, and Chisholm assumed that the increased publicity about weapons in space would make many Americans restless. The launching of an armed satellite seemed to be an affront to the restrained Soviet foreign policy of the Glasnost era.

Other paragraphs contained the type of heavy-handed propaganda he had seen many times before. He scanned to the bottom and confirmed his suspicions. The last line of the "fact sheet" identified the sources—the Institute for Space Sciences in the Public Interest and the local branch of the Revolutionary Communist Party, USA.

After stuffing the leaflets into a lower drawer, he shoved the drawer closed with a clang that could be heard beyond his office. He had a strong bias against such demonstrations, and it was a bias developed long before he had become an officer in the Air Force.

As Chisholm started to attack his in basket with new determination, his thoughts were interrupted by a voice at his door.

"Is it safe to come in, sir?"

Chisholm looked up and saw Rick McClain peering with a smile around the edge of the door. The young engineer, who was a civilian employee of the Air Force, had started a career-broadening tour at the beginning of the year. During his two months at the Pentagon, he had worked for Chisholm. Although McClain's specialty was computers and electronics, Chisholm was pleased at how quickly his new protégé was learning the space business.

"As long as you're not carrying any placards, Rick."

McClain was confused for a moment, then smiled. "I guess you saw the leaflets. I'm here on a friendlier mission." He stepped into the doorway, carrying a box of doughnuts and a mug of coffee.

Chisholm looked at the doughnuts, then at McClain. "Did I forget to rip a couple of months off my calendar?"

The remark caught McClain off guard. "What?"

"The fat pills you're offering? I thought there were three months left until your performance appraisal's due."

McClain smiled as he placed the box on Chisholm's desk. "No bribes, sir. These are because back in January you said you'd bet dollars to doughnuts that those two new pads at Plesetsk were for modified SS-18s. I figure you deserve a payoff."

Chisholm had made his selection when he realized what McClain's remark implied. He set the doughnut next to his coffee cup and asked, "They've put an SS-18 on one of the pads?" He rose from his chair, pleased to have his suspicions about the purpose of the pads confirmed and already wondering what the payload might be.

"Not exactly," McClain said, pausing dramatically before continuing. "They've put an SS-18 on *each* of the pads."

"You're kidding." Chisholm stopped in midmotion, shocked by the revelation. His curiosity about the payload had been overshadowed—Novikov seemed on the verge of violating a basic tenet of the space-launch business. As far as Chisholm was concerned, you *always* conducted a methodical checkout of any new configuration before you even thought about rolling out the second bird. That rule was dictated by common sense and the high costs of failure. There was only one reasonable answer, he decided—there had to be some kind of misunderstanding.

Chisholm began pacing and asked, "When did they go to the pads? Do we have pictures yet?"

"The Operations Center expects to have imagery in a couple of hours, sir. Our noon bird discovered them, but there doesn't appear to be any activity around either booster."

Chisholm looked at his watch. "That puts them on the pads for seven to eight hours, depending on transportation time. Do you have any idea what the booster configuration looks like?"

"Both have a stretched SS-18 core with four strap-ons, that the analysts say are probably RD-107s. The payload fairing is oversized."

Chisholm stopped pacing and stared at McClain. "That ought to be a helluva package if the shroud's bigger than the diameter of an

SS-18. Two, huh? I'll be damned." He picked up his secure telephone and dialed the Air Force Operations Center in the basement of the Pentagon. After identifying himself to the duty officer, Chisholm said, "I'm interested in a pair of space launches from Plesetsk, probably due within the next few days. Put a message in your log to contact me whenever anything goes orbital from the Northern Cosmodrome."

"NORAD called about twenty minutes ago on a Plesetsk launch, sir. Would you—"

"Negative. That wouldn't be the . . ." Chisholm paused, his instincts suddenly in conflict with his common sense. Surely the Soviets wouldn't try launching a new vehicle from a new pad after only six or eight hours. Still, the Soviet prelaunch checkouts of their boosters always were much shorter than the weeks or months that American rockets waited on their pads. Even Soviet manned missions routinely launched within two days of when the boosters were erected on the pads at Tyuratam. "I doubt that's a launch I'm interested in, Captain, but what do you have on it?"

"CINCNORAD's declared it to be a space launch, probably using a new booster combination. The—"

"What kind? What's in the stack?" Chisholm's arms and shoulders had the shivery feeling that came whenever he received an ominous surprise.

"The analysts are still scratching their heads, sir," the captain continued. "After crunching the initial raw data, the computers came up with a greater than ninety percent confidence level that the booster included RD-107 strap-on rockets, and the same level of confidence that an SS-18 was also included."

Chisholm was mystified, completely unprepared to accept that this launch could have been one of the SS-18s that had appeared in the last few hours. After verifying on the telephone that the launch azimuth was similar to many routine launches from Plesetsk, he said, "Captain, I'll take anything else you get on this one and the next few that come from Plesetsk." Chisholm gave his telephone number, then hung up.

As he told McClain of NORAD's assessment, Chisholm picked up the biplane planter and absentmindedly began spinning its propeller.

McClain asked, "You really think this is something to get excited about, sir?"

"I'd have been less shocked," Chisholm said, gesturing with the biplane toward the ceiling, "if you'd told me that this little sucker had flown off my desk and gone directly into orbit. When you're trying something new, Rick, you have to find out what the problems are before you drag out the second copy."

"Of course our competition isn't always as cautious as we are," McClain said.

Chisholm nodded. "Novikov's no conservative, but he's also no fool." He was struck by his own phrasing. Novikov was not a fool. The Soviet general, Chisholm decided, must know something that had not become apparent within the flurry of surprises of the last few minutes. "He must be under the pressures of a mission that can't wait." Suddenly Chisholm wondered if the president's decision to launch Defender was driving Novikov's schedule.

"But if you've got a hot mission," McClain said, "you wouldn't wave a red flag in front of us by suddenly producing two mysterious boosters."

"You're right," Chisholm said as he noticed the time and grabbed the notebooks he would need for his next meeting. "Keep an eye on both pads for me." He picked up his forgotten doughnut and added, "Thanks."

"You ought to be proud of how well you handle that crystal ball, sir."

Chisholm smiled. "Right now I'm more like a guy who's just watched his mother-in-law back over a cliff in his new Mercedes. My feelings are a little mixed."

As he hurried through the halls, he remained preoccupied. He thought about the SS-18s and Defender I on launchpads fifty-three hundred miles apart. He thought about Ambassador Galkin's dramatic departure and how badly the Soviets wanted to stop Defender I. Perhaps, he thought uneasily, after nearly four decades of toleration of the other superpower's satellites overhead, a confrontation for the control of the ultimate high ground was about to begin.

Fewer than two hours later in Cheyenne Mountain, Major Fitzsimmons was startled when the second launch alarm of the morning sounded from a speaker. His eyes darted to his console—Plesetsk again. As he grabbed the hotline to NORAD's command director, he exchanged questioning looks with a nearby captain.

The captain said, "They're full of surprises this morning."

Fitzsimmons nodded his agreement. This was not the first time he had reported two events on the same shift, but in almost every instance, at least one of the launches had been on the forecast. Neither of these was. He looked at the clock—0732 local.

The command director answered the hotline on the third ring.

"Sir," Fitzsimmons said, "looks like we've got another event at Plesetsk. Time fourteen-thirty-two Zulu."

"Standing by for your confirmation."

The next forty seconds were like a replay of the verification procedures run earlier. When Fitzsimmons hung up, he went to his keyboard. By now more information was available on the first launch, and he wanted to take a look.

The Space Surveillance Center, also located deep within Cheyenne Mountain, tracked all active satellites and thousands of pieces of space junk. The first satellite, tagged as Cosmos 3208, was nearing the end of its second orbit about three hundred miles above the earth. He looked at the other orbital parameters and found nothing extraordinary. So far the mission of Cosmos 3208 had not been identified. There was a special note indicating that the launch at 0512 had been the first space launch to use an SS-18 booster. Otherwise Fitzsimmons found nothing indicating the mission had any particular significance.

Perhaps the second launch was unrelated, he thought as he returned to a report he had been reviewing before the latest alarm.

At 1340 in the Pentagon, Chisholm was stuck in a badly bogged-down meeting with more than twenty other people. His last meeting of the morning had run through the lunch hour, so now he wished he had a couple of McClain's doughnuts.

With each passing minute he was growing angrier with Washington politics. A vital upgrade to the avionics of the F-16 fighter force was being held hostage in a congressional committee. A Congressman from New York wanted to guarantee that some contracts would come into his district. Unfortunately for those trying to find a way to satisfy the Congressman, his district did not have any high-tech industry.

Chisholm brightened when he saw his secretary slip in through the side door of the conference room. Maybe there was a crisis, he thought, and she had come to rescue him from the current morass. Moments later he was disappointed. She produced several letters that he had planned to sign during his lunch break. Once she had the signatures, she handed him a folded piece of paper with his name scrawled on the outside, then left.

He turned back to the ongoing argument and put the paper on the table. Then he raised the edge, as if looking at a card drawn in a game of poker. His expression was far from a poker face when he read the message: "Both are up. McClain."

Unbelievable, Chisholm thought, barely able to keep the word from escaping his lips. He folded the paper, grabbed his notebooks, and quietly left the conference room. What really would be interesting, he thought as he hurried along a Pentagon hallway, would be if Novikov put another set of boosters on those pads in the next two or three weeks.

7

Two mornings later, Chisholm was shaving when he received a call from Major Winchell in the Air Force Operations Center. After identifying himself, Winchell said, "We have some of the . . . uh . . . information you requested, sir."

Since they were speaking on an unsecure line, the major obviously was avoiding the subject. Chisholm tried to recall any specific requests. Then he remembered asking to be informed of any space launches from Plesetsk. For an instant he was energized by the possibility that the Soviets had rocketed another modified SS-18 from one of the special pads. He quickly discounted that thought, however, because fewer than forty-eight hours had passed since the first on Monday. More likely, he decided, the Soviets had made a routine launch from Plesetsk, and Winchell simply was calling as requested. Chisholm wished he could ask what the message really meant.

As he finished shaving, he thought through all his unanswered questions about the two launches on Monday. Common sense and experience—his American experience—told him that Novikov couldn't have used one of those pads again so quickly. Yet Chisholm's instincts reminded him that nothing on Monday had made sense. He checked his watch and decided that by skipping breakfast he could stop at the Operations Center on the way to the office.

About forty-five minutes later, Major Winchell was at his console when Chisholm approached. "Sir, we detected a space launch from Plesetsk at 0925 Zulu, and NORAD says this booster's like the pair that went up Monday."

"Jesus," Chisholm said, stunned by the answer. "How certain are they—about the booster, I mean?"

Winchell checked the teletype message that had followed up the initial voice reports on the launch. "That's the first cut, sir, but the computer showed a greater than seventy-five percent confidence level."

Chisholm's list of questions was growing, but he doubted that the major had many of the answers. "What's happening with the two birds launched on Monday?"

"Not much," Winchell said as he turned and typed some commands on his keyboard. A new display of data appeared. "Cosmos 3208, Cosmos 3209—both unchanged, still at three hundred."

Chisholm nodded. Nothing special so far, he thought. Five out of six man-made satellites never went beyond the region known as low-earth orbit, or LEO. LEO's upper and lower boundaries were determined more by nature than by man. Satellites that drifted lower than about one hundred nautical miles were slowed by more and more atmospheric drag. They eventually plunged to a fiery demise unless on-board rockets regularly restored the lost velocity and altitude. When a spacecraft climbed much above three hundred nautical miles, its orbit passed into a belt of trapped radiation that circled the equator like an invisible inner tube around a swimmer's waist. The radiation, which was most intense out to about three thousand miles, posed a threat to any unshielded man or machine that stayed within the danger zone.

Monday afternoon Chisholm had made a quick check of the orbits of Novikov's new satellites. Once their rocket engines had shut down only minutes after launch, the new spacecraft had begun coasting. There was virtually no atmospheric drag at three hundred nautical miles. Therefore, each was following an invisible pathway determined by the satellite's momentum and by the force of the gravity continually pulling toward the mass center of the earth. Chisholm knew of other perturbing influences, such as the solar wind, the oblateness of the earth, and the gravitational attraction of the sun, moon, and planets. Those forces, however, had little effect from one day to the next. So, on Monday he had concluded that without the firing of on-board rockets, each satellite would repeat its same circular orbit indefinitely as the earth slowly rotated beneath.

Since each satellite remained at a steady speed and altitude, those elements offered no special clues. Chisholm decided that each orbit's most interesting element was its inclination angle—the angle between the orbit and the equator as the satellite crossed into the northern hemisphere. These satellites passed over the equator at an eighty degree angle.

Although the inclination angle itself seemed academic, perhaps of interest only to a professor at a chalkboard, it had far more significance. The inclination angle determined how far the satellite's ground track—the path of points on the earth directly below the satellite—went north and south of the equator on every orbit. These ground tracks ranged over the earth from eighty degrees north to eighty degrees south, thereby passing within six hundred nautical miles of the north and south poles on each orbit. From a vantage point three hundred nautical miles high, sensors could see well beyond the poles on every pass. Thus, these satellites were theoretically capable of observing every point on the earth every twelve hours.

Yet he was not convinced that Novikov's new satellites were reconnaissance birds. They were too high for photo-reconnaissance—cameras at one hundred miles made much more sense than at three hundred. Even the Soviet's ocean surveillance satellites followed orbits only about half as high as Cosmos 3208 and 3209. When compared with other Soviet orbits, these most closely matched those of the heavy electronic intelligence (ELINT) satellites. Yet Chisholm knew that the ELINT birds flew even higher to spy on electronic emissions over an even broader area.

So on Monday Chisholm had begun to suspect that these satellites were in temporary orbits known as parking orbits. Perhaps they were waiting for more satellites of the same constellation. Since parking orbits usually were lower, however, he had wondered why Novikov would boost these clear up to three hundred. The most logical answer on Monday had been that Novikov needed months to launch the rest and did not want the earlier birds to sink back into the atmosphere while waiting. Now that a third satellite already had joined the constellation, Chisholm's growing concerns were causing an uneasy feeling behind his belt buckle.

He asked Winchell, "Has NORAD identified a mission for these birds?"

"Maybe ELINT, sir, but that's got about a fifteen percent confidence level. If they're picking up data, they're not passing any back to the Soviet Union. The only electronic signals these birds are putting out so far are the normal postlaunch communications checks."

Chisholm was disappointed that the satellites were so passive. Often a satellite's electronic signature gave him the best clues about its mission. He hoped that Novikov's mysterious craft were something as simple as a new design for gathering electronic intelligence. However, his instincts about that answer set his confidence level at well below 15 percent.

After leaving Winchell, Chisholm checked with the analysts in the intelligence section. So far they knew nothing special about the new satellites. However, one analyst had prepared an envelope in response to Rick McClain's request for all new information on the two Soviet launchpads.

Chisholm took the sealed envelope but did not open it until reaching the privacy of his office. Inside the envelope he found two photos, both showing a launchpad with a modified SS-18, complete with oversized shroud on top. According to an accompanying note, the pads had been empty at midnight. These pictures showed the pads occupied about daybreak.

He was applying the nine-hour adjustment between the local times in Plesetsk and Washington, D.C., when he realized the note said *pads*. During his first glance at the photos, he had thought they were two views of the booster launched within the last couple of hours. Now as he compared details, he confirmed that the pictures showed two different boosters. Novikov was duplicating Monday's miracles, and what was even more astounding as far as Chisholm was concerned, the Soviet wizard had needed only two days.

Chisholm looked at his schedule—some of the mundane things were going to have to go. He checked General Ramsey's schedule and found it to be as packed as usual. Nevertheless, Chisholm knew that the day had come to elevate his concerns to the four-star level.

At 1550 in Plesetsk, the next countdown reached T minus fifteen minutes. Novikov stepped from the launch-control center into snow that was accumulating on the observation deck. The ongoing snow shower obscured *Borzoi IV* behind a wall of swirling snowflakes. Standing in what seemed like the inside of a white cocoon, he realized that his launch schedule was in jeopardy. If ever in his life he needed two weeks of smooth countdowns, this was the time. A delay now would ripple into the schedules for the four remaining *Borzoi* and perhaps even into the schedule for *Zashchitnik I*. Therefore, he was determined to take every reasonable risk to launch *Borzoi IV* on time.

Although Novikov wished that the storm had held off for a few more hours, he was a man who enjoyed taking on the odds—and winning. The hockey games he recalled most often were those in which his team had been behind a goal or two going into the last few minutes. The launches he remembered with special fondness had lingered in doubt until the seconds remaining had dwindled to zero.

"Comrade General," the launch-control officer said over the intercom, "the winds are now two knots over the limit. Should I halt the countdown?"

"No," Novikov said firmly. "Announce the velocity at each minute."

The sting of snow on his face convinced him that it was colder than the last time he had been outside thirty minutes earlier. Looking toward the booster, which was concealed by billions of falling snowflakes, he was more concerned with the winds immediately after launch than with the cold. Initially the wind's speed would be greater than the booster's, and the booster would need a few seconds worth of acceleration to increase its speed well to above that of the wind. Small nozzles in the base of the rockets normally kept the booster pointed in the right direction. Nevertheless, a large gust of wind as *Borzoi IV* was clearing the stabilizing arms could tilt the booster too far for the nozzles to recover.

That thought troubled Novikov more than the risks brought on by the snow. He could afford to lose one *Borzoi*—though he would prefer such a loss to come on the eighth launch instead of the fourth. If this booster toppled out of control and fell onto the pad, the remainder of the launch schedule would take ten days instead of four since the last five *Borzoi* would have to use a single pad.

"The time is T minus thirteen," the launch controller announced. "The peak wind gust in the last minute was twenty knots."

Four knots too much, Novikov thought. He did not like the trend. He also did not like the fact that the sixteen-knot limit had been set using computer simulations. The bulbous fairing that covered the satellite made the booster appear top heavy and made it even more vulnerable to the wind at launch. The winds Monday had been light, so this new configuration had never been launched in winds that were near the limit determined by the computer. His confidence would be greater, he thought quietly, if he had good wind-tunnel data—or if he could have a couple of shots of vodka before making the final decision.

The next three announcements confirmed that *Borzoi IV* remained ready for launch. The wind, however, held at nearly twenty knots.

Just after T minus ten minutes, the weather officer came onto the observation deck. "Comrade General," he said, "I've received updated reports from Moscow."

Novikov brushed aside the snowflakes that had settled on his eyebrows. "Are they predicting spring flowers today, Boris, or do they believe we shall have snow?" When it came to weather forecasting, Novikov had more faith in his arthritic knee and the feel of the breeze on his face than in the bureaucrats in Moscow.

"Snow, Comrade General. Nearly a meter of new snow has fallen on Murmansk, and Archangelsk already has more than thirty centimeters."

Novikov nodded, knowing that the winds often pushed the weather south from the nearby ports across the forests toward Plesetsk. He had checked the satellite pictures periodically throughout the morning. A deepening low-pressure system was moving out of the Arctic, down from the Barents Sea. "I would say we're due for about—" He reached a hand to the part of his kneecap that remained fused in position. Flexing his leg slightly, he nodded a couple of times, as if the answer had just come to him, "—seventy centimeters of very wet snow."

"At least," the weatherman said. "A solid band of heavy snow two hundred fifty kilometers wide is just beyond the Yemtsa River."

Enough to shut them down for the rest of the day and maybe tomorrow, Novikov thought as he scanned his surroundings, straining to see nearby landmarks. A hundred meters to the northwest, the dim outline of trees teased his senses—perhaps there, perhaps only wishful imprints of memories of the previous three launches. Yet two snow showers earlier in the afternoon had swept through like a squall line—a few minutes of a blinding flurry of white, followed by the momentary malaise of an overcast Arctic afternoon. One more break in the snowfall was all he needed.

"Go make me ten minutes of clear weather, Boris. Then take the rest of the day off."

A smile appeared on the ruddy, snowflake-flecked face of the weatherman. "I will do my best, Comrade General," he said, then started toward the warmth of the launch-control center.

Novikov placed his hand against his injured knee, then added, "But be very careful if you go outside this evening, Boris. Tonight's going to be cold enough to freeze things off besides your fingers and toes."

The weatherman's expression changed to an embarrassed smile, but his cheeks were already too red from the cold to show any blush of color.

Novikov paused for effect, then added, "I was referring of course to your nose and ears."

"Of course, Comrade General."

As the countdown continued, Novikov grudgingly accepted that the storm was going to change his plans. He had scheduled a flight to Tyuratam later in the evening. The twinge in his knee assured him that Plesetsk's airfield would be clogged with snow until well after the storm had spent its fury.

At T minus three minutes, the wind had decreased to seventeen knots and the visibility was improving. Although a distant treeline and the image of *Borzoi IV* appeared more like apparitions than physical objects, Novikov at last could rationalize that he had enough visibility. The booster had to be in sight at the time of launch—at least that was what the procedures demanded. This assured that the booster could be destroyed if it malfunctioned in the moments before radar began tracking it. He was willing to make a liberal interpretation of the rules if he had to. After all, it was his signature that had kept that procedure in effect.

Novikov stepped into the doorway at T minus one minute. For a few seconds he watched the gauge that was connected to the anemometer nearest the pad. The jittering needle showed a wind speed varying between fourteen and seventeen knots, but favoring the higher over the lower.

Looking toward the pad, he had to concentrate to see the booster through the falling snow. The visibility was not getting any better.

"Seventeen knots at Ten. Nine. Eight." The launch-control officer's voice began to falter. "Seventeen knots at Five."

Novikov rose on tiptoe, getting a more direct view at the gauge than was available from the launch-control officer's seat behind a console. Novikov's angle made the reading appear closer to sixteen than seventeen. He glanced at the clock. Pressing his microphone button, Novikov continued the count. "Three. Sixteen knots. Two." Taking a quick look at the anemometer gauge, he moved beyond the door. The drumbeat in his temples almost drowned out the sound of his voice as he squinted to get another look at *Borzoi IV.* "One. Zero."

Like millions of suspended prisms, the snowflakes cast shimmering reflections of the flash of yellow and white that erupted beneath *Borzoi IV.* Novikov held his breath, waiting for the noise of the rockets to roar through the mile of snow-filled air that separated him from the pad. As the crackling growl suddenly shook everything around him, the dazzling display of light flashed many times brighter. In that instant his senses overwhelmed his training and rocked him with the false message that the booster had exploded. Immediately he regretted taking the additional risks, pushing against the odds to get the mission off. The feeling was akin to that experienced seven years earlier when he had discovered one of the parachutes had failed, and his spacecraft was plunging too fast toward the rugged peaks below.

Hearing the cheers of those watching from inside, he realized the brilliant glow was moving upward from the pit that had hidden the plume of fire. He shouted into his microphone, "How's it look?"

"Nominal, nominal, nominal," the launch-control officer said, indicating that the booster's performance was matching the predicted thrust and flight path. His voice had returned to its full strength.

Novikov rushed inside and looked ravenously at the readouts that showed *Borzoi IV* racing upward. He would withhold his traditional growl a few more seconds, but he began to look casual, as if the issue had never been in doubt.

Less than an hour later, he was satisfied that *Borzoi IV* was safely in orbit. He also had confirmed that he was stranded at Plesetsk, at least until morning. In addition, the blizzard that had grounded his aircraft was keeping his refurbishment crews off the pads. They could do little until the cosmodrome's maintenance crews cleared away some of the snow, and that would not happen until the storm passed.

"Let me have your attention," Novikov announced sternly to those crowded in the launch-control center. "We have worked continuously for three days, and now I fear that many may want to crawl into some dark corner and warm their spirits with vodka. But these four magnificent launches are only half the work that must be done." He surveyed with amusement the uneasy looks on several faces. Frowning, he looked toward the clock dramatically, then said, "At 1800, I want a meeting of everyone in the lower assembly building. The only exceptions are those who must be on the consoles. I don't want anyone drinking alone in some dark corner." He pulled his coat over his shoulders, picked up his cane, and smiled. "If we're going to drink, we shall drink together. Someone bring something for music."

After leaving, Novikov got a requisition form and listed the supplies he needed—cheese, black bread, tinned meats, salted herring, *baliki* (salted and smoked pieces of sturgeon), marinated mushrooms, fresh fruit, and vodka. Beneath the list he scrawled a signature that was much larger than normal.

He handed the form to Mayor Ganin and faked a serious look. "Tell them that anyone who delays you may find himself riding on *Borzoi V.*"

Ganin accepted the list with restrained enthusiasm, then hurried out with four other members of the general's staff.

As Novikov entered a car for the ride through the tunnels, he appreciated Ganin's unspoken concern. The food and vodka would be drawn from stocks maintained for senior officers and the Party *apparatchiki*. He knew his use of the food would not go without being criticized. Already some men in the Party's local bureaucracy had accused him of the sin of developing a cult of personality. He smiled, knowing that if he got five more good launches from his crews, President Grigoriev would become the ardent leader of the so-called cult. Novikov also understood that if his crews failed, criticism over a few cases of fruit would be inconsequential.

Before joining the celebration in the underground assembly area, he went to his office. His chief of staff, Polkovnik Bobylev, brought the latest contingency plans to Novikov's desk. The two men discussed how the weather delay, now of indeterminate length, would be merged into the launch schedules. If the snow kept his refurbishment teams off the pads for no longer than twelve hours, he could have the next two boosters in position for fueling on Friday—very late on Friday. A loss of twenty-four hours would keep him from bragging that he had put eight *Borzoi* up in eight days. Nevertheless, all nine Soviet satellites could be in orbit less than two weeks after the American announcement clearing Defender I for launch. That, Novikov thought with pride, would be an accomplishment worth bragging about.

Checking the latest pictures from the Meteor satellite, he was convinced that the heaviest snow would not end before four in the morning. Adding in the time necessary to clear the main roads, the taxiways, and the runway, he would be lucky to be airborne by six.

That would work, he thought. He was determined to be in Tyuratam when *Zashchitnik I* rolled out of the assembly building, and his new schedule gave five hours to spare.

Turning to Bobylev, Novikov said, "When the last snowplow moves off the runway in the morning, Vitali, I want its driver to have to maneuver around my airplane." Novikov added with a smile, "And I want to be airborne before the driver has stopped cursing me and my Cossack ancestors."

Bobylev would make sure there were no slipups, even if a hundred different calls were required throughout the night. Now, Novikov thought, he could relax for a few hours, using the unexpected respite to steel himself for the intense challenges yet to come.

A few minutes later Novikov could hear music and singing even before his sedan left the tunnel and entered the main assembly area. The celebration was well under way, and his arrival was cause for a round of cheers. Unlike many Soviet officers, he was popular with his troops. He demanded good performance, but he also found little ways, such as this impromptu party, to reward the extraordinary accomplishments of his launch teams. During his dangerous years as a cosmonaut, he had adopted several philosophies to live by. Work hard, play hard was one.

More than one hundred people had gathered in a section of the assembly area that had been crowded with boosters and satellites three days earlier. Mayor Ganin and his crew were placing food and vodka on empty workbenches. Nearby, a makeshift band consisted of two trumpets, a drum, three guitars, and several other stringed instruments of various ethnic origins.

Novikov picked up a bottle of vodka, then turned to address his people. As he opened the bottle, he took a few moments to look around the crowd, sharing smiles that made the experience seem more personal. "President Grigoriev himself is proud of every one of you. You have worked magnificently for months, and now we shall celebrate—for one hour." He raised the bottle high, then shouted, "To every one of you who has made *Krasnaya Molniya* possible." He took a swallow from the bottle, gestured toward the food and drink, then watched with satisfaction as his people swarmed around the workbenches.

He remained keyed up from the tension of the afternoon, and the vodka added to the warm feeling inside. The fear and excitement he had felt in those questionable seconds after ignition were similar in intensity to his space flights and to his most memorable sexual experiences. Now as the howling blizzard released him from the nonstop schedule he had set for himself, his thoughts turned to Luiza Daukantas.

His rank and position entitled him to almost unlimited prerogatives with the women in his command as well as many others assigned to the Northern Cosmodrome. In the last year Luiza had taken a special place in his life, like a peaceful oasis amid the pressures of developing the weapons of a new age. He took another drink as he looked for her. He eyed the crowd, picking out the women scattered among the predominantly male gathering. That was no easy task since most people wore similar coats in the chilly room.

As the men began to scatter out with their food and drink, he saw Luiza. Barely five feet tall, she was difficult to spot in a crowd. Ten years earlier she had been an eighty-seven-pound adolescent with the potential to become a world-class gymnast. Instead of retaining a skinny figure that could soar with ease over the parallel bars, she had filled out, developing the curves that Novikov found so appealing.

In a few moments the band began playing traditional Russian music, and the longer the vodka flowed, the happier everyone became. Novikov lustily joined in the singing of a few bawdy military songs.

When a few men began the vigorous Cossack dances, he looked on with envy. As a cosmonaut, he had traveled through most of the republics and often joined in the entertainment. He had mastered many dances of the nationalities. In those more carefree days he had been a much heavier drinker, and there was a range just short of total drunkenness where he could outdance the best of the natives. Now he could only clap his hands or tap his cane in time with the music. The thing Novikov regretted most about his injuries, other than his inability to return to space, was that they kept him from being able to dance.

On the far side of the circle surrounding the dancers, Luiza was looking his way. Novikov nodded toward her and gave her the hint of a smile. By the time the next song started, she had moved in beside him. He dropped one arm over her shoulder and hugged her against him as they joined in the singing.

At one minute before seven Novikov moved into the circle and signaled for a break in the music. "There is much important work yet to do, and I expect every one of you to be ready at zero-five-hundred. I understand that Mayor Ganin's wristwatch has just stopped." He glanced toward Ganin, who looked confused. "When he gets his watch fixed in exactly ten minutes, the vodka will stop flowing."

The boisterous crowd voiced its approval of the ten-minute extension.

"Let the music and the successes continue."

The band and the dancers began again, and many people made another pass at the nearly empty food tables. Novikov took Luiza by the hand, and they walked to his car.

His living quarters were near his office in Kochmas. The well-furnished apartment was cold when they arrived, since he had expected to be away for several days. He and Luiza quickly threw off their coats, uniforms, and boots, then hurried into the bathroom. Once beneath the pelting warmth of the shower, Novikov slowed the pace, and they leisurely removed the undergarments from each other. Because of his injuries, and his rank, the shower area of his quarters had been enlarged and enclosed like a steam room. One wall now had a benchlike extension, which Novikov and Luiza had found very convenient.

As the hot water pounded down upon them, he threw off his concerns as completely as he had abandoned his clothing. Novikov made love as if time did not matter. He concentrated only on giving pleasure to Luiza and receiving pleasure from her. Finally, when both were sexually satisfied and exhausted, they sat cuddling, enveloped by the steamy warmth while the heater slowly raised the temperature in the rest of the apartment.

Later Novikov stretched out on his bed while Luiza remained within the dressing area adjoining the end of the bedroom. Now they began what had become an enjoyable ritual for both. As if preparing for a lover who had not yet arrived, Luiza picked from an array of bath powders, French perfume, and lacy lingerie. She took her time, partly to increase Novikov's enjoyment, partly because this was her most feminine interlude within the colorless life of being a woman in northern Russia.

When she finally was ready, she switched off the bedroom light and all but one small light in the dressing area. Silhouetted enticingly, Luiza began the graceful exercises that had been a daily routine for most of the years of her life—although only within the last couple of years had she performed them in lingerie and high heels.

She slowly raised one hand, then the other toward the ceiling. Her flowing movements were reminiscent of the posing between tumbling routines in the floor exercise competitions. Every action played directly to her audience of one, though her eyes never acknowledged Novikov's presence.

For several minutes Novikov watched each motion as carefully as if he were judging her grace and skill as a gymnast. The longer he watched, the more time he wanted to spend with her. Perhaps, he hoped, the storm would stall over Plesetsk and delay his flight for a few more hours. As she continued, he placed a call to the weather office and was disappointed to learn that the weather was following the prediction.

Luiza stretched sideways, sliding her fingers sensuously down her leg until she touched her ankle.

"When we spoke this afternoon, Boris," Novikov said into the telephone, "I believed the night would be unbearably cold. Now my knee is feeling much better, so I predict a much more comfortable night." He extended a hand to get Luiza's attention, and she came to him immediately.

"But, General, the temperatures behind the front are—"

"Good night, Boris," Novikov said as he slipped his arm around Luiza's slender waist and pulled her down to him.

8

The Pentagon, Washington, D.C.
Wednesday, 10 March, 1805 local (2305 GMT)

Chisholm was at his desk when Janice Waters called to say that General Ramsey would be available shortly. Minutes later Chisholm reached the outer office of the vice chief of staff.

"One week and counting, Colonel Chisholm," Waters said, holding up a plastic shamrock decorated with a green and white bow.

Although Chisholm had had little time to think about her invitation to the St. Patrick's Day festivities, he smiled at her gentle persistence. "May ye be in heaven half an hour before—"

"I know," she said with an impish grin, then continued the proverb, "before the devil knows I'm dead. Really, someone you'd enjoy meeting will be there."

Chisholm tried to maintain a straight face as he asked, "Short and always wears green?"

Waters looked confused. "No, she's about medium. . . . I'm not talking about a leprechaun, Colonel."

They both laughed. Before they could continue the discussion, the intercom sounded, and General Ramsey called Waters into his office.

She picked up her stenographer's pad, then said to Chisholm as she walked to the door, "You won't be disappointed if you join us."

"We'll see," Chisholm said.

While Chisholm waited, he thought about what he needed to say. He had great confidence in Ramsey's abilities. The general had been a Rhodes Scholar following graduation from the Air Force Academy thirty years earlier. Although Ramsey was one of the brightest men Chisholm had ever met, the general enjoyed displaying an "ol' country boy" persona in private with favorite subordinates. Chisholm was flattered to be one of them.

As the vice chief of staff, Ramsey dealt with hundreds of weighty topics each week. Few involved satellites and space, so Chisholm provided pertinent background whenever such a problem arose. Ramsey might not know all the basics, but when he did not understand a concept, he was not afraid to say so. And once he had mastered it, he did not forget.

Janice Waters emerged with several folders and said that the general was ready.

When Chisholm entered, Ramsey was signing papers. The general was in his early fifties, trim, and with gray hair neatly trimmed in a crew cut. He glanced up momentarily and said, "I hear you've got a new burr under your saddle, Mike. Do we have a problem with the Defender?"

"No, but maybe yes, General."

"Washingtonspeak if I ever heard it, Mike," Ramsey said as he stopped signing for a moment and looked up with a wary smile. "You're not finally turning bureaucrat on me, are you?"

"No way, sir. The prelaunch processing in Florida's going fine."

"No showstoppers?"

"None, sir. Here's what I'm concerned with." He began by showing pictures of the modified SS-18 missiles that had been on the new launchpads earlier in the day. "I think Novikov's mounting a challenge to Defender."

Ramsey stared for a moment at Chisholm, then said, "We start a rumor like that, and we'll be opening a whole barrel of worms."

"Yes, sir," Chisholm said. "That's why I haven't shared my suspicions with anyone else."

"How certain are you, Mike?"

Chisholm settled into a chair near the desk. "I don't have enough yet to sell anyone on Capitol Hill or at the White House, but I'm seeing things I can't ignore." Then he told of the rapid launches and the three-hundred-nautical-mile orbits.

Ramsey continued signing documents as he listened to Chisholm's description. "The SS-18 angle's interesting, Mike, but you convinced me long ago that the Soviets launch something almost every day. I don't see any 'you can reach out and feel it' connection with Defender."

"I may have found one late this afternoon," Chisholm said, opening a notebook. "I asked Intel what they had on General Novikov's whereabouts for the last couple of weeks. He'd spent most of his time at Plesetsk until last Thursday. That morning he flew to Moscow and stayed at Marshal Murashev's headquarters until returning to Plesetsk on Saturday. Sunday afternoon Novikov went to the Kremlin. Intel thinks he and Murashev attended a meeting with President Grigoriev in which Ambassador Galkin was also included."

"Galkin!" Ramsey stopped in midsignature and leaned forward with great interest. "Hell, that chubby little devil was in Washington until Saturday night. If he was in the Kremlin on Sunday afternoon, Aeroflot must've landed him in Red Square."

"Yes, sir, and the *why* is more important than how he got there. His harangue at Dulles made it clear that he had been recalled because of one subject and one subject only."

"Defender I," Ramsey said.

Chisholm nodded. "Novikov returned to Plesetsk immediately after the Kremlin meeting and put two new birds on the pads fewer than twelve hours later."

Ramsey's expression showed deep concentration. "Ambassador Galkin, President Grigoriev, and General Novikov. You might have something, Mike."

"The CIA believes Novikov's had some kind of development program under wraps for two or three years. Now we see a surge of unusual activity immediately after the go-ahead announcement for Defender I. I don't believe in coincidences, General."

"But would they really risk shooting down the Defender?" Ramsey's expression suggested that he found the idea morbidly fascinating.

"Shooting down isn't quite the right terminology," Chisholm said, expecting a damaged satellite to continue orbiting well after the attack. "But if Grigoriev wants control of space, he has to destroy the Defenders before they're operational and can take care of themselves."

Ramsey pushed the remaining documents aside and started writing in a small notebook. Gesturing toward the photographs of the SS-18s, he asked, "Do you have any pictures yet of the satellites?"

Chisholm shook his head. "So far Novikov's hiding them very well, sir."

"Now even with my airplane driver's mind-set, I know he can't hide satellites from us in low-earth orbit. What are our folks at

SPADATS seeing?" He referred to the Space Detection and Tracking System that continually scanned the skies for new objects in space, then determined their orbits so that the objects could be tracked.

"We're tracking the new birds easily enough, but Novikov's cagey. So far he hasn't jettisoned the payload fairing on any of the birds."

"Is that unusual, Mike?"

"Yes, sir. The fairing minimizes drag during the climb. Once the bird's above the denser atmosphere, the fairing's just dead weight."

Ramsey sat back and looked thoughtfully toward Chisholm. "So Novikov was willing to waste some fuel to keep his payloads hidden."

"Exactly, sir," Chisholm said, pleased that Ramsey recognized that there was a penalty in lifting the fairings to three hundred nautical miles. "Unfortunately, the GEODSS cameras show little more than you're seeing when the boosters were on the pads."

GEODSS, which stood for Ground-based Electro-Optical Deep-space Surveillance System, combined forty-inch telescopes with video sensors. The light reflected by a satellite was converted to electrical impulses, thereby producing an image of what the satellite looked like. The system had proved sensitive enough to detect a reflective sphere the size of a soccer ball at more than twenty-two thousand miles. Therefore, Chisholm had expected to see excellent images of the new satellites passing overhead at LEO, but now was stymied by Novikov.

Ramsey asked, "What's Novikov hoping to gain by playing hide and seek?"

"I'm guessing he wants the constellation built before we recognize what they're doing."

"How long does he need?"

"That's hard to say, General. Last weekend, I'd have bet heavily against seeing even one bird launched from those new pads."

"But now he's got four. Is four enough or does he need forty?"

"Four's definitely not enough," Chisholm said. "I think he's going for four orbital planes with a forty-five degree offset. Right now he's put two birds in the same plane so one of the planes is still empty, but—"

"Speaking of planes, Mike," Ramsey said in a gently chiding voice, "when are you space guys gonna learn to speak plain English?"

"Sir?"

" 'Orbital plane!' As in 'plane geometry'?"

"Yes, sir. A satellite normally orbits in a plane, which includes the mass-center of the earth."

"Well, last time I heard, the earth was spherical, more or less." He gestured to a large globe alongside his desk. "And an orbit goes around it, right?"

"So far you're batting one thousand, sir." Chisholm permitted himself a small smile.

"So enlighten me. How can you talk about a single plane for a satellite that's circling something spherical that's orbiting a sun that's moving through the galaxies?"

"In astrodynamics we make a few simplifying assumptions, sir."

Ramsey gave an exasperated smile. "Seeing as how I'm from the Missouri side of Oklahoma, you're going to have to show me."

"I understand, sir," Chisholm said, familiar with the games Ramsey played in learning from his subordinates. The most unsettling part for Chisholm was that he often was uncertain whether Ramsey was barely keeping up or already well ahead of the point being made. Chisholm went to the globe and touched the circular wooden frame that supported the sphere on a shaft through the north and south poles. "Pretend this frame included clear glass that actually sliced through the globe—sliced flat through it. That glass would be a flat plane, which also would pass through the center of the globe. Fair enough, sir?"

Ramsey chuckled. "Okay, Mike. That's the kind of language an ol' country boy like me can understand."

Chisholm rotated the globe, moving Plesetsk beneath the wooden frame. "Consider that Novikov launched his first satellite from the Northern Cosmodrome and put it into an orbit that follows this frame." He pointed at Plesetsk, then moved his finger northward along the wooden frame as if he were following the path of the imaginary satellite. "If this frame were three hundred miles above the earth—and the frame is pretty close to scale for an earth that has a radius of almost thirty-five hundred nautical miles—the satellite would continue along this frame for years as the earth rotated beneath." Chisholm spun the globe slowly.

Ramsey nodded his understanding. "If he launched another satellite three hours later, the launch site isn't under the first orbital plane anymore."

"Exactly, sir," Chisholm said as he realigned the globe with Plesetsk forty-five degrees—three hours' worth of earth rotation—beyond the frame. "So the second bird would be on a different orbital plane." He moved his finger from Plesetsk toward the north pole.

"Okay," Ramsey said, his expression bright with discovery. "So if he launches a third bird the next day at approximately the same time as the first, it'll be within that first orbital plane—chasing bird number one."

Chisholm nodded. "In this case, he needed two days to get to the third and fourth launches, but number four is doing exactly as you suggest. And I'd expect satellites four and one to remain in, or close to, that plane for the rest of their natural lives."

"Because," Ramsey remarked, "it generally takes more fuel than you carry to move the orbit very far out of its original plane."

"Yes, sir." Chisholm was pleased that Ramsey remembered a concept explained several months before. "It's much cheaper in terms of fuel to change the shape and size of the orbit within that plane. Within those planes he can stretch the orbits a long way. I'm convinced we'll see changes like that when Novikov gets more birds into orbit."

"That brings us back to one of the questions General Bolton's going to ask," Ramsey said, referring to the Air Force chief of staff. "How many birds does Novikov need to pose a real threat?"

"The orbits of satellites two and three suggest we'll see some multiple of four. At least eight. But it could be twelve or even sixteen."

Ramsey smiled and settled back into his chair. "You have a couple of days' data on four new birds, and already you can make those kinds of guesstimates?"

"There's not much guessing as far as those numbers are concerned." Chisholm pointed to the frame. "Consider that this frame is part of a cage that Novikov has started building around the earth. His cage would include three more frames just like it. The orbit for satellite three is perpendicular to the frame, and two's orbit is halfway between."

Ramsey nodded. "With some number of satellites racing around each frame?"

"Yes, sir."

"Like three more frames on the shaft through the north and south poles?"

"Essentially," Chisholm said, trying to keep his example simple. "And the angles between these orbital planes would be similar to what I see on the four satellites he's launched since Monday morning."

"And since he's already put two in one orbital plane, you assume that all four planes will get at least two."

"Yes, sir. How many more, if any, depends on what he wants to cover, how tight he wants the coverage, and how high the final orbits are."

Ramsey leaned back. "So at this point, Mike, you know where he's putting the bars on the cage, but you don't know how much wiggle-room he's leaving us on the inside."

"Right. At three hundred nautical miles, each satellite is within line-of-sight of about ten percent of the earth at any one time."

"So he needs ten satellites for full coverage."

"If he keeps them at three hundred, he'll need more than ten since coverage deteriorates near the edges. Plus, there's overlapping coverage between satellites, especially when a couple of them are passing near the poles. But if he boosts them higher, he'll have greater coverage per bird."

"With twelve or sixteen in orbit, is there any chance they'll run into each other over the poles?"

Chisholm considered offering a short explanation about how hard it was to make two objects collide in space. Instead he decided to explain the real reason there was no chance of a collision over the poles. "Actually, sir, the cage Novikov is building is a little different from the one we hypothesized. The orbital planes are inclined at an angle of eighty degrees, so—"

"So none of the birds actually flies over the poles." Ramsey grinned and shook his head. "And all this hoo-haw you gave me about circular polar orbits was just simplification to a low enough level that a four-star could understand it. Is that right, Mike?"

Chisholm laughed. "It wasn't that I was concerned about you, sir. I thought you might like a helpful example, in case you needed to share your knowledge with any other—"

"I'll tell General Bolton you were thinking of him, Mike," Ramsey said. "Now let's sort through all this high-tech mumbo jumbo and get to the bottom line. If I get this far with the chief, he'll ask what our options are if Novikov really is orbiting a constellation of shooters. You're my brains on this, Mike."

"Our options depend on how tight his coverage is, sir. We might find a path through a hole—but I doubt it."

"Are you really that pessimistic?"

"Novikov knows his business, and he knows the Defenders have to come out of Cape Canaveral. If he builds a constellation of shooters, I doubt he'd leave any gaps for us to punch through without having to blow holes in his coverage."

"But without an American ASAT, how do you propose to do that?"

Chisholm smiled wryly and nodded toward the colonel's insignia on his shoulder. "The ASAT question's well above my pay grade, sir."

"You're implying that that's a question the president should ask our friends on Capitol Hill?"

"They were the ones who decided that an operational American ASAT wasn't in the national interest." The Air Force had developed an antisatellite missile in the 1980s, but Congress had prohibited its testing and deployment.

"We fought that one and lost," Ramsey said with a shrug. "And you think we're finally about to pay the price."

Chisholm nodded. "I'll have a better idea in a week or two, General. In the meantime, I'll be paying more attention to hardware and less to shuffling papers."

"Roger that, Mike."

9

Northern Cosmodrome, Plesetsk, USSR
Thursday, 11 March, 0427 local (0027 GMT)

The telephone in Novikov's bedroom rang and Luiza stirred beside him. He quickly grabbed the telephone so it would not wake her.

The caller identified himself as a duty officer, then said, "The runway will be clear in an hour and a half."

"Good," Novikov said, then dropped the telephone into its cradle.

Looking around the darkened room, he fought the urge to go back to sleep. Luiza's warmth as she snuggled against him contrasted dramatically with the crisp temperature beyond the thick comforters. He was tempted to awaken her to continue the lovemaking they had shared. Instead he gave her a gentle hug and kissed her forehead. A sleepy moan escaped her lips, and she reached instinctively for his arm. He avoided her grasp and slid from beneath the covers, then gently tucked them around her. He kissed Luiza again, completing their unspoken ritual that said he did not want her to awaken.

Not true, he thought as he went into the dressing area and closed the door. He wanted her to awaken—he just didn't have the time to accept the consequences.

As Novikov shaved, showered, and dressed, he pushed aside thoughts of Luiza, replacing them with the upcoming mission. He was not as rested as if he had slept alone. Nevertheless, their lovemaking had liberated him from much of the tension that had increased during the week. Now he was better prepared to face the next few days, which would include what for him was the most distasteful portion of the *Krasnaya Molniya*. He shrugged away the disturbing thought as he crammed his shaving kit full. He was determined to face certain events only as they came instead of mentally rehearsing them a thousand times in advance.

In the darkened bedroom he replaced his shaving kit in the luggage that his orderly had packed for the earlier flight. As he put on his coat, he mentally listed items to be picked up at his office before going to the airfield. He stood silently for a moment and listened. The sound of his car idling in the vehicle shelter told him that his driver was waiting.

He thought again of Luiza and wondered if there was any chocolate in the kitchen. The Belgian-made Godiva, which was available only in the special stores he could shop in, was her favorite. Though he had no obligation, he liked to reward her in small ways that let her know she pleased him. He had been so busy for the last week, however, that until last night he had given little thought to her or sex or chocolate.

Slipping quietly into the kitchen, he found two bars. After placing both on his pillow for her to discover later, he slipped his hand beneath the covers to caress her one more time. Luiza shuddered when his fingers glided across bare flesh, but his lips were on hers before she could speak. She reached up and interlaced her fingers behind his neck, responding as if the kiss were part of a sensuous dream. He lingered a few seconds more, until she rolled toward him. He sensed that she was stretching her legs beneath the comforters, like a cat preparing to rise after a nap.

No time!

Regretfully he pulled back and slowly separated her hands. Again he tucked the covers around her shoulders and kissed her on the forehead.

"Have good fortune, my General," she whispered.

"Sleep in peace, my Luiza," he said before turning away.

As he settled into the back of his car, he felt more invigorated than at any time since the meeting in Moscow. Now he was ready to do battle—with the elements, the Americans, Marshal Murashev, or the capriciousness of fates that favored one launch for success and doomed the next. If *Krasnaya Molniya* could succeed, Novikov was determined to make it so through the sheer force of his will. If *Krasnaya Molniya* did succeed, he thought bitterly, Marshal Murashev would award himself another medal. Novikov tensed in anger against the system that allowed incompetence to reward itself. The last few hours had left him convinced that Luiza's contribution was more deserving of a medal than Murashev ever would be.

Nearly fifteen hundred miles southeast of Plesetsk, Novikov's plane approached the Baikonur Cosmodrome, which stretched across hundreds of square miles of the steppes of Kazakhstan. The base was located north of the ancient village of Tyuratam, now called Leninsk. The cosmodrome's namesake, however, was the village of Baikonur—almost three hundred miles away. Though some might assume that the name resulted from bureaucrats who could not read maps, the intent was more subtle—*disinformatsia*. In the days before satellites could pinpoint the location of any structure on earth, Soviet strategists hoped to confuse targeteers of the Strategic Air Command. Someone had reasoned that the three-hundred-mile error might spare the base if the Americans ever sent bombers and missiles to destroy the cosmodrome.

Baikonur was the Soviet spaceport for manned missions and interplanetary probes, so the base often was compared with the American launch facilities at the Kennedy Space Center on the coast of Florida. Nevertheless, there were major differences—the weather, the absence of an ocean within hundreds of miles, and the fact that Baikonur was nine times larger than Kennedy.

Novikov looked out the window as his aircraft descended for landing. Afternoon temperatures had not risen above freezing during the previous week, so the snows of winter still covered the land as far as he could see. The layer of white, when viewed from higher altitudes, made the area around Tyuratam appear similar to the snow-covered forests of Plesetsk. As the aircraft descended, a difference became obvious—these vast plains east of the Aral Sea were nearly devoid of trees.

Novikov visualized a time in the centuries before massive steel towers had been scattered in clumps across the barren landscape. He imagined his ancestors riding recklessly, their magnificent stallions exhaling diaphanous clouds of white as the animals lurched through deep snow. He wished he could have ridden with them. Smiling, he wished that on Sunday he could ride at the head of a *sotnya*—a squadron of Cossack cavalry. He would bring them to a halt as the countdown for *Zashchitnik I* reached zero. Though the thunderous roar would obliterate his words, he would shout, "Look what I can do!" The feeling was so vivid, he almost said the words aloud as the aircraft touched down on the runway used by the Soviet space shuttle.

Polkovnik (Colonel) Nasedkin, the project leader for *Zashchitnik I*, met Novikov's plane. As they rode eight miles to the assembly building for the superboosters, Nasedkin summarized the events of the last twenty-four hours. The *Zashchitnik I* satellite had been loaded into the cargo pod four hours ahead of schedule. The *Energia* booster, which would carry *Zashchitnik I* into low earth orbit, would start its journey to the launchpad in about five hours. The doors to the assembly building would begin opening as soon as an American reconnaissance satellite passed overhead at 1717. Novikov nodded and set his watch forward one hour to account for the time difference between Tyuratam and Plesetsk.

The car traveled beside railroad tracks that led to, then disappeared into, the largest building in this part of Asia. Without comparable structures nearby to provide perspective, Novikov always had difficulty appreciating the building's size. Today a large locomotive was idling near the doors that made up much of the end of the building. Each door towered more than seven stories high, making the two-hundred-ton locomotive look like a child's toy. Concealed behind the huge doors was a marvel of engineering that impressed even Novikov.

The car stopped near the building, and someone opened a normal-sized door in the base of one of the large ones. When Novikov entered, he stopped for a moment a few feet from the most powerful booster combination that existed anywhere on earth. This was the real thing, he thought. This part of *Krasnaya Molniya* did not depend upon a bunch of hand-me-down ICBMs but upon this heavy-lift booster that was designed from the beginning to lift one hundred tons to low earth orbit.

The *Energia* was lying flat on the gargantuan transporter that soon would be hooked to six locomotives for the six-mile journey to the pad. Even with the booster on its side, the top of the uppermost nozzle was more than forty feet above the cold floor. The scale of everything was misleading until he compared machine to man. The inner diameter of each nozzle on the *Energia*'s central core was large enough for him to stand in. Even at his full height of six feet, he would have to stretch to touch the metal above him. The sixteen nozzles on the strap-on boosters were almost as large.

Novikov walked to the side of the gray and white booster, which stretched almost to the end of the large integration hall. Even un-fueled and lying quietly on its side instead of pointed toward the cosmos, the massive product of the Soviet's best technology excited him. In some ways he envied Podpolkovnik Kalinen—it was going to be one hell of a ride like no cosmonaut had ever experienced.

Novikov walked toward the payload pod, which was lying horizontally on its transporter on a parallel track. Several men were working atop portable scaffolding near the nose of the pod. He spotted Kalinen supervising the loading of his spacecraft. For a moment Novikov considered climbing the thirty feet to the upper platform. However, ladders had become a dangerous challenge, so Novikov called out to the young cosmonaut instead. Moments later Kalinen had bounded down the ladder.

"I hope that wasn't a case of vodka you were sneaking aboard," Novikov said with a wry smile. He noticed that Kalinen was wearing the rank of a mayor.

"Oh, no sir." Kalinen blushed nervously.

"Champagne?"

"No, Comrade General. Just water, some provisions, and all the backup electronics boxes."

"Any problems?"

"No, sir. *Zashchitnik I* will be ready to move to the pad on schedule."

"Is there anything I can get for you? Perhaps something you couldn't get for yourself." Although cosmonauts could shop in stores that private citizens only dreamed of, Novikov had markedly more access to necessities and luxuries.

Kalinen shrugged. "Thank you, Comrade General. There's nothing that I myself need."

Novikov nodded. "Your family? Why don't you make a list of some things your wife might need?"

Kalinen nodded. "That's kind of you, General."

Novikov motioned toward the platform above them. "Do they need you up there for anything else?"

Kalinen hesitated, then said, "No, sir."

"Good," Novikov said, putting his arm around the shoulder of the smaller man. "Then let's go share a meal."

They went to Novikov's office on an upper floor that overlooked the integration hall containing the *Energia* booster. The two cosmonauts shared a leisurely lunch followed by an afternoon of trading stories about missions past and discussing the one scheduled to start in three more days. Novikov periodically checked for any problems with *Zashchitnik I* and with the refurbishment of the launchpads at Plesetsk. Everything was progressing smoothly.

Finally Novikov felt a slight shudder and looked toward the doors at the far end of the building. The center panels had started to inch toward the sides, letting in the light of late afternoon. He stood and pushed aside the heavy glass that kept the noise and cold of the cavernous room out of his office. With the window open, he could hear the grinding, clanking noises of the massive doors being forced aside. He also heard the more distant sound of the diesel locomotives that were idling beyond the doors.

Novikov smiled at Kalinen. "Shall we go watch them move your fine steed?"

10

The Pentagon, Washington, D.C.
Thursday, 11 March, 1715 local (2215 GMT)

Chisholm was trying to clear his in basket when Rick McClain knocked on the door.

As soon as he was motioned inside, McClain said, "Intel's seeing new activity on your two pads at Plesetsk."

Chisholm smiled weakly and placed his pen on the stack of papers he had been reviewing. Picking up the wooden biplane, he leaned back in his chair and slowly turned the propeller. "After what we've seen this week, that doesn't surprise me." In a way he was pleased. The sooner Novikov got the rest of the constellation in orbit, the sooner Chisholm would know for sure what the Defender would be up against.

"Intel said to tell you that the Soviets moved a Big E from the assembly building, whatever that means."

"Really?" The news caused the same tingling sensation Chisholm had felt whenever a fire-warning horn had sounded in his aircraft. McClain's message could mean only one thing: the *Energia*, the Soviet's most powerful booster had entered a prelaunch cycle. "Do they have pictures downstairs?"

"Yes, sir."

Chisholm put the little airplane onto the stack of papers and started for the door. "Let's go take a look. I don't suppose you've seen an *Energia*, have you?"

"Is that the booster the Soviets used to launch their shuttle?"

"You got it, Rick. Just to give you an idea of how big an *Energia* is, the strap-ons it uses are as big as the SS-18s I've been worrying about." Hurrying out into the hallway, Chisholm smiled and added, "When they light that sucker off, you'd think it'd push the earth out of orbit."

Captain Murphy from Current Intelligence greeted Chisholm and McClain, then showed them the latest pictures from Tyuratam. The *Energia* booster had reached the launchpad but remained on its transporter. The six locomotives had been switched to the opposite end of the transporter for the final positioning on the pad.

"It's been a while since we've seen one of these," Chisholm said.

"I'm sure we'd have seen more, sir," Murphy said, "if the Soviets hadn't had so many problems with their shuttle."

"And their economy," Chisholm said as he handed the pictures to McClain, then asked Murphy, "Any hints yet on the payload?"

"Negative, sir. We don't think they're ready to try another shuttle."

"I wish it were their shuttle," Chisholm said. "That'd put a much tighter limit on the size of the payload."

McClain asked, "How else do they use an *Energia?*"

Chisholm took one of the pictures and pointed to the mounting points on the side of the main core of the *Energia*. "They can mate a cargo pod where their shuttle normally attaches. My concern is that the pod's cargo hold is twice as long and has three times as much volume as the cargo bay in our space shuttle."

"I think that's the configuration we'll see in a couple of days, Colonel," Murphy said, "but we've got no idea what they'll put inside."

Chisholm nodded, sharing the same uncertainty. "Could you verify that General Novikov's still on-station at Plesetsk?"

"No problem, sir," Murphy said as he started to one of the computer consoles along the far wall.

Chisholm continued to explain to McClain some of the details visible in the picture of the launchpad at Tyuratam.

In a few moments Murphy returned. "You missed that one, sir. Novikov left this morning and arrived at the Baikonur Cosmodrome about noon."

"You've got to be kidding!"

"No, sir. I'm afraid I'm not."

Sitting on the edge of the desk, Chisholm stared momentarily at the pictures in a way indicating that his thoughts were elsewhere. If Novikov were developing a challenge to Defender, Chisholm thought, the Soviet general's sudden appearance at Tyuratam had to be significant. After all, there were important satellites yet to be launched from Plesetsk to fill the original constellation. Since Novikov's arrival coincided with the unexpected rollout of an *Energia* booster, the mystery had taken on a frightening new dimension. Chisholm's senses suddenly were in touch with feelings from his years as a boy in Texas. He felt as if the skies were darkening, the winds were coming up, and the first heavy drops of a spring thunderstorm were splashing through a muggy afternoon. He now was convinced that nearly half a world away, Novikov was unleashing a storm that would engulf Washington in a whirl of questions no one was prepared to answer.

"I hope Thursday isn't your bowling night, Rick, because we just signed up for some overtime."

McClain, who was not a bowler, looked surprised but eagerly followed Chisholm back to the colonel's office.

Chisholm erased his chalkboard, then said, "I'd bet dollars to doughnuts that before the end of the month, the president'll be asking how to shut down these new Soviet birds."

"Really?"

"I hope I'm wrong," Chisholm said. He really hoped he was.

"But you think you're right, sir?"

Chisholm nodded. "Let's divide the problem into pieces and see what we can and cannot do. Here's the surface of the earth." Just above the chalk tray, he drew a small segment of a very large circle. Then he added a parallel dashed line near the center of the board and labeled its altitude as three hundred nautical miles. "This is one of the circular orbits we've seen so far."

McClain sat on the edge of the desk and watched as Chisholm put an X representing a satellite on the dashed line. "Can we be sure the satellites will stay at three hundred, sir?"

"Negative," Chisholm said, "but it gives us a baseline. If we can't reach a satellite at even three hundred, you and I can go on vacation and let the politicians solve the problem." He wrote the letters DEW and KEW near an upper corner of the board.

"If you were the commander of a fully equipped space defense force, Rick, you'd have a choice between directed-energy weapons and kinetic-energy weapons."

Directed-energy weapons, which finally had moved beyond science-fiction books in the late twentieth century, were the laserlike weapons that struck the target with a beam of energy. Kinetic-energy weapons had been around since stone-age men had begun throwing rocks at each other. Although Chisholm sometimes was amused by the terminology—a bullet now could be described as a kinetic-kill vehicle—these weapons still depended on hitting a target with a mass of something. Yet the space age had added a special twist. The target's velocity—thousands of feet per second for satellites or the warheads of ICBMs—had become a deadly factor in the equation that determined the collision's destructive energy.

"I'm kind of new to all this," McClain said, "but from what I've read, I don't really have a choice of either."

"Right," Chisholm said. "Congress killed our kinetic-energy ASAT, and Perestroika gutted the funding that might've developed a ground-based laser. If we can kludge something together that'll reach that high, my guess is that it'll be a missile." He added a line representing the flight path of a missile from the surface to the satellite. After drawing a circle around the satellite, he wrote Terminal Phase. At the lower end of the missile's path, he added another circle and the words Launch Phase. He wrote Ascent Phase near the midpoint, then said, "The three basic questions are: how do you launch your missile; does it have enough juice to reach the orbit; and can you hit the bird when you get there?"

Tossing the chalk to McClain, Chisholm settled into his chair. After grabbing the small biplane, he propped his feet up on the desk.

Moving to the board, McClain asked, "Where do we start, sir?"

"Your choice," Chisholm said. He had his own answer, but was interested to see how the young engineer would attack the problem.

McClain studied the drawing for a moment, then said, "Launch phase? Obviously we have to position our missile under or nearly under the orbit."

Chisholm nodded. "Good. If we attack, we want it to be at the time and place of our choosing. How do you get there? Land, sea, or air?"

McClain glanced toward the biplane in Chisholm's hands and the Air Force pilot wings above the colonel's left pocket, then said with a smile, "Somehow I feel the answer is air, sir."

"We won't be parochial," Chisholm said, then spun the propeller on the wooden airplane. "But aircraft carrying the missiles to the target area is the most likely answer. Time and distance probably will dictate that."

Chisholm had studied the 1980s operational concept for an "air-launched, direct-ascent antisatellite weapon." A squadron of specially equipped F-15 Eagles would have been stationed on each coast—one at McChord Air Force Base, Washington, and the other at Langley Air Force Base, Virginia. Enough aircraft and missiles would have been available to destroy within hours most of the Soviets' low-altitude reconnaissance and targeting satellites.

However, influential voices in Congress had roared that an American ASAT would be destabilizing. Dire warnings were shouted loud and often that an American ASAT increased the chance of nuclear war—wiping out the Soviets' early warning satellites would blind those whose fingers were on the Soviet nuclear trigger. The fact that the air-launched ASAT could not reach the early warning satellites was not of interest to those who cried that the development program must be abandoned.

When their arguments weren't totally persuasive, they changed tactics. A congressional ban on testing the ASAT could doom the program almost as easily. The argument was that American testing was provocative. After all, the Soviets were arguing loudly against weapons in space, and they no longer were testing their ASAT, which was launched into orbit on a rocket. A "Peace Report" newsletter from an influential Congressman had reported that "no real threat exists from the Soviets in this field." Those who reviewed the photos of Tyuratam knew differently. After each winter storm the pads for the Soviet ASAT launchers were among the first to be plowed clear.

Right or wrong, the test ban had proved to be the death knell for the air-launched ASAT, and no squadrons of special F-15s were deployed.

McClain wrote Air-Launched near the words Launch Phase. "I guess the next question is, What kind of aircraft would we use?"

Chisholm shrugged. "That depends on how big a package it takes to complete the other two phases. In 1985 an F-15 launched an ASAT missile that struck a satellite passing three hundred twenty nautical miles above the Pacific Ocean."

"So the Eagle's a candidate," McClain said, adding F-15 to the chalkboard.

Chisholm continued, "There's a NASA B-52 at Edwards that's air-dropped rockets that've taken satellites directly into orbit. And there's also the possibility of using cargo planes."

McClain had written B-52, then paused and looked toward Chisholm at the mention of cargo planes. "I'm not sure I understand what you've got in mind."

"Back in 1974, Systems Command proved the concept. They rigged up a Minuteman I and let two big white parachutes pull it from a C-5."

McClain looked shocked. "In flight? You're talking about a real ICBM out of the back of a C-5?"

"The ICBM wasn't armed," Chisholm said, "and the missile only carried enough propellant to lift it from eight thousand feet to about twenty thousand. But they proved that an ICBM could be air-launched."

That demonstration had been put together in a little over two months. Chisholm wondered if there would be that much time to develop an ASAT mission.

McClain wrote C-5 beneath B-52 and F-15.

Chisholm asked, "What must you consider for the ascent phase?"

McClain studied the diagram for a moment. "As you said before, whether there's enough thrust to reach the orbital altitude."

"Right. And?"

McClain looked again, this time for much longer. Finally he said, "You've got to get close enough for the warhead's seeker to take over in the Terminal Phase."

"Exactly," Chisholm said with an encouraging tone. "That means we'll need tracking data on the target, and our missile has to keep up with its own location."

"Space Command in Cheyenne Mountain should have the tracking information," McClain said, "and GPS data can solve the missile's navigational problem."

GPS data was continually broadcast from the NAVSTAR satellites of the Global Positioning System. These artificial stars circled the earth every twelve hours at an altitude of about eleven thousand nautical miles. A missile with a GPS receiver would have extremely accurate position and altitude information available throughout the ascent.

"I agree with your GPS assessment," Chisholm said, "but we might have to operate in areas where the data from Space Command isn't as readily available."

McClain wrote GPS beside the missile's upward trajectory, then added Data Links with a couple of question marks. Then he printed Thrust and added a check mark after it. "Sounds like we've already proven we can reach three hundred miles."

"Let's not be in too much of a hurry, Rick," Chisholm said. "When

Major Pearson punched off the ASAT at thirty-eight thousand feet, his F-15 was doing almost Mach One in a sixty-plus-degree climb. We probably wouldn't see that kind of performance out of a C-5."

McClain smiled at Chisholm's understatement and changed the check to a question mark.

Chisholm continued, "And, as you suggested earlier, by the time the president orders us to go after them, they may not be at three hundred anymore. But at least the F-15 shot in 1985 gives us a baseline."

"And the seeker technology has come a long way since then," McClain said as he wrote Seekers near the words Terminal Phase. "There's been a lot of tests on intercepting ICBM warheads, and I've read most of the papers. VHSIC has made a big difference."

Chisholm nodded. Advances in very high speed integrated circuits had put the power of mainframe computers onto microchips. This had reduced the size of the electronics needed to seek out a target and compute a collision course. "I'm counting on your expertise in computers and electronics to get us on target if the president says 'Go.' "

McClain stepped back and looked at the notes on the board. "What about the payload on the *Energia*?"

Chisholm shrugged and spun the propeller on the small airplane. "If its payload is several small satellites, they'll probably stay at LEO too, so that's another version of the same problem. If it's some kind of command and control vehicle, Novikov's probably going to send it up to GEO, and we won't be able to reach it anyway."

GEO—the shorthand version of geostationary or geosynchronous altitude—was a special region of the heavens. Satellites moving east over the equator at GEO appeared to hover in one place instead of racing across the sky. Seemingly a phenomenon more akin to fiction than fact, "stationary" satellites had been proposed in 1945 by the noted science-fiction writer Arthur C. Clarke. He knew that the earth's gravitational force decreased as the distance from the earth increased. Thus a satellite needed less velocity to stay in a circular orbit at higher altitudes. Clarke reasoned that with less and less velocity needed on larger and larger orbits, there had to be an altitude where the time to complete an orbit matched exactly the time for one full rotation of the earth. That altitude was approximately 22,300 statute miles.

Chisholm knew that in the decades since Clarke's hypothesis, much of the world had been linked instantaneously by scores of communications satellites placed at GEO. Other satellites hovered silently, watching for the first signs of a surprise attack from the missile fields of the other superpower. Similarly, Chisholm thought, a satellite over the equator south of Mexico would watch the spaceports in Florida and California—if that was a mission that fit into Novikov's plan.

Beginning with the basic outline on the bulletin board, Chisholm and McClain spent most of the evening brainstorming. They exploited the colonel's background in space systems and the young engineer's knowledge of electronics. Chisholm sought to identify combinations of American missiles, seekers, and warheads that could destroy Soviet satellites at three hundred miles above the earth. He focused on the off-the-shelf hardware that was available. The technical problems would be difficult to overcome, but if Novikov was mounting a threat, there was no time for a ten-year development and testing program.

Chisholm's next objective was to find out how many of the right pieces were available in case the discussion needed to go beyond the what-if stage. Since the question of availability could not be answered in the Pentagon on a Thursday night, he ended the discussion at 2200.

"Sorry I'm late, Sherm," Chisholm said as he opened his apartment door.

A loud scolding, which came from a large four-legged puff of gray fur, assured Chisholm that, as usual, a simple apology would not be sufficient. He bent to pet Sherman—also known as Charmaine whenever Christie visited. However, the fluffy Persian cat permitted only the slightest touch of his long fur before darting toward the kitchen, then pausing to see if his master was following. Chisholm dropped his briefcase on a couch, then hurried toward the kitchen. Sherman led the way, yowling all the time about the unexpected lateness of the dinner hour.

When Chisholm selected a can from the cabinet, the cat changed his tactics. Sherman began frantically intertwining himself around Chisholm's ankles. The meows were no less frequent but took on a tone of impatient encouragement.

"If one of us doesn't let the other get to the can opener, Sherm, we're in for a long, loud evening," Chisholm said as he reached toward the cat.

Sherman permitted another touch, then scampered away unwilling to get involved in any dinner-delaying affection. By the time Chisholm reached the can opener, Sherman was back at the ankles.

The whirring of the opener produced a rumbling echo of approval from deep behind the pug-nosed face and whiskers. Finally the top of the can separated with a metallic clank. Sherman raced to his dish, then danced back and forth around it until Chisholm dropped in the first spoonful.

Sherman had become a member of the family nearly a decade earlier. Christie had been visiting Chisholm during the summer of her tenth birthday. Father and daughter had been walking through a shopping mall when she suddenly exclaimed, "Wait, Daddy! Look!"

She dragged him toward a pet shop window, her full attention was on a tiny ball of animated fur punctuated by enormous whiskers. Chisholm hoped that letting her hold the kitten would be enough, but Christie fell in love at first touch. Finally he almost had to carry her out of the store, and leaving the kitten behind put a pall as thick as winter fog over the daughter-father visit.

Throughout the day he made all the logical arguments about why buying the kitten would be a bad idea, and he intended to remain firm. Yet Christie's undiminished persistence, his guilt about being a summer-only father, and the inadequacies he felt in comparing his salary to the wealth of Christie's new stepfather began to break down Chisholm's resolve. If he and his ex-wife had been on speaking terms, he would have talked to her before buying the kitten. However, they were not, and he rationalized that being a loving father was much more important than being a thoughtful ex-husband.

So back they went to the pet store, and Christie immediately named her new friend Charmaine. Chisholm suggested that other names might be more appropriate for a "boy kitty."

Hugging the kitten to her face, she said firmly, "Charmaine, Daddy. His name is Charmaine."

Chisholm soon decided that the kitten had been worth the investment because the remainder of the visit was their best yet as father and child tried to get better acquainted.

Less than a week after Christie took Charmaine back to Atlanta, Chisholm received a brief letter stating that *his* cat—not their daughter's cat—was en route back to California. There were exaggerated references to the kitten being only slightly less destructive than General Sherman had been in burning Atlanta. If for no other reason, Chisholm decided, he had to love that kitten.

Now the thought of the kitten's short visit to Georgia caused Chisholm to smile, and he spooned an extra portion of cat food past the whiskers and pug nose. Sherman approved, but did not slow down to say thank you.

Chisholm took a long, hot shower, then put on his winter pajamas: a New York Yankees sweatshirt and Washington Redskins sweatpants. Although exhausted, he was still too keyed up over the events of the day to sleep. Instead he went into the apartment's tiny living room, turned on the gas log in the fireplace, dimmed the light, and settled into a comfortable recliner facing the fire. He called the setting his inspiration room, a place of retreat he came to when he needed to clarify his feelings about something. Almost immediately Sherman cut short his own after-dinner bath and hopped up on Chisholm's lap. The cat responded with a whisker-shaking purr as soon as Chisholm started massaging behind Sherman's ears.

At times like this Chisholm enjoyed the companionship even though taking care of Sherman had not always been easy. He had considered offering the kitten back to the pet store. However, by the time Sherman had returned from his round trip to Atlanta, Chisholm had photographs of his ten-year-old Christie smiling broadly and nuzzling her tiny Charmaine against her cheek. Keeping Sherman seemed to be a good way for an absentee father to demonstrate his special love for his daughter. The day he made the decision he also ordered an enlargement of one of the photographs. That picture, showing the little girl and the little cat, now stood on his mantel.

"Take it easy, Sherm," Chisholm said, as the kneading paws of the contented cat put an occasional claw through the material of the sweatpants.

After repositioning Sherman, Chisholm looked at the other items above the fireplace. The most impressive object in the room was a shadowbox that hung on the wall. Lined with blue velvet, the box contained a Silver Star, a Distinguished Flying Cross with two oak leaf clusters, an Air Medal with seven oak leaf clusters, a Purple Heart, and several lesser medals. The display included the insignia of Air Force rank from second lieutenant through captain. The engraved nameplate said Captain Brett Chisholm, 1941–1968.

Beneath the shadowbox a picture showed Chisholm's brother, Brett, dressed in a flight suit and standing in front of an F-4C Phantom. Throughout much of Michael Chisholm's career, he often had made decisions based on what he thought his older brother would have advised him to do.

There were two other pictures on the mantel and a baseball that had been autographed by the 1969 New York Yankees. The picture beside the baseball showed Michael Chisholm with a junior-league team he had coached to the state championship in the year before he had come to the Pentagon. Chisholm used that picture as a reminder of the fun and fulfillment in life beyond the challenges of being on-call twenty-four hours a day.

The fourth picture showed Chisholm and Sandi Turner. He and the beautiful young woman were standing happily on the beach at Waikiki with Diamond Head in the background. Chisholm paused a moment and thought about a discovery made earlier in the day while scanning the *Air Force Times*. Major Sandra Turner's name was in a listing of officers scheduled to attend the fall term at the Defense Systems Management College at Fort Belvoir, Virginia. For the first time since breaking off their engagement, he and Sandi would be assigned within a few miles of each other. He had been too busy during the day to think about the possibilities, but he liked the idea.

Sherman decided that he had bestowed enough pleasure on his master for one evening, so the big Persian climbed down to resume his bath nearer the fire. Chisholm leaned farther back in the recliner, then retrieved an old baseball and glove from an adjacent magazine rack. Slipping one hand into the well-worn baseball glove, he threw the ball into the glove, then grabbed the ball again. He repeated the ritual over and over as he turned his thoughts to the new satellites in orbit, and those yet to come.

Chisholm felt a growing sense of foreboding. Both sides had spent billions in more than a decade of Star Wars research. He had reviewed hundreds of concepts for weaponry that could be carried aboard spacecraft of the twenty-first century. Undoubtedly Novikov had too. Now Chisholm wondered which of those concepts the daring Soviet general might have already installed in the satellites being launched this week and next.

11

Baikonur Cosmodrome, Tyuratam, USSR
Friday, 12 March, 1600 local (1100 GMT)

Friday was passing more smoothly than Novikov had dared to hope. There were, of course, intermittent delays whenever an American reconnaissance satellite was due to pass within range of the launchpad. In each instance all outside work came to a halt, so that no activities were visible to the American sensors.

The schedule had taken these work stoppages into account, so the only unplanned delay came during the loading of the nuclear reactor that would power *Zashchitnik I*'s weapons. The procedure took three hours longer than expected. All unprotected workers had to remain clear of the launchpad during the hazardous operation, so the entire schedule had slipped. Nevertheless, by late afternoon the crew was ready to begin loading fuel and oxidizer into *Zashchitnik I*'s cavernous tanks.

Satisfied that a Sunday launch was possible, Novikov turned his attention to Kalinen and the traditional ceremonies and dinner that preceded any cosmonaut's journey into space.

After a few hours sleep Chisholm was back in the Pentagon on Friday. Following the morning staff meeting, he was taking a few minutes to sort the important items from the never-ending flow of paper that flooded his desk. Sensing a presence in his doorway, he was startled by what he saw when he looked up. At first he wondered if Rick McClain had been in an automobile accident.

McClain's appearance was disheveled. The side of his face and his shirt were stained in red. Chisholm could also see a scrape on a cheek and a slight bruise on the forehead. There was a look that Chisholm had never seen before in McClain's eyes.

"Have a seat," Chisholm said as he rose to assist. "What happened to you?"

"I'm too pissed to sit, sir." He paced angrily in the small area in front of the desk. His voice was deep, and it carried more emotion than Chisholm had ever seen the young engineer reveal. "It's a fuckin' zoo out there this morning!"

Until that moment Chisholm had forgotten that it was Defeat Defender Day. "Are you okay? Do you need to see a doctor?"

McClain reached up and touched the bruise. "Some gal hit me with her sign, so I took it away, and broke it over my knee." He paused as if recalling the recent action. "She didn't care much for that."

"I'd pictured you as getting along much better than that with the ladies," Chisholm said, testing to see if McClain was ready to lighten up a little.

McClain came close to smiling. He rubbed his fingers lightly over the scraped knuckles on his right hand. "I was punching the shit out of her old man at the time." He grinned. "She wasn't my type anyway."

"Are we going to see you on the news at noon?"

"Maybe fight night on the sports network," McClain said with a wry smile. He slumped into a chair. "I know I should've stayed cool, and I was ignoring all the name-calling. But when he started slinging all this red crap—" His voice trailed off.

"Well, policy says we should ignore them when—"

"I know. But I don't buy that their freedom of speech extends to them disrupting my life in any way they choose." He looked at the ruined shirt and tie he was wearing.

Chisholm sat on the edge of his desk. "I understand your frustration, believe me." He paused momentarily trying to decide what, if anything, to share about his brother. Brett's death, more than half a lifetime ago, seemed almost like ancient history. Before that dismal spring, Chisholm's goal in life had been to win baseball games in Yankee Stadium. Brett Chisholm's death, however, had changed every day that followed in Michael Chisholm's life.

He still could picture his father's ashen face on a February afternoon in 1968. Chisholm was fresh off the 1967 season in which he had won eight games as a sophomore pitching phenomenon at his

Dallas high school. Now in his junior year, his fastball had marked him as a major league prospect. On the mound with a zero and two count on the third batter, Chisholm saw his father speak to the coach, then walk right onto the field.

The ferocious fighting of the Tet offensive was in its third week, and suddenly Brett was missing in action in South Vietnam. For the next three days there was no word.

Chisholm had indelible memories of his parents' all-consuming vigil for their number one son. Then the dreaded ringing of the telephone in the middle of the night had brought joyous news—Brett had been rescued from a rugged hillside in the jungles near Khe Sanh. What had not been said was that the antiaircraft fire and the ejection from his burning F-4C Phantom had left Brett badly burned and broken.

By the time Brett was moved to a Dallas hospital, Chisholm had a record of twelve wins and one loss. During the next four months he spent all his free time with his brother. He did not win another game that season. Sharing Brett's last months, Chisholm learned lifetime lessons about another kind of winning and losing.

To Chisholm the most profound insights resulted from the way his older brother accepted, yet worried over, his impending death. Brett often spoke about being willing to give his life for his country, but—and Chisholm had seen it as a large but—he was concerned about the possibility of dying in a war his country did not win. That concern was lost, of course, on Mom and Dad. To them all that mattered was that their son was dying.

Nevertheless, as the two brothers spent many hours together watching televised reports of the war, as well as the riots and dem- onstrations of 1968, Chisholm shared the burden of Brett's growing anger. Before being shot down Brett had flown thirty-two missions in counterattacks against the Tet offensive. By the third week of the offensive, Brett had recognized that the North Vietnamese were sacrificing the Vietcong in a desperate gamble. While the Vietcong were tying up American and South Vietnamese forces in head-on battles that did not favor guerilla fighters, the North Vietnamese were moving divisions of regular troops into the hills around the U.S. Marine base at Khe Sanh.

The immediate objective had been to overrun the isolated base as the Vietminh had captured the French bastion at Dien Bien Phu fourteen years earlier. The strategic objective was to produce a clamor in the streets of America to bring the troops home as had happened fourteen years earlier in France.

By the summer of 1968, Brett could see that the North Vietnamese and Vietcong had fought fiercely but had failed to achieve their immediate objective. As he watched pictures of the clamor in the streets of America, however, he sensed that his enemy was winning a victory that had been denied on the battlefield. By the time he died, his anger and frustration had taken root deep within the soul of his sixteen-year-old brother.

Chisholm faced McClain and said, "I've gotten pretty cynical, though I tell myself that most people out there have honest motives."

McClain bristled. "There was no honest motivation in dumping this stuff all over me."

"It doesn't take much to convert a demonstration into a mob scene," Chisholm said.

He thought of the diatribe-filled leaflets he had thrown into his desk drawer on Monday morning. He had planned to make copies for his liberal friends. Many had difficulty believing that the American Communist Party took an active role in demonstrations against American military and foreign policy. He had less difficulty believing. For years he had studied the Marxist-Leninist dicta on how to gain power.

"This one sure got out of hand," McClain said. "This morning reminds me of pictures I've seen of the sixties."

"Me too," Chisholm said, remembering 1968 in particular. "Sometime when we can get a beer in our hands, I'll tell you about it."

Responding as if that were a cue to end the conversation, McClain stood. "I guess I'd better get to work. I'll see what's happening with the *Energia*."

"I checked," Chisholm said. "They finished erecting it during the night and have the cargo pod on the launchpad. The pod's probably attached by now."

"Any clues yet on the payload?"

Chisholm pulled a picture from an envelope. "Not much. My first question was whether we'd see an escape tower on the nose cone of the pod," he said, referring to a tower with a cluster of nozzles designed to rocket a crew capsule to safety in event of a disaster during launch.

McClain scanned the picture. "None there. Were you expecting Novikov to add a manned bird to his constellation?"

Chisholm sat back in his chair. "Not really. One manned bird in LEO doesn't make much sense." Except for the missions to the moon, manned spacecraft had stayed in LEO below the radiation belts.

"Maybe they're going to launch several *Energias.*"

Chisholm shook his head. "Not likely. If you're going to invest as many rubles as an *Energia* costs, your payload had better justify the expense. I've been assuming we'll see a large command-and-control platform going up to geostationary orbit somewhere over the western hemisphere."

McClain nodded. "How about action at Plesetsk?"

"They've been busy. I imagine we'll see a couple more SS-18s by tomorrow."

McClain smiled. "You're less skeptical than on Monday."

"Novikov's made a believer of me. Anyway, I want you to follow up on our session last night."

"Whatever you need, sir."

"I've added a few more possibilities to the list we put together," Chisholm said, pulling a page from a folder. "Can you travel on Monday and Tuesday?"

"Sure. Where to?"

"I've got some names of people you can see at Eglin and Wright-Patterson."

Eglin Air Force Base in Florida was the home of the Munitions Systems Division, and Wright-Patterson Air Force Base, Ohio, included the Aeronautical Systems Division.

"Anyone I could deal with on the telephone today, sir?"

"We're going to handle most of this face to face," Chisholm said quietly, "at least until whatever Novikov's doing either grabs the headlines or fades into obscurity."

McClain nodded, then asked, "Do I tell anyone what we're concerned about?"

Before Chisholm could answer, his secretary called to remind him that he needed to leave for his next meeting.

"General Ramsey wants us keeping our cards close to our vests," Chisholm said as he grabbed his notebook. "We'll work up a couple of cover stories for our unclassified discussions. We'll have to stay classified when we talk about warhead requirements. There's no way we can disguise that we're asking about anything other than a weapon to be used in space."

"I imagine we'd stir up a few congressmen in a hurry if they learned we were even thinking ASAT."

"I'm more concerned," Chisholm said, "with keeping Novikov convinced that ASAT isn't back into our vocabulary yet."

Saturday the servicing of *Zashchitnik I* continued normally. Huge pipes and hoses slowly added fuel and oxidizer, increasing the *Energia*'s weight during the day toward the goal of more than five million pounds.

Novikov went to the launch-control center at Tyuratam in the early afternoon. Telemetry and voice communications were being transmitted from Plesetsk, permitting him to monitor the prelaunch activities for *Borzoi V*. He wanted to be available to handle any problems that might arise. None did, and the fifth satellite rocketed from the pad at 1318 in Plesetsk. *Borzoi VI* was scheduled to follow in six hours.

Late in the afternoon Kalinen was in the general's office when Novikov said, "Let's go for a ride." When they reached the vehicle, Novikov dismissed his driver and told Kalinen to drive.

Novikov settled into the front seat and acted as a tour guide, giving directions to the first point of interest. For as long as he could remember, he had been stirred by a sense of history. Initially it had come from the old men in his village who had combined stories of the Great Patriotic War with tales of life at the end of the previous century. Within the last twenty years Novikov had come to recognize that the Great Patriotic War was his history, but not his heritage. The war with the Germans belonged to the Murashevs and other dinosaurs who lived rooted in the past rather than with a spirit of the future. Instead Novikov realized that the Soviet triumphs in the battle for supremacy in space were his heritage. He had studied that history extensively, especially during the months of hospitalization following the crash of his spacecraft. He knew where every shrine was located, and most were at Tyuratam.

Directing Kalinen to park on the edge of a snow-covered road, Novikov pointed and said, "This is where we began in 1957. The Americans had been so pompous. Then *Sputnik I* rocketed toward the cosmos from right over there."

Although there was little to see, Kalinen appeared interested.

Novikov continued, "Our predecessors needed half a million

pounds on the pad to put two hundred pounds into orbit. Even though *Sputnik I* had lasted only three months," Novikov said, smiling for emphasis, "those two hundred pounds humbled the Americans and earned prestige throughout the world."

He directed Kalinen to the next stop, which was an operational launchpad. After parking, Novikov and Kalinen walked for a few minutes along the railroad tracks that led onto the pad.

"Imagine what it was like," Novikov said with a tone of awe in his voice, "when Polkovnik Gagarin stepped from the bus with *Vostok I* sitting right there in the morning sun. That's when your heritage and mine really started."

Kalinen smiled. "I can almost sense the excitement."

"His was the most important flight of all."

"But, Comrade General, you made some important—"

Novikov silenced Kalinen with a smile and a wave of the hand. Although Novikov had flown from the same pad on two of his missions, he had no doubt about Gagarin's preeminent role. "The Americans had struggled nearly four years to catch up, but our space program had stayed ahead at every step. In one glorious morning he proved to the elitists that we were not a backward people. The combined heroism of all cosmonauts since has not matched his contribution."

Next Novikov had Kalinen drive northwest toward the launchpad where *Zashchitnik I* stood in the fading sun of late afternoon. When they had traveled about half way, Novikov directed a turn onto a road leading to the second *Energia* pad, which now was empty. In a few minutes the sedan was parked on the accessway to that pad. Novikov stepped outside, and Kalinen followed.

Novikov stood for a few moments looking at Kalinen's booster. It did not seem as imposing at a distance of four miles. In height the two-hundred-foot-tall *Zashchitnik I* was dwarfed by two lightning-arrestor towers that reached six hundred feet skyward on opposite sides of the pad. Closer in, like silent watchmen in the growing darkness, six shorter towers with banks of lights surrounded the *Energia*.

As Novikov started to speak, the first lights flashed on. In what seemed like a chain reaction, hundreds of lights came to full brilliance, bathing *Zashchitnik I* in a dazzling glow.

"Enjoy this moment, Vladimir," Novikov said, "because there's not a launch complex in the world that's more impressive than that."

Kalinen smiled wistfully.

"Actually," Novikov said, turning toward the railing along the opposite side of the accessway, "I brought you here to see something else. By 1969 the race had intensified. We'd landed *Luna 2* on the moon nearly a decade earlier, but the prestige of placing the first footprints on the moon was the prize of the 1960s." He paused a moment, as if studying the ivory inlays in the handle of his cane. "And who can say whether we could've beaten the Americans?"

Kalinen looked interested. "Was there ever a chance?"

Gesturing toward the remains of a long-abandoned pad, Novikov continued with a story that did not appear in Soviet history books. "Two weeks before the Americans left for the moon, our most powerful rocket was less than two days from launch. The SL-15 was magnificent, nearly one and a half times taller than your *Zashchitnik*. The booster was standing right there being fueled when it exploded." Novikov shrugged and smiled wryly. "Who knows? Perhaps Comrade Belyayev would have been standing on the moon to offer vodka to the latecomers."

Kalinen nodded, seeming unsure of the point the general was making.

"We lost that race," Novikov said, "and to this day, the only footprints on the moon are from American boots."

"But the Americans don't go to the moon anymore," Kalinen offered, "and they have not come close to matching our accomplishments with the *Mir*."

"They didn't choose to compete over manned space stations, so we won nothing to offset their victory on the moon. We've remained in their shadow for a quarter of a century—until now." Novikov paused and placed his hands on the shoulders of the shorter cosmonaut. "And now, Comrade Kalinen, on these shoulders rests a great responsibility. You will reclaim our rightful role as the preeminent power in space."

Kalinen shifted uneasily, as if he had never thought of his mission in such grand terms. "But, Comrade General, mine is but one part—"

"Tomorrow you become the most important cosmonaut of all."

"If you say so, Comrade General," Kalinen said, seeming truly flattered by Novikov's praise.

"I say so, so let no one doubt it," Novikov answered, patting Kalinen on the shoulder. "Now let's go see how *Borzoi Six* is coming along."

When they reached the launch-control center well after sunset, thirty minutes remained until the scheduled launch of *Borzoi VI*. An Arctic front had dropped the temperature at Plesetsk by fifteen degrees in the previous hour, but the winds and snow were light. The countdown was continuing without problems.

Novikov got a cup of hot tea and spent most of his time discussing minor problems that had arisen since *Zashchitnik I* had reached the pad.

When the countdown at Plesetsk reached T minus five minutes, Novikov settled into a chair that faced the status screens on the front wall at Tyuratam. He put on a headset and checked in with his team commander at Plesetsk.

Then he sat quietly listening to the count. A few seconds after the controller reached zero, he added the words Novikov had been waiting for, "Lift off." Novikov nodded and watched the telemetry signals. Everything appeared nominal, and he was about to give his traditional growl. Suddenly there was a fluctuation of pressure in the combustion chamber of a strap-on booster, and the pressure dropped to zero on the corresponding turbopump that was forcing liquid oxygen into that chamber.

For an instant Novikov hoped that the telemetry was faulty, but he saw a consistency in a growing pattern of failures. The upward velocity of *Borzoi VI* continued to increase, but not as rapidly or as smoothly as before. The azimuth indicator began spinning from twenty-five degrees, increasing at a rate that Novikov estimated to be about forty degrees per second. He had seen such indications before when unbalanced thrust was caused by the sudden loss of 225,000 pounds of thrust from one strap-on booster. *Borzoi VI* was tumbling, even as it hurtled skyward. He looked at the range-safety plot. The booster was veering off course, but still within the safety zone.

The controller's voice was scratchy and an octave higher. "General, there appears to be a complete failure of—"

Novikov's thumb clamped down on the microphone button. "Blow it!"

"Yes, sir."

Seconds later all telemetry indications became erratic, then went straight-line, indicating a loss of signal from *Borzoi VI.* No one in the command center spoke.

Picturing the fiery debris cartwheeling toward the forests near Plesetsk, Novikov sighed and slowly removed his headset. Then he turned to Kalinen, who looked particularly distressed by the launch failure. "Well, Cosmonaut Kalinen," Novikov said very deliberately, "that guarantees the success of your launch."

Kalinen and everyone else looked puzzled.

Novikov stood and slipped his coat over his shoulders. He looked at Kalinen and winked. "I never lose two in a row."

By the time Chisholm reached his office on Saturday morning, he knew that a fifth SS-18 booster had placed a satellite into low earth orbit, and the sixth was on the pad. He checked the timing of the launch and decided that the newest spacecraft would have entered the same orbital plane as the third satellite. After making a few computations, he decided that the most likely launch window for the next satellite centered on 1018 Washington time.

At 1020 he made a call on his secure telephone. "Have you had reports on anything out of Plesetsk in the last few minutes?"

"Interesting that you should ask, Colonel," the duty officer said. "We just received a voice rep that their second launch of the morning had an oxygen-rich shutdown."

The wording caught Chisholm off guard. "A what?"

"The son of a bitch exploded about thirty seconds into the mission, sir. They probably destructed it, but we don't know for sure."

"Any damage to the pad?" Chisholm hoped that one of Novikov's special launchpads had been knocked out of action. That unexpected break would even the odds in the game of catch-up that Chisholm was playing.

"It's too soon to tell, sir."

"I'll be in my office for the next few hours. Call me when you get anything more on this one."

Lions 5, Christians 1, Chisholm thought as he hung up. He normally felt guilty whenever he was pleased by the failure of someone else's booster. After Novikov's unprecedented string of successes this week, Chisholm felt no guilt.

12

Baikonur Cosmodrome, Tyuratam, USSR
Sunday, 14 March, 1400 local (0900 GMT)

On Sunday at Tyuratam the cat-and-mouse game with the American reconnaissance satellites continued. Novikov was particularly careful about anything that would reveal Kalinen's presence on the mission. The young cosmonaut was taken to the pad in the afternoon when Tyuratam was out of range of the American satellites. Even then Kalinen traveled in a van that routinely transported electronic equipment, instead of using the bus that carried cosmonauts to the launchpads.

After arriving at the pad Novikov rode with Kalinen in the elevator, which lifted them nearly fifteen stories to the level of the payload access bay.

After a brief picture-taking ceremony, Novikov waited in the bay while the technicians strapped Kalinen into his couch. When they finally stepped clear of the crew capsule, Novikov came forward saying, "I'd like a few minutes with Cosmonaut Kalinen. I'll call when I'm ready for the hatch to be secured."

He leaned his cane against the capsule and knelt beside the small opening. His stiff leg made the entry more difficult, and as he struggled in far enough to face Kalinen, Novikov said, "I remember this being easier when I was your age, Comrade Kalinen."

"It was not easy for me either, sir."

"I have something for you," Novikov said. From the pocket of his coat, he removed a set of rank that fit the shoulder strap of a regular uniform. "These were presented to me when I was promoted to podpolkovnik. I would be honored if you would wear these during your mission, Podpolkovnik Kalinen."

As Kalinen accepted the two insignia, he appeared genuinely moved by Novikov's gesture. "Thank you, Comrade General. The honor is mine." He put them on his lap and picked up two small presentation cases. A rubber band held an identical set of insignia and an envelope against one of the cases. "If you could have someone deliver these to my wife, I would be happy. There are some personal things and the mementos from the ceremony with the president."

"Of course," Novikov said. He recognized the presentation cases as those containing the Hero of the Soviet Union medal and the Order of Lenin. "I shall deliver them myself."

For a few more minutes they filled the time talking of things that were unimportant. Finally Novikov handed Kalinen a sealed vial and said, "Here are some pills, in case you experience severe pain."

Kalinen accepted the vial without speaking.

Novikov added, "We'll be keeping close watch."

Kalinen nodded, but remained silent.

"I guess it's time to let you get to work," Novikov said. Though it was hard to maintain balance in the small hatch, he raised his hand to his brow. "Podpolkovnik Kalinen, I salute you."

Kalinen had almost as much trouble returning the salute within the narrow confines of the capsule. He smiled and said resolutely, "I serve the Soviet Union."

"And," Novikov said with a sigh, "I also serve the Soviet Union." They shook hands, then Novikov backed out of the hatch. Turning to the nearby technicians, he said, "Cosmonaut Kalinen is ready for flight."

The technicians moved by to secure the hatch. Novikov grabbed his cane and walked to the elevator without looking back.

Chisholm had just sat down with a cup of coffee and the Sunday paper when his telephone rang.

Major Winchell in the Air Force Operations Center said, "Were you planning to be in the office today, sir?"

For the first time in the last two weeks, the answer was no. "I'd hoped to catch up on a few personal things, like sleep." He recognized that the major's question represented something more than could be said on an unsecure line, so Chisholm added, "I can come in, if necessary."

"I was reading your last note, sir," Winchell said, "and I figured you might be coming to work for a few hours."

On Thursday Chisholm had left a request that he be notified whenever it appeared that a countdown had started on the *Energia*. Once again he wished he had a secure line so that he could ask how much time was left. "How soon would you expect to see me?"

"No rush, sir. You could take an hour or so."

Forty-five minutes later Chisholm walked into the operations center.

"We don't have any pictures of activity around the *Energia*, sir," Winchell said, "so I may have brought you out on a wild-goose chase, but I don't think so."

"What do you have?"

"First of all, the communications have increased significantly, but it's all scrambled with some new codes. The amount of voice and signal traffic indicates they're into a prelaunch cycle."

"What about the mobile service tower?" Chisholm knew that the massive structure would be rolled away in the hours before a scheduled launch.

"The tower was against the booster when our midday bird was overhead, but that data's a few hours old."

Chisholm nodded. "Do the Soviets have birds on other pads at Tyuratam that might be causing the increased comm?"

"They put a routine ELINT bird on a pad last night, but it wouldn't rate the added communications security we're encountering. Also, they're checking out more than the average number of downrange tracking stations."

"Where's the *Gagarin*?"

The *Kosmonaut Yuri Gagarin* was the Soviet's most capable Space Event Support Ship. Its two ninety-foot dish antennas, mounted amidships on high pedestals, gave the ship a distinctive appearance. Built on the hull of a Sofia-class tanker, the forty-five-thousand-ton *Gagarin* was the largest ship in the world fitted-out for scientific activities.

"In position in the Indian Ocean. And the *Nedelin* is on station in the Pacific."

The *Marshal Nedelin* was second only to the *Gagarin* in capabilities as a space tracking and communications ship. The ships' locations were one more clue suggesting that the *Energia*'s payload was going to GEO.

"Have the ships been there a while, or have they been on the move recently?"

Winchell shrugged and turned to his computer console. "No idea, sir, but I'll check." After a short data search, he added, "The *Gagarin* left Odessa a week ago last Thursday, and the *Nedelin* . . . well, it pulled out of Camranh Bay the following morning."

"That works out about right," Chisholm said with a sense of foreboding, since he realized that both ships had left port less than forty-eight hours after the White House had announced the go-ahead for Defender I.

As the minutes remaining until launch dropped into the single digits, Novikov paced, clicking his cane on the floor with each step. He glanced periodically at the displays showing *Zashchitnik I* from various cameras. On the small screens the powerful booster seemed like a scale model. He did not like remaining inside the control center, but there were no provisions for watching an *Energia* launch from outside the bunker.

At T minus eleven minutes the computers had taken over the automated launch sequence. The launch-processing system had been monitoring over forty thousand parameters as the countdown moved through the final hours. Now the focus was on some three hundred critical readings, and the computers were sampling those systems every two-tenths of a second.

Since everything was being monitored from the consoles that filled the control center, Kalinen seldom needed to respond from the capsule. As Novikov paced, he stopped and listened each time Kalinen spoke. Because of the new encryption scheme that mixed the digitized voice transmission with other digital data, the cosmonaut's recomposed words had an electronic edge to them.

Novikov picked up a stopwatch and zeroed the setting. The seconds between ignition and lift-off were going to be the most excruciating he had experienced since being grounded. While waiting for liftoff, he wanted an accurate reference that would let him know how much time had passed since ignition.

His eyes darted from one display to another as the seconds-to-ignition decreased to one. Novikov pressed the button on his stopwatch as the launch controller announced, "Zero."

Immediately every picture of *Zashchitnik I* started jittering. The video from cameras mounted on the pad shuddered more violently as the buildup continued toward the rated thrust of nearly eight million pounds.

Novikov sensed the deep, earthquakelike rumble and heard a muted roar as he studied the display screens. One camera failed due to the tremendous shaking. All the others conveyed the same story—*Zashchitnik I* remained on the pad in spite of the billowing cloud of white that dwarfed the booster and the support towers.

Novikov glanced at his stopwatch—four seconds had passed. It seemed infinitely longer, yet he had to count four more before he would know if the booster was going to leave the pad. He checked the engine data. The chamber pressure on every rocket looked nominal.

Picture frames rattled against the wall and loose items began vibrating off desktops.

Novikov loved the exhilaration as he added his mental energy to the booster's efforts to lift *Zashchitnik I* into the air.

Slowly the millions of pounds began rising on a tail of fire so bright that it blanked out most of the pictures. Nevertheless, Novikov could see all he needed to see—*Zashchitnik I* was accelerating smoothly. He was aware of cheers echoing through the launch-control center, but he continued to watch the engine indicators, silently counting the 150 seconds until separation of the strap-on boosters.

Downrange cameras relayed pictures of the progress of *Zashchitnik I* across the barren steppes of central Asia. Finally the four strap-on boosters dropped away like inverted candles, falling behind the bell-shaped glow of the main engines.

Novikov let out a growling roar and cracked his cane hard across an empty desk. A chorus of growls followed. Hugging the closest technician, Novikov breathed freely for the first time in the last few minutes. *Krasnaya Molniya* was a giant step closer to being operational.

13

The Pentagon, Washington, D.C.
Sunday, 14 March, 1012 local (1512 GMT)

Chisholm was listening on a headset when the call came in from NORAD.

"We've either detected the Tyuratam bird you're waiting for," the voice said facetiously, "or we just discovered an active volcano about twenty miles north of Leninsk."

"If it's the launch I'm looking for," Chisholm said, "our birds should be observing a lot of flame."

"Slightly less than the sun gives off," the caller from NORAD answered. "First cut by the computers is that we were looking at an *Energia*. It blasted out of Tyuratam headed east and appears to have entered a one-hundred-thirty-two-statute-mile orbit about ten minutes after lift-off."

"My guess," Chisholm said, "is that it'll leave for GEO during the second or third orbit. I'd like voice reports on any changes in the orbit and anything significant you learn on this one."

"We'll keep you informed, sir, and be advised we're signing her in tentatively as Cosmos 3220."

After hanging up, Major Winchell offered, "If you want to stay down here, sir, you're welcome to use that desk over there."

Chisholm looked at his watch. "If I can find a wheelbarrow, I'll bring my in basket down and beat on it while I'm waiting."

"Happy Sunday, sir," Winchell said.

Before Chisholm and the duty officer at NORAD had finished discussing the launch, Novikov and some of his staff were on the way to the airfield. His work at Tyuratam was finished. The next critical event of the mission was the engine firing that would drive *Zash-chitnik I* out of its parking orbit. The command that would fire the powerful rockets, and all the commands that followed, would be sent from Novikov's next stop: Flight Control in the Moscow suburb of Kaliningrad.

Less than half an hour later Chisholm was settled at a desk with two computer monitors in front of him. They displayed information from the classified databases maintained by the Space Surveillance Center (SSC) in Cheyenne Mountain. These computerized files provided orbital data on all objects being tracked by the SSC. The data were updated regularly by sightings from the cameras, telescopes, and radars of the Space Detection and Tracking System.

Normally the system provided Chisholm with everything he needed, but there was one shortcoming. There were not enough sensors around the world to continuously monitor satellites in low-earth orbits. Spacecraft such as the huge new satellite known as Cosmos 3220 could be detected only by ground sensors within about a thousand miles of the satellite. In addition, the optical sensors required clear weather and worked best when sunlight was reflecting off the satellite and the ground station was in darkness.

Without continual coverage the tracking system depended upon previous observations to confirm the shape and orientation of the orbit. Once the orbit was known, the computers could readily predict where and when a satellite would come into the view of the next sensor. Chisholm knew—and the Soviets knew—that this worked well when the satellite was coasting. However, firing an on-board rocket changed the orbit and invalidated the predictions. If a firing occurred in a blind spot where the spacecraft had just passed from coverage, the tracking system could "lose" the satellite for hours, maybe even days in extreme cases. Once the spacecraft was discovered again by another radar or optical sensor, the computers would recalculate the orbit then use the new orbit to predict future positions.

Since Chisholm expected major changes in Cosmos 3220's orbit, he was disappointed that it could not be monitored continuously. However, if the new satellite's destination was GEO, Novikov could do little to hide the transfer.

The procedure used to move a satellite from a circular orbit at

LEO to a circular orbit at GEO had become routine. Chisholm knew that the first step would be to add velocity to Cosmos 3220 by firing the spacecraft's on-board rockets. This initial firing would upset the equilibrium that had kept the spacecraft coasting at a constant altitude of 132 miles and a constant speed of nearly five miles per second. The extra velocity would increase the size of the orbit, moving the vehicle along an elliptical path away from the 132-mile circle. If enough velocity were added, the spacecraft could go far enough and fast enough to break free of the earth's gravitational force. More than three decades earlier, however, scientists had mastered these partic- ular equations of motion. Therefore, to transfer Cosmos 3220 to GEO, just enough velocity would be added to cause the new elliptical orbit—known as the transfer orbit—to reach only as high as the geostationary altitude.

Whenever Chisholm analyzed elliptical orbits, he was always in- terested in two parameters that helped define the size of the orbit. Perigee represented the point on the orbit closest to the center of the earth; apogee, the farthest distance from the center. Even before Novikov made his next move, Chisholm already knew the dimensions of the transfer orbit. Its perigee would be 132 miles—the altitude of the parking orbit. Its apogee would be approximately 22,250 miles— the geostationary altitude. He knew one other factor that narrowed Novikov's choices on when and where he could fire the rockets. If the spacecraft were to reach apogee over the equator, the initial firing had to occur as the spacecraft approached the equator.

As the big spacecraft climbed higher, its speed would decrease continually. Cosmos 3220 would trade speed for altitude, much as a baseball does when thrown high above one's head. At apogee the spacecraft's speed on the elliptical orbit would be much less than the nearly two miles per second required to keep a spacecraft in a circular orbit at GEO. Thus a second firing of the on-board rockets would be necessary.

If the additional speed were not added, Cosmos 3220 would con- tinue on the second half of the elliptical orbit and fall back to the original altitude. Dropping toward perigee, the satellite would regain speed just as a baseball does as gravity pulls it back to earth. Since the satellite would be well above the effects of the atmosphere, the force of gravity would have restored all the spacecraft's lost velocity by the time it got back to 132 miles. In that case the huge satellite would repeat the elliptical orbit approximately twice a day between 132 and 22,250 miles. Atmospheric drag at the lower altitude would slow the vehicle a little on each orbit. In the meantime Novikov's technicians frantically would be trying to figure out how to get the rockets to fire as the satellite reached apogee on one of its orbits. If the Soviets were unsuccessful in getting the rockets to fire, a fiery reentry finally would end the spacecraft's useless journey.

Although Chisholm hoped that Cosmos 3220 would experience such a failure, he knew he could not count on it. Now all he could do was wait until the rockets were fired. Then the satellite would blast out of its parking orbit and become visible to more ground stations as it moved higher into the sky. He also assumed that the firing of the rocket on Cosmos 3220 would be visible to the American missile-warning satellites.

So Chisholm concentrated on his routine work, except for the two periods every hour and a half when Cosmos 3220 crossed the equator.

At 1210 he received another call from NORAD. "Sir, we've detected the perigee burn."

Chisholm asked, "Does it look like Cosmos 3220's going to GEO?"

"Yes, sir."

Now that Novikov had committed Cosmos 3220, Chisholm only needed one more piece of information to figure out where the satellite would be when it reached GEO. "Do you have the longitude at the time of burn?"

"Roger. At the start-of-burn the satellite was over the Celebes Sea south of the Philippines and east of Borneo. That's about one-twenty-five east, but I can get the precise coordinates."

"Close enough," Chisholm said. "But call me right away if you see anything suggesting that Cosmos 3220 isn't going to GEO."

Chisholm hung up the telephone, satisfied that he was only two quick steps away from determining the new satellite's next destination. He visualized the new transfer orbit that had its perigee over the Celebes Sea. The elliptical orbit would remain in the same plane that included the earth's center and the circular parking orbit. He knew that the satellite would reach apogee over the equator on the opposite side of the world from where the perigee burn had taken place.

He added 180 degrees to the 125 degrees east longitude he had written moments earlier. Checking the map display, he discovered that the jungles of Brazil were on the opposite side of the world from the Celebes Sea. Not a bad location for a satellite assigned to monitor the United States and its NATO allies, Chisholm thought. However, the ascent to GEO would take nearly six hours, and he had to apply a correction factor to take into account the earth's rotation. During those hours the earth—including the jungles of Brazil—would rotate eastward nearly 90 degrees. Backing up 90 degrees west along the equator, Chisholm had his answer. The new satellite should reach GEO over the Pacific Ocean about four thousand miles west of Quito, Ecuador.

Though not the optimum location for a military satellite targeted against the western hemisphere, Chisholm thought, the Soviets were bringing it into the ballpark. And, once over the equator at GEO, Cosmos 3220 could be moved easily in either direction. Maintaining a geostationary position required a precise altitude with its corresponding speed that would complete exactly one orbit per day. Lowering a satellite slightly below GEO caused it to drift eastward; a higher altitude caused it to fall behind a little each day. Chisholm thought of Defender, which was still a little over three weeks from launch. Clearly Novikov had plenty of time to move Cosmos 3220 to a better location before Defender I would roar from its Florida launchpad.

As Chisholm was gathering his things, Winchell said, "I just got a note from NORAD, sir. Radio Moscow has announced that a solar-observatory satellite was launched this morning from Tyuratam, so maybe that solves the mystery."

"Maybe," Chisholm said, wishing that it would turn out to be that simple, "but I wouldn't bet the rent money on it."

When Novikov entered Flight Control in the space-control complex at Kaliningrad, he scanned a large screen covering much of the front wall. The current display was a computerized map of the world, which showed the positions of many Soviet satellites. He looked at the area east of New Zealand and spotted a marker representing *Zashchitnik I*.

A data screen on the side showed that Kalinen's spacecraft was two hours into the five-and-a-half-hour journey to GEO. Now *Zashchitnik I* was coasting higher and higher, trading off speed for additional altitude. Everything showed that progress on the transfer orbit was nominal, so Novikov felt relieved. Obviously another critical milestone had been achieved: the spacecraft had enough velocity to climb to GEO.

In fewer than four hours *Zashchitnik I* would reach apogee on the transfer orbit, triggering the next critical event—the apogee burn. In addition to the requirement to restore the satellite's speed, the apogee burn was critical for another reason. A major change in direction was required to keep *Zashchitnik I* over the equator. Because Tyuratam was at approximately forty-five degrees north latitude, the orbital plane of *Zashchitnik I* had to be inclined a minimum of forty-five degrees with respect to the equator. *Zashchitnik I*'s ground track had started well north of the equator and had ranged between forty-five degrees north and south since launch. In geostationary orbit, however, the satellite had to travel constantly eastward over the equator as the world turned beneath it. Thus the apogee burn had to change the orbital plane by forty-five degrees, a maneuver very costly in fuel.

Novikov hated paying the price, but he had no choice. All his launch bases were far north of the equator—a mandate of Russian geography that had caused the Soviets to ignore geostationary orbits for many years. This was one of the few times that he envied the French for anything. If he could have launched *Zashchitnik I* from their space center at Kourou in French Guiana, he could have added considerably to the payload.

In addition to having warmer weather, Kourou's location near the equator gave the French base two distinct advantages over the Soviet launch sites. First, satellites from Kourou could be launched into orbits that kept the spacecraft within five degrees of the equator. This meant that the French wasted little fuel in adjusting such orbits to park a communications satellite over the equator at GEO. The second advantage involved the contribution that earth rotation made to the velocity of a satellite. Except for polar satellites that continuously traveled either north or south, almost every satellite was launched eastward to take advantage of the launch site's eastward motion relative to the center of the earth. That earth-rotational effect was greatest at the equator, decreasing to zero at the poles. The easterly velocity at Kourou was more than a third larger than at Tyuratam and more than twice as large the easterly component of earth rotation at Plesetsk. The result was that eastern launches from Kourou were more efficient than launches from the spaceports of any other nation.

Novikov's study of history had told him that attaining warm-water ports had been a motivating factor behind Soviet strategies in the twentieth century. He was convinced that a more worthy goal would be to attain a spaceport nearer the equator. In his opinion the sooner that visionaries replaced the likes of Marshal Murashev and Minister Levchenko, the more powerful the Soviet Union would become.

Returning his thoughts to more immediate concerns, Novikov decided to stay in Flight Control until the apogee burn had been completed. While waiting, he went to the communications console that linked Kaliningrad with Kalinen.

Kalinen was not sleeping, so Novikov put on a headset and asked, "How's the ride, Vladimir?"

"Very quiet now, Comrade General. Earlier it was a little more exciting." His voice had that same tone that came from the electronic scrambling and unscrambling, making the conversation sound more like communications with a robot.

"You seemed excited, Vladimir. During the launch your heart rate was 113, which was almost as high as mine."

Kalinen laughed. "Mine remained so low because I was trying to stay calm. If I'd let myself become excited, the rate would've exceeded the scale of the indicator."

After talking for a few minutes, Novikov ended the conversation so Kalinen could rest. The young cosmonaut would have to be alert after reaching GEO. Then the flight plan called for a sleep period of six hours before the start of an exhausting work schedule.

Novikov spent the next three hours checking the status of *Borzoi VII* and *Borzoi VIII* and reviewing the failure of *Borzoi VI*. The investigation of its loss had revealed nothing that should delay the others. Therefore, *Borzoi VII* was already on the pad at Plesetsk for a launch at 0950 in the morning. The eighth *Borzoi* would be launched twelve hours later.

At 0145 on Monday morning Novikov's concentration was on *Zashchitnik I*. He could have chosen to monitor procedures from the glass-fronted VIP suite on the second floor of the back wall, but he preferred to stay among those who were working on the mission. Therefore, he was wearing a headset and seated at a console in the main room. On the front wall a timer showed the seconds remaining to the scheduled start of the apogee burn. Novikov silently counted the seconds down to zero. Unlike the thunderous displays of fire and smoke at Plesetsk and Tyuratam, there was no immediate indication that reaching zero had any significance.

However, thousands of miles away on the opposite side of the world, on-board computers had activated turbopumps and commanded valves to open on *Zashchitnik I*. The turbopumps sent fuel and oxidizer rushing into the combustion chambers of the rocket engines. Igniting on contact, the dissimilar liquids produced a controlled explosion. The resulting thrust began accelerating the spacecraft to a speed of nearly two miles per second, sufficient to stay in a circular orbit at GEO. The increase in pressure in the combustion chambers also produced a signal that was relayed by communications satellites to Kaliningrad.

Seconds after the timer reached zero, green lights flashed on in Flight Control, acknowledging the increase in chamber pressures on *Zashchitnik I*. Novikov responded with a silent nod, satisfied that the apogee burn had started on schedule. In less than two minutes the green lights went off, indicating that the main rockets had shut down for the last time. Although Novikov's expression did not change as he scanned the numbers describing the resulting orbit, he felt relieved—*Zashchitnik I* was on station.

The mission controller initiated a computerized sequence of commands, and *Zashchitnik I* began configuring itself. First, additional communications antennas deployed. A minute and a half later large solar panels rotated away from the body of the spacecraft. These arrays of solar cells would collect energy from the sun and provide the power used by most of the electronics. In two more minutes sun-seeking sensors activated and began determining the sun's location in relation to the spacecraft.

Once Novikov was satisfied that the sensors were operational, he keyed his microphone. "How are you feeling, Comrade Kalinen?" Some cosmonauts adjusted to the weightlessness and spacecraft motion easily; nearly half suffered space sickness for the first several days. Symptoms ranged from headache, lethargy, and malaise to nausea and vomiting. Novikov wanted to assess Kalinen's condition before letting the cosmonaut intervene in the automated sequences.

"I am ready to work, Comrade General."

Novikov regretted that the electronic tone did not allow him to draw inferences from the sound of the cosmonaut's voice. Kalinen's answer had been immediate, however, so Novikov decided to take him at his word. "We're giving you Primary Systems Two." At the same time Novikov raised two fingers and nodded to the mission controller.

"Understand, Primary Two," Kalinen responded.

Though there were differences, Soviet cosmonauts and American astronauts shared many of the same attitudes. One was a desire to have more control over their spacecraft. This was not unexpected, since many had been fighter pilots and/or test pilots before entering their nation's space programs. Such men were accustomed to guiding their own destinies with one hand on the throttle and the other gripping the control stick. Only grudgingly would they acknowledge that in many situations in space the machines could do the job better. However, all spacemen disagreed with the premise that someone sitting safely on the ground thousands of miles away should control the spacecraft.

Just as Soviet fliers routinely had less operational freedom than American pilots, cosmonauts were used to having less control than astronauts. In this case Kalinen had even less than usual. Originally *Zashchitnik I* had been designed as an unmanned spacecraft. Everything was to be controlled by on-board computers or through electronic signals from controllers in ground stations or on ships at sea.

Unfortunately, some of Novikov's superiors had decided that these spacecraft were too expensive, the goal was too important, and the risks were too high to launch only a machine. Novikov had fought vigorously but lost the argument. Once the decision had been made to include a cosmonaut on *Zashchitnik I*, he had demanded modifications so that many of the spacecraft's systems could be controlled from on board as well as from the ground. Those on-board controls were operable, however, only when corresponding switches were turned on by the mission controller, as Novikov had just ordered for Primary Systems Two.

Novikov asked, "Do you believe you can speed up sun acquisition?"

"Of course," Kalinen said. "The sun is bright where I am."

Within minutes Kalinen had the solar arrays locked onto the sun. Through the remainder of the mission, these large panels of solar cells would automatically track the sun, rotating as needed to produce maximum electrical energy from the available sunlight.

"Good work," Novikov said. He raised one finger so the mission controller could see the signal, then added to Kalinen, "I'm giving you Primary Systems One. The sooner you get earth capture, the sooner we both can get some sleep."

"Yes, Comrade General."

Before a spacecraft was of much use for any mission, it had to be oriented in relation to the earth. Sensors and communications antennas had to be stabilized and pointed in the right directions. The automated system for earth capture had already begun searching for the earth, now a circular image of blues, browns, and whites that differed markedly from the black background of space. The procedure would slowly orient the spacecraft to face its radar toward the earth. Additional scanning would identify the earth's limb, or edge, where the sensors could distinguish the difference between the earth and the background. By computing the midpoint between opposite sides of the limb, *Zashchitnik I*'s sensors would eventually stabilize the satellite with reference to the point directly below.

The automated system would have taken as long as ten hours. However, by using the attitude-control thrusters in Primary Systems One, Kalinen could turn the spacecraft toward the earth without having to wait for the sensors to methodically scan the sky—one small segment at a time—looking for the earth.

As Novikov observed the data coming from *Zashchitnik I*, Kalinen used the small thrusters to change the satellite's attitude. He quickly accomplished manual procedures he had practiced scores of times in the simulator. Within fifteen minutes the spacecraft was almost precisely aligned. Five minutes later the automated system had made the final corrections, and *Zashchitnik I* was stabilized in relation to the point on the earth directly below the satellite.

While Kalinen had been working, Novikov had checked the data on the new orbit. As he had expected, *Zashchitnik I*'s altitude was more than 150 miles below GEO. The length of a single orbit at that altitude was about a thousand miles less than if *Zashchitnik I* were actually at GEO. The speed necessary to maintain a circular orbit at that altitude was slightly higher than the speed required at GEO. Therefore, the higher speed and the shorter distance meant that *Zashchitnik I* would need about fourteen minutes less to complete each orbit than if it were at GEO. So, while *Zashchitnik I* was actually located over the equator, the spacecraft was not yet geostationary. Instead the huge satellite would drift eastward across the vast expanse of the Pacific Ocean at more than three degrees each day. In a week Novikov would raise the satellite to cut the drift rate in half.

He was quite satisfied. Refinements would be made later so that in less than two weeks *Zashchitnik I* would be at its operational location west of Quito, Ecuador, and almost due south of Mexico City. That longitude—one hundred degrees and thirty-five minutes—was halfway between the longitudes of the American launch bases at Cape Canaveral, Florida, and Vandenberg Air Force Base, California.

14

When Novikov entered his quarters, he was exhausted. Instead of undressing, however, he took off only his greatcoat and hat before retrieving a bottle of vodka, a drinking glass, and a tin of crackers from his luggage. Slumping into a large chair in the corner of the room, he slowly opened the vodka and crackers as if a leisurely evening remained ahead. Though those actions seemed to have his full attention, his thoughts were on *Zashchitnik I* and the cosmonaut high above the other side of the world.

Novikov tossed down a large shot of vodka then followed quickly with one of the dry crackers. After repeating the ritual, he leaned back and closed his eyes, thinking of the world's newest spaceman. He downed more than half the vodka before falling asleep.

At 0445 he awoke with a start and looked around the room until he remembered where he was. He finished undressing, collapsed onto the bed, and fell asleep quickly—but not before mumbling a string of curses about Marshal Murashev.

Novikov's telephone rang at seven. Murashev wanted to see him in Flight Control as soon as possible.

Novikov hurriedly shaved and dressed, speculating about what the crisis might be. Since Kalinen should be in his sleep period with nothing happening on *Zashchitnik I*, Novikov wondered if there was an emergency with one of the boosters at Plesetsk. He discounted that possibility—such news would have come from someone on his launch teams, not from Murashev. Thinking with disdain about Murashev, Novikov doubted that the summons was because of a new problem that was any worse than his headache—which was making him wish he had gone directly to bed.

By the time he walked into Flight Control, he had run a dozen possible scenarios through his mind. He checked the status screens on the front wall. Nothing appeared amiss with *Zashchitnik I*. Then he looked around, spotting Murashev in the VIP suite that overlooked the control room.

Starting up the aisle to join Murashev, Novikov called out to a controller at one of the consoles, "Any problems with the *Borzoi?*" Most of the displays for the *Borzoi* were in a nearby control center.

"No, Comrade General," the controller said as he jumped to attention. "The countdown for *Borzoi Seven* proceeds normally."

Novikov nodded as he continued to the VIP suite.

Without as much as a greeting, Murashev asked, "What in the hell is going on, General?"

Novikov was uncertain what Murashev was questioning. Nevertheless, Murashev often was hopelessly confused about boosters and satellites, so Novikov chose his usual tactic of responding with basic answers. "We are building the constellation of satellites that President Grigoriev ordered. So far, we—"

"The failure Saturday," Murashev said tersely. "How could you let that happen? Is *Krasnaya Molniya* doomed?"

Novikov would like to have pointed out that the questions were a day and a half late. However, he knew better than to critique openly— his single skinny star as a general mayor did not come close to matching the marshal's star—a fat star with six diamonds—that adorned the necktie of Murashev's dress uniform. Novikov assumed the old man had spent the weekend drunk at his *dacha* and had learned this morning of the loss of *Borzoi VI*.

"*Krasnaya Molniya* is proceeding well," Novikov said. "I'm sure President Grigoriev would be pleased by our progress, Comrade Marshal. If *Zashchitnik I* is made operational on schedule within the next thirty-six hours, President Grigoriev can declare his blockade before the end of the week."

Though Murashev maintained his gruff exterior, the look in his eyes suggested he was relieved by Novikov's confidence. "Minister Levchenko called this morning. He wanted to know if you can still uphold your promises to President Grigoriev."

Novikov began to understand. The minister of defense had probably spent the weekend with one of his mistresses at his hunting lodge in the woods north of Moscow. If he was so worried, Novikov thought, the minister could have stood with me in the blizzard at Plesetsk or in the control center at Tyuratam as *Zashchitnik I* shook the steppes of Kazakhstan.

Novikov fought to conceal his anger. There had never been a question that *Krasnaya Molniya* had its risks in the technical arena and in the response that might be provoked in the United States. If the operation failed to the detriment of the Soviet government, there would be extreme personal consequences for himself as well as for Levchenko and Murashev. That was understood by all three men. Novikov wished that his bosses would either join the team wholeheartedly or stay out of his way.

In a patient tone Novikov said, "We've always known, Comrade Marshal, that we don't need all eight *Borzoi* to maintain an effective blockade, especially if *Zashchitnik I* works at nearly full capacity. By midnight we should have seven *Borzoi* in parking orbits, and the replacement vehicle for *Borzoi Six* will be on the launchpad sometime tomorrow night."

"But what do I tell the minister about the failure of the booster on Saturday?"

"Tell him if he gets us perfect hardware, my men will give him perfect launches." The response sounded more sarcastic than Novikov intended, but this type of ploy had worked in the past.

"We can never expect perfect hardware," Murashev said as he pulled a Havana cigar from a pocket. "Not even the Americans have perfect hardware."

"I'm sure," Novikov said, knowing he was about to exaggerate Levchenko's abilities, "the minister understands that even if he gives us parts that are ninety-nine point nine percent reliable, we encounter one failure in every thousand parts."

Murashev nodded noncommittally, as he almost always did whenever Novikov went into detail on anything. The marshal began giving more attention to the lighting of the cigar than to the explanation.

"Unfortunately," Novikov continued, "if a booster and satellite have fifty thousand parts, fifty will fail on every mission if reliability is ninety-nine point nine percent." Novikov knew he was taking technical license, but he also knew that the old man would be swamped if details were added to make the explanation accurate.

"Don't let the next one fail, General."

Novikov looked at his wristwatch. "I could return to Plesetsk,

Marshal, if you're available to oversee the configuring of *Zashchit-nik I*."

Murashev hesitated.

Novikov pressed his bluff. "You would need to be here in Flight Control for the next thirty-six hours."

"That is not possible," Murashev said curtly as he stood and picked up his coat. "I must see Minister Levchenko this morning, and I have my own work to do. You will have to complete your work on your own."

Good, Novikov thought as he tried to appear respectful of the older man's work load.

Monday was a busy day for the Soviets. *Zashchitnik I* was the most complex satellite ever put into orbit, and scores of systems had to be activated. There were numerous checklists to follow to determine if any systems had been damaged during the violent shaking that had accompanied the launch from Tyuratam.

Novikov was interested in four of these systems: the nuclear power plant, the radar, the laser weapons with their integrated fire-control system, and the communications computers that would link *Zashchitnik I* with the *Borzoi* and with the command-and-control system at Kaliningrad. Each of the four was markedly more sophisticated than any versions previously put into orbit. In combination they became the first orbital battle station rivaling the imaginative hardware created by decades of science-fiction writers.

Novikov knew that the most critical procedure was the activation of the nuclear generator. Without the megawatts of power produced by the generator, the lasers and the radar would be useless. Once in operation, the nuclear generator had to be extended to the end of a long boom, thereby reducing its radiation effects on *Zashchitnik I*'s electronics.

The radar was an updated version of American designs for space-based radars. The KGB had begun stealing plans for such radars by the early 1980s. Novikov marveled that he could have an operational system ready for combat before its designers had produced even an orbital model of a similar system. The American radars had languished in development for more than a decade because each year's battle for funding had produced little more than another year's delay. He loved the American bureaucracy almost as much as he hated the one he labored under.

Novikov's radar used thousands of sensors aligned in phased arrays instead of relying on a continually moving antenna, like those that had characterized radars for half a century. At GEO *Zashchitnik I* looked down on more than 40 percent of the earth's surface. The spacecraft's huge radar could search the cosmos above that portion of the earth and could see some satellites that were high above areas beyond the visible horizon. The radar could pick out satellites and most large aircraft flying over the sixty-three million square miles of earth within the view of *Zashchitnik I*.

Without computers to sort out the important observations and to identify smaller areas of interest, the radar would deluge its controllers with irrelevant data. Again Novikov had been forced to incorporate American expertise into his satellite. Without the computers procured by Chairman Petruk's agents in the KGB, the radar would be like a keen-sighted observer without a brain.

These computers also provided fire-control for the two chemical lasers that served as *Zashchitnik I*'s main armament. Using inputs from the radar, the computers would determine aim points and firing cycles for the lasers.

Since controllers in Kaliningrad would select targets and give the clearance to fire, communications computers were critical. These computers also could feed targeting data into the *Borzoi* to supplement that from the sensors aboard the smaller satellites.

Throughout the day Novikov followed all progress closely. He had tried to slip away for rest between critical events but had gotten less than a half hour of real sleep.

By late afternoon the long boom was extended to its full length. Then the nuclear plant was activated in its compartment at the aft end of *Zashchitnik I*. As soon as low- and medium-power checks were completed without incident, the heavy generator started moving toward the end of the boom. Less than a quarter of the journey was completed when the cabling jammed. Commands from the ground controllers could not move the generator forward or back.

After forty-five minutes of futile attempts by Kalinen in the spacecraft and the controllers on the ground, Novikov stopped their efforts. He decided to give Kalinen a six-hour rest period while technicians reviewed the blueprints and drawings of the boom and its cabling.

To decrease the effects of radiation on the spacecraft and its contents, Novikov made sure that the nuclear generator was powered down to its minimum level. This was critical because of another compromise in the design of *Zashchitnik I*. Only one side of the generator was covered with heavy shielding. Once the generator reached the end of the boom, mechanical linkages would turn the shielded side toward the spacecraft. Novikov assumed that radiation from a few hours at minimum power probably would not damage the spacecraft's electronics, but he knew the problem had to be solved before *Zashchitnik I* could become operational.

Almost too exhausted to think about solutions, Novikov slumped into a chair. Fortunately, he thought, Minister Levchenko had called for a status report just after the power checks had been completed. Murashev had left work early, reportedly suffering from a cold. With luck Novikov would not have to answer questions from his superiors for the next twelve to fourteen hours. By the time there were questions, he hoped the problem would be solved.

15

Chisholm was sitting with his feet up on his cluttered desk when Rick McClain walked in carrying a cup of coffee. Motioning for McClain to take a seat, Chisholm said, "I figured you were already on the road."

"I've got a flight out of National to Dayton at one-thirty."

"I'm glad you're still here. I've been studying the telemetry on Cosmos 3220, and I have a couple of ideas to bounce off you."

McClain seemed startled. "I thought no one had broken the encryption scheme."

"My suspicions don't have anything to do with breaking the codes. I've been listening to the raw data."

"I would've been surprised if you said we'd solved it," McClain said. "Murphy thinks this is the best encryption scheme the Russians have ever used."

"Why?"

"Why what, sir?"

"The Soviets keep their good stuff hidden in reserve to surprise us in time of war. Why would they expose their best encryption scheme now?"

McClain shrugged as if he had not given that question any thought. "Another indicator that the *Energia* launched something special?"

"You got it, Rick. Very special—something we've never seen before." Chisholm paused and began tapping a pencil on the edge of the desk. Tat-ta-ta-tat. "Now let me hit you with something really outrageous. I believe 3220's manned."

McClain looked confused, then placed his coffee on the safe next to his chair. "I thought you said that astronauts either stayed at LEO or went to the moon, but didn't set up camp anywhere between."

"That's the way it's always been before 3220."

McClain studied Chisholm's expression. "Keeping a crew resupplied at GEO isn't like sending a *Progress* vehicle up to the *Mir* every couple of months."

Chisholm agreed that supporting crewmen on the *MIR* space station at LEO was easier than resupplying a manned satellite at more than twenty-two thousand miles above the earth. Each pound of payload lifted to LEO required 20 to 50 pounds of launch vehicle and propellants on the pad. Each pound taken to GEO could require 150 to 400 pounds at launch, depending upon the efficiency of the rockets. Chisholm recognized that the hundreds-to-one ratio had another deleterious effect on the feasibility of a manned mission at GEO.

Chisholm said, "You'd also have to add enough shielding on the satellite to protect the crew. The weight penalty could cost you most of your payload."

Exposure to radiation had to be considered in the planning of any manned space mission even when nuclear generators were not aboard. The flow of charged particles from the sun, which were a hazard under normal circumstances, could intensify with little warning. Solar storms often triggered outbursts of high energy protons and solar gases that reached the earth very quickly.

The world's population was protected naturally by two radiation belts, known as the Van Allen belts. These geomagnetic belts, which looped out from the earth's magnetic poles, absorbed charged particles thrown off by the sun. Major solar events, therefore, were only a minor inconvenience on earth. In most cases their worst consequences were worldwide electrical storms that temporarily disrupted long-distance radio communications.

Except under certain conditions near the earth's magnetic poles, cosmonauts and astronauts at LEO also were protected by the radiation belts. However, the radiation belts posed a danger to manned missions that had to penetrate these regions of geomagnetically trapped particles. The Apollo missions to the moon had carried enough shielding to safeguard the crews during their quick passages through the radiation belts. However, spacecraft orbiting indefinitely within the radiation belts were likely to accumulate an intolerable dose of radiation.

At GEO satellites such as *Zashchitnik I* were above the heavy radiation in the Van Allen belts but also were above their protection. So no serious consideration had been given to stationing crews at GEO, Chisholm thought—at least not in the American space program.

McClain asked, "What's a good figure for shielding humans? Maybe ten grams per square centimeter? That'd mean . . ." McClain paused a moment, staring toward the ceiling as he computed the numbers in his head.

"At least ten thousand pounds of shielding," Chisholm offered. Tat-ta-tat.

McClain thought for a couple of moments, then added, "Which translates to two or three million pounds on the pad just to lift the shielding."

"So shielding would cost at least a third of the payload the Russians can get to GEO, even with the *Energia*."

McClain shook his head. "That's a tremendous price to pay, but if they didn't, the radiation from one good solar flare could turn their cosmonauts to crispy critters."

Chisholm nodded and said, "So to speak." Tat-ta-tat.

"If you add the weight of the crew and their life support to the shielding," McClain said, "the penalties of man-rating the satellite makes any mission to GEO pretty damned impractical."

The additional costs of making a satellite safe enough to carry humans was one reason that most spacecraft were unmanned.

"I said manned. I didn't say 'man-rated.' " Tat-ta-ta-tat.

McClain looked even more shocked than when Chisholm had suggested that 3220 was manned. Finally his expression softened into a smile. "April Fool's Day is a couple of weeks away, Colonel. You're just testing my coefficient of gullibility, right?"

Chisholm shook his head. "The Russians could have made compromises."

McClain started to answer, then paused. He crossed his arms and stared intently at Chisholm. "I can't believe you're insinuating what you're insinuating, Colonel."

"Believe it. I think the Russians put a man on 3220—and I doubt they paid the weight penalty to keep him there indefinitely." Tat-ta-ta.

"Why?" McClain stood and picked up his coffee. "That's too spooky to think about, Colonel."

"The *why* depends on how badly they needed a man on this mission—and how badly they needed the rest of the weight budget for mission-essential equipment."

McClain paced back and forth across the small office a couple of times, then turned to Chisholm. "Have you shared that thought with General Ramsey?"

"If I can't sell you on the idea, I'm sure as hell not ready to waste his time."

"I wouldn't say that you can't sell me," McClain said with a smile, "but I'm not easy."

"The sequencing of the encrypted data is what made me suspicious," Chisholm said. "We haven't intercepted any voice traffic, but some exchanges of electronic signals have the feel of a conversation between the ground and the spacecraft."

"Maybe 3220 has a robot aboard," McClain said, then added with a grin. "That'd cut down on the vodka and brown bread they'd have to take to GEO."

"I'm serious," Chisholm said. "Compare the telemetry to the mission profile, and you'll reach the same conclusion. There are signals that match engine staging and ignition of the succeeding stages. You can pair up routine commands and responses with no problem. But there are at least a half dozen sequences in those first two hours that have the flavor of a conversation."

"If a crew's setting up housekeeping at GEO," McClain said, "there ought to be quite a few conversations with mission control. I could listen to the current tapes."

"You'll be on your way to Ohio by the time they're available," Chisholm said as he began to look for other answers. "You have any other ideas about how we might confirm the presence of a live body on 3220?"

McClain settled into the chair and closed his eyes for a moment. "There might be a continuous data stream if ground control is monitoring vital signs."

"I've checked. There are long periods with no communications of any kind."

"Maybe on orbit we'll see patterns in these sequences that you believe are conversations. Gaps could indicate sleep periods. However, if several men are on the crew, they might not sleep at the same time."

"That might be a tip-off, because I'm betting there's a crew of one—probably the smallest guy available who could reach the switches."

McClain looked surprised again. "You seem to have this all figured out, Colonel. Why would they send one . . . Hell, why would they send anybody?"

"Suppose you need to orbit some advanced electronics, and you can't risk the whole package not working. If you're a Russian who's a generation or two behind in computers, you might decide that a man in the loop's your best insurance."

McClain's expression indicated that he was catching up with Chisholm. "Somebody to give the black boxes a swift kick if they start off a little cranky in crunching the ones and zeros."

"As the reliability people always say, no one's invented the screwdriver with a twenty-thousand-mile-long handle."

"You're starting to make some of this sound plausible, Colonel," McClain said grimly, "but the 'one-way mission' part bothers me."

"Read their war plans or the histories of the battles on the eastern front in World War II. The Soviets don't hesitate to sacrifice a body or two—or two thousand—if that'll win their objective." Chisholm paused and resumed tapping the point of the pencil on the desk. Tat. Tat. "I need evidence—and the quicker, the better." Tat.

"I could postpone my trip and start listening to the rest of the telemetry. That'll still be pretty circumstantial unless someone in crypto breaks the—"

"The park!" Chisholm stabbed the pencil onto the desktop, sending the bottom half of the pencil flying in scattered splinters. "I need to see pictures of the park!"

"What?"

"There's a cosmonauts' park at Tyuratam. Each cosmonaut plants a tree in the park before going into space."

McClain's expression brightened into an amazed smile. "Damn, Colonel, that might tell us. But would they have planted a tree in this case?"

"General Novikov would. Start digging out every shot we've got for the last four weeks. I'll meet you in the vault," Chisholm said, referring to a vaultlike room where highly classified material could be stored and worked with openly, "as soon as I get someone to take my eleven o'clock meeting."

McClain leaped up. "I'm on my way!"

Twenty minutes later Chisholm and McClain were seated viewing scores of photographs that were scattered out on a table. Some pictures showed the huge cosmodrome spread over the barren steppes east of the Aral Sea. Others revealed roads and paths cutting through the snow-covered hillsides of the neatly kept memorial park with its abundance of trees.

"Nothing," Chisholm said as he tossed a picture onto the table. He leaned back disappointed. "I was sure we'd find a new tree."

"If some top-secret cosmonaut's aboard," McClain said, "the Soviets have to be too smart to plant a tree for us to see."

Chisholm had to agree. Even though Novikov was a man of tradition, Chisholm thought, the general had been enough of a pragmatist to rise toward the top of the Soviet system. Obviously Novikov was aware of what the reconnaissance satellites could see. Chisholm paused—the general also knew how to hide things from the satellites. The surprises of the last week confirmed Novikov's mastery of deception. Chisholm closed his eyes, trying to picture himself wearing the rank of a general-mayor and limping through the park. If he were sending a cosmonaut into space, he knew a tree would be planted before he limped back to his limousine.

Chisholm's eyes popped open. "I need to see more pictures. Everything from just before Govorov and Yefimov were launched in November."

A few more minutes were necessary to retrieve pictures of the park that had been taken before the last team of cosmonauts had gone into space. Back at the table, Chisholm studied a picture taken three days before the November launch. The most obvious difference from those he had seen earlier was a tractor and trailer parked along one of the snow-packed roads. Seven pictures from the following days showed two holes in the ground nearby, then two new trees where the holes had been. The tractor and trailer appeared only in the first picture.

Chisholm let his eyes dart from one picture to another. He tried to find a pattern that could be translated four months forward to the pictures from last week. Suddenly he shouted, "Tallyho!"

In less than two minutes he had the rest of the answer and was on the telephone with General Ramsey's secretary, Janice Waters.

"Janice," Chisholm said, "I've got to have some face time with the general."

"He has people in his office now, Colonel Chisholm," she said. "He leaves with the chief of staff in fifteen minutes for lunch and is booked solid until eighteen hundred."

"He needs to hear what I've got before he sees the chief. Get me in, and you'll be a hero."

"That's heroine, Colonel Chisholm, and you're the third colonel who's tried that line on me this morning."

"But, Janice, you know I'm the only one who ever means it. I've got a real showstopper. Really."

"If you were right here in the office, and there's a break before he has to meet the chief, I might get you in."

"In two minutes, I'm there. Thanks."

As Chisholm crammed the pictures into an envelope so they could be carried through the hallways without security restrictions being compromised, he said, "This is a good chance for you to meet General Ramsey."

McClain appeared nervous. "You don't think he'll mind if you bring me along?"

"No problem, Rick," Chisholm said as they hurried out into the hallway. "General Ramsey and I are on a first-name basis." He waited long enough for McClain to be duly impressed, then added in mock seriousness, "He calls me Mike, and I call him General."

McClain laughed, seeming to shed some of his apprehension about a face-to-face meeting with one of the Air Force's most senior officers.

"Just don't let his Oklahoma-country-boy demeanor fool you," Chisholm said as he started jogging along the hallway. "He's a very smart ol' country boy."

When Chisholm and McClain reached the outer office, Janice Waters was not at her desk. Before Chisholm could check with one of the other secretaries, Waters came out of General Ramsey's private office.

"I warned the general that you were going to try to make him late for lunch," Waters said as she gestured for Chisholm to enter.

"Right," Chisholm said with a wink, "and if we're not out in five minutes, you'd better warn the chief's secretary."

Waters looked concerned. "I hope you're not serious, Colonel."

"Unfortunately," Chisholm said, "I am."

Ramsey was retrieving his uniform blouse from a closet as Chisholm and McClain entered. After McClain was introduced, Ramsey asked, "What's got you all stirred up this time, Mike?"

"Cosmos 3220, General. That's the huge bird the Soviets sent up on the *Energia* yesterday."

Ramsey nodded. "In the boss's staff meeting this morning, the opinions were pretty much mixed on whether or not it's some fancy solar observatory as they advertised."

"I believe it's manned, General," Chisholm said.

Ramsey looked startled. He stopped with the blouse partway off a hanger. "No one suggested that possibility this morning."

"I doubt that anyone else is suspicious, sir."

After a moment's hesitation, Ramsey returned his things to the closet and closed the door. "I think you're right—about me being late for lunch, anyway. Show me what you've got, Mike."

"Yes, sir," Chisholm said as McClain spread pictures out on a table. "The telemetry raised questions, but these pictures were the clincher. I believe they planted a new tree in the cosmonaut's park on the twelfth."

"A tree? In a park?" Ramsey looked at Chisholm, then McClain, then at the pictures. "You need to focus me in a little closer."

"Yes, sir. Here's an overall view of the Baikonur Cosmodrome."

Ramsey scanned the picture. "So far I see fewer trees than were on my grandpappy's ranch in west Texas."

Chisholm pointed at some dark objects in a small section of the first picture. "These are about the only trees you'll find on the entire cosmodrome. This area is known as the cosmonauts' park. Yuri Gagarin planted a tree there in 1961 just before he became the first man in orbit." Chisholm selected a picture showing a closer view of the park. "Here's his tree with more than thirty years' growth. Our astronauts Tom Stafford, Deke Slayton, and Vance Brand joined in the tradition when they visited Baikonur before the Apollo-Soyuz linkup in space in 1975."

Ramsey's expression reflected growing interest. "If there's a crew on 3220, the Russians aren't advertising it. I'm not sure they'd leave such obvious evidence behind if they're trying to keep a secret."

"They've worked pretty hard to hide the evidence, General," McClain said, then gestured toward Chisholm. "But Colonel Chisholm didn't let them get away with it."

"General Novikov believes in tradition," Chisholm said. "That park has trees from more than one hundred cosmonauts. I don't buy that Novikov would break the tradition on this mission, because I don't think this cosmonaut's coming back."

Ramsey took a deep breath. "That puts a hell of a different twist on their game." He paused as if very troubled with the thought. "Where's the tree? I'll need to show General Bolton and Secretary Davis."

Chisholm knew this would be the tricky part as he showed Ramsey the most current view of the park. "The tree's right here, sir."

Ramsey took the picture, looked at it closely, then went to his desk to get a magnifying glass. "Your eyes—or your imagination—must be better than mine, Mike."

"You can't see it, sir, because the tree's covered with camouflage netting."

Ramsey gave a quizzical look that Chisholm had grown accustomed to since coming to work in the Pentagon. Before Chisholm could continue, Janice Waters knocked and opened the door. She did not speak. Her presence was her reminder that Ramsey needed to leave to meet the chief of staff.

Ramsey said, "Jan, please let General Bolton's secretary know that I'll be a little late joining the chief."

"Yes, sir," she said, then cast an I'll-get-you-for-this smile in Chisholm's direction before leaving.

"If Jan discovers we're in here counting trees in a Russian forest," Ramsey said with a broad grin, "she won't let you through that door for a month. Now tell me about this tree I'm supposed to be seeing that I'm not supposed to see."

"These pictures from November finally tipped us to the location of the tree. That's when the Soviets sent cosmonauts Govorov and Yefimov up to the *Mir* space station. This picture shows two new trees a couple of days after they were planted."

Ramsey studied the picture. "Can they plant trees that late in November and get them to grow?"

"I don't know how anything grows any time of the year in most of Russia, sir. I do know they couldn't get the trees in the ground without help." Chisholm selected two more pictures. Pointing to a tractor and a portable power unit parked nearby, Chisholm said, "They had to thaw the ground, and here's the heater-blower they used in November. It's similar to heaters we use to warm up the cabins of parked aircraft in the winter."

"So you've got pictures of a blower nearby in the last few days?"

"No, sir. Novikov was too careful for that. But we can see the ice."

"Ice?" Ramsey gave Chisholm a this-had-better-be-good look. "I can see me trying to explain to the chief that I'm late because of a tree I can't see and ice that I can see?"

"You'll sell him, sir," Chisholm said as he pointed to the second picture. "In this shot from November, the sun was at a lower angle. You can see reflections from ice that's down the slope from both holes where the trees are to be planted. When the heater thawed the snow and the ground beneath it, water ran down the hill, then froze once it got away from the heat."

Ramsey nodded, making it obvious to Chisholm that the general had already reached the bottom line. "And there's new ice this week on the hillside below the camouflage netting?"

"Roger that, sir." Chisholm gave Ramsey another picture. "You can see the ice on the evening of the eleventh, the day the Soviets dug the hole and covered it with a camouflage net. That night Baikonur had several inches of snow, which covered the ice. However, once the ice had told us where to watch, we could tell that something was under the netting on the thirteenth. This final picture's from late yesterday afternoon. You can see the shadow cast by the net draped over the tree. That shadow wasn't there before the twelfth, sir."

"I'll need a couple of these to show General Bolton," Ramsey said as he studied the final picture. "Well, Mike, if there's a man on 3220, why are they trying to keep it a secret?"

"I don't think they're ready to tell the Russian people that one of their beloved cosmonauts has been sent on a one-way mission. I still believe 3220's related to the constellation of low-altitude birds they began launching from Plesetsk on the—"

Ramsey interrupted. "And related to Defender?"

Chisholm nodded. "The timing's too coincidental to be anything else."—

"See what you can find to back that up," Ramsey said. "I think I'll call a meeting of the Space Advisory Council to find out if anyone else is picking up any indicators."

"You might want to go slow on that, General," Chisholm said. "The longer Novikov thinks we're just sitting here fat, dumb, and happy, the more time we have to catch up with him."

Ramsey considered Chisholm's advice for a moment, then said, "You're not suggesting, are you, that we blunder forth and launch Defender without knowing what it may encounter?"

"No, sir, but unless the Soviets are waiting to launch a mate for 3220, I suspect we'll understand what they're up to well before we have Defender ready."

16

Kaliningrad, USSR
Monday, 15 March, 2350 local (2050 GMT)

After discussing *Zashchitnik I*'s malfunctioning cable system with his experts, Novikov had slept for three hours. During that time his engineers and technicians tried to discover why the nuclear generator could not be moved to the end of the boom.

Now Novikov reconvened his team. There was general agreement on the most likely cause of the failure: the cabling, which was to pull the generator into position, had gotten out of its track. Novikov nodded his concurrence. The long boom, which included the cabling, originally had been stowed alongside the body of the spacecraft. There always had been some risk in that design, but there had been no better way to package the boom to withstand the shaking and acceleration during launch. He remembered watching ground tests of the extension of the boom several months earlier. In each test the cables stayed within their tracks and remained free to move. Unfortunately, Novikov thought, mechanical things sometimes did not work so well in the extreme cold, the weightlessness, and the vacuum of space.

He eyed the group of weary men gathered around the conference table. "Do we have volunteers to go up there and fix it?"

Some seemed to be trying to decide whether the general was angered by the failure or just asking for the proposed solution. An older, wispy-haired engineer responded. "The first plan, Comrade General, is to reverse the final steps of the procedure that extended the boom." He showed the hint of a smile, then added, "I first would like to try that from a console here in Flight Control."

Novikov could not think of a better suggestion. "What would you accomplish, Aleksandr?"

"Perhaps, Comrade General, making the cable slack will allow it to slip into the track when we extend the boom again."

"Does this procedure put the reactor at risk?"

"Not if we maneuver only the two outer sections of the boom."

Novikov looked at his other experts, but none seemed ready to offer an alternative. Finally he said, "We're falling behind schedule."

Twenty minutes later Novikov was seated at a console as the boom was being partially retracted. As everyone was quietly awaiting the results, Kalinen's electronically distorted voice came over the speaker. "Sleeping is difficult when you keep shaking my chair, comrades."

Novikov grabbed a headset, then keyed the microphone. "We had hoped to have a surprise for you when you awakened."

"You did, Comrade General. As soon as my heart slows, I will try to help."

Novikov explained the plan to Kalinen. After the boom was extended again, Novikov was ready to activate the motor that ran the cables. As everyone looked on, he raised a clenched fist, then sent the command.

No one spoke while awaiting an electronic response verifying that the nuclear generator was on the move. Seconds later *Zashchitnik I* signaled that the motor had stalled.

"I feel no movement, Comrade General," Kalinen said.

Novikov slammed one fist against his opposite palm, then rested his chin on clenched hands as he tried to think of another solution. Others groaned or cursed.

"I have thought much about the problem, Comrade General," Kalinen continued, "and I propose that I go for a walk and see what can be done."

A spacewalk was an option Novikov had considered before falling asleep. Months ago he had decided to send along an extra-vehicular activity (EVA) suit and a maneuvering unit. Soviet cosmonauts were the unquestioned leaders of the world in total experience in spacewalks outside of spacecraft. However, there always had been at least two, and often three, cosmonauts aboard when it was time to don the bulky suits.

The EVA suit was similar to those introduced more than a decade earlier for use with the *Salyut 6* space station. Modifications had been added to make it easier for one man to seal the entry opening once he was inside. The suit also had a built-in radio transmitter and did not have the umbilical cord that kept the earlier suits connected to spacecraft equipment. A maneuvering unit, stored in an outer compartment, would allow the cosmonaut to maneuver at small distances from the spacecraft.

Even with the changes made to the suit, Novikov knew that some men in Flight Control doubted that a single cosmonaut could get the EVA suit on and move in and out through the narrow hatch by himself. And, Novikov thought, there was the question of the radiation, both from the sun and from the nuclear generator. The material of the EVA suit provided even less protection than the metal walls of *Zashchitnik I*.

"I'd like to find an easier answer," Novikov said.

"I'm here, sir, because I am the easy answer. I am prepared to do my duty."

"But, Cosmonaut-Without-Fear," Novikov said, as much for the benefit of those around him as for Kalinen to hear, "there are other duties for you to do. While you complete those, we will seek other solutions."

"The sunshine here is bright, Comrade General. I am ready for a new day's work."

As a controller with a checklist took over the console, Novikov looked at his watch. It was a new day in Kaliningrad, too, but he did not share the young cosmonaut's enthusiasm—although Novikov knew Kalinen was right about why he had been sent on the mission.

In spite of Novikov's protests that had gone as high as Minister Levchenko, Marshal Murashev had prevailed with his plan to send a cosmonaut on each of the first three *Zashchitniks*. The marshal had argued that unforseen technical problems could jeopardize the entire operation. Studies had suggested that a cosmonaut should be able to survive long enough at GEO to fix any problems that were fixable. Novikov hated to admit it, but the balky generator seemed to validate the judgment of the crusty old marshal.

For a moment Novikov questioned his motives: was he just being a poor loser because he wanted to prove Murashev wrong? If Kalinen could save the mission, Novikov had no right to take the honor away from the young cosmonaut. Novikov hated the dilemma. He also hated Murashev more than ever before.

A few hours later heavy snow was falling throughout the Moscow area as darkness slowly gave way to the dull light of morning. Inside the main room at Flight Control, daybreak on this particular Tuesday came and went without notice.

Novikov was pleased with the computers and the communications equipment on *Zashchitnik I*. Kalinen had removed and replaced several spare electronic modules when the controllers on the ground had encountered problems. Now both systems seemed to be working perfectly. *Zashchitnik I* transferred information readily through high-volume electronic links with communications satellites and with ground stations in Cuba. There was no attempt to establish the links with the *Borzoi* yet. Novikov assumed that American electronic intelligence units already were studying *Zashchitnik I*. Thus he wanted to avoid actions that could reveal any relationship between the *Borzoi* and the larger satellite at GEO.

The routine checks of the circuitry on the radar and the lasers had been successful. The solar arrays, however, did not produce enough electrical power for full operation of the radar. And there were no plans for a full check of the lasers even if the nuclear power were available. Novikov wanted to keep his lasers hidden until a suitable target was chosen for a demonstration of the weapons on *Zashchitnik I*.

The general called a meeting of his team chiefs for a review of the remaining items on their checklists. No one had any other tasks for Kalinen besides the checkouts that could not be completed until the balky nuclear generator was put into operation. Everything else could be handled from the consoles in Flight Control.

A few minutes later Novikov went to the communications console and called Kalinen. "Perhaps the time has come, Vladimir, to find out whether you can get into your EVA suit."

"I know, Comrade General," Kalinen said. "I started the procedure fifteen minutes ago."

"Call us if you have trouble," Novikov said, then leaned back in the chair and waited.

Two hours passed before Kalinen had all his equipment on and checked out. Everything seemed to work perfectly except for the voice-activated switch for the microphone in his helmet. He could transmit only by pressing a button on the belt that controlled other systems within the EVA suit. Inconvenient but workable, he decided.

Kalinen took a long drink from his water tube, then lowered the clear faceplate that sealed the opening on the front of his helmet.

He slipped his right hand into the suit's bulky glove and rotated the glove until the wrist seal clicked into place. When he checked the integrity of the suit, he found that he was successfully sealed within. Already he did not like the claustrophobic feeling. Each movement he made was opposed by the pressure within the suit. Now he had the sensation of floating within the suit as he floated within *Zash-chitnik I* to enter the airlock.

Once he was sealed within the airlock, he held aside a protective cover and pushed one finger against the depressurization button. He waited a few moments as the airlock's breathable atmosphere was vented away with a quiet, sucking sound. When he was satisfied that the differential pressure between the airlock and the near vacuum of space had dropped to zero, he floated up through the narrow passageway to the hatch. Bracing his legs and back, he moved the levers that controlled the manual safety latches. Then he pressed the button that electronically released the locks, and he pushed the hatch open.

"Radio check," he called as he glided out through the opening.

"You're loud and clear, *Zashchitnik I*," the voice from Kaliningrad answered.

The voice had an electronic tone that seemed to echo within Kalinen's helmet. His thoughts about the irritating electronics were forgotten, however, when he emerged into the sunlight and got his first clear view of the scene beyond the dreary confines of his space-craft. Without the filtering of any atmosphere, the sun's brightness was almost blinding. He quickly lowered the sun-filter visor over his faceplate.

Directly beneath him the ocean was several hours from sunrise. That part of the earth blended with the darkness of space like the unseen portion of a crescent moon that hides from observers on the earth. Frostlike swirls of clouds and vast storm systems stretched eastward from the darkness. They appeared first as dull white along the line that divided South America between day and night, then bloomed to bright white closer to the rounded horizon Kalinen saw on the sunlit side of the earth.

In spite of the overwhelming grandeur, he was most affected by the sounds—there were none except those made by his own breathing and his blood being propelled within him. For an instant he felt more alone than at any time since the first few seconds after the hatch had been sealed at Tyuratam.

He had to struggle against the pressures within his bulky suit as he tried to get the maneuvering unit out of its storage compartment. Finally the unit broke free. He turned so that his backpack was against the unit, then clipped the lapbelt around his waist. For a few minutes he tested the jets, maneuvering back and forth out to the end of the tether that connected his suit to the spacecraft. Finally satisfied, he released the tether's clip from the spacecraft, then clipped the line to the maneuvering unit. No longer attached to *Zashchitnik I*, he slowly drifted away. Kalinen smiled, thinking of himself as a human satellite now streaking through the cosmos at more than four times the speed of a bullet from an AK-47.

His efforts thus far had him breathing hard already, so he paused to catch his breath and to take in the unmatched spectacle below. Although the oxygen in the suit was drying out his nose and mouth and making him thirsty, he was determined to enjoy the experience. After all, he thought bitterly, no one had more right to.

He was proud of his accomplishment. He was seeing the earth from a height never before attained by any other cosmonaut—not even Novikov or the noble Gagarin. Only the Americans who had gone to the moon had seen the earth from a vantage point more distant than his.

From more than twenty-two thousand miles away, the earth did not dominate the view from horizon to horizon as in all the pictures from low-earth orbit. Instead *Zashchitnik I* was the dominant object in Kalinen's surroundings, dwarfing the earth, which appeared as if it were a colorful ball suspended on an invisible string. The view made him think of something attributed to an American astronaut about how the earth appeared as a large blue marble—a unified entity when viewed from high in the cosmos. Kalinen was stirred by a similar feeling, but he shrugged it away. If the earth were so unified, he would not have needed to come so far to do what he must do.

He activated the small jets on the maneuvering unit and turned to face *Zashchitnik I*. He had exited near one end of the spacecraft, more than one hundred feet from where the boom was connected at the opposite end. It took a couple of maneuvers to get oriented in the direction he wanted to go. Then he squeezed the controls for two quick blasts on the jets and began drifting toward the far end of *Zashchitnik I*.

He moved along the side of the spacecraft that always faced the earth. The phased-array radar was the dominating feature on the earth-facing side. Kalinen was struck by how magnificent the fifty-foot-long by twenty-foot-wide array appeared with the sunlight casting shadows of the thousands of sensing elements that extended from the face of the array.

The two rotating turrets holding the lasers were on opposite sides of the body of the spacecraft near the middle of the radar's array. Each turret had been briefly cycled through its full range of movement, then returned to the stowed position aligned with the spacecraft. The black camouflage paint made the weapons almost invisible against the darkness of deep space. Unless American sensors had somehow observed the turrets during the tests, there was little to reveal that *Zashchitnik I* was anything more than a surveillance platform or perhaps even a solar observatory.

Near the end of the spacecraft, the boom extended for almost 150 feet, angled away from the earth. He slowly began edging along the boom, inspecting the cabling as he moved away from the main body of *Zashchitnik I*. Though he suspected that it would make little difference as far as the amount of radiation was concerned, he stayed on the shielded side of the nuclear generator as he passed the area where the generator was stuck.

Novikov was awaiting Kalinen's first report on the problem when a call came from Minister Levchenko.

"President Grigoriev wants to schedule the speech at the United Nations on Thursday," Levchenko said. "He's ready to have Tass announce the speech if you don't have any major problems."

Novikov hesitated, quickly trying to assess how major the problem was. Perhaps the nuclear generator could provide enough power to run *Zashchitnik I*'s radar. Passing the data to the *Borzoi* still would make those satellites more deadly than if they were limited to their own sensors. Even if the *Borzoi* had to operate independently, he rationalized, the satellites had a good chance of blockading the American, Japanese, and French spaceports.

Levchenko responded to the lack of immediate assurance. "What kind of problems have you uncovered in your checkout, Petr?"

"Right now we have a mechanical difficulty in positioning the nuclear generator," Novikov said, choosing his words carefully. "I hope Cosmonaut Kalinen will have the difficulty resolved in the next few hours."

Levchenko made a guttural sound of disapproval, then said, "I have already told President Grigoriev that Thursday would be a good day to announce the blockade. You had not told me that there were any problems, Petr." The last sentence was said in an accusatory tone.

In the background Novikov heard Kalinen announcing that he could see what was causing the problem.

Encouraged, Novikov told Levchenko, "If President Grigoriev wants a blockade in place by Thursday, Comrade Minister, he will have one. We can keep the Defender satellite out of the cosmos."

Even without *Zashchitnik I* Novikov felt certain that the Defender would come within range of four or five of the *Borzoi* before leaving its parking orbit. Once the Americans reached that same conclusion, he assumed that they would postpone their launch while computers evaluated all possible ascent profiles. By the time the Americans could devise any alternative launch procedures, he should have *Zashchitnik II* on orbit doing everything that Kalinen's satellite was supposed to do.

"We will count on you to make sure that that promise is carried out, Comrade General."

Novikov hung up the telephone, for the moment almost envying Kalinen—almost.

"The cable," Kalinen said, "is off the track at the third joint from the end." Because of the physical exertion of the spacewalk, his words were halting, grouped into threes and fours with gasping breaths in between.

"If we partially retract the boom," Novikov said, "we should cause some slack in the cabling at that joint. Would that free the cable to get back on the track?"

Kalinen looked farther along the boom as he tried to regain his breath. "Perhaps, Comrade General."

"Before we try," Novikov said, "inspect the rest of the boom for any other failures."

Twenty minutes later Kalinen knew he had found the only problem. As he floated in space a few feet away from the boom, a controller at Kaliningrad sent a command to reverse the boom-extension procedure. The outer sections of the boom began slowly retracting toward the stowed position.

"The cable is becoming slack," Kalinen finally said.

"Watch closely," Novikov said, "and we shall extend the boom."

"I am ready, sir."

The controller sent the opposite command, and the boom started extending.

Kalinen watched the cable pull tighter with each jerk of the motor. "The cable is becoming taut, but it is settling on the edge of the track." The cable tightened on the narrow lip for a few more cycles, then slipped into the narrow crack between the track and the frame of the boom. "It didn't work."

"Hold," Novikov said to the controller. "Stay clear, Cosmonaut Kalinen. We will try again."

The procedure was repeated twice with the same result.

"If I had one of the tools," Kalinen said, "perhaps I could guide the cable into the track."

There were tools in the airlock for making emergency repairs to the outside of the spacecraft. Constructed of special materials, these tools could be used in the near-vacuum of outer space without becoming vacuum-welded to spacecraft.

"Return to the airlock," Novikov said. "Take some rest and recharge the oxygen supply in your airpack. Then we shall decide if that is the best course."

Over the next hour the engineers and technicians discussed what they had learned from Kalinen's spacewalk. There was consensus: Kalinen could use one of the long-handled wrenches like a pry bar, forcing the cable over the edge of the track as the cable pulled taut. The procedure would not be without risk, especially with Kalinen having to contend with the weightlessness of space; however, Novikov could not think of anything better to try.

It was after noon in Kaliningrad when Novikov cleared Kalinen for his second spacewalk.

"You can begin to retract the boom," Kalinen said when he was in position to observe the joint where the cable kept jamming. He watched until the cable was just starting to slip free from beside the track, then said, "Halt, now."

The retraction of the boom did not halt immediately. Nearly a third of a second was required for the electronics to encrypt Kalinen's words and transmit them more than fifty thousand miles to the *Raduga* satellite stationed high over Kenya in central Africa. The upgraded *Gals* military communications package on the *Raduga* relayed the message nearly half as far again to reach the antennas at Kaliningrad. The controller reacted almost immediately to send the stop command over the reverse route to reach *Zashchitnik I*.

When the motors stopped more than a second after Kalinen's voice command, there was more slack in the cable than he would have preferred.

Novikov asked, "How does it look, Vladimir?"

"Do not move anything, please, Comrade General, until I can brace myself with the wrench under the cable. Then extend the boom as slowly as possible."

"The motor has but one speed," Novikov said, then added, "Perhaps we can cycle it on and off."

"That might be best," Kalinen said.

He floated around the boom, looking at the joint from different angles. First he was seeking a location within the framework and cabling where the wrench could guide the cable into the track as the cable tightened. When he found what looked like the best spot, he slipped the wrench into place.

His next problem was to find a position in which he could brace his weightless body to give him leverage. That took longer than picking the spot for the wrench. He had to remove the maneuvering unit so he could fit into the location he had picked. After connecting his tether to the framework near the wrench, he attached the unit a few feet away on the boom. By the time he was ready, he was sweating profusely and gasping each breath.

After resting a few minutes, Kalinen said, "I am ready for you to extend the boom very slowly."

"Beginning now," Novikov said.

The electronic command to the motor arrived at the same time as Novikov's words, and the boom jerked slightly. Kalinen strained against the wrench, but the cable did not move noticeably. The boom jerked again, and the cable came down tighter on the wrench.

Each momentary command to the motor inched the boom toward the fully extended position—bringing more pressure against the end of the wrench. After several cycles of the motor being turned on and off, Kalinen suddenly became worried. The cable, instead of being forced toward the track as the boom extended, was pushing the wrench toward the lip of the track. He tried to get better leverage with his legs, but the muscles in his left calf tightened into a knot. Trying to relieve the pain, he pushed his foot harder against the girderlike boom, while twisting his shoulder to brace himself. Despite his desperate efforts, the next jerk of the boom almost kicked the tip of the wrench over the edge of the track.

"Stop!" Kalinen shrieked, but the word only echoed within his helmet—neither hand was free to activate his transmitter.

The next jerk of the boom drove the wrench over the edge of the cable track, slamming the end of the wrench down like someone jumping onto the end of a teeter-totter. Before Kalinen could react, the wrench whipped free from his grasp. Spinning crazily through the air, the wrench glanced off his sun visor, ricocheted silently off the boom, and hurtled into the darkness of the spacecraft's shadow.

Kalinen screamed in panic. The shock of being hit, combined with the loss of his grip on anything, sent him almost as much out of control as the wrench was. He spun crazily away from the boom until the tether, which was attached near his waist, pulled taut.

For a moment he was frozen with terror, fearing that the life-sustaining pressure was gushing out through a crack in the helmet or a rip scraped in the arm or leg of his suit.

"Are we making any progress?" Novikov's voice was electronically calm.

This time the robotlike sound had a soothing effect on Kalinen. The voice assured him that seconds were passing, and there were no indications yet of catastrophic failure—other than the jagged crack in front of his left eye.

Like a blade on a helicopter, Kalinen's body rotated slowly at the end of his tether. That motion was aggravated by the periodic jerk on the line caused by the pulsing of the motor. Trying to ignore the movements that made his stomach feel queasy, he reached up and slid the shattered sun-filter visor away from the faceplate, which kept the pressure within his helmet. The light of the sun was almost blinding as his eyes tried to adjust. He had difficulty focusing on the faceplate while the boom in the background was rotating into and out of his field of vision. Nevertheless, Kalinen decided that the wrench had not penetrated to the faceplate and that his suit was holding pressure.

He reached out and grabbed the tether so he could climb to the boom. This movement aligned his body with the axis of spin, increasing the rotation rate as a spinning skater does by drawing arms in close to the body. A wave of nausea swept over him, so he let go of the line. The spinning slowed, but the jerking continued unabated.

"What is happening, Vladimir?" Novikov's voice was more insistent.

Kalinen pressed the transmitter button and said, "Stop the motor."

Seconds later the rhythmic jerking of the boom ceased, and Kalinen reeled in the last eight feet of tether line.

"We must try again," Kalinen said, "but first I need a different tool."

He was nearly exhausted, physically and mentally, by the time he strapped the maneuvering unit on his back and began drifting toward the other end of *Zashchitnik I*. Now he felt locked in an endurance struggle that he might not be able to win.

Back in the airlock he picked the biggest wrench that remained. He also noticed a discarded tie-down strap that had been used to secure a large container of spare electronics parts during the launch. Even in the extreme cold of the open airlock, the material remained pliable and strong. He added an extra hour's worth of oxygen into the tank in his backpack, then started out for one more try.

When he reached the boom for the third time, he spent the first few minutes commanding retractions and extensions until the slack in the cable was the amount he wanted. Then he wrapped the tie-down strap several times around the cable and a part of the boom that was on the opposite side of the track. As he secured the strap, he intertwined the wrench handle like a stick used to add pressure to a tourniquet. Then he braced himself and rotated the wrench, tightening the strap and edging the cable over the track.

Once he had supported the wrench on the edge of the boom, he pressed the transmit button and said, "Extend the boom."

The boom jerked a few times, and the cable tightened, sliding this time within the track. Kalinen paused, astounded at how simple the solution had been. After a few labored breaths, he began unwinding the wrench, then the strap, until the strap was clear. Minutes later he maneuvered a few feet away and watched as the signal from Kaliningrad started moving the nuclear generator outward along the boom.

After a few moments, Kalinen said, "The generator moves normally."

"Return inside now, Vladimir," Novikov said. "You have done a hero's work, and the less time you spend outside, the better."

"Thank you, Comrade General," Kalinen said.

Then, for the first time in his fourteen years and four months as a Soviet officer, Vladimir Kalinen intentionally disobeyed the directive of a superior. He sensed that he had already spent too much time near the reactor, so there was nothing more to lose by staying outside a few minutes longer. He wanted to inspect the final positioning of the reactor and of the elaborate piping and fins designed to radiate the generator's excess heat into the cold of space. After all, as his grandmother had taught him, if something was worth doing, it was worth doing well.

He watched the generator move to the end of the boom and jerk silently into the locked position, facing away into the depths of the cosmos. Additional braces edged into place, angling the radiator's fins away from the boom like a partially opened umbrella with its point stuck into the nuclear generator. Satisfied, he fired a couple of blasts on the jets of the maneuvering unit to return to the airlock.

On the earth far below, morning had reached the Andes Mountains. Shimmering off snow-crowned peaks, the reflected sunlight created a sparkling ribbon of lacy-edged white running the length of South America. It was a view that he wished somehow he could share with his grandmother. Then he thought of the crucifix she had never given up, in spite of her years of fear that it would be discovered by the secret police. Perhaps, he thought, she had already seen the view.

17

Novikov sat quietly in the *Borzoi* control center, a console-filled room two doors down the hall from Flight Control where *Zashchitnik I* was controlled. Earlier in the evening he had slept a few hours, and now he was alert, watching the status screens on the front wall. Over Wilkes Land, Antarctica, south of the Indian Ocean, *Borzoi IV* was streaking through the cosmos at nearly seventeen thousand miles per hour.

He checked the clock. Less than five minutes ago, a command had been sent to separate the protective fairing from the main satellite. For more than seven days, that fairing had concealed all details of the payload from the watchful eyes of the Americans. Now the fairing was simply two large pieces of polished metal tumbling slowly behind—dead weight that would not have to be accelerated in the upcoming burn of the rocket on *Borzoi IV*.

A countdown timer, which was located above *Borzoi IV*'s part of the display, reached zero. Thousands of miles away, Novikov thought, fuel and oxidizer should be igniting in the combustion chamber of *Borzoi IV*'s rocket. He moved his eyes to a green light that had not yet been turned on by a returning signal from the spacecraft. Moments later the light flashed on: the injection burn had started on schedule. Novikov smiled and tapped his cane on the floor in triumph.

He turned his attention to an indicator showing the satellite's speed. The number had changed only slightly in the past week as the satellite had circled the earth at three hundred nautical miles. Almost as soon as the green light had illuminated, however, this readout began increasing, slowly at first, then at a rate that turned the last digit into a blur.

In little more than a minute the light went off, indicating that the rocket engine had shut down. *Borzoi IV*'s velocity had increased by about a mile per second. Unlike *Zashchitnik I*, the *Borzoi* did not require another burn of the rocket at apogee. Instead these satellites would continue for years, coasting out to apogee, only to reach the peak and start falling toward perigee. Since the earth was an oblate spheroid instead of a perfect sphere, controllers in Kaliningrad periodically would fire small thrusters on the satellite to keep the orbit's perigee at eighty degrees south. Nevertheless, Novikov felt a sense of accomplishment since *Borzoi IV* was now in its operational orbit.

One down, seven to go, he thought as he leaned back in his chair. He looked at the large screen with the world map and eight blinking lights representing the *Borzoi*. Even though the orbits had been fine-tuned over the last couple of days, the locations of the lights seemed almost random. Two were over land: the mountains of Colombia in South America and the deserts of the Sudan in Africa. The other five were above the world's oceans and seas: the Pacific east of Japan; the ice floes of Antarctica south of the Atlantic; the Pacific east of Guadalcanal in the Solomon Islands; the Sea of Okhotsk between Sakhalin Island and the Kamchatka Peninsula; and the Pacific near Punta Arenas at the southern tip of Chile.

Novikov was confident that the pattern was unrecognizable to anyone other than the chosen few who understood *Krasnaya Molniya*. Within the next half hour *Borzoi VII* would move from over the ocean east of Japan to the cosmos over the fringes of Antarctica. Then *Borzoi VII*'s rocket would ignite thirty minutes after *Borzoi IV* had started its injection burn. The pattern would repeat six more times as the remaining *Borzoi* approached Antarctica from different parts of the world—precisely at thirty-minute intervals.

On Wednesday evening Chisholm worked in the Pentagon until after seven. Then he convinced himself to stop by Houlihan's on the way home. On Monday he had given Janice Waters a "definite maybe" in response to her invitation to the St. Patrick's Day celebration. That had been done partially as a peace offering to atone for disrupting the general's schedule.

When Chisholm reached Houlihan's several miles south of the Pentagon, he found the pub filled to capacity with Irish and pseudo-

Irish revelers. Even though he was more than two hours late, he decided that the party had only gotten bigger and louder during his absence. As he moved slowly through the crowd, he had the sense of trying to tread water in a thick, green sea. Several minutes passed before he spotted Waters at a standup counter alongside the dance floor.

When he finally reached her, Chisholm shouted above the roar of the music and the steady buzz of the crowd, "I'm glad you didn't let anyone start without me."

Waters smiled in recognition, then held up a mug of green beer. Gesturing toward a partially filled pitcher, she said, "I saved you a beer, Colonel." As he poured some into a plastic glass, she added, "I sent the leprechauns out looking for you an hour ago."

Chisholm noticed that her words were a little more run together and less distinct than she normally spoke in the office. "Unfortunately," Chisholm said, as he raised his glass, "bigger leprechauns were keeping me at my desk."

Waters giggled, then said, "I'll tell the general that our first toast was to his health."

"Right," Chisholm said, although Ramsey had never struck him as the leprechaun type.

A waitress pushed through the crowd and Chisholm bought another pitcher of green beer.

"Unfortunately," Waters said, dragging the word out for emphasis, "Monica started without you. She's out there dancing with Major Williams." She gestured toward the mass of people on the dance floor.

Chisholm finally spotted Williams and an attractive redhead. "She looks very nice, but I probably wouldn't be great company for her right now."

"You can't work all the time, Colonel," she said in a gentle, scolding tone, "even though I'm beginning to think you're the exception that proves the rule."

Chisholm nodded, then began to explain what he had recently learned about Sandi Turner's divorce and her upcoming assignment to the Washington, D.C., area.

Waters listened thoughtfully, then said, "I don't know what you're doing here. You ought to get your fanny out to California and tell her some of the things you just told me."

"You know me," he said, raising his glass wistfully. "Duty, honor, country." He took a drink, then added, "Maybe when we get Defender launched, I'll have a chance to head out that way for a few days." Right now there was more than just Defender forcing him to work long hours, of course, but he could not share his concerns about Novikov.

"Who do you think you're kidding, Colonel?" She smiled broadly. "There's always another budget crisis to be fought. The only way you'll have time for a personal life is to make time for a personal life."

Chisholm nodded sheepishly. Waters had lectured him similarly on other occasions. He had recognized long ago that while he was still competitive for promotion—only about fifty colonels were selected each year for the brigadier general promotion list—his personal life could have little priority. Brett would have labored under the same rules in his quest to reach the top. Yet sometimes Chisholm wondered if his fun-loving brother would have made the same personal sacrifices if he had had the opportunity. "California will still be there next month."

Waters nodded toward the dance floor. "But sometimes you miss out when you're only a couple of hours late, Colonel."

"Understood," Chisholm said. As he spoke, he barely recognized the sound of his pager above the noise of the crowded pub. He pulled the device from his belt and found that the indicator light was blinking. The digital display showed that he needed to call the Air Force Operations Center. Flashing a knowing smile, he held the pager so that Waters could read the familiar telephone number.

She glanced at the number, then raised the beer mug and said, "Duty, honor, country, Colonel."

"Roger that." Chisholm kissed Waters on the cheek, then found a public telephone near the entryway of the pub.

Captain John Rodriguez answered Chisholm's call, then said, "Sir, we're seeing some of the changes you were interested in."

Chisholm felt a chill as he realized that Rodriguez probably meant that the new satellites had started moving to their operational orbits. He wanted to ask for specifics, but knew his questions could not be answered on an unsecure line. Hoping an indirect approach would confirm his suspicions about the significance of the changes, he said, "I suppose I could come back in this evening, Rod."

"Yes, sir."

"I'll be on my way shortly," Chisholm said. The sooner he understood the new orbits, the better.

After signaling a farewell to Waters from across the dance floor, Chisholm went to his car. As he was pulling out of the parking lot, an announcement on the radio grabbed his attention. The commentator reported that in the morning at eleven o'clock Soviet Ambassador Galkin would speak at a hastily called meeting of the General Assembly of the United Nations. Chisholm listened carefully and learned that the topic had not been disclosed, but the Soviet press had been playing up the importance of the speech. Undoubtedly, the commentator concluded, the ambassador would announce stronger Soviet protests against the president's decision to launch Defender I.

As Chisholm guided his car back toward Shirley Highway, a feeling of foreboding increased within him. He reasoned that the message from Rodriguez and the scheduling of the UN presentation for just a few hours afterward was no simple coincidence. He was eager to hear what Galkin would reveal about the Soviets' intentions. However, Chisholm wished that the information were coming through behind-the-scenes negotiations instead of in a grand-standing appearance before the world forum.

When he reached the highway that led back to the Pentagon, he turned instead toward his apartment in Alexandria. Within thirty minutes he had fed Sherman, packed a shaving kit, and put a clean uniform into a hangup bag. When he returned to his car, he was also carrying a small portable television.

When Chisholm reached the Operations Center at the Pentagon, Captain Rodriguez said, "The radars at Kaena Point gave us the first hint that the new Soviet satellites were on the move. At about nineteen hundred, our time, one of those birds got tagged as an unidentified when it came within line-of-sight of Hawaii."

Chisholm checked his watch—2135 local. The new phase was about three hours old.

Rodriguez paused to review his notes, then continued, "That was Cosmos 3213. It already had climbed to two thousand miles when it crossed the equator northeast of Australia."

Chisholm nodded, understanding that a sudden change of more than fifteen hundred miles in altitude would cause confusion. "Cosmos 3213?"

Rodriguez looked at the clipboard. "Yes, sir. The fourth bird in the series. Cosmos 3213 was launched a week ago."

"Is 3213 the only one on the move, Rod?"

"Oh, no sir. Last time I checked, four or five had blasted out of their parking orbits. NORAD's now tracking a couple of new pieces of debris in the old orbits, so these satellites appear to be shedding their fairings."

Though his appearance did not betray it, Chisholm felt a twinge of excitement—the game was moving to the next level. "I'll want to see pictures of the satellites as soon as they're available, but make it sound like our interest is routine."

"Yes, sir," Rodriguez said. "No telling, though, when the cameras will have the right lighting for some good shots."

Chisholm nodded. "Do you know how high 3213's going?"

"I didn't notice, sir. An aircraft mishap in England's been occupying most of our time this evening. I can check that right away."

"That's okay. Just get me on a machine that's tapped into the NORAD data." Chisholm knew that he was one of few colonels in the Pentagon who understood the orbital data provided by NORAD's computers. He paused, then added with a smile, "I may be a colonel, Rod, but I can still read the numbers."

"Yes, sir," Rodriguez said with a grin. His tone suggested his full agreement with the implication, though as a captain he would not have raised the subject.

Chisholm settled in front of a computer terminal and called up the current status of Cosmos 3213. Most of the screen filled with words and numbers. A small rectangle in the lower right corner showed a map of the world. A wavy green line superimposed over the map represented the ground-trace—the path that an observer on the earth would follow to stay directly beneath the satellite—of Cosmos 3213's most recent orbit.

Earlier in the evening the firing of the on-board rockets had created an elliptical orbit similar to the transfer orbit that had taken Cosmos 3220 to GEO. So the first readings Chisholm looked for were adjacent to the words *Perigee* and *Apogee*. When he had looked at the data on Sunday, both numbers for the circular parking orbits had been 301. Now he found the numbers 301 and 6603, which represented the satellite's altitude when at perigee and apogee.

He quickly checked the inclination angle—still eighty degrees.

Then he looked for the coordinates for perigee and found that the latitude at perigee was eighty degrees south. A mini-*molniya*, Chisholm thought as he started picturing the orbit of Cosmos 3213.

He knew that in the mid-1960s the Soviets had concentrated on a class of orbits that had become known as *molniya*, the Russian word for lightning. The Soviets discovered that a satellite with a perigee of about 270 nautical miles and an apogee of more than 21,000 nautical miles would orbit the earth twice a day. These highly elliptical—long and narrow—orbits had interesting advantages for an empire that was closer to the North Pole than to the equator. By positioning the orbit's perigee over the southern hemisphere, a *molniya* satellite could spend 11.7 hours north of the equator during each twelve-hour orbit. The differences in geographical coverage was due in large part to the disparity in speed. At perigee a *molniya* satellite was racing through the cosmos more than six times faster than its speed high above the Arctic at apogee. Thus, in contrast to the American reliance on geostationary communications satellites over the equator, the Soviets chose the *molniya* orbits to link its far-north empire with reliable communications satellites.

Satellites that loitered over the northern hemisphere could have deadlier missions than communications, Chisholm thought uneasily. He checked the reading adjacent to the word *Period*—the length of time to complete one orbit. The period for Cosmos 3213 was just under four hours, which told him that the satellite would complete six mini-*molniya* orbits a day. He would make the calculations later, but already he had concluded that these new satellites would spend most of their time north of the equator.

While considering the threatening implications, Chisholm selected displays showing data on the other seven Soviet satellites similar to Cosmos 3213. The computers were indicating a confidence level of greater than 98 percent that four of the satellites already were in similar *molniya* orbits. The tracking system already had observations confirming that another two satellites had left their parking orbits. The computers would continue refining their estimates, but he already recognized the structure of the new constellation. When passing near apogee, each satellite had a field-of-view—or a field-of-fire—that would cover about a third of the surface of the earth. Until pictures came in from the ground sites, he would have to guess at the weaponry aboard the eight satellites. He could think of several good choices that had been in development for a decade or longer. He leaned back in his chair and wondered if Novikov had built a constellation that was invulnerable to attack.

Chisholm spent most of the night playing what-if games, many of which focused on what he might be able to do with the nine new satellites if he were General Petr Novikov. After a four-hour nap on a couch in one of the outer offices, he was awake at six, trying to get as much done as possible before Ambassador Galkin's speech. Just before 1100 Chisholm had his portable television set tuned to a network broadcast originating from the UN. McClain and four others had crowded into the small office.

While awaiting the Soviet ambassador's appearance before the General Assembly, a news commentator spoke in ominous tones about possible implications. "The Soviets have stressed the importance of this speech for the last twenty-four hours, but they have kept the topic a secret. Yet there is little mystery when we recognize that Ambassador Galkin has come directly to New York following his twelve-day recall to Moscow. That recall for consultations was in protest of President Anderson's decision to launch the Defender I satellite. Therefore, Galkin's speech is expected to reveal additional steps the Soviet Union will take trying to dissuade the president from putting military weapons in space. Washington insiders are speculating that Galkin will announce a delay in opening negotiations for this year's purchase of American grain. That move is calculated to draw the nation's farmers into the ranks of those who have been protesting the president's decision."

Great job of analysis, Chisholm thought sarcastically. Nevertheless, he was pleased by the absence of speculation that Galkin was about to declare a form of space warfare.

"Not all the action here today is inside," the commentator continued. "John Tadwell is outside with a report on the thousands of demonstrators who have gathered on this crisp March morning. John."

The picture switched to an overcoat-clad reporter with a clamorous scene in the background. Tadwell held his microphone to his lips and said, "Police are keeping a watchful eye on more than two thousand demonstrators who have been carrying on a noisy protest for the last hour. Their words and placards carry a common theme: Mr. President, keep the Defender satellite out of space. A few minutes earlier, I was—"

"Thanks for that report, John," the commentator interrupted as the picture returned to him, then to Ambassador Yuri Galkin stepping to the podium. Galkin looked dignified in his tailored suit and carefully applied makeup.

"The image makers have done themselves proud," Chisholm said to no one in particular.

After beginning with the normal formalities, Galkin gazed from side to side and said in a most diplomatic tone, "There are no people in the world who are not worried by U.S. plans to militarize space. This worry is well grounded." Galkin paused, then said, "Those are not my original words. They were spoken by General Chairman Gorbachev in 1985. He saw serious reason for concern then just as I see serious reason for concern now."

With a voice rising through the last sentence, Galkin launched into a diatribe enumerating the "reckless and provocative" attempts by the Americans to militarize space. Most charges involved the Strategic Defense Initiative championed by President Reagan in the mid-1980s.

Chisholm listened carefully to the interpreter's choppy translation. Most of Galkin's charges had a thread of truth, though the distortions overwhelmed the facts in almost every example. And, Chisholm thought, the Soviets had pursued similar developments in every case. In some instances the Soviets were better able to support military operations from space; in others, technical limitations had caused the Soviets to fall miserably short of American achievements. Galkin did not mention the Fractional Orbiting Bombardment System the Soviets had tested in the late 1960s. An operational FOBS would have put nuclear weapons into orbits overflying Antarctica and bypassing American radar coverage aimed to the north. Then as the warheads approached the United States from the south on their first orbit, they could have been deorbited, giving almost no warning before striking targets in America.

After nearly thirty minutes Galkin's history of American transgressions reached Defender I. "And this most provocative scheme of all threatens the natural right of every nation to put satellites into space." Galkin banged a chubby fist on the podium.

Even if the charge were true, Chisholm thought, he doubted that anyone cared in Botswana or in a hundred other countries that would never develop a satellite. Nevertheless, Galkin made it sound like something that should bring all delegates to their feet in a common protest.

"Our pleas for reason have met closed ears in Washington," Galkin continued. "Once again I return to words of Chairman Gorbachev, who worked unceasingly to convince those who did not want peace that peace must be obtained. Regretfully he warned, 'If the Soviet Union is faced with a real threat from space, it will find a way to effectively counter it. Let no one, and I say this quite definitely, doubt this.' Although his words were said long ago, they are also mine today. This arrogant determination to put Defender I into the cosmos over the heads of all of us has forced the peoples of the Soviet Union to take decisive action. We have been given no other choice but to meet this aggression in space. Therefore, the Soviet Union has met its responsibility to protect the workers of the world by launching a peaceful satellite we have named Protector."

In the background Chisholm heard Galkin say the word *Zash-chitnik* just before the interpreter said Protector. At least we know the monster's name, Chisholm thought, even if we don't know its capabilities.

Galkin continued. "The peace-loving peoples of the world should think of Protector as a friendly bobby on the street corner, as our British colleagues would say." He paused and looked above his glasses at the representative of the United Kingdom, whose expression did not change. "Like the friendly bobby, this magnificent product of Soviet scientists and workers will protect us all from thugs or ruffians who might threaten the peaceful uses of space."

Vintage cold war words, Chisholm thought.

"If necessary, the Protector can eliminate aggressive weapons and military satellites from the cosmos," Galkin said, "but there are better ways to keep the cosmos free and safe for all."

Chisholm and McClain exchanged glances. Chisholm said, "If he's proposing to knock down the birds we already have in orbit, this is going to get dicey in a hurry."

"The natural answer," Galkin said, "which is clear to every person of common reasoning, is to stop sending military satellites into space. But how can we know whether a new satellite is for peaceful purposes or for aggression?" He paused to let his audience ponder the question. "The answer, of course, is to inspect carefully each device before the hatches are closed on the top of the rocket. And who shall make such inspections? The Soviet Union shall, on behalf of the peoples of the world."

A murmur of voices spread throughout the assembly. Galkin waited with his head raised high and his gaze moving from one area to another, well above the faces of the delegates.

Galkin went on to explain that Soviet technicians would come to inspect each payload within the week before the scheduled launch. "If the satellite is threatening to the peace and security of the world, we shall recommend that it not be launched." He paused to let the audience jump forward to the implications of his statement. "And, of course, those who are foolish enough to persist in launching dangerous satellites will find that their efforts are not rewarded with success."

The response of the delegates was louder than before.

"Perhaps you worry that the Protector could be overwhelmed by those who for decades have been working to develop space weapons. That is worth no concern at all. The Protector has its own protectors, which we have named for the faithful Russian wolfhounds."

Borzoi. Chisholm nodded as he heard Galkin say the word.

"The *Zashchitnik* and its pack of eight *Borzoi,*" Chisholm said. "Interesting."

Galkin closed his folder and looked triumphantly across the room, which was filled to capacity. Then, sounding like a guest speaker closing out a graduation address, he said, "When you go home this evening, tell your children and your grandchildren that they can sleep more peacefully from this day on. The peoples of the Union of Soviet Socialist Republics have made it so."

Galkin stepped away from the podium and disappeared within the cluster of taller bodyguards that moved through the nearest exit.

"Simply extraordinary," the commentator said, looking perplexed as he turned to the analyst beside him. "Obviously the Soviet Union is taking a strong stand to keep military weapons out of space, but he didn't say how this Protector would do that. I don't believe I heard him say that these new Soviet satellites were armed."

"That was not made clear," the analyst said. "But that's definitely what Ambassador Galkin was implying."

The commentator nodded, then turned to face the camera. "We had hoped to interview Ambassador Galkin following this watershed speech, but we've just learned that he's on his way to the airport to return to Moscow. In a moment we will review the key points of the ambassador's address. He gave an answer to how the Soviets are reacting to the Defender I crisis, but he leaves us with a string of new questions that may take weeks to answer. It is difficult to decide where to start."

"I would suggest that you start by thinking in terms of the *Zashchitnik* crisis, Mister Commentator," Chisholm said, smiling at the others who had watched the speech, "because that's what it is."

McClain added in echoing understatement, "He sure injected some extra interest in the Defender launch."

"It's not just a question of Defender anymore," Chisholm said. "We've got a Navstar GPS on the schedule in eight days. The Soviets may consider that our navigational satellites are a military threat."

"Would we permit an inspection?"

Chisholm shook his head. "I don't think so. Anyway, I need a list of every satellite scheduled to blast off a pad in the next thirty days. In addition to whatever we have at the Cape and Vandenberg, find out what the French are working at Kourou."

"How about the Japanese?"

"I suppose you can check Tanegashima and Kagoshima," Chisholm said, "but I think they restrict their launches to February and August."

McClain looked surprised. "Winds? Weather?"

"Fish. Too many fishermen claimed that rocket launches interrupted their fishing."

McClain shook his head in disbelief, then asked with a grin, "Are you interested in what's scheduled at Plesetsk, Kapustin Yar, and Tyuratam, sir?"

"I'm interested in those for different reasons," Chisholm said, "since I'm sure Novikov's birds won't be too militaristic for President Grigoriev's inspectors."

18

The Kremlin, Moscow
Thursday, 18 March, 2004 local (1704 GMT)

Novikov impatiently tapped the head of his cane against the side of the conference table. He was eager to get on with a meeting or to return to Kaliningrad.

A couple of hours earlier while having dinner he had been summoned to the Kremlin by Minister Levchenko. Since arriving, Novikov had spent most of his time alone in the conference room where Marshal Murashev had briefed *Krasnaya Molniya* eleven days earlier. A television set had been added to the furnishings so Novikov could watch a live broadcast of Ambassador Galkin's speech at the United Nations.

Novikov had not been surprised by anything in the speech, so he thought more about its delivery than its content. He was not favorably impressed. If he were the president, Novikov thought, his ambassador to the Americans would have more of the lean, determined look of a Cossack—to confront strength with strength. His message would have been more straightforward: Your Defender represented an unacceptable threat to the Soviet Union's access to space; therefore we have preempted you on the battleground of the future instead of fighting for our sovereign rights on the earth where millions might die. But, Novikov concluded without regret, he was no more of a politician than Galkin was a man of impressive forcefulness.

The general's thoughts were interrupted when the door on the back wall finally opened. President Grigoriev, Minister Levchenko, and KGB Chairman Petruk entered.

After greetings and superficial comments on Galkin's speech, Grigoriev asked Novikov, "Now that you've given us the command of the cosmos, Petr, how soon do you expect an American response?"

"That depends, Comrade President, on how soon we demonstrate our ability to destroy other spacecraft."

"And," Levchenko interjected, "upon *how* we demonstrate that capability. Wouldn't you agree, Petr?"

"Of course, Comrade Minister," Novikov said, noticing Petruk's expression. It seemed, Novikov thought, that Levchenko had scored a point in an ongoing confrontation.

"Now that we've moved from the hypothetical to the real," Grigoriev said, "what would you choose as the first target, Petr?"

Novikov considered his response carefully, aware that this had been one of the most contentious points throughout the development of *Krasnaya Molniya*. Levchenko and Petruk had different opinions. Fortunately, Novikov thought, he agreed with his boss; unfortunately, he disagreed with the chairman of the KGB. Novikov hated giving political answers to straightforward questions but decided this was a time for delicate wording. "There are interesting arguments for several different strategies, Comrade President," Novikov said, hoping to mollify Petruk. "Now that we have the complete range of choices available, I would let our enemies make the choice when they place a satellite on their next booster."

Levchenko nodded, looking as if Novikov had given particularly wise advice.

Petruk shrugged, then responded more to Grigoriev. "Now that we can destroy the satellites that spy on us night and day, we should grasp the opportunity."

Novikov made sure his expression did not criticize the chairman's proposal. That higher-risk strategy, Novikov thought, would provide Petruk with a sudden and decisive advantage in the worldwide game of gathering intelligence.

"But," Levchenko said dryly, "when the wolf realizes you're poking his eyes out with a stick, he may lunge at your throat."

"Without human intervention, all satellites fail at some point," Petruk said, then added sarcastically, "At least, that's what you say every time one unexpectedly stops supplying me with needed information. If certain American satellites suddenly fail, who can place any blame."

Grigoriev sighed noticeably. "These words I have heard already.

I want to know what Petr's decisions would be if he were sitting in my chair."

"The first time someone makes an unapproved launch, Comrade President, I would quietly destroy the vehicle in a way that is obvious to those who would understand. To the rest of the world, I would say nothing. When a second launch is attempted, I would do the same thing."

Grigoriev looked interested. "And what response would you expect the Americans to choose?"

"If I let them choose my targets," Novikov said with a slight smile, "then perhaps they would let me choose their response." Everyone else looked confused by Novikov's logic, so he continued, "I would tell them privately that the Soviet Union has moved the fighting grounds to space, to spare the peoples of the world the horrors of an old-fashioned war for supremacy. If they choose to contend with the battle stations we have put there, we will understand."

A small smile formed on Grigoriev's lips, but Levchenko and Petruk looked even more confused.

Petruk responded first. "You would dare them to attack our new satellites, General Novikov?"

"It's always better, Comrade Chairman, when your enemy attacks your strengths rather than your weaknesses."

Petruk did not look convinced.

Grigoriev said, "If you were within one of our T-eighty battle tanks, Viktor, and your adversaries were armed with spears, you might encourage them to convince themselves that their situation was hopeless."

"Perhaps," Petruk said, his expression showing a greater understanding of the strategy Novikov had suggested, "if indeed I was certain I was so invulnerable."

"Our position is strong," Novikov said. "At this moment, Minister Levchenko has more reason to be comfortable in his chair than his counterparts are in the Pentagon."

"And, Viktor," Grigoriev said in an encouraging tone toward Petruk, "what better way to search out any weaknesses in *Krasnaya Molniya* than to encourage the Americans to find them—as long as your people are closely monitoring the actions of the Americans."

Petruk nodded, seeming pleased to have a critical role in this apparent triumph.

"I will be eager," Novikov said, "to hear of anything that you uncover, Comrade Chairman."

Levchenko said, "But you expect little danger?"

Novikov nodded confidently. "To challenge us today, the Americans needed to continue their buildup of the 1980s. By robbing them of their resolve back then, President Gorbachev assured our dominance in space." Novikov paused, then hastily added with a gesture toward Grigoriev, "Your leadership and commitment have assured that the dominance will continue."

Grigoriev looked determined. "We must maintain control until the satellites of *Cherniy Grom* are in place."

"Yes, Comrade Chairman," Novikov said, aware of how the nuclear-armed satellites could change the balance of power forever. "Then you can destroy—without fear of retaliation—whatever satellites Chairman Petruk suggests."

That afternoon Chisholm was called to General Ramsey's office. As soon as the colonel was seated, Ramsey said, "General Bolton's just been through a string of meetings on this satellite blockade thing. He needs answers, and a few people are suggesting that a preemptive strike by one or two B-ones is the only answer."

Chisholm was shocked. "What do they suggest we strike, sir?"

"The ground facilities controlling the new satellites. They figure the ground net has to be the weak link."

Chisholm shook his head. "That's pretty dumb." For an instant he wondered how many stars were worn by the people giving the advice. Then he decided that the number of stars didn't matter—his assessment stood. "Do the chief's advisers believe they can send a B-one over the suburbs of Moscow without starting World War III?"

"The chief's not committing to anything right now, but he doesn't even have a good place to start."

"Sending B-ones against Kaliningrad and a couple of other sites certainly isn't the answer, sir."

"I don't think so, either," Ramsey said with a shrug. "Your reaction's the same as the chief's. That's why he's casting out a big net for other ideas. We're in a world of hurt if the Soviets can back up Galkin's threats." He paused. "Can they?"

"We don't know what the Soviets've accomplished in the world of lasers or particle beams," Chisholm said. "Ten years ago we predicted they could have a space-based particle beam by now. They've been working hard in those technologies. We know that because those subjects never show up in their scientific literature."

"Lasers demand good optics," Ramsey said, "and the Soviets had a corner on East German optics for almost half a century."

"Anyway, a bluff doesn't make sense. They've spent too many hundreds of millions of rubles on the hardware they've shown off this week."

"You're betting that General Novikov's dealt them the cards they need to control access to space."

Chisholm nodded. "During the night the satellites that Galkin referred to as *Borzoi* changed their orbits from three-hundred-mile circular to a four-hour *molniyas*."

As Ramsey pulled a tablet out of a desk drawer, he said with a wry smile, "You know what I miss about you, Mike? You used to talk like a pilot, and I could listen without my hair roots shorting out from technical overload." Ramsey tossed the tablet across the desk and added, "Let me have a shot at the thousand-word explanation."

Slow down, Chisholm said to himself, as he began to draw a circle near the bottom of the page. "Sorry, sir. Let's begin with the earth."

Adding the new orbits to his picture, Chisholm explained their implications. Ramsey asked a couple of questions but mostly listened.

Chisholm stepped to the globe and tapped the circular frame that held the sphere in position. "If we still consider the supporting frame to be the parking orbit, the new orbit looks something like this." He knelt to touch his pen against the frame near the south pole. Then he swept the pen in an arc that moved farther away from the frame as his hand moved high above the northern hemisphere. He stopped when his hand was almost over the north pole at a distance almost equal to the diameter of the globe. "Apogee is at an altitude that's almost a full earth diameter from eighty degrees north."

"It's a little more frightening when you show it in that perspective." Ramsey studied the scene for a moment, then said, "Looks like they've finally grabbed the high ground."

In earlier discussions Chisholm often had stressed that satellites were the technological answer to the centuries-old tactic of taking the high ground. In the last couple of centuries, the quest to see what the enemy was doing on the other side of the hill finally had gotten airborne. First, observers had gone up a few hundred feet beneath hot-air balloons, then aboard the rickety observation aircraft of World War I. The transition from aircraft to reconnaissance satellites had taken less than half a century. And there had always been another benefit of controlling the high ground. The warrior on the hilltop had a distinct advantage over someone in the valley when the real fighting started.

"Yes, sir," Chisholm said as he held his hand above the Arctic. "What makes these even more threatening is that the satellite spends only fifty-two point eight minutes of each orbit south of the equator. That gives Grigoriev an average of six satellites on our side of the equator at any given time."

Frowning, Ramsey said, "And it looks like each one of them can cover about a third of the world."

Chisholm swung his hand in a slow arc. "Each one is in line-of-sight of thirty percent of the world for about two hours per orbit. That is, if you think of a cone with its point at the satellite, then extending down to the visible horizons. However, any on-board sensors and weapons may not be able to cover the entire area all the time."

"Whatever they can cover," Ramsey said with determination, "we're likely to have a hell of a time fighting our way through if they're all shooters."

"I suspect that the *Borzoi* are shooters, but I can't tell yet how good or how far they can shoot."

"Until we give them something for target practice?"

"Yes, sir," Chisholm said, leaning back in his chair. "The key unknown is the role of the big bird they put at GEO."

"Intel's guessing it's a fancy command-and-control station for the *Borzoi*. I understand it's positioned to see launches from all bases in the western hemisphere."

Chisholm nodded. "I hope that's all it can do. If it's a shooter—and I'd assume Novikov gave it at least a self-defense capability—it'll be tough to take out."

"Guess they've planted their flag on the ultimate high ground with that one."

"It's not the ultimate, General," Chisholm said, "but it has a commanding field-of-fire against anything we launch at it."

Ramsey stared for a moment at a picture on the opposite wall, then said, "I'm not convinced we have anything that could hit it even if it's not a shooter. The chief asked about the feasibility of reprogramming an ICBM to hit a target at GEO." Chisholm looked perplexed, so Ramsey added, "I don't think he's considering that as an acceptable option, but he's getting those kinds of questions from the other side of the Potomac."

Chisholm nodded, not surprised that Galkin's laying-down-the-law type of speech would stir up members of Congress and of the administration. Some would feel the need to become instant hawks; others the need to appear immediately hawkish even though they had no intention of changing long-standing positions on defense. "Even if we could reach GEO with a Minuteman or Peacekeeper, and I'm guessing we can't, you've got a fusing problem to overcome."

"How we'd detonate the weapon once we got it up there?"

"Right, sir," Chisholm said. "And a nuclear detonation in the geostationary belt over our part of the world is like trying to dry your cat in a microwave oven. The electromagnetic pulse from the explosion is liable to cook the insides of a bunch of friendly satellites."

"You're saying we'd have to be willing to ante up heavily before we even think about playing that card."

"Yes, sir. And if Novikov's *Zashchitnik* is a real battle station, he'll zap your warhead before you get within a thousand miles."

"The chief's going to love talking to you," Ramsey said with obvious sarcasm. "Do we just write off the high bird?"

"Not if we're going to break Novikov's seige, sir. I've checked a couple of options. We have two old communications satellites drifting in the vicinity of *Zashchitnik*." He knew that in some cases these satellites were maneuverable even though no longer capable of relaying communications as originally designed.

He went on to explain that old geostationary satellites were boosted to a higher orbit using the same small thrusters that had kept the satellite in the proper position. This reduced the clutter in the narrow ring of space where satellites could stay in synchronization with earth rotation. Drifting harmlessly to the west above the equator, the old satellites were tracked like other space junk by the Space Surveillance Center at NORAD—and perhaps a similar unit at Kaliningrad.

Chisholm added, "One old comsat's less than a week away if we lower its orbit and let it start catching the Soviet bird. When the comsat gets closer, we put it on a collision course."

Ramsey asked, "Does Space Command believe they can reactivate the comsat?"

"I haven't asked yet, sir. I didn't want to start rumors, especially when there was no confirmation that the *Zashchitnik* is a military threat."

"Good," Ramsey said. "We've got to put some contingency plans together in a hurry, but you're right about keeping them very close-hold. Even if that takes care of the whatever-you-call-it, how do we combat the wolfhounds?"

"If we combine some old ASAT parts and can boost them to at least three hundred miles, there's a possibility."

"But you said that these satellites go up more than six thousand miles."

Chisholm pointed toward where the orbit almost touched the earth near the bottom of the page. "We'd attack at perigee, near Antarctica."

"Antarctica?" Ramsey looked surprised. "We can't fight down there. Logistics would be a nightmare. Besides, there's a treaty."

"It is a hell of a long way from here, General," Chisholm said, "but your chair's a thousand miles closer to the South Pole than President Grigoriev's is."

Ramsey nodded as if seeming to recognize that the Soviets would have much more trouble countering an American initiative at the bottom of the world. "What about the treaty?"

"Technically the treaty covers the land and the ice shelves and keeping military forces out of Antarctica, except for scientific purposes. The high seas in that area remain subject to international maritime law."

"So we could use ships but wouldn't be able to use airfields on the ice."

"Right, sir. The mission carrying the ASAT missiles would involve overflight but no landings in the prohibited area."

"What are you planning to use to launch these missiles?"

"I've looked at scores of options, General. The best choice is to airdrop them out of a C-141, then fire the missiles in midair once they're suspended beneath their parachutes."

Ramsey gave Chisholm a suspicious smile. "This isn't just a Chisholm scheme to get away from Pentagon paperwork for a few days, is it?"

"The idea of going along has crossed my mind, sir."

Ramsey leaned back and looked toward a C-141 model that was sitting on a bookcase. "With aerial refueling, a C-141 eliminates the problem of being too far from support bases."

Chisholm grimaced slightly. "Eliminate's a little euphemistic, sir.

Using a C-141 makes the logistics manageable. We'll still need a significant amount of tanker support."

"How much?"

"The primary aircraft would need at least two, maybe three aerial refuelings."

"That's a lot of time in the air."

Chisholm nodded. "The length of the mission depends some on where we can make the last ground refueling."

"Galkin gave us a hot potato to handle. I'm not sure if any of our allies will be willing to help us shoot at Soviet hardware." He paused as if contemplating possibilities, then added, "Do you really think you could take down those eight satellites using a C-141, Mike?"

"Technically there seems to be a pretty fair chance, General. We'd be dropping our missile at about twenty-four thousand feet instead of firing upward like the F-15 with the original ASAT. That means we'd upgrade to the SRAM Two missile for thrust. Rick McClain's matching it up with seekers that use the very-high-speed integrated circuit technology, so we don't require supercooling of the seeker before launch."

"That all means you're putting together something that works?"

"I think so, sir, but it'll be a damned tough mission on the crew. The bird'll have to be depressurized several times above twenty thousand feet."

"Wouldn't it be better to hang your missiles beneath an F-15 or a B-52? That way the airplane stays pressurized and your crew wouldn't be exposed to the dangers of unpressurized flight."

Chisholm already had investigated the same possibilities. "Not enough support hardware's available, sir. Even if we matched a missile to a B-52, we're limited to one shot per mission."

"Too slow, huh?"

"Right, sir," Chisholm said, "especially if Novikov has a warehouse full of backups."

"He's already shown us he can launch five or six a week without breathing hard."

"I doubt that it was that easy, General," Chisholm said, still in awe of what Novikov had accomplished, "but we do have to destroy the eight *Borzoi* quickly."

"Fast enough to convince President Grigoriev that it's a bad investment to supply us with more targets?"

"Exactly, sir. Otherwise, we'll never break through the lower barrier."

"Couldn't we get the job done by hanging ASATs beneath F-15s?"

"Essentially the same hardware-support problem, sir. Each F-15 could carry one missile, and with only one or two ASAT launch pylons in existence, we couldn't get eight shots off fast enough."

"And there are no bases close enough to support an operation at eighty degrees south with F-15s." Ramsey paused, then added, "I wouldn't expect New Zealand to support something like this."

"Even if someone down south offers an airfield," Chisholm said, "we'd be telegraphing our punch when we started deploying F-15s and all their support equipment. C-141s are so familiar that they don't raise any eyebrows wherever they show up."

Ramsey paused, looking for a few moments at the model of the C-141. "I've always liked the concept of hiding in plain sight."

"If we play it right, sir, Novikov won't know we're in the game until his satellites start disappearing."

Ramsey studied the drawing for a couple of moments. "Didn't you tell me once that a satellite travels its fastest when it's nearest the earth?"

"Yes, sir. I've made some rough calculations, and at perigee, the *Borzoi* will be traveling at over thirty thousand feet per second."

"A hundred football fields a second," Ramsey said with a wry smile. "That's almost as fast as the highway patrol clocked my son on his last speeding ticket. You sure we have something that'll catch those hummers."

"We don't plan to catch them, sir. All we have to do is get a chunk of something in their way." Chisholm gestured toward a cluster of quartz crystals that Ramsey used as a decorative paperweight. "Toss your rock in front of one of Novikov's birds, and the energy equivalent's the same as hitting the satellite with a tractor-trailer doing more than one hundred miles an hour."

"If you're right, it sure as hell beats sending B-1s to Kaliningrad. Have you spoken with General Gillette's people about using one of his C-141s for your scheme?" As the commander-in-chief of the Military Airlift Command (MAC) and the U.S. Transportation Command, General Frederick Gillette controlled the DoD's cargo aircraft.

"Not yet, sir," Chisholm said. "If we try the C-141s, the mission can't be set up through normal procedures. It's about a million-step process to put the first warhead in front of the first satellite. Tight secrecy's the only way we'll stay ahead of Novikov."

Ramsey nodded and reached for a telephone that was connected through secure lines to major command posts throughout the Air Force. "Was it old Confucius who said, 'A journey of a million steps begins with the first telephone call'?"

"I'd have to look that one up, sir," Chisholm said with a smile.

After Gillette answered from his headquarters near St. Louis, Ramsey said, "Scooter, I was wondering how soon you were planning to stop at Andrews and visit your folks at the Eighty-ninth?"

The 89th Military Airlift Wing was the presidential support wing headquartered at nearby Andrews Air Force Base.

"What have we screwed up now, Frank?"

Ramsey smiled. "Nothing. The Eighty-ninth is doing great, as usual. I thought you might want to stop by and tell them that."

"You have any particular time in mind, Frank?"

"If you were there tomorrow morning, I could work you into my schedule at lunch and for a little chat afterward. I thought I'd offer you another opportunity to excel." Ramsey smiled and winked at Chisholm.

"You call, we haul," Gillette said, responding with what had been an unofficial motto of the Military Airlift Command for decades. "Anything you want to give me a 'heads up' on now?"

"Negative, Scooter. I'd rather do a face-to-face on this one."

After Ramsey hung up, he said to Chisholm, "Put together the basics of a contingency plan and tell us tomorrow what you'd need if the president were to buy into it."

19

Novikov was sleeping soundly for the first time in several days when he was awakened by the telephone. The caller suggested that the general might want to come to Flight Control to assess something that was happening. Novikov entered the main control room less than twenty minutes later and was met by Polkovnik Nasedkin, Novikov's project leader for *Zashchitnik I*.

"For the last six hours, sir," Nasedkin said, "we've been checking the communications links with the *Borzoi*."

Novikov nodded. He had ordered the checkout as soon as he had learned that Ambassador Galkin had announced a connection between *Zashchitnik I* and the *Borzoi*.

Nasedkin continued, "We've encountered some signal loss between *Zashchitnik I* and any *Borzoi* passing through the region southwest of *Zashchitnik*. More than an hour ago we decided to changeout the control module for that antenna."

Novikov tried not to look impatient, but he did not see a problem that justified awakening him. He was sure that more than one antenna-control module had been included in the spare parts kits aboard *Zashchitnik I*.

"Comrade Kalinen seems to be having more difficulty making the change than we had expected," Nasedkin said, then added quietly, "at least more than we had expected this soon."

The words flashed a sharp pain somewhere between Novikov's conscience and his heart. "What kind of difficulties?"

"He's slow and not very responsive. He speaks very little."

Novikov nodded, then went to the communications console. "Comrade Kalinen," Novikov said slowly. "Are we trying to work you too hard?"

The response was not immediate. Novikov was about to call again when Kalinen answered, "Is that you, Comrade General? On your side of the world, it is a time for generals to be sleeping, not working."

Novikov tried to judge the voice. He cursed the electronics, which had stolen the inflections he counted on in evaluating a man's attitude or condition. "My rest is not as important as yours. How do you feel, Vladimir?"

"I am doing my best, Comrade General," Kalinen said. "Sometimes moving increases the dizziness and nausea, but I will have the module changed in a few minutes."

Space sickness, perhaps, Novikov thought, but that would have appeared on Monday within the first few hours after lift-off. He finally asked the question that he had hoped would not come so soon. "What's the reading on your radiation dosimeter?"

"It's only a number, Comrade General. You will sleep better, I think, if you do not know."

"It might not help my sleeping, Vladimir, but it would help my planning."

"The reading has changed little since I reentered *Zashchitnik*, Comrade General. The electronics are in little danger." He paused, then added, "Unless I now am radiating too many high-energy particles."

"When did the nausea begin?"

"Yesterday, or today, or sometime, sir. Time is confusing. Probably the day after the spacewalks."

Quicker than expected, Novikov thought. It had been hard to estimate the amount of exposure Kalinen would get out near the reactor, but obviously it had been significant.

"Take your time, Vladimir. There is no hurry. You have placed *Zashchitnik I* in a powerful configuration." He waited to see if Kalinen would acknowledge the compliment, then added, "You do remember the pills I gave you?"

"Yes, Comrade General, I carry them in my pocket."

"Let us know, Vladimir, whenever there is anything we can do."

Kalinen did not answer.

Novikov sat back for a few minutes, waiting to make sure that the conversation was finished. He was upset. There had never been any guarantees about how long a cosmonaut would survive on any of the *Zashchitniks*. A violent solar storm could reduce even the most pessimistic estimates, but Novikov had not prepared himself for Kalinen to be at this point so quickly.

Part of Novikov was sad. Another part of him, with which he was uncomfortable at the moment, began considering the other ramifications. Kalinen had done his job and had done it well, even if he was unable to provide three or four more weeks of insurance against on-board failures. Then there was the other concern: while a healthy cosmonaut could fix a damaged spacecraft, there was always the possibility that an unhealthy cosmonaut might damage a healthy spacecraft.

At 0300 Novikov took off his headset and got to his feet. Turning to Nasedkin, Novikov said, "Let me know whenever there are any problems with Cosmonaut Kalinen."

Walking wearily toward the door, Novikov tried to remember if he had any vodka left in his room.

On Friday morning Chisholm was working on his briefing when he got a call from General Ramsey's secretary. Moments later Ramsey was on the telephone.

"Drop what you're doing, Mike, and get to the river entrance," the general said, referring to the entrance on the Potomac side of the Pentagon. "General Stone, General Alexander, and a few of their spear carriers are about to leave, and I told them to wait for you."

"Yes, sir. Any word on where we're going?"

"The Executive Office Building. The vice president has called a meeting at ten hundred. He wants to hear how the DoD and NASA launch schedules are going to bump up against the Soviet's blockade."

"Anything special you want me to do, sir?"

"Mainly be like a fly on the wall and listen for how your project matches with what's said. Your suggestions are being worked through the president's national security adviser, so keep them under wraps."

As Chisholm jammed his materials into a safe, he was concerned about Ramsey's last statement. Too many details were missing for his recommendations to be taken so far so quickly. He feared that if the bureaucrats got involved before he had a tight plan, some of those details would be supplied by people incompetent to make such judgments.

Less than an hour later Chisholm had been cleared through security in the Executive Office Building. Now he was waiting in a conference room, which was dominated by a large mahogany table. Chairs around the table and along the side walls could seat thirty, and almost that many people were awaiting the arrival of the vice president.

Too many participants to get anything accomplished, Chisholm thought as he sat in a chair at one corner of the room. His months in Washington had taught him that nothing substantive ever got decided in a room full of people, especially when they had different turf to protect. And in Washington, he had concluded, the protection of turf—budgets, influence, manpower positions, whatever—was always the first order of business. Chisholm wished he were back at the Pentagon working on the briefing for General Ramsey and General Gillette.

As Chisholm stirred restlessly, he looked around, recognizing about half the people in the room. Several had been at DoD-NASA coordinating meetings he had attended when working on previous space issues. The most senior civilian he recognized was Paul Edwards, who recently had been elevated to an associate administrator position in NASA.

Catching the eye of Edwards, Chisholm said, "Congratulations on your promotion, sir."

Chisholm had been the Air Force representative on a Failure Review Board that Edwards had headed following the loss of a costly satellite three years earlier. The two men had discovered that they had played on sports teams against each other while attending high schools in Dallas. Edwards had liked Chisholm's common-sense approach to the investigation, so mutual respect had developed between them.

"Good to see you, Mike," Edwards called out.

As Chisholm started through the crowd to join Edwards, someone announced the impending arrival of the vice president.

Moments later Vice President Richard Hatcher entered, greeted Edwards and a few of the other senior people, then took a seat at the table. With a mischievous smile, he asked, "Well, gentlemen, who wants to be the first to find out if the Russians can shoot straight?"

Several people responded with nervous laughter. A noticeable silence followed. Finally Lieutenant General Steven Stone, the USAF principal deputy assistant for acquisition, said, "We're hoping, Mister Vice President, that the French may insist on claiming that honor.

They have an *Ariane 4* scheduled for a Monday morning launch from Kourou, and the French don't seem to be delaying their preparations."

"You may be right, General," Hatcher said. "Our reading of things in Paris is that they're going to gamble that this *Ariane* could slip by while the Russians are working the bugs out of their system."

"If the Soviets even have a weapons system to back up the ambassador's warnings," Edwards said. Several people in the room nodded their agreement. "I heard rumors this morning that the pictures of the satellites in the low constellation don't look threatening."

"I haven't seen pictures," Stone said, "but my people told me the same thing. The spacecraft appear to be some new surveillance design rather than a weapon system."

Chisholm suddenly was more interested than he had been a few moments earlier. Before leaving the Pentagon on Thursday night, he had asked about pictures of the *Borzoi*. By that time the GEODSS cameras had not gotten any good shots. Now he made a note to see what the *Borzoi* looked like before his briefing.

"Perhaps, then," Hatcher said, "this meeting is much ado about nothing. Nevertheless, I need to know what the president should be aware of as far as our launch schedule is concerned? General?"

"Mister Vice President," Stone said, "a week from today the Air Force has a Delta Two booster scheduled to put a NAVSTAR Global Positioning System into orbit."

"How badly do we need that launch, General?"

"We can delay if necessary, sir. This satellite's programmed to be an on-orbit spare for our worldwide navigational system. The system's critical, but right now we have a full constellation of working satellites."

Hatcher nodded. "Anything else between now and Defender I?"

"Not from DoD, sir. Defender should be ready the first week in April. Right now all our constellations are pretty healthy."

"Good," Hatcher said. Turning to Edwards, he continued, "And what is NASA's assessment, Paul?"

"Our next shuttle flight's scheduled for the second week in April, sir. Most payloads in our queue are commercial communications satellites. We've got another moon probe due for launch in May."

Hatcher leaned back in his large chair and seemed to be considering the alternatives. Finally he said, "So if we put a hold on next week's NAVSTAR launch, we could wait out the crisis for a couple of weeks?"

There was consensus.

Stone responded, "As long as we don't run into a shutdown like that following the Challenger accident in eighty-six." He paused, then added, "And as long as the Soviets don't attack the satellites that already are on orbit."

"The president understands that quite clearly, General," Hatcher said with an expression that showed he appreciated the seriousness of such a possibility. He asked for the status of preparations for the Defender I.

Stone summarized the most recent progress.

After the senior people seated at the table discussed several other aspects of the blockade, Hatcher asked, "Is there anything else that needs to be covered?"

The vice president's question had been directed at his chief of staff, John Barker, but a man sitting behind Edwards responded. "Has the president considered sorting out the payloads and treating some differently from the others?"

Hatcher leaned to the side, trying to see the speaker. "I'm not sure I understand the question."

Edwards glanced over his shoulder, then said, "Mister Vice President, Doctor Turnhill is the NASA program manager for Moon Base Twenty-ten."

Turnhill stood, giving the vice president a clearer view. "What I'm asking, sir, is if there's any possibility of identifying nonmilitary payloads and getting them cleared for launch."

Hatcher seemed confused, but the din of whispered comments made it obvious that others had found Turnhill's suggestion controversial. The vice president's eyes widened slightly, then he said, "Oh, you're asking if we'd permit the Russians to inspect some payloads. Frankly, we've . . ." He paused, then looked toward Barker and asked, "The participants here are all government? Is that correct, John?"

"Yes, Mister Vice President. No media."

Addressing the group, Hatcher said, "In the last twenty-four hours, the president has considered any number of options. However, I'm not ready to see myself quoted in the *Post* as saying we're considering knuckling under to Galkin's threats. What you suggest, Doctor Turnhill, will have some consideration, but I don't believe it's one of the front-runners."

Hatcher seemed satisfied with his answer, but Turnhill pressed on. "Sir, many in this room have visited Star City and Kaliningrad and the Baikonur Cosmodrome. There are long-standing precedents for sharing information on scientific spacecraft."

Chisholm would like to have challenged Turnhill with a question about who had selected the stops on those visits. A Soviet-controlled tour of Soviet facilities was one thing; a Soviet-dictated inspection of American spacecraft was far from being in the same category. Chisholm wondered whether Edwards was uneasy because his subordinate was pressing the issue so hard. Edwards seemed tolerant, not red-faced as an Air Force general might have been if one of his colonels were putting the vice president on the spot.

"I realize there have been scientific visits, Doctor," Hatcher said, seeming ready to leave the subject. "I'm sure all ramifications will be discussed before any final decisions are made."

"Clearly, Mister Vice President," Turnhill continued, "we have scientific experiments and payloads that should not be delayed because the Soviets are opposed to Defender I."

That statement produced whispered responses throughout the room.

Edwards looked nervous. He glanced toward Turnhill and said, "I'm sure that Vice President Hatcher understands your point."

"Thank you, Paul." Turning away from Turnhill's side of the room, he asked, "Is that about it?"

Turnhill looked as if he wanted to pursue his subject, but finally decided to sit.

Moments later Hatcher brought the meeting to a close and left the room.

Chisholm was curious about Turnhill's role. Was he just a program manager who judged something only in terms of whether or not it was good for his program? Or, Chisholm thought more cynically, had he been more like a shill in the crowd, whose assignment was to raise the possibility of divorcing all NASA payloads from the American stand against inspections? He did not believe that Edwards played the Washington game that way, but then Edwards was not the final authority in NASA.

As the crowd began to file out, Chisholm caught up with Edwards and said, "Looks like you still prefer people who aren't shy about saying what they think, sir."

Edwards gave Chisholm an anguished smile. "You've got to have them in this business, Mike." He paused for effect, then added, "Of course, you don't necessarily have to bring them with you to meetings with the vice president."

"I thought maybe he was your designated sacrificee, chosen to offer NASA's stand on this blockade."

"No, Mike," Edwards said. "If that were the NASA position, I'd have presented it. Doctor Turnhill's just a man with a mission. His program has years to get the moon base established, but he's afraid he can't lose a single day."

"What is the NASA position on the blockade?"

Edwards sighed. "We don't have one yet. Lots of scientists are dusting off their no-military-in-space placards, but right now we're in the wait-and-see mode. You have any easy answers, Mike?"

"Not a one," Chisholm said, certain that his solution would be far from easy.

20

When Chisholm finally returned to the Pentagon, he barely had time to finish the charts for his briefing. Nevertheless, he got copies of the first two pictures of the *Borzoi* satellites. One picture had been taken using the GEODSS telescopic sensors at Maui, Hawaii; the other was from the sensors at Diego Garcia, a remote island in the Indian Ocean.

Chisholm was disappointed with the lack of sharp detail.

First he looked for indications of the amount of electrical power that could be generated aboard each satellite. The pictures showed the winglike panels of solar arrays, which would generate routine amounts of electrical power. He knew, however, weapons on spacecraft required markedly more power than solar arrays produced. One satellite seemed to have a boom with a nuclear generator extended from one end, but the camera angle made it difficult for Chisholm to be sure. He grudgingly concluded that the assessments at the morning's meeting seemed reasonable—both spacecraft looked more like identical surveillance platforms than like the armed satellites he had expected.

He searched for other clues. These spacecraft were unlike any he had seen before, but perhaps not so menacing as he had assumed. Yet, as he looked at the two different satellites, something seemed off. Before he could reach a conclusion, he got a call saying that the generals were ready for him.

Ramsey and Gillette were on a large leather couch in Ramsey's office when Chisholm entered. Under other circumstances Chisholm might have been nervous, but he had earned Gillette's respect years ago when the general had been Chisholm's wing commander.

Gillette smiled and said, "General Ramsey says you've got some grandiose scheme that might end up bending one of my airplanes."

"That wouldn't be my intention, sir," Chisholm said, "but I doubt we'd fly it entirely by the book."

"Well," Gillette said in a tone suggesting he had confidence in Chisholm, "let's hope you have a good story to tell, Mike."

Chisholm placed his charts on a small easel. There were top-secret markings and the words *Spanish Fork* and *Stony Rapids* on the cover sheet.

"Sirs, Spanish Fork and Stony Rapids are two of three contingency plans for an attack against eight military satellites of the Soviet Union. These two, and the actual attack plan called Whitewater Canyon, would be implemented if the president decides these satellites threaten the vital interests of the United States."

Ramsey looked skeptical. "Do you really need three plans, Mike? That's likely to cause confusion."

"I certainly hope so, sir, at least for KGB Chairman Petruk and his agents."

Ramsey nodded approvingly. "Let them catch a red herring or two in their nets?"

"Yes, sir," Chisholm said as he pulled two pictures from an envelope and handed them to Ramsey. As both generals looked over the pictures, he continued, "Here are what a couple of the targets look like."

"All yours, Frank," Gillette said. "I'm just an old stick-and-rudder man. Show me a picture of a satellite, and I'm like a hog looking at a wristwatch."

Ramsey smiled, then said, "I'm not many steps ahead of you on this space stuff, Scooter. That's why I've got Mike as my seeing-eye colonel to explain what pictures such as these mean."

"They might mean that the Soviets are bluffing, sir," Chisholm said, sparking a surprised look by Ramsey, "but I don't think so."

After relating the morning's discussion suggesting that the *Borzoi* might not be armed spacecraft, Chisholm continued, "If they were harmless, Novikov wouldn't have worked so hard to get them into orbit before the Defender. Perhaps the purpose of the low birds is opposite what I'd guessed before. Maybe they're for surveillance to feed targeting information to the big satellite at GEO."

Gillette looked confused, but Ramsey nodded and gave the pictures to Chisholm. "These birds would be the eyes, and the other one's the shooter, instead of vice versa?"

"That goes against my basic instincts," Chisholm said, scanning the two pictures, "but that's the only explanation that comes—"

The shadows are wrong! The words flashed through Chisholm's mind even before he had any conscious understanding of what was wrong with the shadows. For an instant the two generals were forgotten as he rotated one picture so that the bodies of the two spacecraft were aligned.

Ramsey asked, "What did you discover, Mike?"

"The shadows are exactly the same on both pictures, sir," Chisholm said, pointing toward the faint images that seemed to be shadows of antennas and other appendages of the face of each spacecraft.

"I may not know satellites," Ramsey said, "but I've studied enough reconnaissance pictures in my time to see what you mean. Maybe the angles between the camera, the sun, and target happened to work out that way."

Chisholm shook his head. Suddenly he had the answer to what looked wrong. "Negative, sir. The solar arrays tell us exactly where the sun was." He paused, then pointed at the winglike arrays of solar cells and addressed Gillette. "The solar arrays automatically track the sun so that they can generate as much electrical power as possible. You can see that the arrays are oriented in different directions, which means that the sun couldn't be casting identical shadows across both spacecraft."

Ramsey aligned the pictures and studied them for a moment, then said, "But that's what we're seeing, Mike."

"What we're seeing is a picture, sir," Chisholm said. Then noticing that both generals seemed mystified by the point he was trying to make, he added, "A picture in the picture. There's some kind of a cover over the real bird, and they've painted it—with shadows included—to look like normal antennas and surveillance sensors."

Ramsey looked some more, then went to his desk for a magnifying glass. After additional examination, he said, "Well, I'll be damned. I believe you're right, Mike."

"That's why the pictures are murkier than usual," Chisholm said with a new level of respect for his adversary. "The Soviets are masters at camouflaging everything else. Why not satellites?"

"Spooky," Gillette said, shaking his head. "Frank, I'm glad figuring all that out falls in your empire instead of in mine."

"Before this is over, Scooter, you may end up learning more than you ever wanted to know about satellites." Turning to Chisholm, Ramsey added, "Anyway, after yesterday's threats at the UN, we want a contingency plan ready—even if the Soviets are bluffing."

"Yes, sir," Chisholm said, removing the cover sheet with the classified markings to reveal his first chart. "I'll discuss the flying operations, logistics, and security. I apologize for the poor-boy charts, but I haven't allowed anyone else to see the contents of this briefing."

"No problem, Mike," Ramsey said.

Gillette nodded his concurrence.

The first was a crude drawing of the world from a point of view several hundred miles above the south pole. Antarctica was outlined in black, and a blue circle represented the parallel of latitude eighty degrees south of the equator. Four red curved lines—shaped somewhere between a U and a V—came in from the four sides of the page and with their bases barely touching the blue circle.

"Now, Scooter," Ramsey said, "there's a view of the world that I bet none of your MAC troops has ever shown you."

"It's sure one you don't see every day."

"It's the best way to introduce the scale of operations for this mission," Chisholm said as he pointed at the red circle. "This circle at eighty degrees south is six hundred nautical miles from the pole, or twelve hundred miles across. That's roughly equivalent to a circle with Denver on the west, Pittsburgh on the east, Houston on the south, and Winnipeg on the north. During Operation Whitewater Canyon, we'd operate against targets on the periphery of this area of more than one million square miles."

"The area's size isn't your biggest problem," Gillette said. "Flying around down there isn't going to be like shuttling between Pittsburgh, Denver, and Houston. All that white space on all the maps of Antarctica isn't white just because of the snow."

"Yes, sir," Chisholm said, understanding that the maps depicted few surface features because not much of the glacier-encrusted continent had been mapped. "What's on the ground only matters to us if we have to fly low or land, sir, and—"

"He sure isn't planning to land in Antarctica," Ramsey interrupted.

Although Chisholm did not intend to bother the generals with a litany of the problems, there were a host of other challenges that made the mission more risky than flying over the central United States. That briefing would go to the flight-crew members who would have to deal with such things as the cold, the complications of navigating in the polar regions, and solving in-flight emergencies in one of the most remote areas of the world.

Gillette asked, "Just how long's it going to take you to knock off these eight satellites?"

"Anywhere from fifteen to twenty hours, sir."

Ramsey grinned and played with one of Chisholm's favorite phrases, "Depending on how good *and* how lucky you are?"

"Yes, sir," Chisholm said, then added, "and maybe how lucky Novikov is."

Ramsey studied the chart. "With the orbits so far apart and the satellites coming by only every four hours, your time estimate sounds a skosh optimistic."

Chisholm pointed to one of the red curves. "Two satellites are on each of these orbits, so initially one's coming over Antarctica every thirty minutes."

"But those orbits are what, maybe eight hundred miles apart?" Gillette asked. "We'd have to add afterburners and bend the wings back several more degrees to cover that distance in thirty minutes in a C-141, Mike."

"Those distances are a big part of the problem, sir," Chisholm said, "but we pick up a little help from earth rotation."

Gillette slid his glasses down on his nose and looked over them skeptically. "You wouldn't try to fool an old friend, would you, Mike? I've flown one-forty-ones on almost every kind of mission imaginable. No one's ever suggested I was getting any boost from earth rotation, except maybe with the jet stream helping us get home from Japan."

"This doesn't have anything to do with winds, sir. The orbits stay in the same positions relative to the earth, but the earth rotates beneath them." He placed his fingertips on the edges of Antarctica, then rotated his hand clockwise to indicate the easterly spin of the earth. "If we picked a spot under one orbit, we could just fly around in small circles and in eighteen hours, earth rotation would take us beneath the other three."

"But not necessarily at the same time a satellite was passing over," Ramsey said.

"Yes, sir," Chisholm said. "But by bouncing back and forth between the two closest orbits, we can put ourselves under a satellite about every two hours."

Gillette looked concerned. "So that twenty hours you mentioned earlier doesn't include en route time?"

Chisholm nodded. "That's in addition to getting there and coming home. I have a later chart that'll put that into perspective. First I'd like to show you how we'd attack the targets."

Gillette nodded his approval, so Chisholm revealed a drawing that showed the world as viewed from well above Cape Horn at the lower tip of South America. Most of Antarctica was still in view, and the orbit of a single *Borzoi* satellite was pictured.

Pointing toward where the orbit almost touched the earth southwest of South America, Chisholm continued, "The basic plan is to fly the C-141 to a point beneath the path of the next Soviet satellite. A second aircraft, an EC-18B ARIA, will be about a hundred fifty nautical miles up-range, tracking the satellite's approach from the northwest."

The ARIA, or Advanced Range Instrumentation Aircraft, was a jet transport that had been modified to relay telemetry and voice signals from spacecraft. The ARIA often served as a flying radar site to cover space operations or missile tests in remote areas of the world.

"And speaking of ARIAs," Chisholm said to Ramsey, "if the French go ahead with their *Ariane* launch on Monday, I'd recommend that we have an ARIA off the coast of French Guiana to observe."

Ramsey looked interested. "What would you expect them to see, Mike?"

"I hope they don't see anything special," Chisholm said, "but if the Soviets decide to take a shot, the most natural time is during the *Ariane*'s ascent—"

"When the rockets are spewing out a big infrared signature," Ramsey said, making a note. "Sending an ARIA sounds like cheap insurance."

After answering a few more questions about how the missiles would be deployed, Chisholm switched to a chart labeled Spanish Fork, which showed a map of the Pacific Ocean and the adjoining coasts of North America, Asia, and Antarctica. One orange line stretched from southern California to Guam; another from near San Francisco to Hawaii, then southward to American Samoa.

Pointing toward the first line, Chisholm said, "The initial deployment in Spanish Fork would be a NASA B-52, which has been used for drops of aerospace test vehicles. That bird would fly from Edwards Air Force Base to Guam. Within a day or two afterward, the ARIA, a C-141, and two KC-10 tankers would leave Travis Air Force Base for Hawaii." He pointed at the second line, then added, "Later, all four planes will file for American Samoa."

Gillette asked, "And their purpose is to support the B-52 in some way?"

"I hope it'll look that way, General," Chisholm said. "I'll try to make their purpose clearer after I show you a couple of overlays." Over the map he placed a clear sheet labeled Stony Rapids. The new addition had a blue line that now connected northern California to Hawaii to Guam. "The pre-positioning for Stony Rapids involves two C-141s carrying cargo from a stateside onload base through Travis to the Barber's Point Naval Air Station, Hawaii. When the final plan's implemented, these one-forty-ones will be given a destination of Agana Naval Air Station, Guam, with the intention of diverting to land at Andersen Air Force Base, which is just across the island from Agana."

Ramsey asked, "What's the Navy's role?"

"Just a diversion, sir. If the KGB has picked up on Spanish Fork and Stony Rapids by then, I hope Petruk's agents will decide that the one-forty-ones and the B-52 are coming together on Guam for some reason. If we keep the KGB looking toward the western Pacific long enough, Operation Whitewater Canyon will be knocking down satellites before Novikov knows we've started."

Chisholm pulled a clear sheet from an envelope he had kept separate from the other charts. This sheet had three black lines, which connected Hawaii to Antarctica when he placed the clear sheet over the map. One line was bent only enough to pass over American Samoa on its way south. Another angled southwest over Australia and the third went southeast over South America. These represented the potential routes for Operation Whitewater Canyon, but Chisholm had chosen not to name that operation on any of his charts.

"When the president initiates Whitewater Canyon," Chisholm said, "one of the three C-141s in Hawaii will head for Antarctica. Our choice of routes depends on the biggest logistics unknown: where the final staging base, or bases, will be."

"I assume the farther south, the better," Gillette said.

"Yes, sir," Chisholm responded. "As the worst case, we can count on flying out of Pago Pago in American Samoa. But that's about fifteen degrees south of the equator, still four thousand nautical miles from the target area, so we'd like to land the C-141 farther south."

Gillette leaned back and crossed his arms. "An eight-thousand-mile round trip on top of a twenty-hour combat mission? We routinely ask the near-impossible from our maintenance troops and flight crews, but this sounds like you're asking for the really impossible, Mike."

Chisholm shrugged. He had the same concerns about whether the airplane and the crew could hold up that long.

"Australia's a possibility for shortening that down some," Ramsey said, "but all our allies may shy away when they find out what the mission is."

Chisholm nodded. "The choice of a staging base is one problem that's not going to be solved at my pay grade."

"Nor mine," Ramsey said with a smile. "Work up your plan based on using American Samoa, but have options for Australia or South America."

"For security purposes," Chisholm said, "I've put the ARIA and the two tankers into the Spanish Fork plan with the B-52. I expect General Novikov to accept that we're interested in Guam because it's west of the coverage of his big satellite."

"So when the KGB sees an ARIA in American Samoa and the B-52 on Guam," Ramsey said, "Novikov's going to figure your attack is somewhere in between."

"That should appear reasonable to him, since his satellites are well below their maximum altitude crossing over the equator."

"I'd think that'd look a lot more reasonable to the Soviets," Gillette said, "than us sending airplanes to the bottom corner of the world to take them on."

"Anyway," Chisholm said, "Spanish Fork is the first level of deception. Its ARIA and tankers, of course, will go south at the appropriate time to participate in Whitewater Canyon."

"For the mission length you're talking about, Mike," Gillette said, "two tankers won't be enough. If they have to fly out of Samoa, you'll have tankers refueling tankers just to get you and the ARIA some gas."

"Yes, sir," Chisholm said. "We'll be tasking the Strategic Air Command to give tanker support to an exercise of the Hawaii Air National Guard, so extra assets will be pre-positioned." When Gillette and Ramsey seemed satisfied, Chisholm continued, "Stony Rapids will be billed as two C-141s carrying some new torpedoes to the navy base on Guam."

Ramsey smiled. "But when they land at Andersen instead of Agana, the KGB will assume the cargo's some kind of missiles that the B-52 has been waiting for?"

Chisholm nodded. "If they're watching by then, they should stay confused by our diversion at Guam until it's too late to send MiGs after us."

Gillette's attention increased immediately. "Are you considering MiGs a serious threat, Mike?"

Chisholm crossed his arms. "General, if President Grigoriev finds out what our mission is before we get down south, he's got to try to stop that airplane."

Gillette asked, "Where would the MiGs come from?"

"Nicaragua, Cuba, or Vietnam, or maybe even the Soviet Union."

"They don't have that kind of range," Gillette said. "And they don't have many bases they can count on south of the equator, either."

"Yes, sir," Chisholm said. "If secrecy gives me a four-thousand-mile headstart, they'll never catch me in time."

Ramsey leaned back and slowly nodded. "I like it. What's it going to take to get this package on the shelf ready to open if the president decides to implement?"

"Let the normal bureaucracy put together most of Spanish Fork and Stony Rapids under regular security. At the same time, we need a go-ahead to assemble the missiles. We also need some test drops to see how we can get the missiles out the back door of a C-141 and suspended beneath a parachute. And we have to gather cold-weather gear and other things the aircrew would need for Whitewater Canyon. Once those problems are solved, the operation could be implemented within a couple of days after receiving the order."

Ramsey said, "Start putting it together—" The intercom buzzed, and Ramsey went to his desk to answer. After a couple of quick comments, he hung up, then said, "The boss wants me. And I'm sure he'll be interested in those satellite pictures you showed."

"Yes, sir," Chisholm said, putting them into the envelope and handing it to Ramsey.

Turning to Gillette, Ramsey said, "Feel free to use my office for as long as you need, but I suppose you have a few things on your schedule at home."

Gillette answered with a smile, "Let's just say you're not keeping me off the golf course, Frank."

"Mike, get the sneaky parts put together," Ramsey said. He glanced at his watch, then repeated a phrase that Chisholm was used to hearing on a Friday afternoon. "Luckily, there's still two and a half more work days before Monday."

After Ramsey left, Gillette asked, "Who do you need to talk to who works for me, Mike?"

"Chief Master Sergeant Nicholas Oliverio is—"

Gillette interrupted. "Tricky Nick?" His look of surprise changed to one of mild amusement.

"Yes, sir," Chisholm said, suddenly wondering if there would be problems. "I understand the chief's assigned to Traffic at your head-quarters. He'd be in a good position to help get the special equipment gathered on the bird without any fanfare."

Gillette smiled. "You've got that part right. Tricky knows how to get things on airplanes—without fanfare. I think he holds the single-airplane record for cases of Coors taken to buddies throughout the Pacific."

Chisholm laughed. He could not remember an overwater mission with Oliverio in which the chief was not carrying at least one case of beer to someone somewhere. "I'd bet the chief holds the career record too, General."

Gillette nodded. "How long has it been since you've seen him, Mike?"

"Several years, sir. We used to exchange Christmas cards, but that's been a couple of years."

"You might not recognize him now," Gillette said. "Tricky the ground-pounder isn't the same guy that Tricky the flight engineer was."

Chisholm's memories of the chief were of the ultimate professional as far as flying was concerned. Oliverio seemed to live to fly and fly to live. He had been a crew chief on C-141s before volunteering for duty as a flight engineer and knew the C-141 better than anyone else Chisholm had flown with. There was no one Chisholm would rather have sitting at the flight engineer's panel during a life-or-death emergency—and they had shared that experience more than once.

Chisholm had heard of changes three years earlier. On Oliverio's annual flight physical, the electrocardiogram readouts had shown a "slight abnormality." More EKGs and more tests were followed by open-heart surgery. Oliverio's life had been saved but his flying career had died beneath the scalpel.

"It's hard to imagine Chief Oliverio not flying," Chisholm said.

"He's never been accused of being drunk on duty," Gillette said. Then he added, sadly, "But lately no one's accused him of being sober off duty, either."

"Sorry to hear that, sir," Chisholm said. He was sorry in more ways than one. Besides his personal respect for the chief, Chisholm had been counting on Oliverio to carry out an important part of his plan. "Anyway, General, with your permission, I'd like to go to Scott this evening and talk to him. If he can't do the job, he'll know who can."

Gillette nodded. "You're welcome to fly with me in my plane, Mike."

"No offense, sir, but it would be better if we go separately."

Gillette smiled. "Don't want to be seen with me anymore, huh?"

"Not exactly, but yes, sir," Chisholm said with a grin. "The longer we hide the fact that you're giving me special help, the better chance the mission has."

"Sure," Gillette said. "Who else do you need to see?"

"Tomorrow, I'd like to go to Travis to visit your wing commander and Senior Master Sergeant Tony Blake."

"Fine."

"I need to talk to Sergeant Blake about getting a missile out of the airplane and stabilized below a parachute."

"He's the man to figure it out if anyone can. I'll talk to General Case at Twenty-second about putting Tony at your disposal." Referring to the wing commander, Gillette added, "I'll also tell Colonel Stuart to expect a visitor."

"Yes, sir. And if you don't mind, I'll chase down Blake and Oliverio on my own."

Gillette nodded, looked at his watch, then stood to leave. "I assume you won't have trouble finding Tricky on a Friday night."

"I don't expect any problems, sir," Chisholm said, then added ruefully, "as long as I can find the NCO Club."

21

Non-Commissioned Officers Club
Scott Air Force Base, Illinois
Friday, 19 March, 2105 local (0305 GMT/20 March)

Chisholm was wearing civilian clothes when he entered the club. The loud beat of a live band and the drone of conversation told him that Friday night had not yet peaked. He looked around until finding a sign that gave directions to the Top-Three Lounge.

The lounge, which was the private domain of the top three ranks of non-commissioned officers and their guests, was much quieter than the main lounge but no less active. Most people were in civilian clothes, but about a quarter—including a much larger percentage of women than had populated the ranks a few years earlier—wore uniforms.

Chisholm scanned the crowd until he saw Chief Master Sergeant Nicholas Oliverio seated at a table with three other men. Even in the subdued light Chisholm saw differences from the Oliverio he had worked with several years earlier. The chief had a lot less hair. He also carried more weight, which was not well disguised by his loose civilian shirt. Oliverio was absorbed in an animated conversation with one of his companions.

Chisholm approached the table, stood quietly for a few moments until a lull in the discussion, then said, "Good to see you again, Chief."

Oliverio looked up and furrowed his brow, a motion that seemed to be a prerequisite for focusing his eyes. He leaned away from Chisholm as if more distance would help, then brightened. "Well,

I'll be damned. Colonel C.!" He rose unsteadily, jarring the table as he tried to gain his balance.

As Chisholm contrasted the drunk in front of him with the professional he had known so well, he felt sorry for Oliverio. In addition, he felt less convinced that the chief could accomplish the job that needed to be done.

Oliverio's loud statement that a senior officer was present quieted conversations at nearby tables. Chisholm glanced around with a friendly smile, trying to show his awareness that he had entered an area where officers came by invitation only. As his hand was being pumped vigorously, Chisholm said, "I was passing through tonight, Chief, and I didn't want to miss saying hello." His message was more to those nearby than to Oliverio. Chisholm assumed that most of the other sergeants would understand—a colonel had to come to the Top Three Lounge if he wanted to pay his respects to Chief Oliverio on a Friday night.

"I'm sure glad you came in, Colonel C. Whatcha drinking, sir?"

Before Chisholm could answer, Oliverio began introductions to his companions who were senior NCOs at the headquarters of the Military Airlift Command.

When the subject returned to his lack of a drink, Chisholm said, "I've missed dinner this evening, Chief, so I thought maybe—"

"Great coincidence, Colonel C. I think I missed dinner, too. The dining room here burns a great steak."

After brief farewells, Chisholm and Oliverio went to the dining room. The sound of the band seemed only a few decibels quieter than at its source in the main lounge, but Chisholm did not mind. The noise would keep anyone else from hearing their conversation as he tried to assess how much Oliverio had changed.

"Now about that drink," Oliverio said as soon as they were seated.

Chisholm looked above his menu and focused on the chief. "Do you suppose we could get coffee?"

Oliverio glanced toward his wrist as if he were wearing a watch. "It's a little early for me to have coffee, Colonel C." He paused, then added with an off-centered grin, "Normally, I take a gallon intravenously at zero-six-fifteen each morning."

"I thought we might talk a little business later."

Oliverio gazed back, as if his brain needed a few extra moments to process what that might mean. Finally he nodded and said,

"Great," as the waitress arrived. "While the colonel's looking over the menu, Marilyn, would you bring us each a coffee?"

She had started to write, then hesitated, "Is that a *plain* coffee for you, Chief?"

Oliverio looked embarrassed. "Not so loud, sweetheart. You'll ruin my reputation."

She smiled as she wrote the order but gave an I've-heard-everything shake of her head.

Chisholm asked, "Could you bring us a whole pot of coffee, please?"

Oliverio gave an exaggerated roll of his eyes, then patted his midsection. "Stand by, belly. You're in for a surprise this evening."

During the next hour the two men got reacquainted as they enjoyed a leisurely meal. Oliverio told one story after another about happenings in the Military Airlift Command since Chisholm had left. As the food began to absorb the alcohol, the chief became less verbose. His manner was subdued when he began talking about the devastating effect his heart problems had had on his attitude.

Throughout the conversation Chisholm listened carefully. He wanted to help Oliverio, and he wanted Oliverio's help, but the excessive drinking complicated things for both of them. Trying to think of other places besides drinking where Oliverio could have redirected his energies, Chisholm said, "I always figured that if I got grounded, I could spend my first month trout fishing in the mountains of Colorado."

"Oh, I love my mountain spring water, Colonel C.," Oliverio said with a grin. Lifting his hand as if raising a beer can toward his lips, he said, "But preferably without any fish swimming in it."

Chisholm laughed. "But even when you can't fly, Chief, there are other important contributions you can make to the Air Force."

"With all due respect," Oliverio said with a smile that was less lopsided than earlier, "bullshit, sir. You'd never choose shoveling papers around the Pentagon over a flying assignment—if you had a real choice."

Chisholm shrugged, unable to deny Oliverio's assertion. For years he had wanted to command a Military Airlift Wing, but the opportunity had never been offered to him. Although working in the Pentagon held out the possibility of earning a star, he considered the staff job a distant second choice to being a wing commander. Some of his frustration showed through as he said, "But sometimes what we want isn't available in the choices life gives us."

He immediately wished he had chosen different words. They triggered a feeling of regret deep within over being unable to resolve the conflicts with the last true love in his life. Even worse, Oliverio's expression confirmed that the chief had taken the words into a personal context. Years ago the death of Nicholas, Jr., Oliverio's five-year-old son, had been a key factor in establishing the relationship between the two men.

"Yeah, Colonel C.," Oliverio said, clattering the cup down into its saucer. "Sometimes life just sucks."

Chisholm rose and picked up the check. "You have a car, Chief?"

Oliverio nodded, then shrugged. "I've got one, but I don't drive it much anymore." He looked toward his feet as if he were an embarrassed schoolboy. "I picked up a few too many points this year on my driver's license."

"I'll drive," Chisholm said.

They walked to Oliverio's quarters, then left the base, driving east on Interstate 64.

Oliverio looked around. "Where we headed, Colonel C.?"

"Nowhere, Chief. It's just that I need to say some important things that are for your ears only."

Oliverio sat up a little straighter and tried to raise part of his abdomen into his chest. "I'm glad you still have confidence in me, sir."

Chisholm considered leading with his doubts but decided otherwise. "I have a critical job that needs to be done, and you're the first man I thought of, Chief."

Oliverio looked at the stretch of highway leading out beyond the headlights. He cleared his throat, then spoke in a firm voice. "What I told you way back when still stands, Colonel C. Anything you ever need of me is yours."

"I remember," Chisholm said. He vividly recalled the pledge of a grief-stricken father whose son had just died of leukemia. There had been nothing that Chisholm could do to save the son, but he had saved the father's flying career. "I'd need to be able to count on that level of commitment."

"Just name it, sir." Oliverio's voice was softer.

Chisholm hesitated. "This job entails being stone-cold sober for an indefinite period of time."

Oliverio met and held Chisholm's gaze. "Just name it, sir."

While not doubting Oliverio's sincerity, Chisholm remembered a personal struggle to stay sober. He had married his college sweetheart and had started drinking heavily when that marriage fell apart a few years later. "Giving up booze can be pretty damned difficult. I can tell you that."

"I haven't tried to stop, Colonel C., because I haven't had anything worth stopping for." He paused, then added, "Would there happen to be any flying in this project for an old dog like me?"

Chisholm considered the possibilities. Oliverio could not perform duties as a flight engineer—the open-heart surgery had left him permanently grounded. Nevertheless, there was no reason the chief couldn't ride along part way. "The main thing I'd need from you is to get certain cargo together without anyone on the outside being able to recognize what the hell you've done." Oliverio seemed to be trying not to look disappointed. Chisholm added, "I could use someone to keep a sharp eye on things until we get to the jump-off point."

Oliverio brightened. "I'm sure my boss could be persuaded to have me out from underfoot for a while." He paused, seeming to think over his current working relationships. "Course I might need your name and horsepower on the request."

"I've already talked to General Gillette."

"Sir?" Oliverio flashed a wide-eyed expression that caused Chisholm to smile. "You mean about me doing something special?"

"He said that if I needed you for a special project, you'd be made available." Chisholm skipped the rest of the general's assessment.

Shaking his head, Oliverio grinned. "Just like I remember you, sir. When you decide to put on the pressure, you put on the pressure."

"The job's that important, Chief."

"When do we get started, Colonel C.?"

"Monday we'll be setting up the preliminaries," Chisholm said as he slowed for the next exit so he could return to the base. "Your office will start receiving tasking messages to provide support cargo for a routine operation called Sun Prairie. Within a week or so that cargo will be gathered at a base yet to be designated." He had selected the name Sun Prairie as a cover to pull together items needed for Operation Whitewater Canyon.

"Overseas or stateside, sir?"

"This part will be stateside. At some point after that, you'll also receive a separate set of messages labeled Stony Rapids. Then—"

"Sun Prairie and Stony Rapids," Oliverio repeated, searching his pockets for something to write with.

Chisholm shook his head. "Those you'll have to remember. Individually they're unclassified. Write them together on a piece of paper, and you've created a top secret document."

A whistling sound escaped Oliverio's lips. "Uh, Colonel C., I don't have a TS clearance anymore."

"I know," Chisholm said. "That's why you won't be seeing any of those documents. Your job will be to take the containers labeled with their Sun Prairie contents and relabel them to match the items on the Stony Rapids list."

Oliverio smiled. "You ain't fixin' to get us both thrown into Leavenworth, are you, sir?"

"It's all legit, Chief. Maybe not all regulation, but legit." Chisholm paused, then added, "I need to make some cargo invisible to anyone who might become curious about where it's going and what it's for."

Oliverio nodded as he seemed to consider the possibilities. "You have any ideas about how I'm going to pull off this little switch, sir?"

"I don't have a clue, Chief," Chisholm said, grinning broadly. Winking, he added, "But then I'm just the lowly colonel. You're the chief with the eight stripes."

"Colonel C., it's going to be just like . . . well, not *just* like old times working with you, but the challenge sounds like a hell of a lot of fun."

"Give it a lot of sober thought over the next couple of days, Chief." Chisholm reached into his shirt pocket and removed a business card that appeared to be for a pizza delivery firm in Arlington, Virginia. Handing the card to Oliverio, Chisholm added, "If you change your mind about working the project, get to an off-base telephone and call this number, and—"

"Pizza?" Oliverio looked confused.

Chisholm laughed at Oliverio's expression. "Someone else will answer. Anyway, if on Monday you decide it's better for you to be replaced, give us another name. I'll understand."

Oliverio looked disappointed. "I guess if I were wearing the eagles, I'd have the same doubts." He ran his fingers through his thinning hair, then smiled a lopsided smile. "Don't waste money paying someone overtime waiting on that phone to ring, Colonel C., cause I never could stand pizza."

"If that phone doesn't ring, Chief, I'll assume that the job's as good as done." Extending his hand to seal the deal, Chisholm added, "And I could be seeing you again within a couple of weeks."

Chisholm arrived at San Francisco International Airport on Saturday morning. He doubted that the KGB had him under surveillance as a threat to their blockade, but he was being as secretive as possible. For his trip to Travis Air Force Base, which was about fifty miles northeast of the Bay Area, he rented a car instead of requesting to be picked up in a staff car.

En route he picked a public telephone for two quick calls. The first was to Senior Master Sergeant Blake. When Chisholm explained that he was in the area, Blake offered an invitation for dinner. Next Chisholm made an appointment to see Colonel Stuart, the wing commander of the 60th Military Airlift Wing. An hour and a half later Chisholm and Stuart were seated in a room in the complex that included his wing's command post.

Stuart said, "General Gillette told me you'd be coming by to make some requests I wouldn't see in writing."

Chisholm nodded. "In as early as a week, Stu, your wing will be given a special assignment airlift mission with the code name of Stony Rapids. The tasking order will call for a stateside onload, followed by a flight to Hawaii, then to Agana Naval Air Station in Guam."

"Navy support?"

"We hope it'll look that way. When you get to Guam, you'd be smart to have your landing data computed for Andersen instead of Agana."

Stuart shrugged, indicating that changing destinations from the Navy airfield to the nearby Air Force base would be no problem. He started to speak, then his expression changed suddenly. "Did you mean 'you' as in me personally?"

"That's one of my requests," Chisholm said.

"Can you pin down the date?" The duties of a wing commander left little time to devote to real flying. Most wing commanders found it difficult to break away for missions that might require several days away from home base.

"The date's up in the air," Chisholm said. "My guess is that at the earliest you'd pick up the Hawaii-bound portion of the mission in eight or nine days. You should receive at least two or three days' notice, but the actual event depends on things being decided way above you and me."

Stuart asked in jest, "Do you have any other requests that are going to brighten my day, Mike?"

"We'll need some special crews on these missions and a third C-141, under the code name Spanish Fork, that will be scheduled for Pago Pago at the same time."

"No problem. All crews in the Sixtieth are special."

"I mean special special, but we don't want to advertise the fact." Chisholm remembered his days in the flying squadrons. Fliers were always eager to get on any mission that seemed out of the ordinary. It was difficult to keep secret missions secret, especially when the aircrew schedulers were told to pick people with particular qualifications. "The crews need to be qualified for aerial refueling and airdrop, except we won't include navigators."

Inertial navigation systems had been added to the C-141s in the late 1970s, thereby eliminating the need for navigators on most missions. Airdrop crews included navigators because of the requirements for accurate timing and location of the airdrop.

Stuart looked perplexed. "You're making this pretty confusing."

"I hope it'll confuse anyone looking over our shoulders and trying to figure out what we're doing."

Handing Stuart a business card that ostensibly was for an electronics repair shop in Alexandria, Virginia, Chisholm said, "If you can't meet any of these requirements, use a classified phone as if you were dialing the Air Force Secretary's office, only substitute the last four digits of this telephone number."

Stuart looked at the card, then smiled, nodding his understanding.

Chisholm continued, "Tell whoever answers that you have a Yellow Creek message, and they'll get it to me."

"And if I have any questions," Stuart said, "I use the same number?"

Chisholm nodded. "Until you get ready to leave Hawaii, there won't be many more answers available beyond those I can give you now."

Stuart seemed resigned to the fact that he was not on the inside on this operation. "Just another weird chance to excel, huh, Mike?"

"We wouldn't bother you, Stu, if we didn't need you."

Less than an hour later Chisholm was seated in the home of Senior Master Sergeant Tony Blake and his wife, Millie. In these surroundings, which were decorated in a style relying heavily on the rattans and woods of the Far East, Chisholm felt very nostalgic. He still looked fondly upon the days when he and Blake had played on the squadron softball team. Chisholm's fiancée, then-Captain Sandi Turner, and Millie had become close friends while sharing the long hours while the men practiced and played softball. Now as memories flooded back, Sandi was the only one missing from the foursome.

The trio spent the first few minutes catching up on what had happened since being stationed together. As soon as it seemed appropriate, Millie changed to a subject that obviously had been on her mind. With a gleam in her eye, she said, "I suppose you've heard that Sandi Turner isn't married anymore."

Millie's directness made Blake look uneasy.

"That's okay, Tony," Chisholm said to put him at ease. "I had expected the lady's name to enter into the conversation somehow." Turning to Millie, he added with a wink, "Yes, Madam Matchmaker. Actually, Sergeant Matchmaker told me a couple of weeks ago."

Millie smiled at Blake. "I see her every now and then. Sandi's still one sharp lady."

"I wouldn't have believed you if you'd said otherwise," Chisholm said.

She looked wistfully at Chisholm. "You two were so much alike."

"That would have been great," Chisholm said with a wink, "if I'd been looking for a twin sister instead of for a wife. I just don't think I'm cut out to be married to a pilot."

"If I weren't so badly outranked by you and Major Turner," Blake said facetiously, "I'd say it's difficult to imagine two pilots' egos fitting in the same house, but I'm not going to say that."

Chisholm smiled and shook his head at Blake's teasing.

"Tony," Millie Blake said in mock scolding. "They were such a good match."

"Yeah," Chisholm said with a grin. "Like fire and gasoline."

"Now Colonel Chisholm," she said, "if a woman didn't have a little fire in her, you wouldn't be interested."

"Right, but I'd rather that the fire reflecting in her eyes was candlelight instead of an afterburner."

"Maybe you're a bit too particular, Colonel," Blake said. "There's half a wing of pilots on this base who'd be pleased to see any kind of light in Major Turner's eyes."

Chisholm wanted to make a lighthearted response, but none came to mind. "I can't say I'd blame them."

Blake's comment had struck more strongly than Chisholm wanted to admit. Though he had wished Sandi happiness, he had needed a couple of years to stop hurting whenever he had thought about her with someone else. Startled at how quickly the feeling of jealousy returned, he silently chided himself.

Millie seemed to recognize the sudden change in Chisholm's mood, so she immediately added, "But I understand she hasn't found anyone who measures up." Noticing that her husband was smiling, she turned to him and said, "Now go ahead and tell him what you told me." Blake feigned ignorance, so she added, "You know—the nickname."

Blake looked reluctant to explain what his wife was referring to. Nevertheless, he tried to appear serious as he said, "There are those who refer to her as Major Ace."

Chisholm did not understand. "Ace?"

Millie obviously was amused.

"Yes, sir. Ace, because she's shot down more Air Force pilots than the North Vietnamese did."

Chisholm laughed, the comment having assuaged for the moment his feelings of jealousy. "Maybe I should feel honored to have been the first."

"Now you don't mean that," Millie chided. "She's particular—just like you are."

Not quite like me, Chisholm thought. There had been the one big difference after they had called off their engagement. Six months after he had left for Air Command and Staff College, she had been the one to decide to marry someone else.

When Chisholm did not respond, Millie continued, "Now why don't I call Sandi and see if she'd like to join us for dinner. It'd be like old times."

"She's probably busy," Chisholm said in a tone suggesting that he would not try to talk Millie out of calling.

Millie smiled at the obvious progress she seemed to be making. "Well, why don't we see," she said, starting for the telephone.

"Sweetheart," Blake said, "I already called the squadron."

"You two are working pretty fast," Chisholm said, surprised at Blake's admission.

Blake frowned, gesturing that the news was bad. "Major Turner's giving a check ride somewhere between the Philippines and Japan right now."

"Just like the old days," Chisholm said. "This is about as close as we could get to each other for those last four or five months."

Millie grabbed her husband's arm and pulled herself against him. "But it's the times that you can get close that you're supposed to remember. That's how we've always done it."

Blake leaned over and kissed her forehead.

At that moment Little Tony made a rambunctious entrance through the front door.

"I don't see you for a couple of years, and you've gotten almost as big as your Dad," Chisholm said as he gave a manly embrace to his eight-year-old godson.

Chisholm recognized that little Air Force business could be accomplished under the circumstances. So for a couple of hours he cleared his mind of the weight of the last two weeks and played baseball with Blake, Little Tony, and other children of the neighborhood. Then came a meal of hamburgers from the outdoor barbecue. Millie complemented the meal with salads and desserts that increased Chisholm's appreciation for the home cooking he seldom encountered anymore.

When Little Tony had been sent upstairs for his bath and Millie was busy with the dishes, Chisholm asked, "You still have a wood shop, Tony?"

"You bet, sir," Blake said. "I've got a separate room in the back of the garage."

"Let's go take a look," Chisholm suggested in a way that revealed he had something else in mind.

Once they entered the shop, Chisholm turned on the switch for a bench grinder to provide background noise before speaking.

"I've got a hell of a loads problem to work out on a C-141, Tony," Chisholm said as he pulled a small card and a piece of paper from his wallet. Unfolding the paper, he revealed a drawing labeled "Torpedo, aerially delivered." "I need to airdrop something like this without damaging it or ripping out the sides of the airplane."

Blake studied the piece of paper for a moment, then asked, "Do you have its weight and dimensions?"

"I didn't want to write the numbers and draw the shape on the same piece of paper," Chisholm said, "so they're on this card."

Blake read the numbers, then said, "That's a bit lighter than I expected for a torpedo, so—"

"It's not really a torpedo, Tony, but for now, that's what everyone needs to think we're working with."

Blake looked up with increased interest. "Whatever you want to call it is fine by me, Colonel. We could strap it down on a two-pallet train—"

"I'll eventually have to have maybe a dozen on the same aircraft, Tony, so they'll have to be floor-loaded."

Before being loaded into a C-141, most cargo was strapped to pallets, which were flat, ten-foot-square platforms carefully manufactured to slide between rails on each side of the cargo compartment. The pallets allowed cargo to be quickly onloaded or offloaded. When items such as Chisholm's missiles were longer than ten feet, pallets could be linked together in a two-pallet or three-pallet train. The alternative, which he already knew was necessary in this case, was to put the cargo directly onto the floor of the aircraft, letting it slide out on the rollers that were built into the floor.

Blake looked intrigued, but shook his head. "No way, sir. Not at that weight, if you want to drop them in flight."

"You're the loads expert, Tony. How can I do what you're telling me I can't do?"

Blake looked up skeptically, then reviewed the numbers. "First, you've still got a weight problem, sir. The book says that airdrop loads under thirty-five hundred pounds must be rigged on pallets when you're using a C-141. Even with the weight of the chutes, the rigging, you're going to be a little light."

"Parts of the mission I have in mind won't be flown by the book," Chisholm said.

"I never thought I'd hear that from a former chief of stan/eval," Blake said with an exaggerated cringe. Chisholm's last duty in MAC had been giving check rides to other pilots—making sure they understood the rules and flew according to them. Blake grasped his hands against his chest, then added, "Those words are like driving a wooden stake through the heart of a flight examiner."

Chisholm smiled at the vampire analogy, which he assumed had been shared by at least a few unprepared fliers when being faced with a no-notice flight check.

"I'll stay as close to the book as possible, but I need to find a solution if there is one."

Blake took another look at the drawing. "You're talking a fifteen- or sixteen-foot torpedo, or whatever? You'd have to be sure it won't get turned cattywampus and rip out the side of the aircraft."

Right again, Chisholm thought. He had been worrying about such problems for more than a week. Airdrops from the C-141 involved opening the large doors on the tail and releasing an extraction parachute into the airstream. Once an extraction parachute billowed open, whatever the parachute was attached to was going to be yanked from the aircraft. The rails along the side of the cargo compartment were designed to keep the pallets against the floor and to guide them safely from the aircraft. Floor-loaded cargo was less restrained and more unpredictable. If one of the missiles twisted sideways and jammed during the extraction, Chisholm knew that the C-141 could be damaged severely, perhaps receiving enough structural or hydraulic-system damage to become uncontrollable.

"Maybe you could design a shipping container to carry the missile out the back without using regular pallets. And maybe use wooden blocks to build a channel to guide the container out the door."

Blake did not answer immediately. Finally he said, "I could handle the weight problem, and within two or three months, I could rig something that might get the load safely out the door. Of course, I'd need a fistful of waivers from Mother MAC before I'd be able to try my contraption on one of General Gillette's real airplanes."

Chisholm looked at Blake so as not to miss the reaction. "I was hoping we could schedule a proof-of-concept test next Thursday night on the drop zones near Yuma."

Blake stared back for a couple of moments before saying, "You could really let me have five whole days, sir?"

"Good point," Chisholm answered. "We'll need your design for the shipping container by Wednesday morning."

Blake's eyes widened as he seemed less certain that Chisholm was joking. "You're making me think you're serious, Colonel."

"I wish I weren't serious, Tony," Chisholm said. "The flight test program will be run under the code name Toluca Lake, and you'll receive the waiver messages by Tuesday. Once we walk out of this room, you mustn't say or do anything that connects me to Toluca Lake."

Blake looked curious. "Does all this have anything to do with that chubby little Russian's threats at the UN, sir?" When Chisholm's response was a slight smile, Blake added quietly, "At this point, sir, I guess it's best if I just think in terms of torpedo, aerially delivered."

22

The Pentagon, Washington, D.C.
Monday, 22 March, 0547 local (1047 GMT)

In the three days since Galkin's warning at the United Nations, sensationalistic news stories had explored every aspect of the potential showdown in space. Exchanges between diplomats of the United States and the Soviet Union were more private but no less heated.

Publicly the French government had ignored the Soviet threat. On a launchpad at Kourou, French Guiana, near the northeast coast of South America, the French had continued processing an *Ariane 4* booster. Soviet inspectors had not been invited to approve this first launch since the warning, so news teams from around the world had converged at the Guiana Space Centre.

For the last hour Chisholm had been at the Air Force Operations Center. Now he was dividing his attention between a television, the radio chatter on a headset he was wearing, and the Early Bird Edition of Current News, an Air Force summary of news stories.

The television showed a live shot of the *Ariane 4* booster standing quietly on a launchpad. The sun already had risen at Kourou so the booster was readily visible beside its umbilical mast in the clear light of morning. A solid deck of clouds at fifteen thousand feet obscured the sky, but Chisholm was confident that the overcast would not delay the launch. He hoped there would be no delays of any kind because he wanted to see how the Soviets would respond.

Chisholm's headset was linked through a communications satellite to an EC-18 Advanced Range Instrumentation Aircraft (ARIA), which was using the call sign Sparkle Two. The ARIA was above the clouds about sixty miles downrange from Kourou, so there was little

Chisholm could learn at the moment from the ARIA's crew. However, the EC-18's bulbous nose contained the largest steerable radar antenna ever mounted on an aircraft. Once the *Ariane 4* was launched, the crew on the ARIA would have a complete electronic view of the booster's progress.

Several minutes remained before the launch, so most of Chisholm's concentration was on the Early Bird. The twenty-two-page handout quoted from weekend news reports, and Chisholm found many that were of interest.

He was pleased to see that Galkin's speech had had a chilling effect on the anti-Defender rallies, which already had been scheduled in several American cities. Attendance at the weekend demonstrations fell far short of the masses predicted before the ambassador had hinted at a Soviet military presence in space. On several televised news programs, American supporters of Defender I had hammered away on a theme that had received little credibility only weeks earlier: the Soviet Star Wars program was an iceberg, only the tip of which previously had been revealed. The approval rating for President Anderson and Defender I had jumped to more than 70 percent in polls conducted over the weekend in the United States.

Chisholm was not surprised to learn that Soviet spokesmen had refused to confirm the existence of armed satellites in orbit. Instead their statements included heavy-handed inferences about the technical risks in any launch. The implication was that the prelaunch inspections by Soviet experts could not help but increase the likelihood of success. Tass and *Pravda* had one dominant theme: the president's reckless determination to militarize space was the sole cause of the rise in tension. An echo of similar stories in many European newspapers had fueled numerous anti-Defender rallies—including some in France—on Sunday.

When the countdown entered the final minute, Chisholm put aside the Early Bird and turned his attention to the television. Although the French had a good record of success with the *Ariane 4*, the booster appeared fragile and top heavy. Its second and third stages were thinner than the thirteen-foot diameter of the nose fairing and vehicle equipment bay at the top of the stack. He could see that this booster was the 44LP configuration: a first-stage core of four Viking V engines surrounded by two solid-fueled and two liquid-fueled strap-on rockets. The French rated the 44LP as capable of rocketing more than eight thousand pounds to GEO. The morning's payload included two satellites: a tactical-communications relay satellite for the North Atlantic Treaty Organization and a commercial satellite for a European consortium.

The television audio switched to the launch controller, and a French-accented voice started counting down from fifteen seconds. Continuing a superstitious habit that dated back to the first launch he had attended, Chisholm tapped his pen lightly against the desk in time with the count.

Torrents of nitrogen tetroxide and unsymmetrical dimethylhydrazine ignited on contact as they surged into the Viking V engines and into the liquid-fueled strap-on rockets. Almost simultaneously the two solid-fueled strap-ons ignited as well. Chisholm watched two churning white towers of exhaust billow from twin tunnels leading out of the flame pit beneath the *Ariane 4.*

Seconds later, as the *Ariane* rose majestically, the television commentator spoke melodramatically of the absence of Soviet interference. Chisholm chuckled to himself, wondering if the newsman had expected the Soviets to zap the booster before it cleared the umbilical mast.

Almost immediately the first report came from a controller in the cabin of the ARIA. "Sparkle Two has acquisition at T plus seven seconds. No visual contact yet."

The television commentator droned on with details that long ago had become commonplace for Chisholm.

In a few moments a French-accented voice cut in. "Guiana Mission Control confirms solid-booster burnout at T plus thirty-four seconds. The vehicle is at a height of two point four four kilometers. Velocity now is five hundred meters per second."

Thanks for the metrics, Chisholm thought facetiously. He calculated that the booster had reached an altitude of something over eight thousand feet, and he was not interested enough in the velocity to make a conversion.

When the booster and its trail of flame disappeared into the clouds, the television picture switched to the umbilical mast, now standing alone near the columns of dissipating exhaust. Seconds later the Air Force observer on the ARIA announced, "The flight crew reports visual contact with the *Ariane.* Looks like a normal burn."

Across the room from Chisholm, a controller waved his hand to attract attention. When Chisholm pulled aside his headset, the controller said, "Sir, ELINT sources report increased transmissions between Cosmos 3220 and two *Borzoi* that are within line-of-sight of Kourou."

"Keep me posted," Chisholm said as he felt a chill raise the hairs on his arm. He wondered if he were about to witness the first tactical engagement of the space age. "Be sure the people on the ARIA know."

"They know, sir," the controller responded.

Chisholm started tapping the pen again, wondering if a countdown had started for something as spectacular as the launch he had just witnessed. He was frustrated by the fact that he was deep within the bowels of the Pentagon instead of being with the ARIA on the scene of the real action.

"Guiana Mission Control confirms burnout and separation of the liquid strap-on boosters at T plus one hundred and thirty-six seconds," the French-accented voice proclaimed. "*Ariane* is now at a height of thirty-seven kilometers at a downrange distance of thirty-three kilometers. Velocity is one thousand five hundred eighty meters per second."

The announcer sounds pretty calm, Chisholm thought, but then things in the control center at Kourou probably looked good. He wondered how much different that voice would be if the Frenchman were aware of the increased Soviet activity.

Less than a minute later the French voice reported the successful separation of the first-stage booster. The Viking IV engine of the second stage had ignited normally at an altitude of seventy-six kilometers.

About 250,000 feet, Chisholm thought, well above most of the atmosphere. At any time Novikov could show what he's got.

One hundred twenty-five miles beyond the South American coast the Viking IV engine was propelling the upper half of the *Ariane* farther into the northeastern sky. The first stage was falling farther behind with each passing second. Reflecting the morning sun and the fiery tail of the Viking IV engine, the first stage slowly tumbled, venting excess fuel and oxidizer.

Suddenly two red beams flashed down from unseen sources far to the north and met on the seventy-foot-long cylinder that had been the *Ariane*'s first-stage booster. For an instant it was as if two glowing red strings were supporting the tumbling cylinder of tanks and pipes. Then the abandoned first stage disintegrated in a silent explosion.

"*What was that?*"

The excited question from the ARIA interrupted Chisholm's concentration and stopped his pen in midmotion. The tone of voice gave him his second chill of the last couple of minutes. He wanted to ask for an explanation but decided to stay off the radio.

"Sparkle Two, Dominion," the controller across the room from Chisholm called on the radio. "What's going on?"

"We're not sure, Dominion. A couple of redlike flashes, maybe beams, came out of the northern quadrants. It's the damnedest thing, though. They converged on the first-stage booster."

"Confirm that they missed the *Ariane*, Sparkle Two," the controller said.

"So far," the voice from the ARIA said. "But the beams sure blew the hell out of the spent booster. Looks like leftover fuel and oxidizer in that section detonated."

Chisholm was enthralled—the Soviets had locked onto the wrong target. His mind raced, trying to pinpoint what would have caused such a failure. Software—he would bet almost anything that it was a problem with the computer software. He was certain that the Soviets were no more successful than anyone else in eliminating the software problems that plagued advanced weapon systems. Yet the bright glow of the second-stage engine should have made the spacecraft the easy target. Chisholm had trouble imagining a programming blunder bad enough to cause the fire-control system to lock onto a spent booster instead of the spacecraft. Maybe Novikov and his boys weren't ten feet tall after all.

"Keep a close watch on the *Ariane*, Sparkle Two," the controller said.

"Roger that, Dominion."

Chisholm pressed his mike button and asked, "Sparkle Two, are you positive that there were two beams?"

"You bet. They were gone almost before they appeared, but everyone has the same sense of what happened. A beam from the northeast and one from the north-northwest converged simultaneously."

The coordination was impressive, Chisholm thought, even if they were locked onto the wrong target. He felt uneasy as he tried to imagine two fire-control systems locking onto a false target. Closing his eyes, he tried to picture what the observers on the ARIA had seen.

"Guiana Mission Control confirms jettison of the payload fairing at T plus two hundred ninety-six seconds," the French voice said in a tone of bored self-assurance. "*Ariane* is at a height of one hundred twenty kilometers and at a velocity of four thousand six hundred fifty meters per second."

He's still happy as can be, Chisholm thought.

"They're trying again, Dominion!" This time the message from the ARIA had been shouted into the microphone.

The controller asked, "What's happening, Sparkle Two?"

"We're not sure, Dominion," the voice on the ARIA said. "There wasn't even a wiggle in *Ariane*'s track. The beams were closer to where the fairing is tumbling, so looks like they fired late again."

Screw that thought, Chisholm said to himself as he suddenly came to a frightening conclusion: Novikov was taking target practice! A hell of a discrimination system, Chisholm thought excitedly as he squeezed the control for his microphone. "Sparkle Two, are you tracking the fairing and the first-stage booster?"

"Negative, Dominion. We're concentrating on *Ariane*."

"Get on the fairing and first stage immediately, repeat immediately! We need to know exactly where they go into the ocean."

The controller in the command post looked questioningly at Chisholm.

Chisholm shouted across the room, "We need to recover the damaged pieces if we can."

The controller's expression changed to one of understanding. "As evidence of an attack?"

"That, too," Chisholm said, "but I'm more interested in evidence of the type of kill. If we're going to defeat the dragon, we need to know what kind of fire he breathes."

Chisholm pictured the debris now plunging toward the Atlantic Ocean. Some pieces were marked with clues about the type of beam that had focused deadly energy onto the booster's skin. He understood enough about directed-energy weapons—lasers, particle beams—to know that they normally used one of three kill mechanisms. A thermal kill—similar to letting a magnifying glass focus the rays of the sun on a piece of paper—occurred when the concentrated energy burned its way into the target. An impulse kill was more like the knockout punch of a boxer—a strong pulse of energy striking the surface and sending in a shock wave that caused the target to collapse. In a functional kill the weapon used a beam of subatomic particles—

such as protons, electrons, or neutral atoms—to destroy the functioning of the target's electronics. The result was similar to plugging a 120-volt appliance into a 220-volt source of electrical power.

The controller across the room asked Chisholm, "But can you determine anything from pieces that've fallen fifty miles, sir?"

"I hope so," Chisholm said. Perhaps, perhaps not, he thought. Nevertheless, finding the damaged pieces was the first step and pinpointing their splashdown was critical, if any search was to be undertaken. Novikov had planned his little demonstration without realizing that an ARIA would be there with its unmatched capabilities to track the pieces. Chisholm smiled—the Soviets had made their first mistake.

"Guiana Mission Control confirms third-stage ignition and the separation of the second-stage booster at T plus three hundred forty-five seconds." The voice continued as before.

You wouldn't sound so smug, Chisholm thought, if you were broadcasting from the ARIA. He waited another fifteen minutes until the *Ariane* payload was established in a parking orbit at an altitude of more than one hundred miles. Minutes later he was in General Ramsey's outer office waiting for the general to arrive for the day.

The darkness of another evening was slowly engulfing Kaliningrad and four limousines parked outside the main entrance to Flight Control. The dignitaries, who had arrived a few minutes earlier, now were in the second-floor VIP suite that overlooked the main control room.

Novikov was on the main floor, checking tracking data on the two satellites that had been launched on the *Ariane 4*. Both spacecraft now were more than halfway to GEO, coasting upward a few hundred miles apart on separate transfer orbits. He had chosen the NATO tactical communications satellite as the historic first target. As he turned to verify that *Zashchitnik I* was ready for combat, he saw Minister of Defense Levchenko approaching.

"Chairman Petruk brought an interesting report that I want you to see," Levchenko said, extending two pieces of paper and nodding back toward the VIP suite.

As Novikov accepted the report, he glanced toward the other dignitaries who had gathered to witness the first attack by the huge Soviet satellite. KGB Chairman Petruk was in an animated conversation with Ambassador Galkin as President Grigoriev looked on. Marshal Murashev was seated, barely visible to Novikov.

"Vice President Hatcher held a strategy session last Friday morning," Levchenko continued. "This summarizes what was discussed."

Novikov quickly scanned the first page, half-listening to Levchenko's ongoing summarization of the summary. Finally, Novikov smiled and said, "Nothing here threatens *Krasnaya Molniya*, Comrade Minister. They're waiting to find out if we're bluffing."

"And we won't keep them waiting much longer," Levchenko said.

Novikov sensed that the minister was referring to those waiting in the VIP suite as well as to the Americans. "Only a few minutes more, Comrade Minister." Looking at the second page of the report, he scanned the list of attendees at the Washington, D.C., meeting. He recognized about a third of the names, and only one—Colonel Michael T. Chisholm, USAF—caused him to pause. Perhaps, Novikov chided himself, he had been relying too much on the invulnerability of his spacecraft instead of concentrating on men who would try to discover weaknesses. "Do we know why Colonel Chisholm was at this meeting?"

Levchenko shrugged. "Chairman Petruk did not mention him. Is he of special concern?"

"Perhaps," Novikov said. "I've read papers he's written on strategy and space warfare. He's much more like me than like bureaucrats who think only of politics."

Levchenko stiffened, and his expression suggested that he had taken the words personally. "What does that mean?"

"Like me," Novikov said, gesturing toward the aviation titles and badges on his own tunic, "he brings a pilot's understanding of tactics to the use of spacecraft. Few in the Washington cliques appreciate such subtleties." His appraisal of the Moscow *apparatchiki* was identical, but not reflected in his pleasant smile.

Levchenko seemed satisfied. "Is Colonel Chisholm someone Petruk's agents should be monitoring?"

"Yes," Novikov said without hesitation. "If the Americans try to counterattack, they will need such wisdom. His movements may tell Chairman Petruk where to concentrate."

Levchenko nodded, then took back the report and underlined Chisholm's name. "Will this take much longer, Petr? I have other things to do this evening."

Novikov had been on the verge of suggesting that Levchenko fire the first shot, but immediately decided that the minister did not deserve the honor. Glancing toward the status boards on the front wall, Novikov hid the resentment that flashed in his brown eyes. "We'll be ready as soon as you join President Grigoriev."

"Good," Levchenko said, turning toward the VIP suite.

Novikov settled into a chair at a control console, pulled on a headset, and entered the commands that passed the tracking information on the NATO satellite to the fire-control computers. In little more than a second, electronic signals confirmed the movement of the turrets aboard *Zashchitnik I*. Two seconds later a pair of green lights went on, indicating that the lasers were locked onto the NATO spacecraft and ready to fire.

Novikov activated the communications channel to *Zashchitnik I* and asked, "Vladimir, would you like the honor of firing the first shot?"

There was no response until after Novikov called a second time. Finally Kalinen said in a halting voice, "No, Comrade General. I leave such things to you or to Marshal Murashev."

"Fine, Vladimir. Be ready. We'll fire in a few moments."

"I know," Kalinen answered. "I felt the shuddering as you positioned the lasers."

Novikov activated the speakers in the VIP suite, then announced in a professional, almost detached, tone, "There will be a ten-second countdown, then a volley of two shots, seven seconds apart."

He nodded to Polkovnik Nasedkin, who started the count.

Novikov exposed the firing buttons by lifting a spring-loaded guard made of hard plastic. When the count reached zero, he pressed one button. The green status light for the first laser blinked off, then came on almost immediately. Seven seconds later he pressed the second button, and the other light responded identically.

Novikov turned to Nasedkin and said, "Prepare for the second target."

As Nasedkin went through the procedure, Levchenko's voice came over Novikov's headset, "Well? What has happened?"

"I believe, Comrade Minister," Novikov responded on the circuit into the VIP suite, "that the NATO alliance has experienced a failure of its newest satellite."

"Is there proof? We saw nothing."

"The positive proof will come through some of Chairman Petruk's agents when they relay reports of a loss of signal at . . ." Novikov paused to check his watch, then added, "at 1901 this evening, Moscow time."

Levchenko seemed disappointed. "I would like something more definite."

I would like a lot of things, Novikov thought, but the physics of the cosmos and the politics of the Soviet Union keep me from having most of them. He continued in a confident voice, "The radar on *Zashchitnik I* may confirm some fragmentation of the satellite if its pieces begin to disperse. The French control at Kourou should be trying to reestablish contact, so our ELINT satellites should have confirmation within the next few minutes."

Levchenko did not bother to answer.

Novikov watched as the five men in the VIP suite spoke briefly. Then Grigoriev led them out the back door. What had they expected to see, Novikov wondered—flashing lights and simulated pictures of burning spacecraft? They should watch the American newscasts, he thought angrily, assuming such pictures would be broadcast within the next few hours.

Novikov returned his attention to the second shot. He was deeply disappointed that Grigoriev and the rest seemed unimpressed with how flawlessly he had committed an act of war against the once-powerful NATO alliance.

About half an hour later it was nearly noon in Washington, and Chisholm was still trying to break away to have breakfast when his classified telephone rang.

"Colonel," a duty officer said excitedly, "the French have lost contact with both satellites they launched this morning."

Thoughts of food disappeared. "How long ago?" He was concerned that there had been another attack soon after the launch, and no one had told him.

"The first was at sixteen zero one Zulu, and the second was about four minutes later, sir."

Glancing at his watch, he realized that the loss of signal had come minutes, not hours, ago. "I need rough positions and altitudes on the birds when contact was lost."

"Just a minute, sir. I'll check."

Chisholm was surprised by the timing. Both satellites should have been well on their way to GEO—well above the orbits of the *Borzoi* satellites that had fired at the booster and fairing.

"Sir," the duty officer said, "NORAD advises that both birds were over the Amazon basin around sixty degrees west longitude at thirteen thousand miles."

Bingo, Chisholm thought—well above the *Borzoi* and almost perfectly aligned for a shot from Novikov's *Zashchitnik*. He hung up and was dialing General Ramsey's secretary when another call came in on the classified telephone. When he switched phones, he was surprised to find that General Ramsey himself was on the line.

"Mike, I've got two minutes before a meeting with General Bolton. What's your assessment of this loss-of-signal thing on the new NATO bird?"

"I think President Grigoriev just sent a message to the president," Chisholm said.

"Which is?"

"The big satellite at GEO's a shooter," Chisholm said, "and Grigoriev can deliver on the threats made last week at the UN."

Ramsey asked, "Which puts the Defender I launch at risk?"

"Roger that, sir."

"Any way this loss-of-comm thing could be a routine glitch that'll clear up in a few hours?"

"Negative, sir," Chisholm said. "Zapping both birds makes the message unmistakable. They're not going for the headlines, but they're not trying to be sneaky about it."

"Grigoriev wants us to understand that he can wipe out four hundred million dollars," Ramsey said, snapping his fingers, "just like that?"

"Just what I predicted this morning, General," Chisholm said, "only they used the bird at GEO for the kill."

"That's cheerful news," Ramsey said sarcastically.

"Today's demonstration's only the beginning, sir."

"That idea of yours about using an old comsat to bump the big bird. Is that still viable, Mike?"

"The probability of success is slim, sir, but I haven't thought of a better way to get something to GEO."

"They seem to have thrown down the gauntlet, while diplomatically giving us the cold shoulder. Their message seems to be to take our best shot at their new birds, so the old comsat may have to do."

Ramsey paused, then added, "And you're still hot on the idea of trying to recover the booster and fairing."

"You bet, sir. I've done some checking this morning. The continental shelf off South America is pretty wide. Those pieces from the *Ariane* may be in less than six hundred feet of water."

"I'll press your case, Mike. Gotta go."

On Monday afternoon Chisholm learned that the readiness level of American military forces had changed from Defense Condition (DEFCON) 5 to DEFCON 4 at 1510. Fifteen minutes later he was called to General Ramsey's office.

"The diplomats are really screeching at each other now," Ramsey said, "and the president's got his hackles up. He's using the attack on a NATO asset as justification for taking swift action."

Chisholm was encouraged by the president's recognition of the seriousness of the Soviet threat, but wondered if swift action were possible. "Does that mean we'll try to recover the pieces of the *Ariane*, sir?"

"Not only that, but he's given a go-ahead on everything including accelerating the launch of Defender I."

Dangerously optimistic or naive, Chisholm thought. "I hope he realizes, sir, that we need to destroy nine Soviet satellites and any replacements before he can launch Defender."

"That's understood," Ramsey said, "but he wants Defender available if a window of opportunity opens. In any case, Defender's at least ten days from being ready, no matter how much presidential interest it receives."

Chisholm nodded. "Ten days is probably sooner than we could attack the low birds even if something could be done by then against the high bird."

"He's ordered us to proceed on both operations," Ramsey said. "Space Command's trying to reactivate an old comsat this afternoon. With any luck, we'll know in three or four days if it can bump their shooter at GEO."

Chisholm thought about his conviction that a cosmonaut was aboard. "Is anyone concerned that we may be attacking a manned satellite?"

"It's been mentioned in passing," Ramsey said. "But the Soviets certainly aren't raising the issue."

"I believe it's manned," Chisholm said.

"But we don't know that for sure, Mike," Ramsey said. "Besides, if you strap on the pearl-handled revolvers, and walk into the streets and start shooting the citizens, you gotta expect a little lead to be thrown your way."

"This is a first," Chisholm said, thinking about his suggestion that now provided the method of attack. He wondered how far Brett would push that issue if he were making the recommendations. "I guess I'm more enthusiastic about killing satellites than killing cosmonauts."

"It'd be our machines fighting their machines, if the Soviets had chosen to play it that way, Mike. But, they raised the stakes when—or I should say if—they put a man aboard. This doesn't belong on your conscience."

"I understand, sir," Chisholm said, wondering how he would feel in a spacecraft awaiting a counterattack.

"Anyway," Ramsey continued, "as we speak, the bean counters are shoveling money into a contingency fund. By this afternoon you should be able to buy twelve of your ASATs and the other gear you'd need for your Whitewater Canyon plan."

The mention of the mission to Antarctica brought to mind something Chisholm had thought of a few minutes earlier. "Now that the president's making noises about strengthening forces in Europe, there might be a good use for a carrier battle group that's making a port call in Sydney."

"I imagine they're busy gathering up sailors by now and preparing to leave Australia," Ramsey said.

"Right. Perhaps the secretary of defense could order that group temporarily to the South Atlantic to free up the Atlantic groups to concentrate on Europe."

Ramsey looked confused. "I think the president's just bluffing as far as any real challenge to the Russians in Europe."

"I understand, sir," Chisholm said. "What I have in mind is to have our aircraft carrier run interference for us between South America and Antarctica."

Ramsey leaned back seeming to consider all the ramifications. "I assume the Navy'd like to get a piece of the action, and a few F-14s might discourage anyone coming after you from Cuba."

"Once we're finished," Chisholm said, "the carrier battle group can head back into the Pacific."

"I'll start working that. Any other thoughts, Mike?"

"Just that it's a refreshing change, sir, to see something happen quickly in Washington."

"I hope the right things are happening."

"So do I, General," Chisholm said, "but in any case, it stands to be a hell of an interesting couple of weeks."

23

During the last hour Novikov had been monitoring *Zashchitnik I*. For the first time in the mission, he had given the controller a set of codes that activated four hidden microphones in the spacecraft. Now he eavesdropped, hearing Kalinen alternate between rage-tinged delirium and an eerie silence.

After listening to several bitter denunciations of Marshal Murashev, Novikov keyed his microphone and asked, "Cosmonaut Kalinen, can you hear me?"

The ravings stopped. There was silence, then the sound of Kalinen moving clumsily within the spacecraft.

Novikov called again, "Vladimir, can you hear me?"

Finally Kalinen answered, "Why, General? Why must we do such things?"

"It is necessary, Vladimir," Novikov answered without enthusiasm. "You would feel better if you strapped into your couch and took the pills I gave you."

"I want to go to Star City. I do not like this place and its electronic voices."

"Do you still have the pills, Vladimir?"

"No. Murashev has them."

"What?" For an instant, Novikov was thrown off by the answer.

"I gave them to Murashev," Kalinen said, dragging out the marshal's name.

"You must get them from him, Vladimir. You will feel much better."

"I want to go home to Sofya. I don't want to die here."

"You must do your duty, Vladimir," Novikov said, "just as I must do mine."

Novikov leaned back, angry and frustrated with the role he had been forced to play. Clearly he must protect the spacecraft from damage caused accidentally, or intentionally, by a delirious Kalinen. Yet Novikov was repulsed by the idea of coaxing another man into suicide—but that was his least distasteful alternative. He possessed another secret code. If transmitted, the electronic signal would open an external hatch in an equipment bay. Within seconds the atmosphere within *Zashchitnik I* would disappear into the cosmos. Kalinen's death would be similar to that of the cosmonauts Dobrovolsky, Volkov, and Patsayev during the return of *Soyuz 11* more than two decades earlier. Yet Novikov would know of one big difference—this death would not be accidental but would be directly on his own hands. As he listened to the rapidly deteriorating situation on *Zashchitnik I*, Novikov knew he could not delay much longer.

Just as Kalinen started another rambling statement about Murashev deserving to die, Novikov saw Murashev enter Flight Control.

"Cut the backup microphones," Novikov quickly said to the controller. "If Kalinen asks for me, tell him I've been called away for a few minutes."

Novikov hurried toward Murashev to meet the marshal as far away from the communications console as possible.

Without even a greeting, Murashev asked, "What's the status aboard *Zashchitnik I?*"

"I believe Comrade Kalinen is in his final hour," Novikov said in a way that did not hide his discomfort about the roles he and Kalinen had been given.

Murashev seemed without emotion. "When your house is next to the cemetery, you cannot weep for everyone."

Novikov almost blurted out more than would have been prudent. Instead he said, "But, Comrade Marshal, I never lived by a cemetery."

"I know," Murashev said with disdain tingeing in his voice. "That's the problem with you boy-generals. You never learned what killing is about."

"I never learned that it was about killing our bravest officers," Novikov replied sharply.

"If brave men did not die," Murashev said, "there would be no heroes for the people."

"But, Comrade Marshal," Novikov said, "will the people ever know of Cosmonaut Kalinen's heroism?"

"Today, or tomorrow, or whenever," Murashev said as he tapped his fingers against his breast pocket. "The announcement is already drafted. Kalinen died a hero trying to save his training aircraft over the steppes near Tyuratam."

Under Murashev's watchful eyes, Novikov stiffened, then bit his lip.

Murashev continued, "I only need the date and time of his accident, which you will supply."

"Cosmonaut Kalinen deserves to have the people know of his real heroism, Comrade Marshal."

"Some day that can happen," Murashev said as he removed his gloves.

"When?" Novikov did not try to disguise the blunt challenge.

Murashev eyed the general warily, then shrugged. "When the people are able to understand the great triumph he helped achieve." He paused, then added, "Now I must attend the meeting I came to Kaliningrad for."

After Murashev left Novikov returned to the radio. Kalinen had stopped broadcasting. Novikov had the other microphones reactivated and heard only the hum of electronics.

"Vladimir," Novikov said, "this is General Novikov, and I order you to strap into your couch for the safety of the spacecraft."

"I have already done that, Comrade General," Kalinen said quietly.

"And do you have the pills, Vladimir?"

"Yes."

Early Wednesday afternoon the Tass news agency announced, with regret, the death of Vladimir Kalinen in an aircraft crash northwest of Tyuratam. Even though there was little that required Novikov's presence at Kaliningrad, he delayed his visit to Kalinen's widow for nearly twenty-four hours.

When Novikov arrived at Star City on Thursday, he found the wives of several cosmonauts at the apartment with Kalinen's widow, Sofya. Novikov carried the items he had been given just before the launch at Tyuratam. His aide delivered a large basket of fruit and meat. In the few minutes of innocuous conversation that followed, most of the women seemed intimidated by Novikov's rank. Then he asked Sofya if there was some place they could speak privately.

In the apartment's small bedroom Novikov gave Sofya the medals, the insignia of the new rank, and the letter, which he had read to make sure it disclosed nothing about Kalinen's mission. Novikov had decided that if she cried, he would share tears with her. She was stoic, however, as if any show of emotion would degrade Kalinen's memory.

During a few additional moments of awkward conversation, Novikov was fearful that Sofya would ask for details about how Kalinen had died or why he had been promoted. She did not, and Novikov was relieved, because he did not want to lie. Sensing that she was interested in being alone to read the letter, he excused himself and left fifteen minutes after his arrival.

Once outside the cramped apartment, Novikov appreciated the freshness of air that did not hang heavy with mourning. He walked for a few minutes across the spacious grounds between the buildings of Star City. Years before, this parklike setting had been his home. Star City had been an exciting world as distant from the life of the common citizen as the moon was from the earth. He had been filled to overflowing with a cosmonaut's idealism—much more carefree than he felt at this moment. Then, he had been burdened with only two worries: being incinerated by thousands of kilos of rocket fuel in a failed launch or dying like a fiery meteor reentering the atmosphere. His shaving mirror never had looked back accusingly at him as it had done this morning.

He paused beside a statue that had been his favorite. The statue had a vertical ring more than twice his height. Soaring through the ring was the beautiful image of a cosmonaut with his arms outstretched like the Superman of American films. Instead of wearing a cape, this flier had another ring—the sculptor's impressionistic view of a space helmet—touching the back of his collar and circling his head. On many occasions Novikov had claimed that the ring represented a cosmonaut's fallen halo that came from drinking too much vodka. That, of course, was back when Novikov often posed beneath the statue claiming to his assembled friends that the sculptor obviously had Novikov in mind when creating the work of art.

Looking up at the perfectly formed figure, Novikov tried to picture Kalinen soaring freely, representing the dedication, courage, and idealism that Novikov used to feel. The statue refused to return his gaze. Instead its vision remained above the horizon, above the compromises Novikov had made in his personal quest for power.

Knowing that there was nothing at Flight Control that required his return, Novikov went to his quarters and drank vodka until he passed out.

By Thursday afternoon Chisholm was receiving one cryptic message after another as pieces of Sun Prairie, Spanish Fork, Toluca Lake, and Stony Rapids were coming together throughout the United States and overseas.

He received confirmation that a B-52, which years earlier had been modified by NASA to drop flight-test craft over the California deserts, suddenly had been pulled from its current test program. Chisholm's timetable for Spanish Fork called for the B-52 to leave Edwards Air Force Base in less than forty-eight hours for Andersen Air Force Base, Guam. Only cursory attempts were being made to conceal that the special aircraft was going on a higher priority mission.

The NASA B-52 had a history of space-related successes. In the 1960s experimental X-15s had dropped from beneath its wing and rocketed away on suborbital missions to the fringe of outer space. In the 1990s the same B-52 had air-dropped the forty-one-thousand-pound Pegasus booster, which could put satellites weighing nearly a thousand pounds in low-earth orbit. Chisholm was counting on the aircraft's capabilities and reputation to convince the KGB that Guam had some significance in the American plan to break the blockade.

A classified message from McClain reported the successful checkout of a command-and-control module used previously to support missile tests. The room-sized cube of computers, electronics, and control consoles could receive telemetry and radar data from other aircraft such as the ARIA that had monitored the launch of the *Ariane 4*.

Chisholm planned to carry the module in the cargo compartment of a C-141 and feed data through cables to the missiles he planned to airdrop. For now, the module would be marked like regular cargo for shipment to Guam. He hoped that any suspicions about its purpose would be linked to the Spanish Fork B-52 and to other Stony Rapids equipment destined for the island in the western Pacific.

Reports from a classified manufacturing site in Utah told Chisholm that everything was progressing ahead of schedule. Four ASAT missiles were already assembled, and the checkouts on the full dozen should be complete within three days.

At Wright-Patterson Air Force Base, Ohio, modifications were nearly completed on an ARIA so that its electronics could pass data directly to the computers on the ASATs while the missiles were in flight.

Oliverio was at Hill Air Force Base near Ogden, Utah. His message reported that he already had more than half the Sun Prairie items that Chisholm was shipping in from various supply points.

Blake was on a C-141 en route to southern California with a dummy missile and the shipping container. The Toluca Lake test plan called for the first test drop sometime between sunset and midnight.

Nearly half a world away, the carrier USS *Nimitz* had left Sydney, Australia. Although the carrier and its battle group had set an easterly course to pass north of New Zealand, the *Nimitz* was not yet committed toward the South Atlantic. Those orders would come when the scheduling for the C-141 mission became more definite.

Chisholm was pleased with the progress, impressed by what could be done when given enough priority and money. He was beginning to believe that the missiles could leave Utah on the following Tuesday.

24

When Novikov entered Flight Control, Nasedkin immediately came to the general and said, "Within the last few minutes, Comrade General, the proximity sensors on *Zashchitnik I* have made an interesting contact. Another satellite seems to be following us."

Very interesting, Novikov thought. He had equipped *Zashchitnik I* with sensors to detect other objects that were at approximately the same altitude. Since the radar was aimed downward and could not warn of potential collisions with other geostationary satellites, such sensors were necessary. "What satellite, and how far away?"

"We have not yet identified it, sir, but it's following *Zashchitnik I* through the geostationary belt, and it has closed to within ninety-five nautical miles."

"It's catching us from behind?"

"Yes, sir."

"Good," Novikov said, knowing that if the unidentified satellite was moving faster than *Zashchitnik I*, it had to be lower—closer to being within the coverage of the lasers. "I need the identity of the satellite and the rate of overtake, Comrade Nasedkin, and I need that information quickly."

Nasedkin hurried away, and Novikov considered the possibilities. The Americans had not launched any new satellites, so the mysterious satellite must be one that already had been nearby. Suddenly he was hit with an unsettling thought: What if Defender I was not the first American satellite to carry weapons into space? Perhaps, he thought with growing concern, the current adversary was an armed satellite, orbited years earlier to attack Soviet early warning satellites in the event of an American first-strike on the Soviet Union.

Not likely, he thought, even though he had been taught for years that the militarization of space was the only goal of the American space program. In any case, he decided, he would waste no time in destroying this new American threat.

A few minutes later Nasedkin returned and said, "The satellite appears to be an old defense communications satellite that has not been used for more than a year. Our tracking station in Cuba confirms that that satellite is missing from its predicted position."

"Good," Novikov said. "Do you have information on the closure rate?"

"That is uncertain, Comrade General," Nasedkin said, "but the rate seems about one degree per day."

"Excellent," Novikov said.

He had enough experience in moving geostationary satellites to know that a drift rate of one degree per day occurred when the satellite was about forty-five miles below GEO. He concluded, therefore, that the mystery satellite's orbit was about that far below the altitude of *Zashchitnik I*.

Novikov closed his eyes. He pictured the dark skies above the Pacific with the American spacecraft racing ninety-five miles behind and forty-five miles below *Zashchitnik I*. At the moment the enemy satellite was well outside the cone-of-coverage of *Zashchitnik I*'s radar and lasers. If the Americans were smart, he thought, they would ease their satellite higher as it closed in. That would reduce the rate of intercept, but would remain clear of *Zashchitnik I*'s kill zone. However, Novikov concluded with a smile, changing altitudes was a game two could play.

"Since they're trying so hard to catch us," Novikov said, "I think we should help. Boost *Zashchitnik* fifty miles higher."

"But, that will reduce the drift—" Nasedkin stopped short. He obviously recognized that while raising *Zashchitnik I* would slow its drift toward its operational location, the fifty-mile increase in altitude would significantly change the angle between the American satellite and the weapons on *Zashchitnik I*. "Immediately, Comrade General," Nasedkin said enthusiastically.

Novikov tapped the head of his cane against the palm of his hand.

"Prepare for an attack as soon as the other satellite enters the kill zone."

Major John Vance was in charge of the night shift in the Space Surveillance Center in Cheyenne Mountain when he received a call from one of the orbital analysts.

"Sir, it looks like Cosmos 3220 has reached its operational location," the analyst said.

Vance recognized that Cosmos 3220 was the huge Soviet satellite that Washington wanted destroyed. He had spoken earlier in the evening to someone about the old Defense Satellite Communication System (DSCS) satellite that was chasing Cosmos 3220. "What do you have on 3220?"

"The Soviets have killed the drift rate to almost zero," the analyst said. "Looks like they're parking her at about one hundred five degrees west longitude."

Vance wondered why the Soviets would park the satellite almost due south of Cheyenne Mountain. Interesting, he thought, but not as strategically significant as if the satellite were directly south of one of the launch bases—or exactly halfway between. Why had they picked 105 degrees west? He had discovered long ago that the *why* behind Soviet actions often was more interesting than what had been done. Suddenly he ma le the connection: stopping the eastward drift meant the Soviets had raised the satellite. Maybe the cat-and-mouse roles had just switched in the game taking place more than twenty-two thousand miles above the equator.

Vance asked, "How long ago did they start raising Cosmos 3220?" He grabbed another telephone and punched the button for the duty officer at the Consolidated Space Operations Center (CSOC) east of Colorado Springs.

"Some time after we recorded the last position an hour ago," the analyst said.

"C-SOC." The duty officer on the other line used the common acronym for the operations center.

Vance quickly asked, "Do your guys know Cosmos 3220's climbing?"

"What?" The duty officer sounded more confused by the question than astonished by the implications.

"The Soviets are raising your target," Vance said excitedly. "If you don't boost your DSCS immediately, you're going to run right under him—right in front of whatever it is he zaps satellites with."

"Understand! Stand by."

Vance was disappointed that his news seemed to be such a surprise.

A couple of minutes later, the CSOC duty officer returned to the phone and said, "What can you tell us about 3220's current orbit? We've lost contact with the DSCS bird on all normal frequencies."

Chisholm was called into Ramsey's office at 0610 on Friday morning.

"I feel like we're running around with a baseball bat and trying to sneak up on Godzilla," Ramsey said. "If that bird can blast anything we send up and everything that's already at GEO, what can we do besides capitulate?"

"That may be the only choice Novikov's given—" Suddenly Chisholm realized there was a potential solution he had overlooked. "NASA has something else up there, General. Do you know Paul Edwards? He's an associate administrator at NASA."

"If NASA's got something that'll break the blockade, we can go directly to the White House, Mike."

"It might go smoother if you invited him for a visit first, General. Maybe cover his visit by having someone tell the Pentagon to host another meeting to review the launch schedules."

"First," Ramsey said, "just what are we talking about, Mike?"

"NASA's Moon Base Twenty-ten program, sir. The Prospector probe on the moon."

Several months earlier NASA had sent Prospector to the moon as the first step in establishing a permanent base by the year 2010. Since then, the craft had been exploring the proposed site and collecting samples that were to be returned in the summer for analysis.

"Sierra Hotel!"

Later in the morning Edwards joined Ramsey and Chisholm in a small conference room in the Pentagon.

"We seem to have proved this morning, sir," Chisholm said to Edwards, "that Cosmos thirty-two twenty isn't vulnerable from the sides or from below." When Edwards nodded, Chisholm added, "Our only chance is to attack from above."

"Mike tells me, Doctor Edwards," Ramsey said, "that the only American assets above thirty-two twenty belong to NASA."

"We're giving the president the B-52, but—" Edwards stopped as he obviously recognized the answer. A look of understanding crossed his face, then changed to a pained grin as he glanced from Ramsey to Chisholm.

"Sir, it's either bring your Prospector spacecraft back from the moon," Chisholm said, "or we surrender the sovereignty of the American space program for the foreseeable future."

"Even if Prospector were a viable option," Edwards said, "you have eight other satellites to contend with."

"The president's put the low birds on the DoD's to-do list," Ramsey said, "but that information stays in this room."

Edwards nodded, then gave Chisholm a frustrated smile. "Ask me to give you the firstborn of my next five generations, Mike. That'd be easier than telling Doctor Turnhill that he's about to lose the rocks he's been collecting."

"As long as Cosmos thirty-two twenty commands the high ground," Chisholm said, "the good doctor won't need the samples because he won't have a program."

"I understand," Edwards said, "but telling him would be like slamming a chip shot in a tile bath."

"Going to bounce off a few walls before he settles down," Ramsey said with a concerned expression.

"With a two- to three-day transit time from the moon," Chisholm said, "we can't afford a leak."

"If Bill finds out we want to butcher his baby," Edwards said, "he could make a broken fire hydrant seem like a tiny leak."

"That'd kill the whole plan," Chisholm said. "Novikov should be able to outmaneuver us if he knows when we're coming."

Edwards nodded. "Prospector's designed to rendezvous with a shuttle, not to chase down a maneuvering target."

"Maybe," Ramsey offered, "we keep Doctor Turnhill from knowing about it until it's over."

"He's like a mother hen at his operations center," Edwards said. "If we try to slip Prospector off the moon, he's bound to discover something's going on."

Chisholm asked, "How about if we send him to Guam?" When the other two seemed to find the idea an interesting possibility, Chisholm added, "Maybe even lose him en route for a couple of days."

"We could send him the long way through Japan, just to throw off the KGB, of course," Ramsey said with a wink.

"And based on where Cosmos thirty-two twenty is parked," Chisholm said, "Guam's the best location for relaying final corrections as Prospector swoops in. Since Doctor Turnhill's the expert, Guam might be the right place for him when those corrections are made."

"If I could get him down off the ceiling in time," Edwards said with a sigh, "once he finds out what's happening."

"We'd make our radars and other facilities on Guam available to you, Doctor Edwards," Ramsey said, "if you think there's a chance that Prospector could help break the blockade."

Edwards seemed to consider the possibility for a moment, then said, "You understand, of course, that I can't make a commitment now on behalf of the administrator."

"Sure," Ramsey said, "but we don't have much time."

"What kind of timetable are you working on, General?"

Ramsey sat back in his chair and said, "I propose that we tell the president this afternoon that Prospector would come off the moon four or five days from now in an operation we'd call Diamond Bay."

25

The Pentagon, Washington, D.C.
Monday, 29 March, 0715 local (1215 GMT)

A few minutes after seven, Chisholm and General Ramsey had been called to the chief of staff's office to brief General Bolton. Chisholm was on his second chart when Bolton asked, "What's the bottom line, Mike? When can we kick this thing off?"

"Some of our diversions are already started, General," Chisholm said. "The ASAT missiles will be at the onload base by tomorrow night at midnight, our time. If we don't run into any big problems, we could airdrop our first missile sometime Friday morning."

"And the business with NASA," Bolton said. "How soon can they be ready?"

"NASA has already sent their B-52 to Guam. They're awaiting a firm timetable as far as the Prospector moon probe's concerned. As soon as the president says go, they'll start moving some personnel." Chisholm exchanged a glance with Ramsey, who smiled but did not volunteer any information about why the move was necessary. "There's only one window each day when the moon's properly aligned—"

"How soon?"

All the options for Operation Diamond Bay were displayed on a later chart, but Chisholm had the information memorized. "A go-ahead this morning would get the president a launch from the moon on Wednesday evening. The *Zashchitnik* spacecraft could be attacked on Saturday morning. That would be within a few hours after the launch of our eighth missile against the *Borzoi*."

"And," Ramsey added, "the accelerated schedule for Defender I puts it ready for launch late Friday evening."

Bolton stood. "I have to leave for a meeting at the White House that I was just invited to. Start putting numbers into your schedules. Assume you'll have the go-ahead by ten hundred this morning."

At 0932 Chisholm received a two-word message from Ramsey— Do it! In less than an hour Chisholm had sent out all the messages with the updated times for the various deployments. Once he had set the schedule for the C-141s to leave Hawaii on Wednesday evening, he made his plans for traveling from Washington, D.C., to Honolulu. He assumed that the KGB and the CIA were working overtime to discover their opponents' intentions. However, he had no way of knowing if the Soviets were paying any attention to him. If they were, he was determined to use their surveillance to add to their confusion.

Guam, he decided, was the key. If the misleads he had woven into the Spanish Fork diversion were working, the Soviets already should be focusing on Guam.

He checked his watch. The NASA B-52 would have completed its flight from Edwards Air Force Base, California, to Andersen Air Force Base, Guam, six hours earlier. He speculated that the Russian trawler stationed near the end of the runway would not have missed the arrival. Unlike SAC's camouflaged B-52s, which had been a part of the Guamanian landscape for more than three decades, this particular B-52 still was painted gray. A gold stripe on the tail fin displayed NASA in bold black letters. Beneath its right wing this B-52 had the special pylon with its history of carrying rockets that could reach orbit.

By now, he thought, the big aircraft should be parked within a closed and guarded hangar—Spanish Fork called for the B-52 to be temporarily displayed for only two hours after landing. He also assumed that any agent worth his rubles would have discovered that an adjacent hangar had been cleared and put under guard. The obvious implication was that other special aircraft were yet to reach the Pacific island. And, Chisholm hoped, the KGB might decide within the next couple of days that one of those special aircraft would be bringing him to Guam.

He had thought a lot about his travel plans. If he made them too obvious, the KGB could become suspicious that he was trying to lead them to Guam. Therefore, to cover his absence from the Pentagon, he filled out a request for a week of ordinary leave at his home in Virginia. Not likely that the Soviets would discover this mislead, he thought, but if they did, they should think it highly suspicious that he would take time off in the midst of the crisis.

In making reservations, he chose Baltimore-Washington International Airport as his departure point instead of Dulles or Washington National, the airports he normally used. He chose an itinerary that included a change of airlines at Dallas-Fort Worth and at Los Angeles. He made the reservations in a different name for each leg of the flight to Honolulu.

Satisfied with this first layer of deception, Chisholm focused on the second layer. He wanted the KGB to discover him in Hawaii and eventually link him to a C-141 that would depart Barber's Point Naval Air Station for Agana Naval Air Station in Guam. Therefore, he made sure that his secretary used his correct name and rank in her contacts with protocol at Hickam Air Force Base near Honolulu. She requested a room for him in the base's quarters for distinguished visitors. At the same time she provided the number of his flight from Los Angeles so that a staff car could pick him up at Honolulu International Airport. He had a couple of other tricks in mind, but they would have to wait until he reached Hawaii.

Novikov spent most of Tuesday afternoon in Flight Control reviewing intelligence reports. The latest ones carried a common message: the Americans were busily preparing an attempt to break his blockade. Since several reports focused on Guam, he did also, trying to discern any advantage of launching an attack from the Pacific island.

Why, he wondered, would someone with Chisholm's expertise choose the remote island nearly a thousand miles north of the equator and more than two thousand miles west of the international date line. Since *Zashchitnik I*'s coverage barely reached the date line, Novikov recognized the choice as an attempt to separate his *Borzoi* from the protection of *Zashchitnik I*.

A reasonable first step, he thought, but the second was more doubtful. His *Borzoi* never were lower than two thousand miles over the northern hemisphere. In addition, there was no evidence of an American ASAT that could reach that high—even if launched from the special B-52 now concealed at the airfield on Guam. He studied all the available information on the B-52 and its long record of successes. Finally Novikov concluded that there was little more to learn until the aircraft emerged from its hangar with some kind of rocket hanging beneath the wing. One analyst had reported that more than a half-dozen American tankers, cargo planes, and space-support aircraft were en route or due to leave shortly for Hawaii and Guam. As Novikov put the reports aside, his instincts said he wouldn't have to wait much longer.

He also spent nearly an hour reviewing the KGB file of background information on Chisholm and the technical files that included reports written by the American colonel. In several Chisholm had emphasized the need for an American ASAT as a hedge against a Soviet offensive in space. Novikov recognized with some satisfaction that none of the writings addressed how to counter a force as formidable as his *Borzoi* and *Zashchitniks*.

Novikov was about to leave Flight Control for the evening when he received a call from Minister Levchenko. As Novikov hurried to the telephone, he hoped that the minister had learned what the Americans were planning.

"Petr," Levchenko said, "I just spent five minutes listening to Viktor Petruk ridicule me about wasting his agents' time."

What now, Novikov wondered, wishing that he could stay clear of the petty competition between the minister and the KGB chairman. "There are answers we need that only his agents can provide, Comrade Minister."

"Petruk made a mockery of your interest in Colonel Chisholm. The colonel has been working normally at the Pentagon and has decided to go on vacation to his house in Virginia."

"When, Comrade Minister? And for how long?"

"Starting tomorrow," Levchenko said. "He will be off duty a week."

Right, Novikov thought facetiously, recalling the intelligence report about several aircraft suddenly on the move. "Then perhaps, Comrade Minister, this would be a good time for me to take a few days in Odessa. I've barely seen the sun in three weeks."

"This is hardly the time," Levchenko said curtly. "The Americans are getting ready to try something, and whatever it is, I want you here to stop them."

"Maybe American intelligence will be fooled if we tell them I'm taking seven days in Odessa, Comrade Minister."

"That makes no sense—" Levchenko stopped cold, then roared his laughter. "You're telling me that Petruk is a fool."

"No, Comrade Minister," Novikov said as he felt a chill at Levchenko's phrasing. "I would never say that. However, if we stop watching Colonel Chisholm and he appears mysteriously in Guam, President Grigoriev will think we all were very foolish."

Chisholm felt very unsettled as he sat alone in the evening quiet of the Pentagon. Even though he had an early morning flight out of Baltimore-Washington, he was still at his desk at 2030.

For the last four hours he had worked furiously trying to tie up all the loose ends. The only interruption had come when he had been summoned to Ramsey's office for a short farewell. Ramsey had also provided letters signed by General Bolton and General Gillette. The letters gave Chisholm the wartime authority to waive almost any regulation that might keep him from accomplishing his mission.

Most of his time had been spent on several important projects and many minor ones. They had languished in his in basket for nearly three weeks, awaiting his recommendations while he focused instead on the growing crisis. This evening he had written scores of memos and intermingled them into a stack of papers six inches high. Now those papers were in a safe drawer that served as his out basket when he worked late.

He looked at his to-do list that had grown to more than two pages since he had set the firm schedules yesterday morning. Now only three items had not been crossed out. Picking up extra food for Sherman and dropping off a key to a neighbor would be the last to be accomplished. The third item remaining was a letter to Christie, which he was determined to write and to put into the mail before leaving the Pentagon.

After writing the date and the salutation, he paused. He suddenly realized that he didn't know what should go into the letter. After all, it might be the last contact Christie would ever have with her father. He sat back and picked up the small biplane from his nearly vacant desktop. As he began to spin the wooden propeller, he began to understand the source of the uneasiness that had plagued him.

Was he just afraid? Not yet, he decided, although he was certain he would be when there was time to think. So far he had been too busy to worry about whether or not he would come back. Still, Chisholm knew that fear didn't affect him like many of the people he had flown with. That was one of Brett's gifts to his younger brother. Brett had given permission to be afraid. Chisholm still remembered Brett saying, "If a man isn't afraid when he should be, then he's a fool, and I don't want him flying on my wing." Several times in his own flying career Chisholm had experienced the exhilaration of facing death at arm's length. There had been an unforgettable near-miss— close enough to see whether the other pilot was wearing clear or tinted glasses. An engine had jammed in full reverse on landing, threatening to take his C-141 off the side of a narrow runway at eighty knots. In his thousands of hours of flying, he had experienced more in-flight emergencies than he could remember.

There was a difference between then and now, he thought. In those cases the joy he always experienced in flying had been interrupted with little or no warning. Then the solution had been to confront the emergency, handle it, and brag about it to your buddies at the bar. Now, however, for the first time in his life, he was facing a mission that very well could be his last. And, as he gazed toward the nearly blank piece of paper, he realized that his real concern was what to say to Christie.

Spinning the propeller one more time, he smiled wistfully as he remembered another piece of Brett's advice. "Make your letters sound like you expect to live forever, kid. Don't cause the family to fret the rest of their lives because they thought you were worried about dying."

Chisholm put the biplane aside and picked up his pen. Now the words for Christie came much more quickly than he had expected. He began with the normal couple of paragraphs about Sherman. Then came the proposal of a late spring or early summer visit to England. Perhaps she could get away for a weekend to Paris or Copenhagen or Vienna. Planning a couple of months ahead might not sound like he expected to live forever, he thought, but it was close enough. Next came words about how proud he was of her and an apology for not being around to say that often enough.

Guilt stirred within him, and Chisholm leaned back in his chair. He frequently had felt guilty because his devotion to the Air Force had taken away so much from his personal relationship with Christie. After all, he could have resigned his commission and found other work near wherever his ex-wife had chosen to live. Then the court-approved visitation of every other weekend and every other holiday could have meant something. But he always came back to a long-held conviction—helping keep the country free served Christie in ways that she would never fully appreciate. This week, more than ever before, would give meaning to his years of dedication—and sacrifice.

He looked at the wooden biplane with the two flags attached to the wing struts, then quickly removed the small Air Force flag. His next paragraph told of how the flag had flown in space and how he wanted her to have it. He told her that the flag should serve as a reminder that by being such a special daughter, she had also contributed to the success of the Air Force. He paused, then added a couple of extra sentences about how much he loved her. He was sorry that their living apart had kept him from saying that as often as he would have liked, but decided that one apology per letter was enough.

After reading the letter once, he pulled a stamped envelope from his briefcase and sealed the flag and the letter inside. Then he removed the American flag from the biplane and placed the flag in his briefcase.

He locked all his safes and gathered everything he was taking with him. Then he wrote a quick note to his secretary about the paperwork he had finished. As was his custom, he put the note in the middle of the desk, then placed the aviator's bust on top. For the first time in years he looked at the inscription on the wooden base—words composed by his people in his last flying assignment.

We wish you a blue sky, a bright sun, a fresh breeze on your brow, and hopefully, fond memories of these halcyon days.

Glancing around at the shelves that were overloaded with reports, he realized how much he missed the blue skies, bright sun, and fresh breezes of a Hawaiian afternoon. Although the next few days were likely to be anything but tranquil, he looked forward to an exciting glimpse back into the world of those fond memories.

26

When Chisholm arrived in Honolulu, he was met by a young airman from the motor pool at Hickam Air Force Base. Standing with the uniformed airman in the baggage claim area, Chisholm seemed casual enough, but he wondered if anyone from the KGB had noted his arrival. The luggage he retrieved from the baggage carousel included a hangup bag that had been made by a tailor a few blocks outside the Kadena Air Base in Okinawa. Before draping the bag over his shoulder, he unfastened the latches so that it extended to its full length. Then he made sure that the brightly embroidered words Michael T. Chisholm, Colonel, USAF, showed clearly as he walked toward the staff car.

A fifteen-minute ride brought Chisholm from the international airport to the Base Operations building at the neighboring air base. As he stepped out of the car, he noticed three aircraft of particular interest on the adjacent parking ramp. One was the EC-18B ARIA from Wright-Patterson Air Force Base in Ohio. The aircraft's bulbous nose and other strange appendages seemed to defy everything Chisholm had learned in his study of aerodynamics. Whenever he saw an ARIA, the strange aircraft made him think of a jet tanker that was suffering from hives.

As far as Chisholm was concerned, the most significant things about this ARIA were that it was part of Operation Spanish Fork and the crew members were in their seats, starting the engines. They were on schedule, due to take off in twenty-five minutes for Pago Pago International Airport in American Samoa.

Chisholm also saw crewmen performing the preflight inspections on two KC-10 Extenders, the tanker version of the DC-10 jumbo jet. Both were scheduled for takeoff in an hour and would be following the ARIA to Pago Pago.

Satisfied, Chisholm entered Base Operations and went to the airlift command post for the Military Airlift Command (MAC). After showing his identification to the controller, he was cleared inside the command post. While retrieving a copy of travel orders from his briefcase, he scanned the status boards used by the controllers to keep track of USAF aircraft scheduled through Hawaii. He immediately spotted listings for his three C-141s. Two had arrived that morning and were still on the ground at Barber's Point Naval Air Station, about ten miles west of Hickam. Their next destination was Agana Naval Air Station in Guam, although their departure time was listed as TBD—to be determined. His third C-141 was on the parking ramp at Hickam. Its departure time for Pago Pago also showed TBD.

"I'll be leaving on one of the C-141s at Barber's Point," Chisholm said, handing his orders to Major Yeager, the senior controller on the afternoon shift.

The mention of the aircraft at Barber's Point seemed to increase Yeager's interest. "Maybe you can help me, sir. Colonel Stuart said you might know the alert time for those two birds. The crews are legal for alert this evening at 2200, but MAC still hasn't set a departure time."

After landing, MAC crews were given twelve hours for crew rest. Then, three hours before the crew's next takeoff, controllers such as Yeager were responsible for alerting the aircraft commander and the NCOIC (non-commissioned officer in charge). Usually there was no confusion because the schedule was set by MAC headquarters long before the aircraft reached Hawaii.

"I'm not sure when the alert time is," Chisholm said, choosing his words carefully to avoid a lie. He assumed that for security MAC was holding back announcing the departure time until shortly before the crews were to be alerted. He added the cover-story answer, which he had thrown in to keep MAC controllers from asking too many questions. "There could be a coordination problem with the Navy."

"Right," Yeager said, seemingly satisfied. "I just don't want to get tagged for a delay because someone's late in telling us the schedule."

"I wouldn't worry about that, Major."

"That's easy for you to say, Colonel," Yeager said with the knowing smile of a conscientious controller who worked hard to keep the big planes moving on schedule. "I doubt you can tell me anything about the Samoa-bound C-141 here at Hickam with an indefinite departure time. No one can give me a fix on its schedule either."

"Can't help you," Chisholm said honestly. Eager to change the subject from his three C-141s, he pulled a sealed envelope from his briefcase. Ripping open the outer envelope and revealing another that had Top Secret markings, he added, "But I believe you can help me. I need to store this in your TS safe."

While Yeager was opening the safe, Chisholm looked for other aircraft on the status board. There was no indication of any maintenance problems with the ARIA and KC-10 tanker that he had just seen on the parking ramp. Three more Strategic Air Command (SAC) KC-10s from March Air Force Base in California were due to land in two hours. The words *Silver Tiger* were scrawled in the remarks section for the three tankers. Silver Tiger supposedly was a SAC exercise deploying tankers to support training for the Hawaii Air National Guard. Chisholm assumed that he was the only person in Hawaii who knew that the tankers really were inbound because the fiftieth state was two thousand miles closer than California to his tanker staging base in American Samoa.

After the transfer procedures were completed and the envelope was locked in the safe, Chisholm said, "Where do you have the crews quartered?"

"The pilots are on-base here at Hickam. The enlisted members of both crews are at Barber's."

Good, Chisholm thought. He needed to brief the aircraft commanders on all three C-141s, and that would have been difficult with two crews at Barber's and one at Hickam. Also, it was better having the enlisted crewmen closer to the aircraft so that there would be no delay in starting the preflight inspections once the crews were alerted. "Do you have any messages for me from Chief Oliverio, Sergeant Blake, or anyone in Washington?"

Yeager checked, then said, "Negative, sir."

Satisfied that everything in Hawaii was on track, Chisholm only had one other question: Had the Prospector left the moon yet? The launch window had opened a few minutes earlier, but he assumed he would get a message only if there was a problem.

He checked out a beeper then went to the distinguished-visitor quarters. After dropping off his luggage in his suite, he found Colonel Stuart coming out of the door of another.

Stuart, who was dressed in walking shorts and an Aloha shirt, offered a few words of welcome, then said, "I borrowed a van from a friend, and we're driving to Waikiki in a few minutes to have dinner. You're welcome to join us."

"Great," Chisholm said, eager to be seen with the crews of the C-141s scheduled for Guam. If anyone was tracking him, he wanted them to conclude that Guam was his next stop.

"I'm meeting the other pilots at the club."

The two colonels walked the short distance to the Hickam officers club. Once inside, Chisholm slowed to look at the historic displays on the walls of the entryway. There were pictures of the triangle of runways that had been Hickam Field in the midst of pineapple fields more than a half century ago. Other pictures showed burning airplanes and burned-out hangars, evidence of the price Hickam's airmen had paid in 1941 when the Japanese had attacked the adjacent U.S. Navy base at Pearl Harbor.

Moving through the quiet club, they found most of the activity on the lanai in back. The staff was setting up for a Mongolian barbecue, which was the club specialty on Wednesday evenings. Three groups of people were gathered at tables enjoying the gardenlike setting that separated the club from the channel leading to Pearl Harbor.

Stuart looked around then started toward a nearby group of four men and a woman. "There's Major Griffin. He's the aircraft commander on your bird." Chisholm was wondering who the woman might be when Stuart added, "You'll also be riding with the prettiest pilot in the wing."

"Wait. We can't—" Chisholm's words stopped when the woman leaned back in her chair and looked directly at him. He was stunned to see Major Sandi Turner.

Though his astonished expression did not reveal it, his first thought was that she looked even better than he remembered. Her sandy-blonde hair was longer and set off a healthy-looking tan and a sprinkle of freckles. She was wearing a two-piece outfit made of a soft white material with Hawaiian flowers in pastel shades. The halter-style blouse ended a few inches above the wraparound skirt, offering an enticing view of a tanned and toned body. With an orchid in her hair and wearing high-heeled beach sandals, Sandi Turner did not look like the typical MAC pilot with thirty-five hundred hours of flying time.

Her reaction showed as much surprise as Chisholm felt. For an instant he thought he saw a look in her eyes that, in happier times, had accompanied her playful flirting. Her expression rapidly became neutral, but he sensed she was pleased to see him.

Though long-suppressed feelings stirred within him, he was appalled by this unexpected discovery. How could a female pilot have been placed on the hand-picked crew for this mission? Stuart must know that the law prohibited women on combat aircrews.

As Stuart began the introductions, Chisholm tried to remember their conversation of a week and a half earlier. I screwed it up, Chisholm thought, recalling that he had intentionally avoided saying that the second aircraft might become engaged in direct combat. Whatever the cause of the misunderstanding, Chisholm knew the law. He could not allow a woman on the secret mission. Yet he had to avoid calling attention to the crew in any way that could reveal that the next stop was not going to be Guam.

Chisholm's preoccupation showed through, especially to Sandi. By the time he realized how antagonistic—perhaps even hostile—he must have appeared to her, it was too late. Her expression reflected the professional courtesy due a senior officer, but the look in her eyes had changed. He recognized the fiery anger that had become familiar in the last few months he had shared with her. Chisholm turned away, trying to avoid looking as upset as he felt. He checked his watch and added five hours to Honolulu time. It was nearly 2200 in Washington, D.C., but he would have to place a call anyway.

Stuart had not recognized that there was a problem. "Is everyone ready to go downtown?"

"There's a problem I've got to work at the command post," Chisholm said. "Could you drop me there?"

Stuart seemed surprised. "I thought you were ready to go to Waikiki."

The other pilots started inside, with only Sandi seemingly aware that Chisholm's problem had arisen within the last few moments.

Moving close so that only Stuart could hear, Chisholm said, "There's a restriction on the second bird's crew that I couldn't tell you about earlier. I can't take any women along."

Stuart looked puzzled. "You asked for the best, and Sandi's one of the top pilots in my wing. What in the hell are we into here, Mike?"

"I can't tell you anything else, Stu, until we get alerted. But I've got a problem, and I need to see how General Ramsey wants it handled."

"But—"

"We can't argue about it here, Stu."

During the ride to the command post, the other pilots carried the conversation, trying to make a favorable impression on their wing commander. Sandi remained quiet, seemingly more interested in the homes and buildings beyond the windows of the van. Chisholm also sat in silence, torn between telling her what was wrong and maintaining the security that the operation demanded. In spite of the pressure he felt to resolve the situation quickly, he kept thinking that thirty-something looked even better on Sandi than twentysomething had.

When they reached Base Operations, Chisholm stepped to the pavement, and Stuart said, "We'll wait a few minutes."

"Good." Chisholm assumed that after his call to Washington, D.C., he would need to discuss how to replace Sandi. He also wanted a chance to explain to her that his reaction did not reflect his personal feelings.

As Chisholm sat in a soundproof booth waiting for his call to be put through on a secure line, he found himself thinking more about Sandi than about the problem her presence had created. Special feelings were returning more strongly and more quickly than he expected. The intensity, he decided, reflected their strength—and the strength with which he had suppressed such feelings once he had learned of her marriage.

Ramsey's voice suddenly boomed through the earpiece. "I'm glad you called, Mike. There's a little good news and some that's disappointing."

Chisholm thought immediately of the launch of the moon probe and wondered immediately if Operation Diamond Bay had been delayed.

Ramsey continued, "First, the Navy's picked up pieces from the *Ariane*, so we have evidence. I'm told the Soviets used some kind of laser but the experts need the hardware in the lab for any real analysis."

"Great," Chisholm said. "It'd be nice to know what type of laser they're using, since some can reach down farther into the atmosphere than others."

"Is that a threat to your bird?"

"I doubt it," Chisholm said. "Even if they could reach down and get us, they've got a target-acquisition problem. We'll be barely within the line-of-sight of the *Zashchitnik*, and at low altitude the *Borzoi* will hardly get a look at us before they get zapped."

"If you're satisfied, I am," Ramsey said. "However, we've run into a snag on your clearance."

Chisholm was relieved that the problem didn't involve the Prospector, but he was confused for a moment by the general's phrasing. Then he decided that the reference was to the clearance to land at Santiago, Chile, and his problem with Sandi suddenly faded in importance. The mission would have to be planned all over if the C-141 could not land in Santiago. He started thinking about substituting a landing at Pago Pago and immediately thought of more problems than could be solved without delaying the mission at least twenty-four hours. Avoiding any mention of the Santiago, he asked, "Is it a problem I can work on from here, sir?"

"Negative," Ramsey said, "it's pure politics and diplomacy. This evening our ambassador was told that your prospective host wants a little *quid pro quo* for granting landing rights for this particular flight. Anyway, it looks like we won't have a signature on the agreement before tomorrow morning at the earliest. Will a delay of a few hours blow your schedule?"

"As long as our support aircraft show when we need them, we should be able to do our part of the job."

Chisholm tried to think of any other problems. Since a *Borzoi* passed over Antarctica every thirty minutes, Chisholm's plan always had been to attack the first one the C-141 could get in position for. Arriving one day instead of another would only affect the sequence of targets in his plan of attack. His most serious concern was that any delay gave Novikov that much more time to discover the real American plan.

Ramsey continued, "The president there wants us to release some aid money that's been frozen by Congress. The speaker of the House understands the importance and is working this evening on getting an agreement. We're hoping to get a call from the White House within the next couple of hours."

"That wouldn't be a problem, sir," Chisholm said, looking at his watch. "We're not due to get alerted for nearly four hours."

"In a couple of hours," Ramsey explained, "we may have the agreement to release the funds. But once the first square's filled here in Washington, we have to fill the second, which is to consult the other government in the morning. I'd guess we're eight or ten hours away from a firm commitment for your refueling."

Chisholm wondered if the attack against the *Zashchitnik* satellite also was being delayed. "Will that change the timing of anything else?"

"Negative," Ramsey said firmly. "The other schedule has been firmed up and it won't change."

Chisholm understood the implication—Prospector already was on the way. He kept his voice from betraying the excitement he felt. "Good. Perhaps we can make up a little time as we go along."

"Delaying you some may be helpful as far as your fighter support is concerned," Ramsey said. "The Navy reports that the *Nimitz* and her support ships are into their third day of heavy seas now that they're near Antarctica. They're already about five hundred miles behind where they had expected to be."

Not good, Chisholm thought, but that wouldn't matter if the Soviets didn't discover what the C-141 was doing. "With luck, we'll never need them anyway, sir."

"Right," Ramsey said. "Anyway, Mike, we're talking on your nickel, and I haven't given you a chance to say anything."

"I've discovered a significant problem with my crew, and—"

"The female pilot?"

Chisholm was surprised. "I didn't realize you knew, sir!"

"We discovered her name on the crew orders late this afternoon, so it's been hashed out pretty well at this end."

"How do you want me to handle the change?"

"We don't want you to change anything," Ramsey said.

For an instant Chisholm assumed he had misunderstood the general, but the phrasing was too clear to be misinterpreted. "I didn't believe that we could keep her on the airplane, sir. There's too much chance of the Soviets sending someone after us."

"The potential for combat was discussed in detail, Mike. The decision was that her presence enhances the cover story that your plane's on a routine delivery to Guam."

Chisholm suddenly was angry. He had always had mixed feelings about the law that prohibited female members of the armed forces from being assigned to combat roles. Part of him said that true equality meant accepting equal risks as well as equal rewards. Yet his upbringing had infused him with a protective sense with regard to women. The last few months of discussions with his brother, Brett, had convinced Chisholm that women should not have to face the risks and brutality of war. In this case he was angry that someone else had made a decision saying it was okay to make Sandi Turner face such risks. He fought to conceal his anger and to pick his response carefully. "I assumed the Air Force didn't have a choice, sir. Once we start picking off their *Borzoi,* my C-141 becomes the Soviet's number one target."

"We're not discounting the risks, Mike," Ramsey said, "and it wasn't an Air Force decision. The president, the speaker of the House, and the Senate majority leader were all in on it."

Chisholm was shocked by the revelation. "What about *her* feelings, sir? Did they consider *her?*" The questions sounded more like a challenge than he intended them to. For an instant, he considered acknowledging his personal feelings, but decided against it—neither he nor the general should let how he felt about Sandi influence the decision.

"I'm not sure how the discussion went, Mike, but they gave us the authority to leave her on the crew."

"I believe, sir," Chisholm said, "that's a decision that should have her concurrence, at the very least." His tone was forceful, and he realized that as much as he wanted to deny it, he was speaking from personal feelings as well as professional. When Ramsey did not respond immediately, Chisholm began to suspect he had pushed too hard.

Finally Ramsey said, "Are you saying we should take her off the crew anyway?"

Personally that was Chisholm's first choice. Professionally he understood that her presence might further confuse the Soviets. In any case he felt that the decision should be Sandi's—not Washington's. "I suggest we give her the option of taking herself off. We could invent something to ground her medically for a couple of days."

"Can you get a replacement pilot on such short notice?"

"The crew was set up to look like a check ride," Chisholm said, "so there already are two other pilots. I wanted three because this mission's going to be a killer, but I can spend time in one of the pilot seats while someone else rests."

"You feel pretty strongly about telling her, don't you, Mike?"

"Yes, sir. She's a good officer, and as such, I believe we owe her the consideration."

Ramsey hesitated, then said, "This has been pretty much your show from the git-go, so use your judgment. If she chooses to come off the crew, make it look reasonable."

"Thank you, sir."

"You better get some rest, Mike. With any luck we'll be pulling you out of there in the middle of the night."

When Chisholm exited the soundproof booth, Stuart was waiting in the command post. The two colonels moved to a corner of the room, and Chisholm said, "I need to talk to Major Turner for a while, so I suggest that the rest of you go on to dinner."

"We can wait," Stuart offered.

"No. I want to create as little appearance of disruption as possible."

"What can I tell the other pilots? They'll be curious."

"Just tell them to hold down the speculation and to get to bed early this evening."

Walking out to the van, they discussed the details of getting together when the crews were alerted. Stuart got aboard and spoke for a couple of moments to Sandi.

Looking once toward Chisholm, she seemed to consider what Stuart had told her. Then she acknowledged the others with a "See you later, guys," and stepped out of the van, accompanied by an exaggerated chorus of hisses and boos.

Remembering Sergeant Blake's comments about the wing's other pilots, Chisholm wondered if any of Sandi's more ardent admirers were among the men in the van.

As Chisholm and Sandi silently watched the van pull away, he tried to decide where to go to explain. The command post was the natural place, but there would be little privacy. He feared that the professional demands of the moment had already revived personal conflicts of the past. If he and Sandi started shouting at each other, he did not want that witnessed by everyone in the command post.

Turning to Sandi, he said, "We need to go somewhere to talk very privately."

She looked skeptical. "If that's meant to be a line, Colonel, it's not the first time I've heard it from another pilot."

Here we go again, Chisholm thought, remembering the quarrels that had crowded out the lovemaking in their last few months. Looking beyond her while searching for a patient response, he suddenly discovered one answer he was looking for. About a hundred yards out on the parking ramp, cargo was being unloaded from a lone

C-141. Near its nose a power unit was generating electricity for the aircraft. He had learned years ago that conversations next to a noisy generator could be very private, if you could even hear each other at all.

"Do you have your line badge with you?" He assumed that in civilian clothes they would attract attention walking onto the parking ramp. Display of the line badge—a photo-ID card that authorized access to a military flight line—was required and was the easiest way to satisfy the curiosity of the security police, aircrews, or maintenance personnel.

Sandi looked surprised by the sudden shift in subject. "Of course," she said, gesturing with the small purse in her hand.

Motioning toward the C-141, Chisholm said, "Let's go there and talk."

As they walked into the vast openness of the parking ramp, Sandi immediately encountered problems with the wind. Her shoulder-length hair was free instead of pulled tightly into one of the more restrictive styles required when in uniform. As she tried to keep her hair from blowing across her face, a gust whipped her skirt wildly. Chisholm caught a glimpse of a well-conditioned thigh and the hint of white lace before she recaptured the edge of the wraparound skirt.

"Looks like you still do a lot of jogging," he said, remembering how much they had enjoyed their long runs together.

A hint of a blush colored her cheeks as she gave him an exasperated look. "But not in wind like this or in an outfit like this."

As they approached the C-141, a sergeant in a flight suit came out of the crew entry door and down the ladder. He gave a questioning look toward the new arrivals, then smiled as he recognized Sandi. "Good afternoon, Major. You giving a little orientation tour?"

"No, Sergeant Jackson," she said. Gesturing toward Chisholm, she added, "The colonel's already had a trip or two on a one-forty-one. We just need a little privacy."

Jackson looked surprised by the answer, but said, "Help yourself, sir."

"The discussion's official," Chisholm said, then cursed himself for saying something that sounded like a cover-up. He was getting more flustered than he had expected.

"Whatever, sir," Jackson said. "I'll be at the back if you need anything."

As Sandi started around the nose of the aircraft, she said, "You can talk to me without everyone assuming it means something sexual, you know. Female crew members aren't so unusual anymore."

"I know," Chisholm said as they reached the noisy power cart. "This is a mission that wasn't supposed to have any female crew members."

She turned toward him and shouted above the roar of the generator, "What was that? I couldn't hear what you said!"

Great, Chisholm thought with increased annoyance. None of this is working out. He leaned close to Sandi and distinctly repeated his words.

She stepped back and fixed him with a fiery glare. "Why the hell not, sir? I don't understand why there'd be any question about my going."

For a moment, they stood glaring at each other. Then Chisholm said, "There are things I can't tell you, but there are valid reasons for you to stay behind."

"Professional or personal."

"What?"

She let go of her hair for a moment, took hold of his neck, and pulled him toward her. "Are your reasons professional or personal?"

"Professional," he said, realizing the answer was the truth, though not the whole truth.

After studying his face for a moment, she said, "You don't look too sure, Colonel."

"I don't want you subjected to the risks," he said, then added, "That's my professional opinion and personal preference."

"So what's new? You never wanted me taking the risks that you were willing to take."

"The difference is there's more of a chance you'd get killed this time!" Chisholm paused, then said, "Let me explain."

He cupped his hands around his mouth, then touched them lightly around her ear so he would not have to keep shouting. Her perfume was distractingly inviting as he revealed details from his discussion with General Ramsey. He chose his words carefully, trying to explain the presidential involvement without specifically mentioning combat.

She stepped back, seeming to consider what he might be holding back. As she pushed her swirling hair out of her face, she knocked the orchid free. The wind caught the fragile flower, carrying it toward a spot of oily fuel beneath one of the C-141's inboard engines.

Chisholm hurried after the tumbling flower, catching the orchid before it reached the fuel. He turned and saw Sandi watching. She had one hand entwined in her hair and the other trying to keep the two edges of the skirt together. Not a good place to impress a lady, Chisholm thought as he flicked a little dirt from a petal of the flower.

"Truce," he yelled as he approached.

"What?"

He started to replace the flower in a clip above her ear. She reached to take the flower, but the wind caught her skirt, and she quickly grabbed the soft material instead.

"I said truce," Chisholm repeated, leaning near her ear as he continued to work with the flower. Again the fragrance of her perfume made him want to stop quarreling. Never before in his career had he felt so pressured by the clock. "I'd like a little time for us to get reacquainted, and I'm not sure when we might have another chance."

She looked interested. "No more quarreling?"

He shrugged. "Who am I to overrule the president? If he says the decision's up to you, it's up to you."

She nodded. "A truce sounds fine as long as it'll get me out of this wind."

"Let's go to the club," he said, moving to the upwind side and taking her arm.

After they had escaped the openness of the flight line and the unhindered force of the breeze, Sandi ran a brush through her hair a few times, then said in mock seriousness, "Next time you take me for a walk on a windy flight line, I'd rather be wearing a flight suit."

Chisholm shrugged noncommittally. "Any response I can think of might be construed as sexist or a violation of the truce." He paused, then added, "But I do like the outfit you're wearing."

"Thank you," she said in a tone that was more proper than friendly.

Chisholm struggled with what to say next as they walked in silence for another block. If he had had any idea that they were going to meet, he would have rehearsed everything he wanted to tell her. Unfortunately, the schedule left little time for courtship rituals aimed at slowly getting reacquainted. He knew that when the mission started in just a few hours, special emotions would have to be forced aside. Finally he decided to take the risk and be direct. "I hadn't imagined you'd look as great to me as you do."

She seemed pleased with the compliment but unwilling to let him fan the flame of old feelings too quickly. Moving a couple of steps to the side, she exaggerated a careful look over him from head to foot. "Not bad, but it sure doesn't look like anyone's feeding you too much home cooking."

She was probing, he thought, since she knew less about his situation than he knew of hers. "That's what prison food and long hours and no tender loving care will do. You'll understand when your career sucks you into the Pentagon."

"Truce, remember?" For emphasis she stopped walking and assumed a combative posture. "My career's off limits this evening."

"Fair enough," he said, then decided to reassure her, in case she had missed the point. "You're right about the lack of home cooking."

She started moving again. After a few steps she looked directly into his eyes and said, "Seeing you today was such a surprise, but you looked exactly as I had imagined."

Her words stirred a warm feeling within him, and he pushed aside thoughts of why he had come to Hawaii. The shyness of her smile reminded him of their earliest days together. Then he had been the major, and she had been an insecure lieutenant fresh from pilot training. Initially he had had to draw her out, but soon she no longer had been intimidated—or inhibited—by the difference in their rank. He wished that somehow they could recapture the love and closeness of what clearly had been the best period of his life.

When they reached the next curb, he took hold of her hand and continued holding it long after they had crossed the street.

The dining room in the officers club was almost empty, but Chisholm hardly noticed. Throughout the dinner he found himself captivated again by Sandi's charm and self-assurance. She seemed cautious at first. Soon their conversation became as carefree as in their earliest times together, and her laughter came more frequently.

In an hour that passed much too quickly, Chisholm felt released from the pressures of the previous weeks. The empty loneliness of the last few years seemed as if that time had been part of someone else's life.

Walking outside, they found less privacy. Many people were having dinner on the covered patio, with its overhead fans slowly stirring the air of early evening. He led Sandi across the parklike setting of tall trees and short, well-trimmed grass that separated the patio from the channel to Pearl Harbor. Moving beyond the last line of palm trees, they had a clear view of the channel and the western sky. It was nearly dark, but streaks of multicolored tropical clouds decorated the western sky and reflected dimly in the water.

"I think we missed a beautiful sunset," Sandi said.

Chisholm took her hand and started walking along the road that paralleled the water. "But that's the closest we've come in years to sharing a sunset."

"I know."

They walked quietly for a few minutes, leaving behind the noise and the people. Passing through a darkened shadow, Chisholm suddenly pulled her to him. She stiffened and tried to turn away, but his lips found hers and stayed with them.

Chisholm enjoyed the feel of her pressed against him again. She was not responding as he had hoped, so he relaxed the embrace. Nevertheless, he let his lips linger lightly on hers for an extra moment—the way she had liked to end a kiss in happier times.

"No fair," she said. Stepping back, but not completely out of reach, she added, "That wasn't part of our truce."

"You didn't read the fine print in the associated protocols."

"Colonel," she said with her facetious smile, "I think you've been a bureaucrat in the Pentagon too long."

"I didn't realize that my being out of practice was so obvious," he said with a mock pout.

She placed a hand gently on his shoulder and said, "That's not what I meant, and you know it."

Chisholm liked her reassurance. "In Washington, negotiations are an unending process, and the agreement likely depends on how someone felt the handshake. What kind of restrictions did you see in the truce?"

"Talk, for one." Chisholm looked confused, so she added, "Less talk." She slid her hand behind his neck and pulled against him, raising her lips to his. This time her kiss was enthusiastic.

Chisholm eagerly wrapped his arms around her. When he slipped one hand down to the bare area of her back just above her skirt, she made a sound of approval and accentuated a shivering motion against him. As he continued the kiss with a passion he had not felt for years, his hand played lightly across her skin in a rhythm that she responded to immediately. Intertwining the fingers of his other hand in her hair, he moved his fingertips lightly against her ear.

Her breathing deepened, and her kiss became more demanding. Finally she leaned away. "You haven't forgotten how to press the right buttons."

"I had, but it's coming back in a hurry."

As Chisholm kissed her, he let his other hand glide down across her hip and onto her thigh.

Suddenly both were startled as the pager attached to his belt shrieked a series of annoying beeps.

"Damn," Chisholm uttered as he reached to silence the pager.

At the same time Sandi made a frustrated growl and pulled back. Shaking her head in disappointment, she said, "Just remember, my career wasn't the only one that intruded."

He nodded and kissed her lightly on the cheek. "And you just remember where we left off." He took her hand and started toward the officers club to find a telephone.

After Chisholm had identified himself on the telephone, the duty officer in the command post said, "Let me start by saying I'm just the messenger, sir, because I have no idea what this means. I was told by a captain in the Pentagon to tell you that the first square was filled."

Chisholm was stumped. "That's all?"

"Yes, sir."

Then Chisholm remembered General Ramsey's statement about needing to get the square filled in Washington before the final agreement could be reached in Chile. Now it was a matter of what time the right officials opened for business in the morning in Santiago. "I understand, Captain."

Turning from the phone, he saw Sandi sitting gracefully in a chair in the entryway of the club. She had replaced her lipstick and changed her hair slightly. Why, he wondered angrily, hadn't the fates allowed her to reenter his life a month ago instead of four hours ago? His fanciful thoughts fled in the face of the mission that now was only hours away.

Seeing him approach, she rose from the chair and asked, "Well?"

"There's good news, and there's bad news," he said as he led her through the large entry doors. Standing on the porch of the officers club, he put an arm around her waist, pulled her close, and leaned down to her ear. He paused for a moment to appreciate the fresh perfume, then whispered, "The good news is that it's time to go to bed."

"Now wait a minute," she said, stepping back. "That wasn't in the fine print."

Miming an expression for silence, he raised a hand. When she relaxed enough for him to slide his face against her cheek again, he whispered, "The bad news is that it's also time to go to sleep."

She smiled, looking embarrassed that she had reacted too soon. "I thought you were playing things a little fast and loose, Colonel."

He took hold of her hand and began walking toward the transient officers' quarters. "I'd know better how fast to play things if I knew how much time we had."

She looked at him and seemed to sense for the first time that he genuinely was worried.

Stopping in the shadow of a tree near her building, Chisholm hugged her without speaking. At that moment he wanted her more than he had wanted any woman since they parted. He really wanted to convince her to let him go inside with her, but he knew they would get little, if any, rest before being alerted in the middle of the night. Even more than that, he wanted to convince her to stay behind in Hawaii.

"Sandi," he said, "don't go with us in the morning."

She stiffened, and all playfulness disappeared from her voice. "Don't you dare ruin this evening."

"I'm sorry," Chisholm said, "but I couldn't be true to myself if I didn't try to convince you."

She gave him a look of disappointment. "And I wouldn't be true to myself if I let you." She rested her head against his shoulder and added, "I'm afraid we can't gloss over the old problems."

"Well," he said as he turned her face toward his, "we did a pretty damned good job for a few hours."

He pressed his lips lightly against hers. This time the embrace was more reserved—but no less genuine.

He moved his cheek against hers and whispered, "Once we get alerted, most of the time I'll have to treat you like one of the guys."

"Fair enough," she said, grazing her lips against his ear in a way that put chills through his shoulders. Then she squeezed her arms tighter around him and added, "Just as long as it's only most of the time."

27

Ministry of Foreign Affairs, Santiago, Chile
Thursday, 1 April, 0655 local (1055 GMT)

Mercedes Roche, a senior secretary at the Ministry of Foreign Affairs, got a surprise when she arrived for work. Normally she and four clerks had the office to themselves for the first couple of hours each morning. Today she opened the door and collided with Norman Perkins, the United States Ambassador to Chile, who was leaving in a hurry.

A few minutes later, an aide came out of the foreign minister's office and said, "I have a memorandum that needs to be taken to the Ministry of Transport and Telecommunications."

"I can take care of it," she offered.

"Seal it in an envelope," the aide said, "and deliver it directly to Minister Escobar's secretary."

She placed the piece of paper on her desk. As she retrieved an envelope and carefully adjusted it in her typewriter, she scanned the memorandum—an authorization for an American C-141 to refuel at Arturo Merino Benitez International Airport, departing no later than 0700 the following morning. She noted that full security was to be provided, and all customs requirements and inspections were waived.

Once she had sealed the envelope, she called her cousin, Cesar, and told him she needed a ride. That was her normal procedure whenever she came across anything that might be of interest to Cesar's contact in the KGB.

Chisholm awakened abruptly at 0100 as the clock radio near his bed blared to life. He turned off the radio, uncertain for a few moments if his memories of Sandi were real or part of a deliciously cruel dream. In the darkened room the lingering taste of her lipstick caused him to think of what might have been.

Then he remembered why he had set the alarm. Before going to bed he had decided that if he weren't alerted by 0100, he would go to the command post and call the Pentagon for an updated estimate of the departure time.

When he entered the command post at 0137, he learned that a call to Washington D.C., was unnecessary.

Captain Whittaker, the senior duty controller on the night shift, said, "We've been trying to alert you for a zero-five-hundred departure, Colonel. MAC told us to alert a half-hour early since the crew bus has to drive you all the way around Pearl Har—"

"I understand," Chisholm said, now ready to take over. He pulled a special copy of orders from his billfold and gave it to Whittaker. "These orders assign me as the mission commander on the Barber's Point-Agana leg of this mission. Colonel Stuart will be my deputy. We'll be filing as a two-ship flight with him in the lead aircraft, and I'll ride in number two."

"A wing commander's going to be just a deputy?" Whittaker made the statement more out of astonishment than as a challenge. Nevertheless, he stood a little straighter and suddenly seemed to hold Chisholm in higher regard.

"Roger that," Chisholm said, "and the new departure time is zero-four-thirty." Chisholm assumed that the crew members at Barber's Point had not been alerted yet, since they did not require the long bus ride. "Have your sergeant alert the engineers and loadmasters, based on the new departure time."

Whittaker looked almost overwhelmed by the way this Pentagon colonel had suddenly disrupted a routine night. "I'm sorry, sir, but we can't change the departure times. I'd need concurrence from Twenty-second Air Force, or MAC, and I'd have to give them a good reason if I made the request."

"You already have MAC concurrence, Captain. You'll find General Gillette's signature at the bottom of those orders."

Whittaker's expression showed his surprise—CINCMAC normally did not sign such orders. "Gee, I don't know, sir. I've never seen—"

"Captain, it's about zero-five-forty-five in Illinois, so we might catch General Gillette in his office. But I don't think you or I or your boss really wants you to waste the general's time asking if he really meant what he signed."

"Yes, sir," Whittaker said. After telling his sergeant to alert the men at Barber's Point, Whittaker said, "We'll never get you and the other pilots to the aircraft in time."

Chisholm copied a telephone number from his notebook, then continued, "Call this number on a secure line. Tell them you have a Stony Rapids mission alert and you need a Blackhawk helicopter here at Base Ops. in forty-five minutes."

"For crew transport, sir?" Whittaker said the words as if he did not believe that could really be the answer.

Chisholm nodded as he pulled the pager from his belt. "As soon as you've made that telephone call, I'll trade you this beeper for my package that's in your top-secret safe."

While Whittaker was making the call and retrieving the classified package, Chisholm studied the status board showing other MAC aircraft and crews. He spotted his third C-141 that was scheduled for American Samoa and noticed its depart time also was 0500.

Chisholm cut away the covering from his top-secret package and removed a set of classified orders that authorized him to change the schedule of the Samoa-bound C-141. He grinned at Whittaker and said, "I'm afraid we're about to go another round, Captain. You need to alert Major Easton's crew for a zero-four-thirty departure. Any connection between Easton's aircraft and the two birds at Barber's is classified secret, so don't say anything outside of here on an unsecure line."

Whittaker scanned the orders, nodded, and passed the instructions to the sergeant.

"Now," Chisholm said, "I'll stay out of your way until Colonel Stuart and Major Griffin report to your window. Your main responsibility at the moment is to act as if this is just another routine night."

Whittaker gave a helpless smile. "I'll do my best, sir."

While Chisholm waited, he checked the weather for Santiago, Chile, and other potential emergency airfields along the west coast of South America. April began the first full month of autumn in the southern hemisphere, but each airfield was calling for good weather during the next twenty-four hours.

The other pilots arrived at 0200. Moments later Chisholm was in a back room of the command post passing out briefing folders to Stuart, Griffin, and Whittaker. Chisholm sat back, amused at the pilots' expressions as each man read through what he was required to do. The two-page explanation included procedures that would switch Major Easton's C-141 with Chisholm's in the early morning skies southwest of Honolulu.

Stuart dropped his copy on the table in front of him and smiled. "If this isn't some weird April Fool's joke, Mike, I must be the highest paid decoy in the whole U S of A."

"Your part of the deception's important because we have to keep the focus on Guam for the next day or two." He paused, then added with a mischievous smile, "While you're there, you may need to entertain a Doctor Turnhill of NASA for a few hours."

Stuart looked disappointed at drawing the diversionary portion of the mission. "Mike, I don't understand why you don't file a flight plan for Pago Pago and let Easton head for Guam." He paused, then added, "And why were you so concerned about Sandi Turner going along to Pago?"

"Sorry, Stu, but right now you don't have the 'need to know.' "

Major Griffin asked, "How about me, Colonel Chisholm? If I'm going to be flying you, don't I have a valid 'need to know'?"

Chisholm lifted another manila envelope that was sealed with tape. "There's a whole other package you're going to get to read after we're airborne, but we're taking things one step at a time."

"And my job, sir," Whittaker asked, "is just coordination?"

"Coordination and rumor control," Chisholm said. "I want Major Easton's C-141 on the runway here at Honolulu five minutes or so before we're cleared on at Barber's. As long as that's happening, you just sit and watch. If there are delays here or at Barber's, you delay the other takeoff by broadcasting an appropriate message from your instructions."

Whittaker nodded his understanding.

Chisholm continued, "And no one says anything outside this room that connects his flight with ours. Understood?" After the other three nodded, Chisholm added, "Your flight plans have been filled out as much as possible. You'll need to add the times."

Chisholm answered a few more questions, then Griffin and Stuart got up to leave. Stuart called Chisholm aside and asked, "Do you think we ought to call in Sandi Turner and give her another chance to drop out?"

"Negative," Chisholm said vigorously, although he wished there were a way to change her mind.

When Major Easton arrived a few minutes later, he was told to come inside the command post. Chisholm introduced himself, showed the orders that granted his special authority, and briefed Easton on the plans for switching destinations after takeoff. The major studied the documents, asked a few questions, then seemed satisfied.

Several minutes after Easton walked out, Chisholm left the command post. First he checked the parking ramp and saw the Blackhawk helicopter and its crew waiting for the flight to Barber's Point. Then he went to the flight planning room where the pilots for all three C-141s were completing necessary paperwork. He saw Sandi standing at the NOTAM board, checking the notice-to-airman listings of current problems with navigational aids or airfield equipment.

She looked at him, offering a pleasant—and professional—smile. As soon as he smiled in response, she returned her attention to the NOTAMs.

For a couple of moments he could not take his eyes off Sandi. Her military appearance contrasted sharply with his memories of the previous evening. Now her hair was pinned above her collar, and her lipstick was a couple of shades lighter. The Air Force-issue flightsuit clung to her trim waist and hips, although its seven pockets obscured some of the smooth lines of her figure. The fit was more like that of a jumpsuit one might see on the streets in Beverly Hills than that of the loose, baggy suits worn by the other pilots. Hers obviously had received additional tailoring at one of the shops in Okinawa or Korea.

Major Griffin was seated at a large table, which had an aeronautical chart displayed beneath a Plexiglas tabletop. Chisholm was only partially successful in getting Sandi off his mind as he approached and asked Griffin, "Any problems, Major?"

"Negative, sir. We're ready whenever Colonel Stuart is."

Looking up from his flight plan and other forms, Stuart said, "I'll be ready to file in a couple of minutes."

Once the forms were filled out, the next step was to file the flight plan with the dispatcher in the Base Operations section. In this case a single flight plan covered both aircraft in the formation.

While waiting, Chisholm walked to the NOTAM board and started scanning the teletype listings. He asked Sandi, "Finding anything of interest?"

"The ILS at Agana is NOTAMed off the air for the next four hours," she said, "but it should be in service by the time we arrive in Guam."

Chisholm nodded as if the status of the instrument-landing system at the Naval Air Station was of interest to him. Flipping through the sheets of international NOTAMs, he smiled inwardly. He was sure that everyone who noticed him would come to the same conclusion: glancing through the NOTAMs was the Pentagon colonel's official-looking excuse to make small talk with the attractive major.

Pausing a few moments with the teletype sheet for South America exposed, he said, "I trust that you had a pleasant evening, Major."

She looked at him with a suppressed grin. "I've had some better ones, Colonel, but I've also had worse." As she pushed her pen into the pocket on her shoulder, she added quietly, "I'm sure you remember some of each."

Releasing the sheets of NOTAMs, he turned to her and nodded. As he focused on her and her words, he mentally tucked away the other piece of information—there were no significant NOTAMs affecting the main airport at Santiago, Chile.

Colonel Stuart stood and called to Chisholm, "We're ready to file."

The others began following him through the glass doors to the Base Operations dispatcher across the hall.

"And I do remember," Sandi said in a more seductive tone as she started walking away.

Chisholm followed her, uncertain about what she had said. "What was that?"

She hesitated until he caught up, then said quietly, "I remember exactly where we left off."

Chisholm recognized the look in her eyes and wished he could turn the clock back to last night.

28

Honolulu Center, Honolulu, Hawaii
Thursday, 1 April, 0240 local (1240 GMT)

A few miles from Hickam, Chuck Manalo fidgeted impatiently in the administrative office adjacent to the main control room of the Air Traffic Control Center. His shift as a controller had ended at midnight, but he had not gone home. Now, for the second time in the last hour, he started thumbing through a notebook that contained recent updates to procedures. He appeared to be completing a review required periodically by all controllers, but on this cycle through the notebook he was just killing time.

On the desk beside him a computer monitor showed routine data on active flight plans for aircraft on the ground at airfields under the control of Honolulu Center. The list increased when another pilot filed for a proposed flight and decreased when a pilot called for his Air Traffic Control clearance before starting engines. For the last couple of hours Manalo periodically had glanced at the monitor, looking for two specific aircraft. He had been a controller at Honolulu Center for more than thirteen years. For the last eight he had been providing special information, on request, to the KGB.

Now he looked up from the notebook and noticed a new entry for a flight plan filed at Barber's Point Naval Air Station. He picked up his nearly empty coffee cup and studied the monitor as he sipped the cold coffee. The column designating aircraft type showed C-141B/2—a flight of two C-141s. The tail number on the lead aircraft matched one of the two numbers he had memorized earlier.

Though tired, Manalo was relieved—this was the flight plan he had been looking for since the middle of his shift. The proposed departure time was two hours away, but at least the end of his wait was in sight.

He stood, tossed his coffee cup into a trash can, and decided to go to the snack bar. He needed to kill the next couple of hours without raising anyone's curiosity about why he had not gone home.

The Blackhawk helicopter swept in low at Barber's Point, then hover-taxied to a parking spot near the two C-141s. With their skins of green and brown camouflage reflecting little of the artificial light that illuminated them, the two aircraft looked more menacing than Chisholm remembered. Perhaps, he thought, it was because he had always flown them on support missions. This morning's mission had a different ambience, and the darkly camouflaged C-141s added their own special flavor.

Chief Oliverio and Sergeant Blake were standing beside the crew entry door near the front of Chisholm's C-141. As Sandi and the other two pilots went aboard, Chisholm stayed outside.

He was glad to see that Oliverio, who was wearing a flight suit again, appeared almost as he had in the old days. "That green bag doesn't look so bad, Chief. After seeing you at Scott, I was afraid you'd need a tie-down chain for a belt."

Oliverio smiled, trying to suck in his stomach. "You've ruined my whole metabolism, Colonel C. I'm down twelve pounds since your visit."

"The chief's a mere shadow of his former self," Blake added.

"I wouldn't go that far, Tony," Chisholm said, then winked, "but I did notice that the brewery stocks took a hell of a plunge last week."

Oliverio nodded and tried to appear serious. "If we don't hurry and finish this project, Colonel C., they may have their worst year in recent memory."

Your participation in this mission is finished, Chisholm thought, but he wanted to tell Oliverio privately. Instead, he said, "You're looking much better, Chief. Now let's see what goodies you two brought to paradise for me."

With both sergeants following, Chisholm climbed the ladder to the crew entrance door. Stepping inside, Chisholm felt almost as if he had never been away from flying. He stood for a moment, looking around at what had been a familiar setting for him. To his left a bulkhead marked the forward end of the cargo compartment. A waist-high ladder, which was built into the bulkhead, led up the forward compartment that was variously called the cockpit, the flight station, or the flight deck. Chisholm would end up there for takeoff, but now he was more interested in the cargo.

Everything aft of the bulkhead was the realm of the loadmaster, who often was the most junior member of the crew. Most loadmasters made their first flights only a few months after finishing high school. Nevertheless, they soon shouldered a heavy responsibility: making sure that the cargo was positioned and tied down in ways that would not make the C-141 unsafe to fly. Chisholm knew that this would be a particularly tough mission since more than twenty thousand pounds of cargo would be dropped during flight. As each missile was launched, the weight near the tail would decrease by twenty-five hundred pounds, and Sergeant Blake had to make sure that the C-141's center of gravity stayed within limits throughout the flight.

Turning right, Chisholm walked past the comfort pallet, a cubelike unit with the galley and two latrines. Next was the command-and-control module, McClain's portable room that had been added to work with the missiles.

The usable interior of the C-141 was about one hundred feet long, and most of the floor space was covered. Aft of the command-and-control module there were two rows of seats. The loadmasters and any passengers normally stayed in the cargo compartment during takeoffs and landings. In this case, Chisholm thought, Rick McClain was the only passenger, ostensibly a tech-rep accompanying the module to Guam.

A husky sergeant, who was working on the aircraft weight-and-balance form, jumped to his feet as the three men approached. Blake introduced him as Sergeant Willie Claremont, the crew's loadmaster, who ostensibly was receiving a flight check from Blake. As they went through the "How's everything going" conversation, Chisholm was impressed with the size of the boyish-faced sergeant, who was built even more powerfully than Blake.

Walking away, Chisholm said quietly to Blake, "When that youngster grows up, you'll think there's been an eclipse of the sun when he walks by."

Blake gestured toward four large shipping containers that were side by side on the floor. "You can't expect me to move around these two-thousand pounders without having a little beef to put behind them, sir."

"Understand," Chisholm said, knowing that even with the rollers built into the floor, moving the missile-laden containers would not be easy.

Each was nearly sixteen feet long and carried a single missile. The containers were marked as Explosives, Class A. When Chisholm stooped to check the shipping documents, he found the contents were identified as explosive torpedo instead of rocket motor. He had made sure that although the cargo manifest was completely phony, its fake listing included corresponding types of dangerous cargo. Although Chisholm was willing and authorized to break various rules, he did not want to jeopardize lives any more than necessary: if they crashed somewhere, he wanted the firefighters to have a warning that the cargo was dangerous.

Boxes, crates, and oxygen bottles were stacked nearly to the ceiling just aft of the four missiles.

"Looks like you've got a lot of work ahead of you and Sergeant Claremont," Chisholm said to Blake, recognizing that at least two of the missile containers would have to be moved past the stacks of cargo.

"I had to put some heavy stuff near the middle, sir," Blake said, "or we'd never have gotten the takeoff CG in limits."

"If I had expected this to be a simple mission," Chisholm said with a smile, "I wouldn't have invited you along."

Blake shrugged to show some concern. "Keeping the CG within limits near the end of the mission may get tricky. We'll have to slide the command-and-control module back a ways to compensate."

Difficult but manageable, Chisholm thought.

Oliverio, who had been listening with interest, began to nod. "You're not talking about—"

"We're not talking about anything, Chief," Chisholm interrupted, knowing that Oliverio had made the airdrop connection. "At least nothing for you to be asking about."

Oliverio glanced at Blake.

"Don't look at me, Chief," Blake said, gesturing with his hand to show he did not have all the answers. "I'm just the guy who packed the freight."

"Right," Oliverio said, obviously convinced that Blake knew more than he was saying.

Chisholm moved to the first stack of cargo and checked the shipping documents attached to one of the crates: blankets for Agana Naval Air Station. Cold-weather gear, Chisholm thought, as he pictured the list that cross-referenced the real and the dummy manifests. He glanced at Oliverio. "Did you have any problems, Chief?"

"Nothing to it, Colonel C.," Oliverio answered with a smile.

Moving beyond the two stacks of cargo, Chisholm saw the shipping containers that carried the other six missiles. More crates were on the ramp, which was part of the system of tail doors at the back of the C-141. Surveying the area, he saw nothing to indicate that the aircraft and its cargo were not destined for Guam.

"Looks good," Chisholm said to Oliverio, then asked, "Is Rick McClain around?"

"I think he's in his box," Blake said, motioning toward the command-and-control module in the forward part of the cargo compartment.

There was a door on the back wall. Chisholm knocked and asked, "Anybody home?"

There were indications of movement, then an unlatching sound. McClain opened the door and welcomed Chisholm inside.

"There's not much to see until we get the rest of the antennas and cabling connected," McClain said as he started a quick orientation.

The module included two identical work stations, each with four monitors, a printer, and a computer keyboard. There were numerous control panels. Some were for radios; others, now concealed beneath Plexiglas covers, controlled computers that would provide data to the missiles once the cables were connected. Now, however, nothing outside the module indicated that it was anything more than cargo on its way to Guam.

After his brief visit to the module, Chisholm found Oliverio and invited the chief outside.

As they walked beneath the wing of the C-141, Oliverio was the first to speak. "You're not fixing to leave me here in paradise, are you, Colonel C.?"

"You've done a great service, Chief," Chisholm said. "I wish I could take you along, but your part's finished."

"Even though you can't use me at the engineer's panel," Oliverio said, "I could come in handy if you need a good wrench-bender."

"You've got too many stripes to get your hands greasy anymore, Chief," Chisholm said, then added, "Let me have a copy of your orders."

Oliverio unzipped a pocket, pulled out several pieces of paper, and gave one to Chisholm.

"Go lose yourself in Waikiki for about thirty-six hours, Chief," Chisholm continued as he scribbled, "Authorized 48 hours delay in Hawaii," and his signature on the bottom of the orders. "I don't want to advertise to anyone that you've been bumped from the crew."

Oliverio looked over the note, then asked, "You think they'll buy this at the command post when I finally come looking for a ride home, Colonel C.?"

"Just find a duty officer named Whittaker," Chisholm said, then added with a smile, "He'll recognize my name."

Blake leaned out through the crew entry door and yelled, "Major Griffin says it's almost time to fire 'em up, Colonel."

"Right away, Tony," Chisholm said, then turned to Oliverio. As they shook hands, Chisholm said, "Tell your boss that I'll need you to come in for a debriefing when I get back to the Pentagon."

With his lopsided grin, Oliverio said, "I'm looking forward to finding out what I've done, Colonel C."

When Chisholm got to the flight deck, he found the crew already was running the Before Starting Engines checklist. Missions on the big transports were team efforts, and using checklists was how the team made sure everything was done, and done at the right time.

It had been years since Chisholm had flown on a C-141. Even though the cockpit was crammed with enough dials, gauges, controls, handles, knobs, and circuit breakers to make visitors wonder how anyone could remember what everything was, Chisholm still felt at home. Up front, just aft of the windshields and instrument panels, the two pilot seats were separated by a center instrument console.

Each pilot position was equipped with a control yoke—similar to a steering wheel with the lower part and most of the upper part cut away—rudder pedals, and a set of four throttles. The C-141 could be flown from either position. Nevertheless, the left seat was designated the pilot's seat; the right, the copilot's seat. As the aircraft commander, Major Griffin was in the pilot's seat and Major Sandi Turner occupied the seat to his right.

Captain Jon de Luca—a third pilot assigned as a flight examiner, or check pilot—sat just behind the center console on a flimsy seat called a jump seat.

Two other crew positions were behind the pilots. On the right the flight engineer's panel included monitoring gauges and controls for such things as the fuel, electrical, and pressurization systems and the auxiliary power unit. Master Sergeant Bill Jacobs, one of the crew's two flight engineers, was at the panel. He alternated duties with Technical Sergeant Jack Ingalls, who currently was acting as the scanner—the observer who made sure all the outside procedures were done correctly.

The navigator's station was behind the pilot's seat on the left side of the cockpit. This crew did not have a navigator, so Chisholm strapped into the navigator's seat and pulled on his headset.

"Colonel Stuart's about ready if you are, sir," Griffin said on the intercom.

"Roger, that," Chisholm said, then added with a look of anticipation, "Fasten your seat belts, folks, 'cause the fun's about to begin."

An hour later Rick Owens, the air traffic controller responsible for the sector southwest of Oahu, was talking to Chuck Manalo about fishing. The morning rush from Hawaii's airports was another hour or so away, but Manalo was careful not to distract Owens. Whenever Owens' attention was on an aircraft, Manalo stood quietly in the background—observing the progress of the flight of C-141s from Barber's Point. Everything appeared routine, Manalo thought, wishing that he already was home in bed. After wasting nearly five hours, he had nothing more significant to report than the departure time of the two C-141s.

As Manalo was convincing himself that he had seen enough, he noticed something unusual: the C-141s were overtaking another aircraft that was cruising at thirty-five thousand feet. He had learned long ago that the military transports flew slower than most commercial jets, so C-141s seldom overtook anyone at cruise altitude.

He saw nothing to warn Owens about since the aircraft being overtaken was four thousand feet higher. Instead Manalo moved to the side to see the data on the other aircraft—MAC 50249, another C-141. No big deal, he thought, realizing that a slightly higher headwind at thirty-five thousand could explain why the single C-141 was falling behind.

Scanning the rest of the data, he saw that 50249 was routed from Honolulu International Airport to Pago Pago. Nothing sinister about that, Manalo thought. All aircraft from Hickam used the runways at the international airport, and the airfield in American Samoa was a routine refueling stop en route to Australia. Yet the flight plan was taking the C-141 a little northwest of the normal track for Pago Pago, and this wasn't the right time or day for the weekly C-141 to Australia. Manalo also remembered the two KC-10s and the special electronics airplane that had left Hawaii for Pago Pago during his shift. Perhaps, he thought, the Air Force was doing something in American Samoa that would interest the KGB.

As Owens laughed loudly at the fish story he had been telling, Manalo chuckled, then began his own story so he could watch the radarscope for a few more minutes.

In the darkened cockpit of the single C-141, Major Easton also watched a radarscope—the one on his center instrument panel. In the lower part of the display, his aircraft was represented by a greenish-blue line at the center of six concentric circles of dots. The closest circle represented a distance of four thousand feet from his aircraft, with each successive circle being four thousand feet farther away. The only other items displayed were a small yellow circle and a small yellow square, each with a dot in the middle representing one of the other C-141s. Both were up and to the left of Easton's position. The yellow circle, which represented Colonel Stuart's C-141, was inching forward onto the third ring of dots, meaning that the lead C-141 had pulled ahead almost two nautical miles.

Easton looked out his window to check the positions of the two aircraft that had overtaken his within the last few minutes. He could see the navigation and anticollision lights of both C-141s, four thousand feet below at eleven o'clock.

Easton placed his hand on the throttles and said to his copilot, "Stand by with the transponder."

Reaching toward the back of the center console separating the pilots, the copilot grasped the switch that controlled the IFF transponder. The IFF was an electronic system designed to identify friend from foe. Though it was badly outdated for use in combat, the IFF had become an indispensable tool in air traffic control. The aircraft's black boxes would respond with coded position and altitude information whenever interrogated by ATC radars. Whenever the IFF was not working, the radars picked up only energy reflected from the surface of the aircraft.

For the next few moments Easton divided his attention between the radarscope and the flight command repeater, a small rectangular panel near the center windshield. As the circle representing Stuart's C-141 centered itself on the radarscope's third ring of dots, a tone sounded in the headsets. Simultaneously an amber arrow, with its head pointed down, lighted on the flight command repeater. The tone and arrow were in response to electronic commands sent from Stuart's C-141—it was time for Easton to descend from thirty-five thousand feet.

Easton took a deep breath—he had never before intentionally violated an air traffic control clearance as he was about to do by leaving thirty-five thousand feet. He would have felt much more comfortable if they had filed tactical flight plans that were not as specific on the actual altitudes and flight paths. Pushing those concerns aside, he pulled the outboard throttles to Idle, leaving the two inboard engines at the cruise setting to maintain pressurization during the descent. "Transponder," Easton said.

The copilot rotated a switch on the IFF and said, "To stand by."

Satisfied that the IFF would no longer respond to an interrogation by the radar at Honolulu Center, Easton clicked off the autopilot and said, "Spoilers coming out." He took hold of the handle that controlled the spoilers—the C-141's speed brakes. When he eased the handle down from the closed position, thirty-six panels rotated out from the upper and lower surfaces of the C-141's huge wings. Initially the mild vibration was hardly noticeable. However, Easton moved the handle to the flight limit, and the shaking increased to a coffee-spilling shudder.

Easton banked slightly and forced the nose down as the airspeed started decreasing. The C-141 plunged into a steep descent as Easton homed in on a position less than a half mile behind Colonel Stuart's aircraft.

If Chuck Manalo had not been watching the Samoa-bound aircraft, he would have missed the sudden failure of its IFF. That C-141 now appeared only as a faint blip—known as skin-paint—which was returning from the reflective surfaces of the aircraft. His sense of what was happening was further complicated by the nearby flight of two aircraft. Since all three aircraft were nearing the limits of the radar, it took a trained eye to pick out the skin-paint so close to the return coming from the IFF on the leader of the C-141 flight. Manalo's eyes had had years of training, and he sensed that the single aircraft had started to converge on the other two.

"Rick," Manalo said, "I think you just lost the transponder on MAC five-zero-two-four-nine."

Owens looked, then nodded. "You're sure being old eagle-eyes tonight." He promptly broadcasted, "MAC five-zero-two-four-nine, Honolulu Center. Squawk Ident."

"Two-four-nine, Ident," Chisholm said in response from his aircraft, which was not 50249.

Owens and Manalo watched to see if an enhanced electronic signal from the IFF would replace the faint blip. After waiting a few seconds, Owens said, "Two-four-nine, Center, we seem to have lost your parrot. Would you recycle, please?"

"Understand," Chisholm said. "We're behind a couple of aircraft that look to be down at about flight level three-one-zero, if that helps any."

"Roger," Owens said. "That's a flight of two, company traffic. They'll be continuing straight ahead at Choko," he added, indicating the next reporting point.

Chisholm asked, "Do you have any other traffic in our area, Honolulu?"

"Negative, Two-four-nine. You MAC guys are the only people in paradise who get up this early to fly."

"Understand," Chisholm said. He almost added the line about MAC standing for Midnight Air Command, but assumed that the controller had heard it before. Instead he asked, "Is our parrot squawking again yet?"

"Negative."

"We'll recycle a couple of times," Chisholm said. "If that doesn't fix it, Honolulu, we'll send an engineer downstairs to kick a couple of black boxes."

"Roger, Two-four-nine," Owens said. "We'll keep looking until you get to the limits of our coverage." Then he began working another aircraft that had entered his sector.

Manalo watched and listened quietly. As he studied the area near the IFF return of the flight leader, he began to pick out a faint blip of a skin-paint return. It was about the same distance behind the flight leader as the blip had been right after the IFF had failed. Manalo noticed one difference—the single aircraft was on the left of the other two instead of on the right.

For the next couple of minutes the blip continued inching back from the IFF return. Then the three C-141s reached the small symbol on the radarscope that represented the reporting point called Choko. From that time on, each sweep of the radar antenna showed the blip headed southward on the track that led toward American Samoa.

Manalo leaned against the wall and tried to interpret what he had seen. Why, he wondered, would he see such variations when comparing aircraft that already were established at cruise altitude and cruise airspeed? It was almost as if the single C-141 had gained speed in a descent then lost speed climbing again. Or— He held back a gasp that nearly escaped his lips. It could have been one descending and another climbing—he had to get to an outside telephone.

"I've done about enough damage for one night," Manalo said, forcing a yawn.

"You can't fool ol' Rick," Owens said, sending an immediate shiver through Manalo's shoulders and neck. Then Owens added with a grin, "Anytime a lazybones like you hangs around for five extra hours, he's got to be bucking for controller of the month."

"Then I suppose," Manalo said with a relieved smile, "the campaign posters I was planning to put up would probably be too obvious."

When the maneuvering finally was over, Sergeant Blake made a standard query that had been delayed by the deception. "Anyone up front ready for coffee?"

Griffin turned to Chisholm. "Is there anything else critical coming up right away, sir?"

"Negative," Chisholm said. "I need to give everyone a mission briefing, but this is a good time for a break. Loadmaster, nav seat will take a coffee, black, no sugar." Chisholm used the crew position he occupied to identify himself on intercom, which was the standard procedure on multiplace aircraft.

As the other crew members on the flight deck took turns announcing their requests, Chisholm removed the last sealed envelope from his briefcase. He did not look up a couple of minutes later when someone climbed the ladder and placed a cup of coffee on the table at the nav station.

Chief Oliverio stood for a moment beside Chisholm, then said, "I thought you always took two sugars, Colonel C."

Chisholm reached for the cup and said, "Once I got to be forty, I—" He jerked his head around and faced Oliverio. "What in the *hell* are you doing here, Chief?"

Though he had not spoken on intercom, Chisholm was loud enough to get the attention of almost everyone in the cockpit.

Oliverio looked sheepish. "April Fool, sir?"

Chisholm knew he should be angry. Part of him was, but most of him wasn't. "You can be thinking April Fool when you feel my boot on your butt as you go out the back door, Chief." He hesitated, then added, "With or without a parachute."

The worried look on Oliverio's face eased as he heard the last remark. "Colonel C., would you buy that I was having a couple of beers to celebrate doing such a good job for you and fell asleep and . . ."

"Good try, Chief, but no cigar."

29

Novikov was in the *Borzoi* control center discussing orbital data when a commotion erupted in the back of the room. He looked up and saw that several of his men near the door were standing at attention. In a moment Victor Petruk, chairman of the KGB, emerged from the group as people hurriedly stepped aside.

Novikov was startled by Petruk's unexpected visit, but disguised his apprehension well. "Good evening, Comrade Chairman. Welcome to Kaliningrad."

Petruk nodded, then said in a businesslike tone, "I have a question that we need to discuss privately."

The words sent a chill through Novikov, but he forced himself to retain a confident appearance. After all, Novikov rationalized, he had been too busy for the last several months to get into any trouble with the KGB. For an instant he thought of his impromptu celebration for the workers at Plesetsk, but he was certain that that indiscretion would not bring a visit by the chairman.

"We can use the technical library," Novikov said, motioning toward a room beyond a window.

Novikov led the way, but he could not easily push aside his four decades of fear of the secret police. As he stopped to open the door, he turned and looked back. Petruk's bodyguards had stayed behind. Perhaps the chairman's surprise visit was nothing personal, Novikov thought as he tried to will his heart rate to normal.

When the door opened, three engineers were gathered around a table studying a diagram of one of the communications modules on the *Borzoi* satellites. Each man had a look of respect when he noticed Novikov. Their expressions changed to wide-eyed fear when they recognized Petruk. All jumped to their feet simultaneously. The tallest man, a middle-aged engineer from Sverdlovsk, knocked over a cup of coffee as his legs lifted the table momentarily. He looked petrified, torn between remaining at attention and trying to stop the spreading pool of coffee.

"The chairman and I need to use the room for a few minutes."

Novikov was pleased that his voice remained steady. He was amused—the three could not have cleared out more quickly if he had yelled, Fire. As Novikov closed the door, Petruk opened a thick notebook.

"An agent in Honolulu has reported a strangeness about the flight of American C-141s that are carrying war materials to Guam."

"What kind of strangeness?" Relieved that the question had not been personal, Novikov replaced his fear with the thrill of being engaged again in the game with the Americans.

"There was a clumsy attempt at deception. There seems to have been a switch between one of those aircraft and another that was flying from Hawaii to the American colony in Samoa."

Novikov tried to remember where Samoa was. "Why would the Americans choose to send some of the materials to this new place?"

"I had hoped I could ask the questions and you, General, would have the answers." Petruk sighed and closed his book. "I have no idea why the Americans would waste time flying south from Hawaii if their real objective is to try to attack your satellites from Guam."

South, Novikov thought. Samoa must be south. "Perhaps your agent was—" Novikov stopped cold. South! He experienced a chilling sense of dread nearly matching that inspired earlier by Petruk's unexpected appearance. Novikov had known all along that Guam was the wrong place to base an attack against the *Borzoi*. Perhaps the Americans also understood. "How long ago did the airplanes leave Hawaii, and where is this colony called Samoa?"

Petruk seemed surprised by the sudden change in Novikov's reaction. The chairman's voice was more forceful as he restated his earlier question. "Why would they send some of the materials to Samoa?"

"Perhaps the Americans have decided that they need to be farther south to attack the *Borzoi*." Novikov's mind was racing ahead of the conversation. Could they? Would they? Why not? If he were trying to attack such an American constellation of satellites, he would base his forces in Antarctica. Damn! Chisholm should have reached the same conclusion—and maybe he had weeks ago! Novikov was angry that he had not played the devil's advocate more forcefully when he first had heard about the B-52 and other American forces gathering at Guam.

"Samoa is near the equator," Petruk said. "Perhaps they are preparing to attack *Zashchitnik* while the others will try to attack the *Borzoi* from Guam."

"Perhaps," Novikov said absentmindedly, thinking of an attack from closer to Antarctica. He was impatient to learn of the C-141's destination in relation to bases farther south. "Perhaps Samoa is a stepping stone to Australia or New Zealand or South America."

When Novikov added the words South America, he noticed a slight twinge in Petruk's expression. Perhaps it had been nothing, Novikov thought, but he sensed that the motion was as close as the KGB chairman ever came to flinching.

Petruk crossed his arms in front and seemed to be deep in thought. In a few moments he asked, "What would the Americans expect to do in South America?"

"They may hope to attack the *Borzoi* when the satellites are at perigee," Novikov said. He gambled that the term perigee would confuse Petruk and lead to a more balanced exchange of information. "Such an attack would require a base far to the south, in somewhere like South America."

Novikov had expected Petruk to question the word perigee, but the chairman seemed lost in his own thoughts. Why, Novikov wondered, did Petruk not take the bait and ask more about the potential American attack?

A few moments passed without a response from Petruk, so Novikov continued, "Can you tell me, Comrade Chairman, when the American aircraft left Hawaii for Samoa?"

"When?" Petruk's train of thought obviously had been interrupted. He glanced at his watch, then said, "About two hours ago."

Novikov decided to be direct. "Is there anything I should know about South America, Comrade Chairman?"

"You know all that you need to know, General," Petruk said brusquely as he pushed his notebook into his pocket and went to the door.

Novikov hesitated, but knew he had to ask. "Would you indulge me one more question, Comrade Chairman?"

Petruk stopped, looked impatiently at Novikov, then nodded.

"Do your agents know if Colonel Chisholm was on the C-141 that has turned away from Guam?"

"Is that important?"

"He is an expert in C-141s, and he understands my satellites."

Petruk's eyes darted down to the doorknob, then back to Novikov. "He is on that airplane."

Everyone jumped to his feet as Petruk emerged from the technical library and joined his bodyguards.

The three KGB men had almost reached the exit from the *Borzoi* control center when Novikov called out, "Come back any time, Comrade Chairman."

Several men near Novikov looked astonished. Petruk nodded over his shoulder toward Novikov, then disappeared through the door. For the next few moments the only sound in the room was the buzz and hum of the computers.

Novikov called out loudly, "I order everyone to start breathing again." Amid nervous laughter, Novikov slapped a couple of people on the shoulder, then hurried away to find an atlas.

With the C-141 headed south toward American Samoa and with all ten people crowded together on the flight station, Chisholm was ready to give his briefing. He picked up the small American flag, which he had removed from the biplane in his office, and slowly rotated the flag staff between his thumb and forefinger. "I'm not going discuss Mom and apple pie, but I am going to talk about the American flag. This one's logged more miles than most of you." He moved it around making sure everyone had a look. "It flew aboard a space shuttle for nearly a hundred orbits around the earth. What we do in the next couple of days may determine whether any more of these go into space without having an 'approved by the USSR' hammer and sickle stamped on them first."

Chisholm looked around at the faces he could see. Only Rick McClain smiled at the poetic license Chisholm had taken. The rest of the crew seemed surprised, curious to learn more.

Handing Griffin a piece of paper, Chisholm said, "Here's the flight plan for the first leg, which calls for a turn toward South America in about ten minutes."

"South America?" Griffin and Sandi said the words at the same time. Griffin continued, "That's got to be twelve or fourteen hours from here. We're only carrying fuel for an eight-hour flight to Guam."

"Total flight time on this first leg is about fifteen hours," Chisholm said. "In about five hours, you'll rendezvous with King zero-one, a tanker out of American Samoa." Chisholm briefly outlined the mission, stressing throughout the need to maintain security over the radios and during the refueling stop in Santiago.

Griffin looked warily at the flight plan, then asked, "Who's this filed with, sir? I mean, having us wandering around crossing airways without anyone knowing we're out here could be dangerous."

"One person at FAA headquarters in Washington has a copy and knows our crossing time at Choko. He's looking for conflicts with other aircraft and will take care of any he discovers. There's not much cross-traffic anyway, and once we pass the airways between Los Angeles or Mexico City and the south Pacific, we're on a route where no one flies."

Griffin seemed satisfied, so Chisholm pulled more papers from his briefcase and handed Griffin a copy of the waiver signed by General Gillette. "This gives us the authority to waive any MAC regulation that would prevent the accomplishment of the mission." Chisholm used the word *us* to emphasize that they were working as a team. However, there was no question in his mind that he, not the aircraft commander, would make the final decisions. "The first one we're waiving is the limitation on crew-duty day. We're going to fly for as long as it takes to get eight good shots off."

Griffin looked up from the waiver. "How many hours are you talking about, Colonel?"

Chisholm shrugged. "The leg out of Santiago should take thirty, maybe thirty-five more hours, depending on where we land."

Only McClain did not look surprised. Griffin asked, "How liberally are you planning to waiver other safety-of-flight considerations?"

"Obviously a crash isn't in the interests of mission accomplishment," Chisholm said, realizing that his words sounded more bureaucratic than he intended. "We won't be reckless, but we'll take risks when risks seem appropriate."

Griffin nodded noncommittally as he handed the waiver to Sandi.

"Although the cargo manifests say otherwise," Chisholm said, "everything in back is for this mission. This manifest tells what's really in the crates. Use it for cross-reference, and if there's any confusion, ask our stowaway to straighten it out."

Handing the new manifest to Blake, Chisholm faked a stern look in Oliverio's direction. The chief tried to look appropriately contrite.

Chisholm continued, "Before we reach Santiago, everyone should get fitted with a set of cold-weather gear because it'll be bitter in here every time we depressurize. One of the large crates has a false front covering a set of storage containers. Select your gear, then hide it away so that when we land in Santiago, nothing's in the open that will give away our next destination." Glancing around, Chisholm saw that no one seemed confused. "The cargo includes some special parachutes and a paratroop kit. While you're wearing your cold-weather gear, fit a parachute over it." Crew members on airdrop missions normally inspected a parachute and adjusted all the straps before takeoff so that the parachute could be used immediately in an emergency. "After we depart Santiago, Sergeants Blake and Claremont will complete the installation of the paratroop kit."

The final instruction produced several questioning looks. The kit included hardware needed when as many as 155 paratroopers would jump from a C-141.

Griffin asked, "This mission doesn't have anything to do with paratroopers, does it?"

"No," Chisholm said, glancing at Griffin, then fixing his gaze on Sandi, "but the mission may have something to do with air combat. These chutes are equipped for a barometric release, so if we have to abandon the aircraft at high altitude, I prefer to have us on the static lines."

By hooking a static line between one of the release mechanisms on a parachute and a cable in the aircraft, the parachute canopy would deploy automatically. If the static line activated the barometric release, the parachute would not open until reaching fourteen thousand feet. Thus, the slower part of the descent would occur where there was enough oxygen to keep the person conscious. If the aircraft were being abandoned during a low altitude emergency, the static line would be attached to the D-ring, and the parachute would start deploying immediately after the jumper cleared the aircraft.

Everyone looked somber, so Chisholm said, "I didn't come all this way for a parachute jump. Some of the other crates contain chaff and flares in case there's been a breakdown in security."

The chaff and flares, commonly referred to as countermeasures, were to counter the radar-guided missiles and the heat-seeking missiles carried by enemy fighters. Chaff was bundles of aluminum-foil-like strips. The strips had been cut to specific lengths to send confusing returns back to fire-control radars. The flares, which shined with an eye-threatening brilliance, were designed to float beneath small parachutes. The purpose of the flares was to attract those missiles whose infrared seekers homed on the hot exhaust of an aircraft engine. Countermeasures had been part of the natural evolution as aerial warfare moved into the missile age. Unfortunately, Chisholm thought as he considered the effectiveness of his makeshift defenses, the Russians had had nearly three decades' worth of experience in developing counter-countermeasures.

"We'll keep them hidden until after we leave Santiago," Chisholm said, "but then I want every engineer and loadmaster to learn how to kick out the chaff and flares in a hurry." He scanned his list of items. "There's extra food, bedding, oxygen bottles, and long intercom cords for roaming around within the aircraft. What else?"

"The antennas," McClain said.

"Right," Chisholm said. "On the ground at Santiago we need to hook up a couple of antennas. One lets us talk long-range and secure through communication satellites. Unfortunately, we'll be flying in a region without one hundred percent coverage. The other antenna lets us receive data from the ARIA that will be working with us. The antennas are in crates along with tools and instructions."

Oliverio asked, "How about the weapons, Colonel C.?"

Chisholm nodded. "We have a dozen M-sixteen rifles and some nine-millimeter pistols. If an emergency forces an unplanned landing, we'll serve as our own security force until some decisions are made."

"I just hope it'll be our people making those decisions, Colonel C. A few M-sixteens ain't going to hold off much of a crowd for very long."

"Agreed," Chisholm said. Seeing nothing else to discuss on the cargo list, he continued, "Use this leg to get as much rest as possible. There will be a few more easy hours right after takeoff from Santiago, then we'll be depressurizing every couple of hours."

Blake shrugged. "No one's going to get much rest during that part of the mission."

Chisholm nodded, glanced at his watch, then said, "It's just about time to turn toward Santiago."

Using a rubber band, Chisholm attached the small flag staff to a knob on the navigator's panel. Then he followed McClain downstairs to the command-and-control module to start refining the targeting timetables. The other crew members started setting up work/rest schedules.

A few minutes later Sandi climbed down from the flight deck and saw Oliverio fixing coffee at the galley.

"Chief, I'm not sure what kind of magic you have with the colonel," Sandi said, "but I half expected him to convene a court-martial when you showed up a while ago on the flight deck."

Oliverio gave her a lopsided grin. "Maybe Colonel Chisholm is part Chinese, sir."

Sandi gave him a quizzical look.

"The Chinese believe you're responsible for someone after you save his life. Colonel C. and I go back a long way, Major." He paused, then added, "Even longer than you and he go back."

She shrugged. "Your name came up a few times, Chief, but he never mentioned saving your life."

"Actually, I'd about killed him first," Oliverio said with an embarrassed smile, "so I don't suppose either of us do much bragging about it. He never told you about that wild landing we survived at Altus?"

"Never, Chief," she said, her expression showing obvious interest.

Oliverio leaned against the galley and took a sip of coffee. "He was a captain then, on loan to the training school as an instructor pilot, and I was a shiny, young maintenance man trying to become a flight engineer. I had a few other things on my mind and screwed up the fuel panel. All that did was shut down two engines."

"Two?" Sandi's eyes widened. "I hope you weren't close to the ground."

"I left him with maybe four hundred feet," Oliverio said with a sarcastic smile. "We were in the base turn on a landing pattern."

"Great timing, Chief," Sandi said, matching his sarcasm.

"Colonel C. managed to keep us out of that red Oklahoma dirt," Oliverio said, "but when he pulled off onto the taxiway, it wasn't any court-martial on the flight deck. I thought we were going to have a lynching."

Sandi laughed. "He does have a touch of temper when he's provoked, but now I'm even more confused about this bond the two of you seem to share."

"I already had a pretty good string of screwups at the school. So when we finished the flight, I figured it was washout time for me, and I was destined to drag a toolbox around for the rest of my career." Oliverio paused and took another sip of coffee as his expression became more serious. "Later that evening he happened to see a note that my wife had called from Wilford Hall. When he learned that she was in San Antonio with our son in a cancer ward, Colonel C. decided I should be in Texas instead of screwing up airplanes in Oklahoma."

"That sounds more like him."

Oliverio nodded. "I'd been scheduled to go to his squadron in California, so he made a few phone calls, sent me to be with my son, and got me back into engineer's school during one of the remissions."

"Did your son—"

Oliverio shook his head. "Colonel C. was one of the pallbearers." Oliverio dumped out his remaining coffee, cleared his throat, then took on a more mischievous expression. "Colonel C. promised that I could be one of the sword bearers at your wedding, Major, and I'm still waiting."

Sandi forced a smile, then said, "I think we were both disappointed that that was a promise he couldn't keep."

At that moment Sergeant Blake called from farther back in the cargo compartment. "Chief, we need to get into some of these crates. You want to help us find all the things you've hidden?"

"Right away, Tony," Oliverio said, then turned to Sandi. "I've still got my sword all shined up, Major, in case you two ever decide to make good on that promise."

She smiled. "I'll remember that, Chief."

Novikov carried the atlas into Flight Control and went immediately to the console for the radar on *Zashchitnik I*. Displaying a page showing the Pacific ocean, Novikov pointed and said, "I want a search for aircraft along a line between Hawaii and American Samoa. Start five hundred miles south of Hawaii and search for one hundred miles either side of that line."

While waiting for the results, Novikov studied other maps in the atlas, trying to determine how credible an attack in the south might be. In a few minutes he started feeling better, having concluded that the gods of geography and orbital mechanics had smiled upon him. His requirement to cover the northern hemisphere had forced a choice of orbits that, quite serendipitously, had put their only vulnerable segment over one of the most remote and inhospitable regions of the earth. Yet, he thought with a sigh, Chisholm had to understand geography—he had logged enough hours flying to remote places in the world—and the American adversary did not seem deterred.

Novikov's thoughts were interrupted when the radar controller reported, "There is one target, Comrade General. It's nine hundred seventy miles south of Hawaii."

The distance was about right, Novikov thought. "Its direction of flight?"

"Northeast, sir."

"It's flying toward Hawaii?"

"Yes, sir."

"Search once more," Novikov said, "and verify that that aircraft continues northward."

Novikov settled into a chair and put his feet on a desk. He opened the atlas to a map of the world. As he looked at South America, he thought about the chairman's evasiveness. Novikov was convinced that Petruk had held something back—and that something had to do with South America.

Minutes later the radar controller reported the same results as before, except that the one plane had moved fifty miles closer to Hawaii. Novikov drew a line between Hawaii and the westernmost point on South America. "Give me another search beginning on this line at five hundred miles from Hawaii. Cover a width out to one hundred miles north of the line and three hundred miles south."

While the radar controller estimated the geographical coordinates for the search, Novikov wondered if he was wasting time and effort. There could be scores of aircraft over the vast expanse of water separating Hawaii and South America. He wondered if an aircraft such as the American C-141 could fly that distance.

Novikov told an aide to locate information on C-141s, then went to a globe that was on a stand in a front corner of the room. After having someone bring him a long piece of string, he used a trick learned years earlier for estimating distances on a global scale. Holding one end over the Hawaiian Islands, he stretched the string across the surface of the globe. He took hold of the string where it touched the westernmost point of South America. The length of string between his hands was a measure of the distance he wanted to estimate.

Holding the string tightly, he lifted it temporarily from the globe, then placed one end of the string on the equator. Extending his other hand toward the north pole, he found he could reach seventy-five degrees north, and he knew that each degree north from the equator represented sixty nautical miles. Multiplying sixty times seventy-five, Novikov concluded that a flight from Hawaii to South America would be at least forty-five hundred nautical miles, or more than five thousand statute miles.

As he returned to the radar controller's console, Novikov considered the implications. Long-range jet transports could cover that distance, although they would have to fly somewhat farther to reach an airfield. He figured that a C-141 would require at least eight hours to reach South America. He was relieved that he had a few hours to develop a counterstrategy, if indeed Petruk had some other intelligence about a mission to South America.

"There are four targets, Comrade General," the radar controller said.

"Show me," Novikov said leaning over the controller's shoulder.

The computer screen was blank except for faint reference lines of latitude and longitude and returns from four aircraft. Three bright blips were in the lower right third of the monitor, and one was nearer the left edge.

The controller said, "These three aircraft appear to be flying between America and Australia or New Zealand. Two are headed northeast and the other southwest." The controller pointed toward the single blip and continued, "This target is flying toward South America, almost parallel to the line you drew."

"What's its speed?"

"The radar estimates a groundspeed of about four hundred thirty knots."

Novikov nodded. If that blip was the C-141, it would need more than ten hours to cover the forty-five hundred nautical miles. He was pleased to have gained two more hours over his previous estimate, but his sense of dread was growing—the Americans might be mounting a real threat to the *Borzoi*.

Novikov wrote the coordinates, then turned to the controller. "Track it!"

"Yes, sir!"

There was one more check to make before he decided to sound

the alarm. Combining the coordinates of the blip with the string and the globe, he found that the unidentified aircraft was nearly a thousand miles from Hawaii. That distance could be covered in about two hours and twenty minutes cruising at 430 knots. Novikov looked at a clock on the front wall. It was 2015, so the C-141 had left Hawaii almost three hours ago. Taking into account the climb to cruise altitude, Novikov concluded, the blip could be the C-141, and it certainly wasn't headed for the American colony in Samoa.

Novikov went into the VIP suite and dialed the secure telephone. When a sergeant answered, Novikov asked for Marshal Murashev, though there was little reason to expect him still to be in his office.

"He is not available this evening, Comrade General. Can someone else help you?"

That was the standard answer whenever the marshal had had too much to drink or had left instructions not to be bothered at home. That was also the answer Novikov had hoped for. There was no time to waste with Murashev, but Novikov had been obliged to make the effort. "No, Sergeant. I will handle it another way."

Novikov dialed the number for the office of Minister of Defense Levchenko. The call was automatically transferred to the command post deep beneath the ministry.

"I must talk to Minister Levchenko on a matter of grave urgency," Novikov said to the duty officer. When the man at the other end of the line seemed hesitant, Novikov added, "Check your list. The minister will accept my call."

Ten minutes passed before the call was transferred and Levchenko answered on a secure telephone in his residence. "Have we finally prodded the Americans into action, Petr?"

"Yes, Comrade Minister. I believe we have."

Novikov told of the encounter with Chairman Petruk and of the mysterious flight of the American C-141. Levchenko interrupted intermittently to curse Petruk's scheming but asked no questions until Novikov finished.

"Can the Americans hurt us, Petr?"

"I don't know, Comrade Minister. The Americans are trying very hard to hide that C-141 from us, so what it carries must be very precious."

"Perhaps it is carrying communications equipment to establish a support base."

"Perhaps," Novikov said, "but if Chairman Petruk can connect the C-141 with a planned attack against the *Borzoi*, I recommend that you order the American aircraft destroyed."

There was a long pause. "That may be a hard order to execute, unless your *Borzoi* can reach into the atmosphere."

"I'm afraid not, Com—" Novikov stopped, realizing he was about to answer before considering all the possibilities. "It would be a difficult challenge, Comrade Minister, but if necessary, we could try."

His mind already was racing. Some instincts said yes; others were more cautious. He began scanning the screens to see where the *Borzoi* were. By chance, *Borzoi IV* was passing about halfway between Hawaii and the unidentified aircraft.

"We will hope that does not become necessary, Petr."

"If we were to try," Novikov said, "the next few hours may be the best chance. The airplane is over a very remote stretch of the ocean and—"

"Don't get too anxious, Petr. For all you know, you may be watching an aircraft that's carrying only pineapples to South America."

Novikov conceded that Levchenko was right about the lack of positive identification. That was one reason that the *Borzoi* had not been designed as a weapon to be used against aircraft. "Perhaps Chairman Petruk will be able to verify the target, especially if he has some intelligence on the C-141's destination."

"I must make some calls," Levchenko said.

"I was hesitant to press Chairman Petruk too hard, Comrade Minister, but it is important that his information about threats to *Krasnaya Molniya* be shared with me."

"I shall try to convince him to share that information with me," Levchenko said, then added, "and I shall not reveal that the suggestion came from you."

"Thank you, Comrade Minister." Novikov wanted to avoid Petruk's wrath, but if the Americans were mounting a real threat to the *Borzoi* and the chairman withheld intelligence on that threat, everyone could lose. "I cannot counter such threats if I do not know about them."

"The president and I depend heavily upon you, Petr. We will keep you informed."

Levchenko replaced the receiver into its cradle and slumped back in his chair. It was sufficiently bad that the Americans were doing something dangerous enough to worry General Novikov. But if Viktor

Petruk were meddling, the situation was even worse. Levchenko picked up the telephone and dialed the number for President Grigoriev's residence. Levchenko was determined to get to the president before the KGB chairman did. Perhaps Grigoriev also was aware of the piece of intelligence that Petruk was guarding so closely.

When the president got on the line, Levchenko said, "General Novikov is starting to see some interesting reactions from the Americans. I thought you would want to hear of them, Comrade President."

"Of course, Aleksei," Grigoriev said. "Chairman Petruk has been sitting here telling me some fascinating things. Come join us and tell me your opinions."

"Right away, Comrade President," Levchenko said without letting the grimace on his face show through in his voice.

A few minutes later Levchenko was ushered into Grigoriev's study to join the other two men.

As a servant prepared brandy for the minister, Grigoriev said, "Viktor tells me we may have a serious problem with *Krasnaya Molniya*."

Petruk smugly sipped his coffee as he studied the minister of defense for his reaction.

Levchenko wondered what Petruk knew and what he had told the president. The minister tried to act more composed than he felt as he took the brandy. "We expected an American response. Now that we have seen it, we will let them play into our hands." He raised the brandy, but only let the flavorful liquid touch his lips. Petruk already had enough of an advantage, Levchenko thought.

"It seems to me, Comrade Minister," Petruk said, becoming more mocking as he continued, "that you have failed to see the Americans slipping through your fingers. Perhaps the threat to the *Borzoi* is because you play into the hands of the Americans."

Levchenko bristled, but held his anger back. "What real threat can they be to the *Borzoi?*" He knew that Novikov did not have a definite answer to that question, so it was unlikely that Petruk did—unless the KGB chairman had new information from a highly placed source.

Petruk shot back, "You discount the danger of the American mission to South America?"

Levchenko raised the brandy, took a small sip, then spoke as casually as he could. "*Zashchitnik I* is tracking the American C-141 flying from Hawaii to South America." He paused, pleased by the surprised looks on the faces of his two companions. "Would you like me to inform you when and where the aircraft lands, Chairman Petruk?"

"I have already told the president where the airplane will land," Petruk said, reddening at having been upstaged. "Any schoolboy could compute an estimate of the landing time."

Levchenko started to respond but deferred at the sound of Grigoriev clearing his throat.

"Since we all seem to know that the Americans are secretly flying to South America," Grigoriev said, "Santiago, Chile, to be precise, what do we do about it?"

Levchenko was pleased that he had learned that piece of information without having to be deferential to Petruk.

"If the minister is convinced his satellites are invulnerable," Petruk said, "perhaps nothing needs to be done. Why interrupt an American plan that cannot succeed?"

Levchenko shrugged. "I am confident of the *Borzoi's* safety. I rely, of course, on the chairman's annual reports that consistently assure us that the Americans have no antisatellite capability." Levchenko took a small sip of brandy. "If, Comrade Chairman, you've come this evening to confess the inaccuracy of your reports, I would feel less confident."

Petruk stiffened. "I have not, Comrade Minister! The reports—"

"Perhaps," Grigoriev interrupted, "the Americans have been as successful in hiding the continued development of an antisatellite missile as we were in hiding *Zashchitnik* and the *Borzoi.*"

"If there were even the slightest possibility of such a secret ASAT," Levchenko said in a more conciliatory tone, "then I recommend that the C-141 be destroyed in an appropriate way."

Grigoriev nodded. "And what way would you suggest?"

"There are many anti-imperialists from Mexico on south who would like to deal a blow to the *Yanquis.*"

Petruk responded in a chiding tone. "You would risk the billions of rubles of *Krasnaya Molniya* on—"

"We will put the responsibility for success into hands that we know," Grigoriev said. "Chairman Petruk has suggested that we may already have the right leader for the mission exactly where we need him." He turned to Petruk and waited for the chairman to continue the explanation.

"Lyashko," Petruk said as he opened his notebook. "KGB *Mayor* Andrei Lyashko traveled for several years as a javelin thrower on the national team. He had three years of combat in Afghanistan, being wounded there in 1988. Lyashko currently is assigned under cover as a clerk in the Romanian Embassy in Santiago, Chile."

"And," Grigoriev added, addressing Levchenko, "you should find him favorable because he trained originally in your own *Spetsnaz.*"

Levchenko nodded. A member of the Special Forces would be his choice to head such a team, if he were putting the team together. However, this would be Petruk's team—and Levchenko did not want to spend the months ahead being reminded of how the KGB had saved *Krasnaya Molniya.* "Before my recommendations were interrupted by Chairman Petruk, I was about to suggest that our allies would offer landing fields and aircraft. These would permit Soviet pilots to cause the American aircraft to disappear where it wouldn't be found."

Grigoriev appeared interested. "Where would that be?"

"The aircraft's ultimate destination must be Antarctica," Levchenko said as if that answer had never been in question, "and General Novikov assures me that it would not attack before getting there. The waters off Antarctica are even less hospitable than our northern seas, so an aircraft easily could disappear there."

Petruk responded, "I believe—"

"I believe," Grigoriev interrupted, "that it is time for both of you to put your people to work. Viktor, you will direct a clandestine attack on the ground at Santiago. It should appear to be an attack by revolutionaries against government targets." Grigoriev paused until Petruk nodded curtly. "Aleksei, you will find planes and pilots, and you will get them into a position to destroy the aircraft in a suitable way, as you said earlier."

"Yes, Comrade President."

"And," Grigoriev continued, "that suitable way should not connect the loss of the aircraft to this room." He paused, then added, "But if Petr Novikov believes the aircraft must be destroyed, destroy it. We will worry later about explanations."

"Yes, Comrade President," Levchenko repeated.

"And, Viktor, your people will do everything possible to assist the ministry of defense."

"Of course, Comrade President."

"Both of you will make sure that petty infighting does not cause us to lose the advantage we have over the Americans." He stood, signaling that the meeting had come to an end. "If you allow bickering to continue, I assure you that there will be no winner."

30

Augusto Cesar Sandino International Airport
Managua, Nicaragua
Thursday, 1 April, 1347 local (1947 GMT)

The weather was insufferably hot and muggy. *Podpolkovnik* (Lieutenant Colonel) Gennadi Berezin crouched with his back against a maintenance building as the sun slipped behind a line of clouds. The air moved sluggishly off the waters of Lake Managua to the north and did little to relieve the press of humidity. Instead the breeze carried the stench of raw sewage. Berezin hated the smell. He disliked many things about his assignment to Nicaragua, but he hated that smell and the heat most of all. He longed to be home in Russia. He missed waking to the crisp cold of an April morning in Kiev instead of the eighty degrees and eighty percent humidity of the Russian compound in Managua.

Berezin was killing time—again—on the parking ramp for military aircraft at the international airport. He was scheduled to take off in ten minutes. At the moment, however, the engine on his Hind-D was missing a few parts, which were scattered in the dust on the steel matting beneath the helicopter.

Sandinista maintenance of the Hind-Ds was another thing Berezin hated about this assignment. Five or six days a week he flew as an "adviser" in the powerful helicopters, which the Soviet government had supplied to the Sandinistas. On three or four of those days— sometimes on all six—there were delays because his helicopter, or his wing man's, was not fit to fly.

Berezin had had mixed feelings when he had left Russia fourteen months earlier. Leaving behind the first-class fighters he had flown for ten years was a disappointment. However, he had been enthusiastic about helping an oppressed people protect themselves from the evils of the capitalists, especially when those people were almost on the doorstep of the United States.

Now as he chewed on a piece of sugar cane, he still missed flying well-maintained fighters, but his idealism was gone—melted away in the Nicaraguan heat. He had grown to dislike the Sandinistas, whom he considered lazy, unmotivated, and undisciplined. He was certain the dislike was mutual. Listening to his sergeant arguing with the other maintenance men, Berezin was indifferent as to whether they repaired the helicopter or not. The combat missions against the disorganized bandits who opposed the government offered little challenge or results, and he expected this afternoon's mission to be as unproductive as the rest. If the men could not fix the helicopter within the next several hours, he wished they would hurry up and reach that conclusion. He was ready to return to the compound, away from the heat that was reflected and intensified by the steel matting.

In the distance Berezin saw a rusty jeep approaching along a taxiway. He recognized the vehicle as the one belonging to the detachment of Russian fliers, and the driver was in a hurry. Berezin stood as the jeep jerked to a stop near the helicopter. *Kapitan* (Captain) Vasily Pokrovskiy was the driver who jumped from the jeep.

As soon as Pokrovskiy saw Berezin walking toward the helicopter, Pokrovskiy rushed toward him. The kapitan saluted, then said, "Comrade Podpolkovnik, your flight has been canceled. We are to return to the compound immediately for new orders."

The cancellation pleased Berezin, but he was surprised that the decision had been made by someone unaware of the condition of the helicopter. He was also curious about the mention of a new mission. Walking to the jeep, Berezin asked, "Why the change?"

"I don't know, sir, but everyone's excited."

As the jeep bumped along the road between the airport and the Russian compound, Berezin wondered what had happened. He knew that the Americans were making irresponsible threats because of recent Soviet achievements in space. If there were going to be provocations against Soviet interests in the western hemisphere, Berezin assumed the American threats would come against Cuba. "Perhaps we are going to Cuba, Pokrovskiy," Berezin said as he braced his feet against the floorboard to stay seated in the bouncing jeep.

"Is Cuba better than here, sir?"

"Of course," Berezin said. After a short pause, he added, "It has to be."

When Berezin and Pokrovskiy reached the Russian headquarters, they were sent to the inner compound. That area normally was restricted to officials of the KGB and to the senior members of the diplomatic mission to Nicaragua. The activity inside the communications center surprised Berezin. Every senior Russian official in Nicaragua was in the room. He recognized Ambassador Markelov seated behind a desk cluttered with pages ripped from the teletype machines. Markelov had tossed his suit coat aside in a futile effort to keep cool in the stuffy, overcrowded room. Beads of sweat glistened through the sparse strands of hair combed across the barren crown of his head.

Berezin routinely attended meetings with Markelov at least twice a month, serving as the ambassador's main adviser on tactics that involved aircraft.

Markelov noticed Berezin and called him over. "Podpolkovnik Berezin, you are to lead a very important mission."

"To Cuba, Comrade Ambassador?" Berezin wanted to show he had already been thinking about the upcoming mission.

Markelov looked surprised, then said, "To Peru. You will take four MiG-25s. In Peru you will receive additional orders."

Berezin was confused. He was not certain where Peru was, but he thought it was south, away from the United States. Even at his rank he was seldom shown more of a map than was necessary for the mission at hand. Such precautions might stymie defectors, Berezin thought, but provided poor preparation for missions to distant countries. He could not imagine why a flight of MiG-25s would be needed in Peru and why a mission away from the United States would cause so much excitement.

"I will need maps, sir. When do we take off?"

"Maps will be available. Right now we are arranging for the MiGs. Once we make the agreement, they must be armed and configured for long-range flight. You will leave as soon as the planes are ready, sometime before midnight."

The mention of armament increased Berezin's interest. The MiG-25s had been designed in the 1960s to shoot down the American B-70 bomber. Although the B-70 was never produced, Berezin considered the supersonic MiG-25s to have been the best in the world in their time. Their top speed was over two thousand miles per hour, and two decades earlier a MiG-25 had set a record by climbing to over 118,000 feet. A MiG-25 in the hands of a good pilot—and Berezin considered himself one of the best—was still a formidable fighter. If he were going against American pilots, however, he would rather have the maneuverability of a MiG-31, like those he had flown on his last assignment. A 1980s aircraft, the MiG-31 had better armament, fire-control systems, and range than the older MiG-25.

As Berezin continued trying to imagine the upcoming mission, he was curious about who would control his flight of MiGs once they got to Peru. In Russia the ground controllers always guided the MiGs toward their targets. He wondered if there were any Russian controllers stationed in Peru.

He also wondered about the airplanes. He knew of eighteen MiG-25s parked in locked hangars and warehouses. Ostensibly they belonged to the Nicaraguans and were maintained by Nicaraguans. However, the MiGs were flown only periodically at night by the Soviet pilots. Berezin suspected that the real purpose of the MiGs was to provide air cover in contingency plans for attacking the Panama Canal from Cuba. Now he was concerned whether or not the planes would fly well on a real mission after sitting so long. Like humans, Berezin thought, airplanes needed to be exercised. These MiGs had not gotten much exercise while he had been in Nicaragua.

Berezin asked, "We'll be using the local MiG-25s?"

"Yes." Before Berezin could ask the obvious question, Markelov added, "They will be checked over well by Russian mechanics."

"Perhaps there are MiG-29s or MiG-31s in Cuba," Berezin said.

He assumed that since secret MiG-25s were in Nicaragua, something better was hidden in Cuba. Almost as soon as he asked, however, he cursed himself for raising the subject. If Markelov decided to use Cuban MiGs, he might also use Soviet pilots stationed in Cuba— leaving Berezin mired in Nicaragua as he had been before the sudden excitement.

"There's not enough time."

Berezin nodded, relieved that he had not talked himself out of the job. "Who will fly the other three MiGs, Comrade Ambassador?"

Markelov searched through the papers on the desk until he found one with four names scrawled in pencil. "These are the men assigned to your flight."

Berezin looked at the paper, then read the other names aloud. "Kapitan Kovalev, Leytenant Yashin, and . . . Kapitan Pokrovskiy."

He looked toward Pokrovskiy, who was standing close enough to hear the conversation. The kapitan seemed pleased, and that pleased Berezin. Of the three, Pokrovskiy clearly was the best—aggressive, quickminded, obedient—and Berezin was glad the young kapitan was on the list.

Berezin turned to Ambassador Markelov. "Will there be more information before we leave for Peru?"

"We know few details. I do know your mission has the personal interest of President Grigoriev." Markelov paused as if thinking of adding more. "I suggest you and the other pilots try to sleep now. You may not sleep again for quite some time."

"Yes, Comrade Ambassador," Berezin said.

Sleep would come easier, Berezin thought, if there had been no mention of the personal interest of President Grigoriev. Perhaps, Berezin thought, the mission was important enough to earn an advancement to a better assignment in Russia.

Someone else needed the ambassador's attention, so Berezin moved toward the door.

Pokrovskiy walked beside Berezin and asked, "Is Peru in Cuba?"

"No," Berezin said. He was tempted to add, "I don't think so," but instead spotted a faded map tacked to a wall. He gestured toward the map and said, "You show me."

The discolored map was of the western hemisphere. Berezin had not seen such a map during his entire tour in Nicaragua. He needed a moment to get oriented, finally locating Nicaragua in the narrow strip of land connecting North and South America.

Pointing, Berezin said, "You know we are here?"

Pokrovskiy studied the area near Berezin's finger, then said, "Yes, Comrade Berezin. A moment, please. I have not seen such a map since training at the academy."

Pokrovskiy seemed fascinated by the map.

Berezin was beginning to remember that Peru was a country in South America where many Soviet advisers were assigned. Studying the map, he spotted Peru on the west coast. He was pleased to have found Peru before having to acknowledge his uncertainty to Pokrovskiy. However, Berezin was immediately concerned—Peru looked to be hundreds of miles from Managua, and much of that distance was over the waters of the Pacific Ocean. In more than eighteen years of service, Berezin had never flown a mission like that. He had felt a growing sense of adventure since learning of the new mission.

Now the excitement was tempered by a twinge of self-doubt at being so ill prepared.

"Well, Comrade Pokrovskiy?"

The kapitan shrugged, so Berezin pointed toward Peru.

Pokrovskiy looked surprised. "How will we fly our MiGs all the way down there?"

"For you it will be easy," Berezin said, smiling as he turned for the door. "Just follow the lights of my MiG."

He was pleased that Pokrovskiy had the sense not to ask how the lead MiG would find its way. Berezin did not have a good answer to that question.

After leaving the communications center, he told Kapitan Kovalev and Leytenant Yashin of the mission. Before going to bed, Berezin packed some clothes and a few personal items in a canvas bag.

Now he lay on sweat-soaked sheets as he watched the overhead fan squeak slowly through each revolution. For twenty minutes he had tried to fall asleep in spite of the midafternoon heat that blanketed the Russian compound. Too many thoughts competed for his attention. Two months had passed since his last proficiency flight in a MiG. He doubted that the three younger pilots were any better prepared. Berezin decided that he would lead the first element with Kovalev as wing man. Pokrovskiy would be the second element leader with Yashin on the wing.

Although confident in his skills as a fighter pilot, Berezin still worried about his lack of experience in long-range, overwater navigation. He kept trying to imagine how he would lead the flight of MiGs to Peru—and beyond.

Loud laughter came from a room down the hall. The evening card game had started early. Berezin was a regular participant except on the evenings when he was flying. Perhaps if he joined them for a few hands of cards and a couple of drinks, he could get relaxed enough to fall asleep. He smiled as he rolled onto his side. If he joined the game, he would still be playing when someone came to tell him the aircraft were ready.

In the muted light Berezin could see the picture of his wife and son on the table beside the bed. He missed the twelve-year-old boy, Stepan. Even at Berezin's rank, he was not permitted to take all of his immediate family on an assignment outside Russia. Someone was always kept back to counterbalance thoughts of giving in to the temptations of the capitalist regimes. Since either his wife or son had to stay behind, Berezin had chosen to leave both. As time passed, he wished he had brought Stepan. Berezin's marriage had been one of convenience, though not without some rewards. His son was the most worthwhile result of the marriage. If Stepan had come to Nicaragua, Berezin was sure his son already would have learned to appreciate Russia even more.

But tonight it was good that Stepan was home, Berezin thought as he rolled again to stare at the dirty ceiling and dusty fan. Another outbreak of noise made him think of the card game. Seldom did he have trouble falling asleep, especially after playing cards. But then, seldom was he totally sober when he collapsed on his bed at whatever hour.

As Berezin lay studying the fan, he decided that he was too sober to sleep. And the mission depended upon getting some sleep, he rationalized as he got up and found a bottle of vodka. He filled a shot glass, then tried to find something to eat. A soft tortilla, which had dried out since lunch, was the closest thing to food in his room. He hated tortillas, he reflected as he broke off a chunk.

Berezin exhaled sharply, then threw his head back, tossing the vodka down his throat in one quick swallow. He quickly followed the vodka with the piece of tortilla. As he chewed the stale mass, he realized how much he missed the brown bread of Russia. He had started to cap the bottle before he noticed there was barely enough left for one more drink. Sleep would come twice as quickly, he rationalized, if he had a second drink. He drained the vodka into the glass and repeated the ritual.

He settled into bed and soon a feeling of warm contentment was spreading through his body. His mind cycled through some of the same questions as before, but now he felt more like a spectator than the man responsible for the answers. Noise from the card game erupted more often, but he had lost interest. Perhaps with five drinks, he could go to sleep five times faster. Unfortunately, he would also awaken five times slower, he thought as he rolled over and faced the wall.

The knock on Berezin's door came at 2130 in Managua. His excited anticipation and a quick shower readied him for the mission even with just a few hours of sleep. Before leaving he added the family picture and an unopened bottle of vodka to his travel bag.

When Berezin reached the communications center, he was surprised to see that Ambassador Markelov had been joined by *General-Mayor* (Brigadier General) Aleksandr Tatlin. Berezin had heard rumors that General Tatlin had been working undercover for several months in Cuba, but there had been no confirmation. Tatlin's sudden appearance in Nicaragua was one more indicator that something important was happening.

Berezin and the other three pilots gathered around General Tatlin as the ambassador watched. Tatlin spread a couple of aeronautical charts on a table. The charts were in English with a few notes in Russian scrawled in open areas. Berezin was surprised to notice the eagle symbol of the American Department of Defense marked prominently on the front of the charts.

"External fuel tanks have been added to all four MiGs," General Tatlin said. "Both element leaders will be armed with two AA-eight and two AA-seven missiles. The wing men will carry three missiles each."

A total of fourteen missiles, Berezin noted. He wondered how many enemy aircraft General Tatlin expected the MiGs to go up against.

Tatlin continued, "You'll fly due south for the first hour and a half. You must stay well west of Panama to keep from drawing the attention of the Americans there."

"Yes, Comrade General," Berezin said.

"But," Markelov interjected, "if you stay too far west, you will miss South America completely."

"Right," Tatlin said, then continued, "The radar warning receivers and the electronic countermeasures transmitters have been activated in the two element lead aircraft. Also, both aircraft have additional navigational radios."

Berezin was accustomed to flying without a full complement of electronic equipment. The primitive facilities and shortages of spare parts combined with the heat and humidity to create a maintenance officer's nightmare. Nevertheless, Berezin had not been hampered in combat by a lack of operational equipment. The counterrevolutionaries in the jungle were even less well equipped. Yet air-to-air combat was different, and he was disappointed that the warning systems and countermeasures were not fully operational on all four MiGs.

General Tatlin took a small blue booklet from his briefcase. As he thumbed through to locate a page near the center, Berezin could see the front. Again, the printing was in English, and the U.S. Department of Defense seal was on the cover. Berezin saw that the booklet contained information on airfields in the Caribbean and South America. He also saw a set of dates that caused him some concern. The information was more than a year out of date.

Tatlin held the open booklet so that all four pilots could see. "You will refuel at Jorge Chavez International Airport in Lima, Peru. These diagrams show the airport's location. The KGB will meet you and have additional instructions. Right now you should copy the radio frequencies and any other information you need. Ambassador Markelov can help with the translations. Do not write the name of the airfield or that your destination is in Peru."

Before Berezin could start making notes, General Tatlin picked up the chart showing South America and called Berezin aside. Tatlin said, "The Americans are trying to cause a great provocation. You may be the only one who can stop them."

As a fighter pilot, Berezin had fantasized about air-to-air combat with the Americans, but he had never imagined having a unique role in the struggle against capitalism. The possibility excited him even though he had little understanding yet of what that role might be. "I eagerly serve the Soviet Union, Comrade General."

"An American plane flying into Santiago, Chile, must be destroyed." Tatlin pointed several hundred miles farther down the coast from Lima.

Berezin was relieved that he did not have to admit he had no idea where Santiago was.

"President Grigoriev hopes that the aircraft will be destroyed in Santiago," Tatlin continued, "but if the Americans are not stopped there, your MiGs must stop them. Otherwise, their aircraft will do extreme damage to the forces of socialism."

Berezin wanted his chance, so he hoped the Americans would not be stopped in Santiago. "What kind of aircraft is our target?"

"A C-141 cargo jet."

"A C-141?" Berezin could not conceal his surprise. He assumed the target would be a B-1 bomber, although he could not imagine how a B-1 in South America could threaten vital Soviet interests. He was familiar with the characteristics and appearance of the C-141, since the aircraft was similar to the Ilyushin Il-76 in the Soviet Air Force. "What kind of fighters are escorting it, and how many fighters will we encounter?"

"There are no fighters. The Americans evidently hoped to disguise the C-141's importance by sending it alone."

"I don't understand, Comrade General, why a single American cargo plane can be such a threat."

"You don't need to understand it. You need to destroy it."

The general's tone did not reflect the importance Berezin had started to feel about his role. Berezin decided to be more careful. "Yes, Comrade General."

"Can you destroy the C-one-forty-one if you arrive over Santiago while it's on the ground?"

Interesting question, Berezin thought. He was unsure of the answer and knew that General Tatlin, who was not a pilot, would be less sure. "That is difficult to say for certain since we carry only air-to-air missiles. If we had the thirty-millimeter gun of a MiG-29, I could guarantee the destruction of the aircraft on the ground or in the air." That sounded more boastful than Berezin had intended, but he hoped to impress Tatlin.

"But you don't have the gun. Could you do it with what you'll have?"

"If his engines are running, the heat-seeking missiles might home-in on an engine."

"Would that destroy the aircraft—and the cargo?"

"Probably, Comrade General. If thousands of kilos of jet fuel burn, the cargo should also burn."

Tatlin nodded his agreement. "And if the engines are not running?"

"There would be too much ground clutter for my radar to lock onto a parked aircraft. Success is more likely if we wait until the C-141 takes off."

"You may not have the fuel to wait," Tatlin said firmly. "If you get there, and the aircraft is on the ground, you must not leave without destroying it."

If it came to destroying the aircraft on the ground, Berezin thought, his Hind-D was more capable than a fighter such as the MiG-25, which was designed as a long-range interceptor. However, Santiago obviously was beyond the range of his helicopter. General Tatlin was asking for an answer to a difficult problem.

Berezin said, "A low-level attack from the side, sending all missiles in at close range, could set the fuel on fire." He assumed that the missiles tearing into the side of the C-141 would do enough damage to cause fires. He doubted that his missiles would explode. They would not have time to arm if he pressed in close enough ensure he could not miss.

"I hope that when your aircraft reach Lima," Tatlin said, "we already will have good news from Santiago. If so, you will simply refuel and return to Managua. Your flight plan to Lima reports that you are Puma Flight, ferrying four MiG-21s to Peru. That will get you by the Americans in Panama."

For years, MiG-21s had been a major Soviet export into the third world arms market. No other supersonic fighter had been more widely exported. Therefore, the reported movement of MiG-21s would trigger much less American interest than the sudden appearance of MiG-25s.

Knowledgeable observers would not mistake a MiG-25 for a MiG-21, Berezin thought. The single-engine MiG-21 was much smaller than the twin-engine MiG-25. From any angle, the two aircraft looked considerably different. If the American pilots from Panama did not scramble for a close look, however, no one would recognize the deception before the MiG-25s landed in Peru.

Berezin gestured toward the chart. "Can we take the map, sir?"

Tatlin hesitated. "This is the only copy I have. It is best that you not carry evidence of where you're going or where you've come from."

Berezin asked, "Will our contact in Lima provide maps?" Tatlin's look suggested that less information was likely to be available in Lima. Berezin continued, "If the Americans are already gone when we reach Santiago, I will need something to help me find them."

Tatlin looked at the chart for a moment, then handed it to Berezin. "You must not fail. If you destroy the Americans, the president himself will pin the medal on your tunic."

"I will not fail you, Comrade General."

31

Near Arturo Merino Benitez International Airport
Santiago, Chile
Friday, 2 April, 0150 local (0550 GMT)

Two time zones east of Managua, Chisholm's aircraft was landing at the international airport at Santiago, Chile. As Major Griffin let the C-141 settle toward the runway, he misjudged slightly in the darkness. The C-141 touched the runway, bounced, and floated airborne for the length of a football field. Griffin eased the aircraft down a second time. His expression was an embarrassed frown as he pulled the throttles into reverse thrust to slow the big aircraft.

After a few moments of silence, Sergeant Blake's voice boomed over the intercom, "Everyone's okay back here, sir. As soon as we pull up our socks, we'll be ready to go to work."

Griffin looked more embarrassed. In the copilot's seat, Sandi tried to stifle a smile.

From the navigator's seat Chisholm said into his microphone, "Brutal, Sarge." There was one unfortunate thing about a bad landing in a C-141, he thought. The pilot usually had at least a half dozen intimate witnesses.

Blake asked facetiously, "Did you make that landing, Colonel?"

"That's a negative, Sergeant Blake."

Griffin pushed the throttles out of reverse thrust, then let the C-141 coast toward the end of the runway. With a perturbed grin, Griffin said, "Must be the Coriolis effect. I've never made a good landing south of the equator."

Chisholm was amused at the pilot's reference to Coriolis, the nebulous acceleration that caused such things as clouds and water to swirl in opposite directions above and below the equator. Since the flight from Honolulu had taken more than fifteen hours, Chisholm worried that Griffin's slight misjudgment might mean that fatigue already was a factor. Counting preflight activities in Hawaii, the crew had exceeded the normal MAC standards for the length of the crew-duty day—and the real mission had not even started.

Griffin guided the C-141 onto the taxiway at the end of the runway and started the after-landing checks.

A "follow-me" truck led the C-141 to the main parking ramp, where a tan staff car and two jeeps waited. A machine gun was mounted above the backseat of each jeep. Chisholm could see that the men in the jeeps all wore uniforms of the Chilean armed forces. The three vehicles started accompanying the C-141.

As Sandi announced the completion of the after-landing checklist, she studied the armed jeeps moving near the wingtip on her side. She smiled mischievously. "I hope the police aren't here because of your landing. That'd make interesting reading in the critique of your check ride."

Griffin sighed. He followed the truck to the southeast corner of the parking ramp. That parking spot was the farthest from the terminal and other aircraft—a normal precaution for servicing an explosives-laden aircraft.

Chisholm watched the other vehicles as the C-141 parked and the crew went through the final checklists. The tan sedan and one of the jeeps stopped in front. The other jeep went out of sight somewhere behind the aircraft. Two Americans in civilian clothes got out of the sedan.

Before going outside, Chisholm wanted to talk about the outbound fuel load. He did not want the discussion on the intercom, however, where it might be monitored by equipment for gathering electronic intelligence. When the checklists were completed and the crew members removed their headsets, Chisholm said, "We need a full fuel load."

Sergeant Jacobs, seated at the flight engineer's panel, said, "That'll put us well above the recommended takeoff weight for normal operations, Colonel."

"I understand, Sarge," Chisholm said, making sure that Major Griffin was listening too. "We don't have a choice on this one."

Jacobs nodded, flipping open his C-141 Flight Manual to the page covering the gross-weight limitations. "This'll be the first takeoff I've ever been on with a gross weight in the Emergency War Ops range on the chart."

"Let's hope you'll never need to again, Sarge," Chisholm said as he got out of the jump seat.

Sergeant Blake was waiting in the cargo compartment when Chisholm and Griffin stepped down from the cockpit. "You suppose the major would feel better, Colonel," Blake said with an evil smile, "if we told him about that landing in Singapore?"

Chisholm's look of mock seriousness confirmed that he knew which landing Blake referred to—and who the pilot had been. "He probably would feel better, Sarge, *if* one of us had the bad judgment to tell him about it."

Blake continued smiling as he said to Griffin, "Major, what the colonel's saying is that your landing's not the worst one he and I have survived together."

Griffin looked pleased.

"Don't feel too relieved, Major," Chisholm said with a wry grin, before stepping out through the crew-entry door and starting down the external ladder. "You'll have to outlive Sergeant Blake before you'll be permitted to forget this one."

Lieutenant Colonel Dale Finnegan, the American air attaché in Chile, met Chisholm at the bottom of the ladder. Finnegan said, "Glad you got here okay, Colonel."

"And you'll be even happier to see us gone," Chisholm said with a smile.

"The sooner, the better, sir," Finnegan responded, "but no later than sunrise."

"You're making me feel like Cinderella."

"If you're still on the ground at sunrise, Colonel, we all may turn into pumpkins. Ambassador Perkins had to make some sacred promises even to get you here at all."

"We're shooting for a ground time of no more than three hours," Chisholm said.

"No problem as far as we're concerned, sir." Finnegan gestured toward an approaching fuel truck. "Your gas is on the way."

"We'll refuel first. Then we've got to wire up a couple of antennas before we take off." Chisholm paused, then asked, "Is there any message traffic indicating that the Soviets are paying attention to us yet?"

"Negative, sir. I did get a strange message from General Ramsey's office about twenty minutes ago. The message said to pass the word *cocoon* to the next arriving flight."

"Good," Chisholm said. Ramsey's real message was that the mission's cloak of secrecy seemed to be intact. If the Soviets stayed fooled for the next few hours, Chisholm thought, the mission just might succeed. He nodded toward the closest jeep, with its gunner standing by. "Any local threats?"

"The jeeps are routine whenever a plane's carrying explosives. There are a couple of antigovernment groups that'd love to get a shot at you, but you should be long gone before they discover you were here."

Oliverio walked up and said, "Colonel C., we've got a lot of oil dripping off number two."

Instantly Chisholm was concerned. There were compromises he was willing to make to keep moving, but he knew that the mission could not be flown on three engines. "How serious, Chief?"

"I'm not sure until we get the cowling open, sir, but there's more oil than I like to see."

Chisholm turned to Finnegan. "How are you fixed for maintenance troops?"

"We don't have many. For serious engine maintenance, Mother MAC sends a team of wrench-benders and their equipment down from Charleston."

"We don't have time for that," Chisholm said as he led Finnegan and Oliverio toward the number two engine.

By midnight Berezin had left the stench of Managua far behind. Now he was level at thirty-seven thousand feet with the other three fighters following closely behind. Ahead of the sleek nose on his MiG-25 he saw little but the stars above and some clouds scattered below. Near the horizon back to the left were a few lights of villages in Costa Rica. Those lights, and his navigational radios that no longer pointed toward Managua, were his only connection with land—with the real world. When those lights disappeared, he would see no others for nearly a thousand miles. Actually, the next landfall ahead of his MiG was Antarctica, more than five thousand miles away. He remembered the ambassador's warning as they had discussed the route: if the MiGs stayed too far west, they would miss South America.

Berezin still felt unprepared for the navigational challenges ahead of him. He had ferried aircraft across vast stretches of Siberia on two occasions, but never before had he piloted an aircraft so far over an ocean where he was beyond the sight of all land. There were many areas in Siberia where the ground references were no more helpful than the waves now below him on the dark ocean. In Siberia, however, he had always flown above the watchful eyes of *Voyska* PVO, the Troops of Air Defense. Then he had not worried about getting lost— *Voyska* PVO made sure Soviet pilots did not stray far from the planned flight.

Now, flying through the darkness above the Pacific Ocean, Berezin knew he was well beyond the watchful eyes of any controllers on the ground. Never before had he been turned loose to fly so freely with so much fuel. He hoped none of the three young fliers with him would be overwhelmed by the sudden feeling of independence. He knew the three well. All were considered loyal. Otherwise they never would have been assigned overseas to such a distant place as Nicaragua. He had noticed that each pilot had been excited before takeoff, but the emotions had seemed to be the excitement of sharing a new adventure. None of the three had any maps, so he was certain they would stay close in the air, like geese flying south in the autumn. Once they landed he would have to keep an eye on his charges. He could not afford to have the mission—and his career—jeopardized by the defection of one of his young companions.

For the first hour Berezin maintained a course due south. Once certain he had passed well clear of the American bases in Panama, he turned his MiG southeast.

He was happy with his airplane. It flew well, and almost all the equipment it was fitted with seemed to be working. Although it was impossible to get a full checkout of his threat warning receiver (TWR), the system that would warn of enemy radars seemed intermittent at best. Fortunately, the TWR on Pokrovskiy's MiG seemed fully operational.

While Berezin had been sleeping in the late afternoon, two navigational radios had been added to his MiG. The VHF Omnidirectional Range, or VOR, receiver would give him the direction to VOR stations on the ground. The Tactical Air Navigation, or TACAN, receiver would give direction and distance to TACAN stations. He had used such radios in ferrying aircraft from one base to another, but that was long before he had left Russia.

Berezin was not confident that he could navigate using these radios alone. In Russia the ground controllers always provided headings to guide his aircraft. In Nicaragua he had guided his helicopter using ground references—the lakes, rivers, beaches, and mountain peaks that he had come to know so well. This mission to Peru would be entirely different. He hoped the weather at Lima was good. Berezin had little confidence that he could use the radios to guide his MiG into an airfield covered with low clouds.

He thought of Kapitan Kovalev flying on his wing. Kovalev's MiG had no navigational radios. If they were flying in Russia with MiG-25s of the Soviet Air Force, Berezin thought, all four pilots would have operable Instrument Landing Systems (ILSs). With a good ILS each pilot should be able to find a runway when clouds were down to four hundred feet above the ground. Unfortunately, the maintenance crews in Nicaragua had given up long ago on trying to keep the ILS receivers operable for the MiG-25s. If the weather in Lima was bad, Kovalev would have to fly very tight formation as Berezin tried to find the runway for both of them. He wondered how long it had been since Kovalev had flown tight formation in bad weather.

After sleeping for five hours in his room in the Romanian compound in Santiago, *Mayor* (Major) Andrei Lyashko was awakened at 0200 by his alarm clock. He dressed in camouflaged fatigues and pulled an oversized set of dirty coveralls over them so that he would look like a laborer. He was lacing his combat boots when a guard knocked on his door.

"The airplane is at the airport," the guard said.

"What?" Lyashko was pleased to confirm that the mystery aircraft really had come to Santiago, but he had been told to expect the landing at about 0300. "How long has it been there?"

"I don't know," the guard said.

"Quickly tell my driver that I'll be ready in five minutes," Lyashko said as he hurried with his boots.

Obviously someone had screwed up, he thought as he slipped the rest of his personal gear inside his pockets. He had planned to watch the aircraft land, then slip onto the airfield as soon as he saw where the Americans parked. Now there was little time to waste.

Stopping at the embassy's armory, he collected three canvas bags containing the equipment he and his accomplices would need. Together the bags weighed more than one hundred pounds, but Lyashko lifted them as if they carried no more than workout clothing for a visit to the gymnasium. The excitement of the impending mission added to his strength.

Lyashko was eager to get started. Although he had worked on several clandestine missions for the *Spetsnaz* and the KGB, this would be his first combat as anything more than an adviser since being wounded in Afghanistan.

He was driven in a van from the embassy to a rendezvous with the other two members of his team. He fretted because additional time was lost as the driver made sure they were not followed. Finally the van reached the meeting point on a dark street in a barrio near the airport.

A dilapidated bread truck was parked in the shadow of a large tree. After using the van's lights to exchange identification signals, Lyashko's driver pulled up to the back of the truck. Francisco Morales and Mario Gonzalez, dressed similarly to Lyashko, opened the truck's back doors. He handed the bags to the two men, then jumped aboard.

Morales and Gonzalez were full-time members of the Revolutionary Left Movement, a guerrilla group opposing the government of Chile. Each man had a small, wiry build, and the two together were hardly as large as Lyashko. Morales had spent two years in prison after being caught in a sweep of revolutionaries. Both men were eager to deal a blow to the government and to the Americans.

For a few minutes the truck traced a circuitous route to ensure that no one was following. The drive gave Lyashko an opportunity to see that the American aircraft was on the parking ramp near the south end of the runway. Finally the driver entered a dead-end road near the southern perimeter of the airport. He turned the truck around at the end, as if he had taken the wrong road. In the moments that the truck was changing direction, Lyashko and the two Chilean guerrillas dropped onto the dirt road. Each man carried a bag as he sneaked into nearby underbrush.

After moving well away from the road, Lyashko stopped the team in a small clearing. All three men stripped away the coveralls, revealing their camouflaged fatigues. Lyashko removed tubes of brown and green face paint from his bag. After spreading the greasy substance over his face and neck, he put on a shapeless camouflage hat.

Lyashko's bag included three rocket-propelled grenades and an RPG-7 launcher. The RPG-7 was a thirty-nine-inch-long tube with two sights on top and two handgrips beneath. The forward grip included the trigger used to fire the five-pound grenades, which were loaded one at a time. The rocket, which was built into the projectile, could propel the grenade as far as nine hundred meters. However, their effective range—the range within which a hit was likely—was five hundred meters. Thus his first goal was to get within that distance of the aircraft, then assess whether the team could work in even closer. He assumed that a single hit on the thin skin of the C-141 would disable the aircraft, since the grenades had been designed to penetrate more than twelve inches of steel on the front of a tank.

Setting the RPG-7 aside, he removed other items from his bag. There was an Avtomat Kalashnikova AK-47 assault rifle, a field pack, three additional clips of ammunition and a sealed plastic bag. The waterproof bag protected a U.S.-government-issue olive-drab flight suit—complete with USAF captain's insignia and a patch of the Military Airlift Command.

He put the flight suit and ammunition into the pack, then fitted it on his back and loaded the rounds for the RPG into the top of the pack. Hanging the AK-47 by its sling over his left shoulder, Lyashko grabbed the RPG-7 and was ready to go.

Morales and Gonzalez had made similar preparations. Both were armed with AK-47s and carried satchel charges of high explosives. In the confusion following the attack on the C-141, Morales would run among the other aircraft and destroy as many as possible.

When all three men were ready, Lyashko led off through the underbrush and over the fence that marked the perimeter of the airfield.

32

Over the Pacific Ocean
Friday, 2 April, 0050 local (0550 GMT)

Berezin had spent half an hour familiarizing himself with the navigational radios. Now they were set on the VOR frequency and the TACAN channel for Talara, a ground station in northern Peru near the western tip of South America. Since his MiG was not within range of the station, the pointers on his instrument panel rotated aimlessly, seeking a signal on the selected frequencies.

As Berezin kept checking the rotating pointers, he began to wish someone else had been appointed to lead this important mission. The longer he sat in the dark with no real grasp on anything beyond the cockpit of his MiG, the more he wished he were in Managua playing cards and drinking vodka. He felt guilty about how much the three other pilots flying close behind were depending upon him. He decided that if they knew how uncertain he felt, they also would wish to be in Managua.

After another twenty minutes the pointer for the VOR radio began to swing erratically then pointed ahead and to the left. Almost immediately the TACAN pointer stabilized in the same direction. A few seconds later the distance indicator steadied on 192 miles then slowly decreased as Berezin's MiG continued streaking through the darkness toward Peru. He felt much better. He had found Talara. He was confident he could find Lima nearly seven hundred miles farther down the coast.

On the parking ramp in Santiago, the maintenance work began in earnest once the C-141 was refueled. No problems were encountered in installing the new antennas. These antennas were for communicating through satellites and for receiving data from the ARIA that would join the C-141 over Antarctica.

Replacing the oil pump on the number two engine posed a tougher problem. The War Readiness Spares Kit included a pump, but replacement was difficult—and slow. Oliverio led the effort with the aircrew's two flight engineers and the local maintenance personnel assisting.

Chisholm sent Finnegan to the American embassy to pass word about the delay. General Ramsey—and others—needed to know. Somewhere in the darkness between American Samoa and Antarctica, the ARIA and a KC-10 tanker orbited lazily. Both crews were awaiting word of the C-141's departure from Santiago. Then the ARIA would top off its fuel and head south to rendezvous with Chisholm's C-141. The KC-10 would return to American Samoa for more fuel.

The delay in leaving Santiago would mean that the satellite chosen as the first target would be well past perigee by the time the C-141 arrived at eighty degrees south. Chisholm knew, therefore, that he needed to work on that problem, so he joined Rick McClain inside the command-and-control module. Together they started creating targeting charts that took into account a takeoff as late as sunrise.

Progress for Lyashko, Morales, and Gonzalez had been painfully slow. It had been necessary to crawl much of the way from the perimeter road, since most of the grass near the runway was short, dead, and brown. Twice the three men had lain frozen in the shadows for ten minutes as a security patrol moved slowly through the area.

Now the attackers had reached cover in the weed-choked ditches that drained the airfield's vast area. Although Santiago had received only three inches of rain in the last six months, most had fallen in a first-of-the-season thunderstorm the previous afternoon, so the ditches now were wet and studded with water-filled holes.

Lyashko had never been stopped by a little adversity, and in the darkness of early morning most things were going his way. A steady breeze from the south had helped him keep from getting overheated. The wind also helped mask the sounds of his team's movement through the weeds.

Nearly five hundred meters south of the C-141 he stopped for a few moments to assess the situation. He had reached his first objective, which was to get within range of the American airplane. Unfortunately, he was behind the C-141, where the profile was much smaller than from the side. A broadside shot would be much better.

The last several times he had looked toward the quarry, he had noticed maintenance men hovering around one of the engines beneath the left wing. He also had seen an armed jeep on guard behind the aircraft. Surprise was on his side, so the men on the jeep did not worry him—his two companions would take them out as he fired an RPG into the enemy aircraft.

Now he decided that the ideal firing position was the drainage ditch alongside the aircraft, between the parking area and the runway. If the Americans started the engines before he reached his next goal, he would simply fire from wherever he was.

"We will move closer," he said quietly as he loaded the first round into the RPG-7.

"We must get much, much closer," Morales responded. "All the airplanes are too far away."

Lyashko understood. Morales' goal was to attack Chilean aircraft, and for some reason, the C-141 had been parked several hundred meters from other aircraft.

"After the American plane is destroyed," Lyashko said, "you can take the jeep to attack aircraft parked near the terminal."

Morales nodded and seemed satisfied.

Lyashko would have been indifferent about the Chilean aircraft except that he wanted Morales to continue with what Lyashko had considered all along to be a suicide mission. Morales' attack would cause additional confusion, thereby giving Lyashko a few moments to slip into the American flight suit and—to kill Gonzalez. Lyashko hoped to sneak away as a frightened American crew member while the Chilean forces were left only with the bodies of the two members of the Revolutionary Left Movement.

Fourteen hundred miles north of Santiago, Berezin's MiGs were nearing the end of the flight from Managua. Lima, Peru, was one time zone west of Santiago, so the sun was well below the eastern horizon when the four MiGs started a long descent to Lima.

Although the controller's headings kept the MiGs offshore, Berezin could see lights along the coast as the MiGs continued southward. After descending below ten thousand feet, he began to notice occasional lights above him to the left. Either they were strange stars, Berezin thought, or there were some very high mountains nearby.

Ahead and to the left the lights of Lima contrasted sharply with the darkness of the sea that stretched endlessly to the right. Finally Berezin was told to switch to the control tower at Jorge Chavez International Airport. He called the tower and asked for landing instructions.

"Puma Flight," the tower operator said in heavily accented English, "you are cleared to enter a five-mile initial for runway one-five. Right-hand traffic at fifteen hundred feet. Winds are one-eighty at fifteen knots."

In Managua Berezin had gotten used to listening to English spoken by tower operators whose native language was Spanish. Here in Peru the accent was much heavier, so Berezin had to think more about what had been said before he could translate the words to Russian. Fortunately, he had anticipated most of what the tower operator would say.

Berezin was leading his flight in for a visual traffic pattern, and the instructions said to line up on the runway at least five miles from the end. That was no surprise. The heading for runway one-five was 150 degrees, parallel to the coast. He checked the information being received from the Lima TACAN and found that the descent controller had positioned Puma Flight almost on course, about fifteen miles from the end of the runway. Right-hand traffic meant that he would turn to the right once he was over the runway. That would take his flight over the water and away from the mountains as each pilot extended the landing gear and slowed for landing. Fifteen hundred feet was the assigned altitude until the MiGs were ready to descend in the final turn around to the runway. The winds from 180 degrees would provide a right-to-left crosswind.

Now that Berezin had the landing instructions, he needed to change his flight's formation. During descent the four MiGs had flown a fingertip formation: the aircraft were aligned like the tips of the four fingers on his right hand. Berezin was in the lead with his wing man to his left in the same relationship as the tips of the middle finger and the index finger. Just behind his right wing Pokrovskiy and his wing man were positioned like the tips of the outer two fingers of his right hand. However, Berezin needed all the aircraft behind him and to his left when they reached the runway.

Berezin gave the order over the radio. "Puma Flight, left echelon." After a pause, he added, "Now!"

Two—Three—Four echoed in quick succession as the other pilots acknowledged the command. Pokrovskiy and his wing man eased back their throttles. Those two MiGs slipped a few feet farther behind, then crossed under to the other side of the leading MiGs. Pokrovskiy's wing man continued drifting left until he was on the outside of a straight line of four aircraft slanted back to the left.

As Berezin approached the airport, he looked across the other three aircraft. Their lights were perfectly aligned, and he felt a surge of pride. With little preparation, they had come over fifteen hundred miles in the darkness. Now his flight was in a formation that he would be proud to show off over Red Square on May Day. He wished it were daylight so he could demonstrate to the peoples of Peru the superiority of Soviet airmen.

Flying over the runway's threshold, Berezin began the landing pattern by pitching-out—rolling his MiG briskly away from the other three. With his wingtip pointed toward the dark ocean to the right, he held a sixty-degree bank and pulled the throttles to idle. He maintained enough back pressure on the stick to keep his MiG at fifteen hundred feet above the ocean. The turn and the reduction in power would slow his MiG so that he could extend the flaps and landing gear.

When Berezin had turned nearly 180 degrees, he rolled the wings level. For a few seconds, he flew parallel to the runway in the opposite direction—the downwind leg of the traffic pattern. While lowering the flaps and landing gear, he checked the other aircraft. Four seconds after he had pitched-out, his wing man had mimicked the maneuver. Pokrovskiy and his wing man had followed after additional intervals of four seconds.

The pitch-out had two purposes. First, it provided the spacing needed between aircraft for landing. Second, as Berezin had come to appreciate in Afghanistan, staying high until close into the runway was much safer. Flying a long, low final approach to the runway over land controlled by guerrillas offered a tempting target to the bandits.

Berezin was satisfied with the spacing separating the four aircraft. His men were doing well, considering that they had not flown jet fighters for weeks and that they were landing in the dark at an unfamiliar airfield. The runway was more than eleven thousand feet in length with an uphill slope, so Berezin planned to land long. That would put his MiG a little farther down the runway as the others came in behind him.

As his MiG passed the end of the runway and Berezin began a

descending turn, he noticed that the wind had pushed his aircraft closer to the runway than he wanted. He added bank and back pressure on the control stick to increase the rate of turn. Berezin did not like "bending it around" to salvage a bad approach, but he also did not want to have to make a "go-around" and start all over.

Approaching the threshold of the runway, he took another quick look at the other MiGs. They were closer than he would have liked.

Touchdown was long and hot—he had more airspeed than the flight manual called for—but Berezin was satisfied. Considering it was his first night landing in a MiG in a long, long time, he had no complaints. He tested his brakes, then let the aircraft roll, slowing of its own accord for the next mile. Behind him Kapitan Kovalev also had overshot slightly. His aircraft slid across to the east side of the long line of approach lights, then corrected back over the lights beyond the end of the runway.

As Berezin watched, Kovalev's MiG landed smoothly. By then Berezin was more concerned with the lights of Pokrovskiy's MiG. The young kapitan had tried to fly a tight pattern, staying in close to the runway. The wind had blown him even closer, and he had overshot badly. His aircraft was nearing the approach lights but too far to the side for a safe landing behind Kovalev. Go around and try again, Vasily, Berezin thought.

Pokrovskiy announced his decision. "Puma Three's on the go!" His voice was excited, and he kept the mike button depressed a couple of extra seconds.

Berezin heard the sound of the kapitan breathing rapidly into his oxygen mask.

Bright tongues of flame lit the darkness behind Pokrovskiy's MiG as the afterburners lit off on the two Tumansky engines. Seconds later the MiG roared overhead at three hundred feet as Berezin's started to turn off at the end of the runway.

Berezin checked the fourth MiG. Leytenant Yashin had flown a much bigger pattern, and his airplane was well positioned just beyond the approach lights. Berezin's attention was jolted away from number four by an excited radio call on the tower frequency.

"Negative, Puma Three! Right traffic! Right traffic!"

The voice of the tower controller was high-pitched in the same heavy accent that had been difficult to understand before. This time the words ran together almost like the sound of bullets from a machine gun.

Berezin did not understand the word "negative" as he spun his head around toward Puma Three. When he spotted Pokrovskiy's aircraft, the message became clear. Unexplainably, Pokrovskiy had turned the wrong way. He had pulled up to the left and was climbing over the city.

The tower operator shouted, "Overflight over Lima not authorized! Stay west of the runway!"

Too late, Berezin thought. Pokrovskiy was already over Lima— and not very high above it at that. Berezin could see many lights on hillsides higher than where he sat in his MiG on a taxiway.

U.S. Air Force Colonel Kirby Welch lived in Lima in a hillside home overlooking Jorge Chavez International Airport. He was awakened instantly by the sound of Pokrovskiy's MiG-25 passing less than a quarter mile away. Jet fighters *never* flew over the city—at least they never had in the nearly two years Welch had served as the air attaché at the U.S. Embassy in Lima. As was common in many third world countries, flying over the capital was prohibited and normally did not happen except during a coup.

Welch wondered if the roaring jet signaled the beginning of an attempt to overthrow the Peruvian government. He had learned long ago that in Latin America, unexpected military maneuvers in the middle of the night sometimes initiated a new struggle for power. However, nothing during the previous day had suggested an imminent coup.

As the sleep cleared further from his mind, Welch remembered a top secret message that had arrived late in the afternoon from Washington, D.C. That message had ordered every American embassy in Latin America to report any unusual aerial activity observed during the next forty-eight hours. Certainly the overflight of the city by a jet fighter was *unusual*, Welch thought, but he could not imagine a connection between the mysterious aircraft and the message.

As Welch got out of bed, he noticed the clock: three thirty-three. He grabbed a set of binoculars from the top of a bureau as he hurried to the double doors leading from the bedroom to an adjacent patio.

By the time he stepped outside, the sound from the aircraft was fading. No other jets were screaming by in quick succession as he would expect in a coup. This particular aircraft was continuing up the coast, so Welch decided that the pilot must be trying to land at

Chavez. That made little sense to Welch as he searched the sky for the aircraft's lights. Peruvian jet fighters used the airfield at Las Palmas, twelve miles farther down the coast. Besides, he thought, Las Palmas did not open for normal operations until 0600, so this jet would not have taken off from there.

The accented English of the tower operator came even faster than before. "High terrain! Over five thousand feet within eight miles east of the runway centerline!"

Berezin needed an extra couple of seconds to interpret the words. He wondered how much of the information, if any, Pokrovskiy was understanding.

"Keep it in tight, Puma Three," Berezin called on the radio.

"Yes, Comrade," Pokrovskiy said.

Again he left the microphone active longer than normal. Berezin interpreted that as a sign that the young kapitan was very distracted. Pokrovskiy was breathing even faster.

"Steady, Pokrovskiy. Just—" Berezin said over the radio.

"Right traffic! Flying over Lima is forbidden!"

Berezin wished the tower operator would shut up.

"I've lost the runway," Pokrovskiy shouted, speaking this time in Russian.

An airport's main lights are directed toward approaching aircraft, so runways often are difficult to see from the side at night. Berezin had a better view of Pokrovskiy's MiG skimming above the hills of Lima than Pokrovskiy had of the airfield. It appeared that the MiG had flown far enough.

"Start your turn, Puma Three," Berezin said in Russian. "The runway's at your eight o'clock low." He was confident that once Pokrovskiy turned toward the runway, he would spot the approach lights. Berezin's main concern was that the MiG seemed to be going too fast. Perhaps Pokrovskiy was too distracted to accomplish the normal prelanding checks. "Check your gear, Three!"

"Roger, Comrade. Landing gear coming down."

Pokrovskiy should have extended the landing gear again before starting the turn. Catch up with things, Kapitan, Berezin urged silently.

The crosswind, the extra airspeed, and the delay for the landing gear took the MiG even farther from the runway. By the time Pokrovskiy had reversed course, his MiG was at least three miles beyond the approach lights. Berezin barely could see the MiG's lights angling back toward the end of the runway.

Berezin asked, "Do you have the runway?"

"Yes, Comrade," Pokrovskiy said in a tone that was slightly less excited. "I am ready to land."

As Berezin listened and watched, the lights of the MiG disappeared behind a patch of darkness about a mile short of the runway. Berezin blinked, trying to refocus. The MiG's lights remained hidden. He shouted into his microphone, "Pull up, Three! Pull up!"

A flash lit the darkened mass from behind, outlining an unlighted ridge that rose more than three hundred feet above the elevation of the runway threshold. Pieces of flaming wreckage skipped over the top. An orange fireball rose above the ridge, then transformed into a billowing black column of smoke barely visible in the night. As Berezin watched the reflections of flames shimmering off the smoke, he cursed into his oxygen mask. Suddenly he felt exhausted.

Noises carried clearly in the darkness, since most of Lima was sleeping—or had been before the jet thundered overhead. Having heard other aircraft on the ground at Chavez, Welch had been looking that way when he was startled by the crackling roar of the engines on the airborne jet surging into afterburner. He turned and saw burning wreckage bouncing across the top of the ridge even before the sound of the crash reached him.

For a few moments Welch was mesmerized by the flames leaping skyward. Then, recognizing that his duty day already had started, he shed the special shock pilots feel after watching the gut-wrenching aftermath of a plane crash. He focused his binoculars on the airfield and found three aircraft at the south end of the runway. He could not identify what type of aircraft were on the unlighted taxiway, but the separation between the lights on the wingtips told him that the three aircraft were fighters. He wondered where the fighters had come from and why they were landing at the international airport.

As Berezin waited for the ground crew to put safing pins in the missiles beneath his MiG, he listened intently to the radio. Perhaps Pokrovskiy had ejected before his MiG-25 smashed into the hillside.

The hoped-for call on the emergency radio never came.

After the missiles had been rendered safe from being accidentally fired on the ground, Berezin taxied his MiG behind a jeep, which led to a nearby hardstand for parking. He shut down his aircraft, then climbed slowly from the cockpit. His enthusiasm for the mission had died along with Pokrovskiy.

Welch showered, shaved, and dressed quickly. Minutes later he returned to the patio carrying a thirty-five-millimeter camera with a telephoto lens. Scanning the airport, Welch was surprised to see the three fighters parked not far from where he first had seen them. They were in a remote area with two fuel trucks nearby. Even before focusing the camera, Welch reached an unexpected conclusion—the aircraft were being kept from the normal parking areas because the fighters were armed. He was even more surprised when he looked through the camera—the three jets were MiG-25s, and even in the dim lighting their markings appeared to be Nicaraguan. Welch snapped five pictures of the aircraft then hurried to his van. He would get closer pictures on his way to the American embassy.

Refueling trucks were waiting and the ground crew connected hoses to the MiGs even before Kapitan Kovalev and Leytenant Yashin climbed down from their aircraft. Berezin was surprised by the number of Russians that swarmed around the three MiGs. He had not imagined that so many were stationed in Peru. Most wore civilian clothes, although he noticed a few maintenance men wearing work uniforms of the Soviet Air Force.

The three pilots were somber as they quietly discussed what had happened. While they talked, a van pulled up, and its Russian driver invited them aboard. Berezin wanted to go to the crash site, but the driver had been told to take the pilots to the Soviet ambassador. Berezin nodded his concurrence, then turned back into his thoughts as the driver raced along the taxiway that paralleled the runway. After a few moments the van turned onto the main parking ramp near the terminal, then in among hangars and warehouses.

The driver guided the van into a large warehouse and stopped. Everything within the building seemed Russian, Berezin thought as the driver led the three pilots to the office area. Stepping inside the Soviet operations center at Jorge Chavez International Airport, Berezin encountered a scene as frantic as the one in the communications center in Managua.

A tall, distinguished-looking man noticed the arrival of the three pilots and came immediately to them. Berezin wondered if the man was the ambassador.

Gesturing toward Kovalev and Yashin, the man spoke first to the driver. "Take these two to get some food and bring enough for Podpolkovnik Berezin." Once the driver and the two younger pilots walked away, the man turned to Berezin. "I am General Alekseev, KGB. The ambassador had to leave to discuss the crash with the local government."

Berezin was surprised to find such a high-ranking KGB official in Peru. He shrugged, thinking of the loss of the young kapitan. "Yes, Comrade General. I don't know what we can do. I don't believe the pilot—"

"What you're going to do," Alekseev said, "is leave as soon as your aircraft are refueled. Are there any maintenance problems on the three remaining MiGs?"

The directness of Alekseev's response caught Berezin off guard. He had been engrossed in his thoughts about the loss of Pokrovskiy and had assumed that the crash would delay the mission. Obviously that was not the case. He struggled for a moment to remember any problems. "There is difficulty with the threat warning receiver on my MiG."

"For that we have no spare parts," Alekseev said. "Anything else?"

Berezin thought again. The other two pilots had not mentioned anything, and he doubted that it mattered if they had. "No major problems that I know of, sir."

"Good," Alekseev said as he led Berezin toward a nearby table that had maps and charts spread across it.

"We do not know yet if our men in Chile have succeeded. If they do not, your target will almost certainly be airborne by the time your MiGs get to Santiago."

Berezin asked, "Where is the target going from Santiago, sir?"

"To Antarctica."

Alekseev briefly explained the messages from Moscow about an American attempt to destroy Soviet satellites as they flew over Antarctica.

Berezin was shocked but fascinated by the concept as he studied the map, trying to estimate the distance to Santiago. He guessed that he would need nearly three hours to fly that far since the MiGs were slowed by the external fuel tanks.

"If the C-141 takes off quickly," Berezin said, "it'll be out of range before we start. How are we to catch the craft?"

"You will fly to Río Gallegos. That's an airfield in Argentina at the tip of South America."

Alekseev pointed. Berezin was concerned about how far away the next airfield was. He was unsure the MiGs could fly that far even with the extra fuel.

Before Berezin could share his concern, Alekseev continued, "Besides the distance, there is one other complication. You will have to cross Chile."

"Does Chile prohibit overflights, Comrade General?"

"Your flight plan does not show you flying anywhere near Chile. It shows you are to remain off the coast near Lima."

Berezin had not expected to fly across international borders without a flight plan—except in time of war. He wondered if he would have to use his missiles before he caught up with the Americans. He asked, "Does Chile have air defense fighters?"

"Just some Mirages stationed near Santiago," Alekseev said referring with disdain to the French-made fighters. "If you stay well off the coast until you're south of Santiago, they won't come after you. Your course is marked on this chart."

Berezin saw how narrow Chile was. He could cross from the Pacific Ocean to Argentina in five or six minutes. "What about fighters in Argentina, sir?"

"Air traffic control in Argentina will learn you are coming." As an afterthought, Alekseev added, "The Argentineans owe us for assistance in their war against the British. You will depart Lima using the call sign Puma Flight. When you reach Argentina, your call sign will be Jaguar."

Berezin worried that the attempts at secrecy could endanger the mission. He wondered if the Americans could be fooled, especially after the crash of Pokrovskiy's aircraft.

33

Arturo Merino Benitez International Airport
Santiago, Chile
Friday, 2 April, 0505 local (0905 GMT)

Oliverio had been working on the engine for almost two hours when Chisholm came outside. The chief was tightening a nearly inaccessible nut, and he had oil on his face and forearms. Though it would not have been obvious to the casual observer, Chisholm sensed that Oliverio was enjoying himself.

"Chief," Chisholm said, "I realize it's been years since you've fondled one of these things, but are you making any progress?"

"We got beyond the foreplay about an hour ago, Colonel C.," Oliverio said with a mischievous grin. "We'll be ready for an engine run in twenty minutes."

Chisholm checked his watch. Less than two hours remained until the sunrise deadline. If the chief's estimate didn't slip, Chisholm thought, there was plenty of time for the engine run. The pilot would start the number two engine and run it for a few minutes with the cowling open, then shut down the engine. Oliverio would check all connections to ensure that no leaks remained then close the cowling so that normal preflight checks could continue.

That schedule would work, Chisholm decided, as long as the oil leak was fixed. Since they were getting toward the point where there would be little time to spare, he began to consider contingencies.

"Any chance we can go without the engine run, Chief?"

Oliverio continued to strain with the wrench but smiled. "I realize us chiefs are supposed to be perfect, Colonel C., but I'm not too proud to run a quick test." He paused. "That's what the book calls for, sir."

"Whatever you think, Chief," Chisholm said. He would follow the book—up to the point where the mission was in jeopardy. Then he would throw away the book and start operating on experience—and instinct.

In dealing with hundreds of maintenance problems on scores of parking ramps throughout the world, he had learned many lessons. The most practical was that pilots should stay out of the way while the sergeants were fixing the aircraft. He noticed Sandi and de Luca standing near a jeep in front of the C-141. The Chilean driver and gunner were explaining the operation of the American-made M-60 machine gun mounted on the jeep. The driver was working hard to speak English. Sandi was responding in Spanish, when necessary, to bridge the frequent gaps in the young soldier's understanding.

Chisholm joined as an observer. He watched partly out of curiosity, but mainly because there was little left to do but kill time—something he had also learned a lot about in his years of flying.

In a drainage ditch one hundred meters away, Lyashko had paused for a few minutes before the final push. As he rested from having carried his weapons through the underbrush, weeds, and mud, he decided to go forward for ten minutes more. Then he would climb the side of the ditch and take whatever shot was available. He tapped his boot against Morales' shoulder as a signal to move out.

When Lyashko had crawled another twenty meters through the edge of the water, he put his hand on something that unexpectedly slithered away into the water ahead of him. Startled, he flinched and slipped off the bank, splashing into a muddy pool and dipping the RPG-7 launcher into the water for the first time.

Lyashko did not like snakes. Cursing quietly, he scrambled onto the bank. The RPG-7 was a rugged weapon, but this would be an unfortunate time to damage it. In the dim light that reached out from the nearby parking area, he surveyed the launcher. The sights were still in place. The weapon appeared wet and muddy but undamaged.

As he pulled a damp handkerchief from his pocket to wipe the mud from the launcher, Morales and Gonzalez crawled beyond and continued moving along the ditch. Lyashko thought about having them wait but decided that if another snake were to be encountered, Morales could have his turn.

Lyashko was wiping mud from the launcher and blowing water from its sights when Morales hit a trip wire. There was a small flash, a pop, and a rising hiss as a flare hurtled skyward. Almost before Lyashko could look up, the flare burst into a brilliant yellow-white light suspended beneath a small parachute.

Lyashko cursed silently because he had lost the element of surprise. He yelled in a loud whisper, "Freeze!"

The flare was a couple of hundred feet in the air, floating on the wind in the direction the team had been moving. Lyashko expected the flare to descend to the ground in less than a minute. Then he would attack.

The sudden flash of light in the sky startled the five people gathered at the jeep in front of the C-141. All were mesmerized for a moment by the flickering light and the jittery shadows it cast. Then the driver yelled in Spanish, started the jeep, and roared away in a sweeping turn toward the edge of the parking ramp. He drove a few yards onto the grass, then stopped.

Chisholm tried to see the area beneath the flare, but his view was blocked by a maintenance van in front of the C-141's right wing. He ran to the van, then moved cautiously beyond where he could see the grassy area between the aircraft and the main taxiway. Sandi and de Luca followed.

Chisholm hoped that a coyote or some other Chilean predator had tripped the warning flare. However, he saw the gunner yank back the bolt on the M-60 and heard the metallic click of the first round being forced into the firing chamber.

In the ditch Lyashko had been surprised to hear engines start on two jeeps—a second jeep and machine gun made his mission even tougher. He extended the RPG-7 in front of him as the sound of one jeep got noticeably louder. Even though the flare had not yet reached the ground, Lyashko decided to wait no longer. He whispered loudly that there were two jeeps, then added, "Spread out and get the gunners."

As Lyashko edged up the side of the ditch, Gonzalez rolled several times to his right, distancing himself from the other two. Morales rolled back almost to Lyashko. Then both Chileans crawled rapidly up the slope.

Gonzalez was the first to see the C-141's defenders. Taking quick aim at the jeep beside the aircraft, he fired half a clip of bullets. Even before looking for results, he rolled partway down the slope, out of the line of fire of the machine gun.

The jeep's driver died instantly. A plate of steel in front of the machine gun deflected bullets that might have hit the gunner. He returned fire, raking the top of the slope where Gonzalez had appeared.

Chisholm had seen the lone figure emerge above the slope, but was unable to shout a warning before sparkling flashes erupted from the gunman's AK-47. Scrambling for cover, Chisholm ran headlong into Sandi. He grabbed her around the waist, then stiff-armed de Luca, herding both of them behind the maintenance van. As Chisholm knelt to watch from beside the front bumper, he reached a sickening conclusion. His efforts to keep the mission secret had failed—the Soviets knew where he was and understood why he was there.

The jeep behind the C-141 raced across the grass. Morales rose to attack just as the gunner sprayed machine-gun fire along the slope. Four bullets ripped into Morales, spinning him sideways and killing him before he hit the ground.

Although Morales' abbreviated scream was drowned out by the roar of the jeep and its machine gun, Lyashko saw the small Chilean tumble limply toward the ditch. Choose, Lyashko prodded himself— the aircraft or the jeep! He released the safety on the RPG-7, aimed at the onrushing jeep, and fired.

The jeep disintegrated in a thunderous explosion.

Simultaneously Gonzalez emptied the rest of his first clip at the other jeep. Bullets tore into the gunner's leg and groin, knocking him over the side. Gonzalez rolled out of sight, his breathing coming in panting spurts as he tried to yank the empty clip from his AK-47. For a few moments he was shaking so much he could not disengage the clip.

Fearing that the next RPG round would destroy the C-141, Chisholm stood and shouted, "Stay here!"

Racing from behind the van, he used the jeep as a shield between himself and the nearest attacker. He stepped over the wounded gunner, then vaulted into the jeep. Chisholm saw Morales' body near the ditch in front of the burning hulk of the other jeep. The dead guerrilla was near the source of the first RPG round, so Chisholm grabbed the pistol-like grip beneath the M-60 and fired a quick burst over the body. Then he turned, ready for the killer of the driver whose body now was sprawled across the seat in front of Chisholm.

While Lyashko was loading the second round into the RPG-7, Gonzalez replaced the empty clip in his AK-47 and came above the slope firing.

Chisholm fired as soon as he saw movement. The bullets from his M-60 cut Gonzalez nearly in two before the young Chilean had fired twenty rounds. Those slugs from Gonzalez's AK-47 ripped into the jeep and ricocheted off the metal shield, which protected Chisholm from his hips to his shoulders. Flinching, he closed his eyes and hunched behind the shield—but kept firing for a couple more seconds. Before he stopped he realized someone behind him had cried out in pain.

Chisholm turned and saw de Luca stagger forward, reach out, and slump over the back railing of the jeep. Already blood was oozing from a dark hole in the front of his flight suit. Fifteen yards farther behind, Sandi was sprawled in the grass, covering her head with her arms.

Wondering if she had been wounded, Chisholm wanted to rush to her but knew he must not. He could not even reach out to stop de Luca's bleeding. His first responsibility was to protect the airplane and its irreplaceable cargo. Swinging the machine gun toward Morales' body, Chisholm began firing short bursts.

Lyashko edged forward as bullets zinged overhead. The big T-tail of the C-141 towered above the battle, and Lyashko could see the tail even before he could see the fuselage. Now he was panting. From the moment the flare had rocketed into the night sky, he had acted on instinct. Time had seemed to rush by at high speed, but he had stayed calm—even when blasting the onrushing jeep. He could remember several closer calls in Afghanistan—and during live-fire training exercises in Russia. However, seeing Gonzalez being torn apart made Lyashko realize for the first time that he might fail—for the first time.

Suddenly he recognized that the tail could be his next target since destroying the controls on the tail would keep the aircraft from flying. Even better, he could disable the aircraft without exposing himself to the gunner whom Gonzalez had failed to silence. After that shot, Lyashko decided, he could drop into the ditch, hurry several meters farther away from the gunner, then fire the last grenade into the fuselage.

Lyashko rolled onto his side and pointed the RPG-7 toward where the flat, winglike structure was mounted on top of the big vertical stabilizer.

In the grass just beyond the body of one of the attackers, Chisholm saw something rising, shimmering and shiny. In an instant he felt a shudder within his chest. He was seeing reflections of the burning jeep glittering on a silver cone—the front end of a rocket-propelled grenade atop a launcher that protruded above the slope.

Furiously he jiggled the handgrip beneath the M-60 and held the trigger against the back of the trigger guard. A spiraling line of fire reached out, peppering hot metal into the ground around the body and the launcher.

Just as Lyashko was squeezing his trigger, twenty-five pounds of high explosives detonated in the satchel charges beside Morales' body. Shrapnel ripped into Lyashko, knocking him backward. The RPG rocketed over the C-141 and arced high above the parking ramp.

The shock wave from the satchel charge jarred Chisholm, and for an instant he was terrified that the C-141 would be riddled. Most of the shrapnel, however, fell well short of the parking ramp. When he recovered from his surprise, he stopped firing and prepared to fight off the next attack.

Behind him he heard the sound of approaching sirens. As more seconds passed without evidence that any attackers had survived, he sensed that his battle was over. A quick glance told him that de Luca was alive, and Sandi seemed okay. She had crawled most of the way to the jeep.

Chisholm cringed. If he, Sandi, and de Luca had been killed or wounded, only Major Griffin would have been left to pilot the C-141. The loss of three pilots would have been almost as crippling to the mission as losing the aircraft. He began shaking and fought to suppress the chills spreading through his body. He breathed deeply. He often got more excited after an emergency than while responding to it.

Several vehicles loaded with Chilean army troops raced up, and Chisholm directed them toward the drainage ditch. He stayed ready to fire until the soldiers were spread out through and beyond the areas where he had killed the two attackers. Finally he turned and saw Sandi trying to stop de Luca's bleeding. Chisholm was relieved that she was okay, but he was angry that they had disobeyed his order to stay behind the van.

Chisholm asked, "How is he?"

"I think he's got broken ribs and a lung wound," she said. Her voice was strong, but her face was very pale. "He needs a doctor. There's not much I can do."

Chisholm could tell without touching that the driver was dead. The gunner was unconscious but breathing. He also was pale, but his lack of color was from the loss of blood. Chisholm jumped from the jeep and tried to stop the bleeding, which already had covered most of the gunner's uniform from the waist to the knees.

Chisholm was angry at himself for letting Sandi come along. These were the types of risks he did not want her taking. "Running out here was brave but dumb, Major!"

Sandi glared back. "You or me, Colonel?"

"You—and him!" Chisholm nodded toward de Luca. "The mission's dead if we'd lost both of you."

"What about losing you, Colonel?"

"The mission requires qualified C-141 pilots. It doesn't require me."

Before Chisholm and Sandi could argue further, several members of the aircrew rushed up and began helping the wounded. Moments later the first ambulance joined them. As the medical personnel took over, Chisholm focused on Oliverio. "How close are we on the engine, Chief?"

"I was installing the safety wire when the shooting started," Oliverio said. "I'm five minutes from being ready for the engine run."

"Is the oil leak *really* fixed, Chief?"

"Yes, sir. The engine run should verify—"

"Skip the engine run. Button up the cowling as soon as you can, Chief."

Major Griffin was listening. Normally the aircraft commander made the decision whether an aircraft was ready for takeoff. Chisholm's special authority put Griffin in a difficult position, and the young major looked uneasy with Chisholm's decision. In peacetime, safety was the overriding consideration that Griffin was to use in determining whether his aircraft left the ground.

Griffin asked, "Do you think that's safe, sir?"

"Safe enough," Chisholm said. He knew that the engine would not lose oil quickly enough to fail during takeoff. If the engine had to be shut down later, they might be able to complete the mission. Chisholm knew from experience that the C-141 flew well on three engines.

"I've never taken that kind of shortcut before, sir," Griffin said.

"You've never flown a mission like this before," Chisholm said. He gestured toward the soldiers who were searching the drainage ditch. "I'm concerned about safety, and one of my worries is that more than one team of terrorists may be out there."

Griffin nodded. "Yes, sir."

"Sir," Oliverio said to Griffin, "we'll wipe away all the old oil and make one more good check underneath after we've got the engine started."

A reasonable precaution, Chisholm thought. If Oliverio had left a line disconnected, the new leak would appear as soon as the engine was running.

"Have the crew make a good inspection for bullet or shrapnel holes, Major," Chisholm said to Griffin, then addressed everyone. "The sun'll be up in little more than an hour. I want to be airborne in thirty minutes."

34

Chisholm stayed by the battered jeep until de Luca was lifted into an ambulance and driven away. As Chisholm walked to the C-141, he noticed the air attaché's sedan speeding across the ramp toward the airplane.

Finnegan jumped out of the car and hurried over. "Sounds like things are going to hell in a handbasket, Colonel."

"Here or everywhere?" Realizing that his deception had been unsuccessful, Chisholm wondered if the Soviets were taking other actions.

"Right here," Finnegan said. "But there's going to be turmoil in several sections of the city once word of this attack spreads. How soon can you get out of here, Colonel?"

"Don't we have until sunrise?"

Finnegan raised a hand and crossed his fingers. "I think we can hold to that—but don't count on anything longer. If leaders of the opposition party find out you're still on the ground, the government may be forced to seize your airplane."

"What happens then?"

"Let's not find out, Colonel."

"I suppose if we run into trouble down south," Chisholm said, "we shouldn't count on getting any help at Punta Arenas."

The Chilean airfield at Punta Arenas was near the southern tip of South America, almost fifteen hundred miles closer to Antarctica.

Chisholm wanted the option of refueling there if he missed a rendezvous with an aerial tanker.

"After what's happened here, Colonel, I'd hate to see the ambassador even raise that question."

Chisholm nodded his agreement. "You'll see that Captain de Luca gets what he needs?"

"Yes, sir," Finnegan said. "We alerted the embassy's medical staff as soon as we heard there were American casualties."

"I hate to leave him behind. The young man's got guts, and you tell him I said so." Chisholm paused, then added, "I'd like an armed escort when we taxi to the other end for takeoff."

"We'll stick with you until you're airborne," Finnegan said.

Chisholm started to go aboard the aircraft, then thought of one other thing. He wanted to make sure Ramsey knew that the operation had emerged from its cloak of secrecy. "Call General Ramsey's office. Tell him you have a personal message from Blackjack. The message is 'Butterfly'."

"Butterfly? Is that all, sir?"

"He'll understand."

"What if he's unavailable? Not many four-stars sit around waiting to take *my* calls from Santiago."

"He may not be waiting for yours," Chisholm said, "but I'm sure he's got a duty officer sitting around this morning waiting for mine."

As Chisholm spoke, Oliverio joined them.

"This bus is about to leave, Colonel C.," Oliverio said.

As Chisholm and Oliverio walked to the crew-entry door, Chisholm said, "I'm glad you came along, Chief."

Oliverio had a twinkle in his eye along with his usual grin. "I'm starting to remember why my old pappy told me never to volunteer, sir."

"You can stay here with Colonel Finnegan, if you'd like."

"I'll think about that, Colonel C.," Oliverio said. He grabbed the extra intercom cord and headset that was lying beside the crew-entry stairs. He put on the headset and began extending the long cord that would let him monitor the interphone while still outside the aircraft. "I'll let you know if I want to stay, sir, when we get to wherever the hell we're going."

Chisholm got aboard the aircraft and strapped into the jump seat behind Griffin and Sandi. As he pulled on a headset, he discovered that the crew was already running the Before Starting Engines checklist. Good progress, he thought.

Sandi glanced at him as she changed the frequency on one of the radios. Her icy look was one he had become familiar with. Usually he had deserved it—as he did now. He regretted having yelled at her. She had been frightened but brave, and she deserved praise instead of criticism. He owed her an apology, and he wished they could get away from everyone for a few moments. He also wished he had left her in Hawaii.

When Griffin called out that he was starting number two, Chisholm watched the engine instruments. The engine started without a problem, and everyone in the cockpit looked relieved.

"Number two looks perfect," Sergeant Jacobs said as he checked additional indicators on his flight engineer's panel.

"I'll look her over while you're starting three and four," Oliverio said from beside the idling engine.

"Good," Griffin said. "Starting number three."

"Number three's clear," Sergeant Ingalls responded. As the outside scanner, Ingalls was monitoring the engine-starting sequence from beyond the nose of the C-141. One of his responsibilities was to ensure that the area in front of and behind each engine was clear before the pilot started the engine.

Moments later Chisholm noticed that Sergeant Jacobs was leaning forward from his flight engineer's panel. He was straining to see the starter button for number three. Chisholm moved aside to give Jacobs a clearer view.

Jacobs looked back toward the engine RPM indicators on his panel and said, "Engineer's got no rotation on three, sir."

Chisholm looked toward the other set of engine instruments on the panel between the two pilots. The RPM indicators gave the same message: the starter was not turning the compressors on the number three engine.

"Scanner has no sign of rotation out here either, sir," Ingalls said. From his position in front of the C-141, he had a clear view of the big compressor blades in the front of the engine.

Damn, Chisholm said without pressing the microphone button that would have broadcast his assessment to the rest of the crew. Ingalls' response told Chisholm that they had a bigger problem than faulty indicators on the instrument panels.

Griffin hesitated, then said, "Stopping start on number three." He pulled out the starter button that he had pressed a few seconds earlier. "See what you can find out, scanner."

"Roger, sir," Ingalls said, hurrying to the number three engine.

"Number two looks good," Oliverio said. "I'll button up the panel and join the scanner."

Chisholm remembered without having to ask that a lack of rotation was a normal symptom of a broken starter shaft. The starter's purpose was to rotate the engine's compressors, pulling enough air through the engine for the pilot to add fuel and ignition. Sometimes starter shafts broke because the crew had been careless. Chisholm knew they usually broke simply because starter shafts break. The same thing had happened to him on half a dozen C-141s—but never at such a critical time. Whatever the cause of the failure, that starter was not going to spin the compressors fast enough.

Chisholm's mind was racing. He assumed there was a spare starter in the parts kit, and Oliverio could install the new starter in . . . maybe forty-five minutes. Chisholm looked at his watch. He did not have forty-five minutes to give to the chief.

There might be one other answer, Chisholm thought as he grabbed a booklet of information on the airfields of South America. Opening to the diagram for the airport, he sensed that he was about to make an unpopular decision. He glanced at the data, confirming that the runway for Arturo Merino Benitez International Airport was long and without any significant slope from one end to the other. So far, so good, he thought. He already knew that the runway was dry, and he recalled a steady breeze from the south when he had been outside earlier. The headwind and the long, dry, level runway would help them get airborne. At major airports a C-141 seldom needed even half the runway available. He assumed that in spite of a takeoff weight of almost 350,000 pounds, there was a reasonable chance the C-141 could get airborne on three engines.

"Engineer," Chisholm said, directing his question to Jacobs at the flight engineer's panel, "how about giving me a figure for the takeoff ground role for—"

"It's written on the margin of the data card, sir," Jacobs said, pointing toward the takeoff and landing data he had given to the copilot. The takeoff ground roll for a four-engine takeoff was marked in the margin.

"The number I'm curious about is how much runway we'd use on a three-engine takeoff."

Everyone in the cockpit turned toward Chisholm.

"We're at max gross weight, sir," Griffin said.

"I know," Chisholm said, "but don't excite yourself until we hear if the problem's fixable."

Griffin was shaking his head in disbelief. Sandi looked fascinated that Chisholm had raised the subject.

"You can bet the problem's fixable, Colonel C.," Oliverio said, "but if it's what I think it is, it isn't fixable in time to get us out of here before sunrise."

Chisholm asked, "Starter shaft?"

"That's the odds-on favorite, sir. We'll know for sure in a minute."

"Sir," Jacobs said, "the ground run for a three-engine takeoff is nine thousand nine hundred fifty feet—assuming the head wind holds at ten knots and nothing goes wrong. Without the wind we need eleven thousand three hundred feet."

"Copilot," Chisholm said to Sandi, "get a new check on the winds, current and forecast, for the next hour."

She nodded and turned to make the radio call.

"Bad starter shaft, Colonel C.," Oliverio said.

"Roger," Chisholm said grimly. He tried to think of any other possibility he had overlooked.

"Maybe we could get airborne on three, sir," Griffin said, "but have you thought about what happens if we lose another engine on takeoff."

"Sure," Chisholm said. "Lose another, and we'll crash and burn."

He was more direct than he would have been under other circumstances. Although he wanted to hear the counterarguments, he did not plan to spend much more time talking.

Griffin studied the airfield diagram for a moment, then said, "We'll have ten thousand three hundred feet of runway ahead of us when we line up, and we need nine thousand nine hundred fifty of that to get airborne. Frankly, Colonel, I've never heard of such a thing."

"My dad used to do that all the time," Sandi said. When everyone else looked toward her, she continued, "He flew tankers. He told me that on hot days during the Vietnam War, they sometimes loaded on so much fuel that they didn't get airborne until they were on the overrun."

Many airfields had an additional thousand feet at each end of the runway to provide an added margin of safety. While pilots seldom planned to use the overrun, the additional concrete or asphalt occasionally saved airplanes.

Chisholm asked Sandi, "What did you learn about the winds?"

"Steady at eleven knots, right down the runway, sir."

"Good," Chisholm said. A steady head wind would make the takeoff possible.

"I hate to be the one to disturb this little tête-à-tête," Oliverio said, "but sunshine's not far beyond those mountains."

The Andes Mountains, which towered magnificently to the east of Santiago, would delay the local sunrise, but dawn had already reached the airfield.

Griffin frowned. "Colonel, I want to go on record that I believe a three-engine takeoff at this weight is too risky."

"If you're not willing to make the takeoff, Major, I will," Chisholm said firmly. He gestured toward the pilot's seat, which was normally occupied by the aircraft commander on dangerous missions. "But I'd rather have you in the left seat, Major, because you're better qualified than I."

An anguished look covered Griffin's face as he struggled to make the difficult choice.

Chisholm decided it was time for a rallying speech. If the crew did not buy it, he would start giving direct orders. "This crew was handpicked for this mission because you're among the best the Air Force has at what you're trained to do. Captain de Luca's lying on an operating table somewhere because he tried to make sure the mission wasn't stopped here." Chisholm paused and looked around at the other crew members in the cockpit. "Taking risks at times like this is part of the heritage that goes with putting on these flight suits."

Griffin sighed, then asked, "Just what do you propose, Colonel?"

"Start number four and get the scanners aboard. Then I'll temporarily take the copilot's seat so Major Turner can make her check of the new takeoff data while we taxi to the end of the runway. If she or the engineers discover anything in the data that says we can't make it, we'll cancel—but at the end of the runway and not sitting here!"

"Number four's clear to start," Oliverio said in an obvious attempt to prod the cockpit crew into action.

"Chief," Chisholm said, "explain to Colonel Finnegan what we're doing and that it's all being done under my orders and in accordance with my waiver authority."

"Yes, sir," Oliverio said. He put his headset on the ramp beside Sergeant Ingalls, then hurried to Finnegan's sedan, which was parked farther in front of the C-141.

Chisholm added to the rest of the crew. "I'll say two more things that I hope will make some of you feel more comfortable. First, I don't have a death wish, and second, I plan to start number three when we get enough windmilling RPM during takeoff roll."

Once the C-141 was moving, air would flow into the front of the engine, turning the compressors as the wind turns a windmill. The procedure was a little like starting a standard-shift car by rolling it downhill and releasing the clutch when the car was moving fast enough. At some point during the takeoff roll—and Chisholm was unsure how fast the C-141 would have to be moving—the compressors would be rotating fast enough for him to add fuel and ignition. In seconds the engine would light off and accelerate to idle. Chisholm expected to have all four engines at takeoff power by the time the aircraft lifted off near the end of the runway.

Griffin turned away from Chisholm and reached for the starter button for the number four engine. "Starting number four, scanner."

"Four's clear," Sergeant Ingalls responded.

Within a couple of minutes Oliverio and Ingalls were aboard and the C-141 was ready to taxi on three engines.

Chisholm stepped back from the jump seat as Sandi unstrapped from the copilot's seat. As she tried to pass him, he took hold of her elbow and stopped her. He leaned close to her ear and said, "My comments outside were asinine. I'm sorry."

Her look was noncommittal, as if she were trying to judge his sincerity.

He squeezed her arm slightly and added, "That was brave, and you're a good officer, Major."

He assumed that she preferred to hear his professional appraisal, instead of his personal concerns about her safety. There was no time for discussion, so he moved into the copilot's seat before she responded. She sat on the jump seat to make an independent computation of the takeoff data.

Fastening the lap belt, he thought about how good it felt to be back at the controls of a C-141, even though this was just to taxi. Now that de Luca had been lost from the crew, Chisholm expected to take his turns in one of the pilot's seats during the long hours ahead.

Finnegan's sedan and five armed jeeps accompanied the C-141 as it taxied the two miles to the north end of the runway. Griffin parked while Sandi, Oliverio, and Ingalls computed the final parameters that had to be checked before takeoff. While waiting, Griffin and Chisholm discussed how the number three engine could be started and advanced to takeoff power. Chisholm easily could reach the Fuel and Start Ignition panel, so he would start the engine while Griffin continued the takeoff. Once number three reached idle, Chisholm would advance the throttle and remove any rudder trim Griffin had used to offset the lack of thrust from number three.

After comparing the figures, Sandi said, "The only problem—" She smiled, self-consciously, then continued. "Well, not the only problem, but the one place we can't match the required performance is in rate of climb on three engines. If you don't get number three started, we'll be at least two hundred feet low at Maipú."

Maipú was the first navigational fix, eight miles beyond the end of the runway. Chisholm was not worried since the minimum crossing altitude at Maipú gave several hundred feet of terrain clearance. He would have been much more concerned on a cloudy day when the pilots would be unable to see the ground. "We should see the terrain well enough to stay out of the trees. Anything else?"

Sandi answered, "We've got a real 'go speed' of one hundred thirty-four knots. On this takeoff go speed is based on refusal speed, and it's fourteen knots before rotation speed."

Chisholm nodded, understanding what might seem like gibberish to those unfamiliar with flying jargon. Refusal speed was the speed the C-141 could accelerate to and still stop on the remaining runway. Thus he interpreted Sandi's words as meaning that once the C-141 had used up enough runway to attain 134 knots, there was barely enough runway remaining to stop—and the C-141 would be still well short of flying speed. On most takeoffs a C-141 quickly reached rotation speed—the speed at which the pilot pulled on the yoke to raise the nose off the ground. Therefore a C-141 pilot routinely could stop if a serious emergency occurred anytime during the takeoff roll before the aircraft became airborne.

In this case when the crew continued beyond the go speed of 134 knots, they were committed. Griffin would have to try a takeoff no matter what malfunction might occur while the C-141 was accelerating to 148 knots so that it could lift its weight from the runway. Chisholm assumed everyone was dealing with the same thought—

an engine failure during that fourteen-knot window would doom them to a crash if engine number three was not running by then.

"I don't guess you see a real go speed very often," Chisholm said.

"About as often as we see three-engine takeoffs, Colonel," Jacobs said from his flight engineer's panel.

Chisholm got out of the copilot's seat so Sandi could strap in for takeoff. Before Chisholm strapped into the jump seat, Oliverio tapped him on the shoulder.

"I understand I missed something you had to say about a death wish, Colonel C.," Oliverio said without using the intercom. "Did you say you had one or you didn't?"

Chisholm smiled. "Does it make any difference one way or the other to you, Chief?"

"Not really, sir," Oliverio said with a look of anticipation, "because either way, we're in for one hell of a ride—and I wouldn't miss it for a fifty percent interest in a Coors brewery."

With Sandi in position and the new takeoff data available, Griffin gave the takeoff briefing. Though briefings for takeoffs in good weather were almost ritualistic, he had several items to emphasize throughout the briefing.

"The copilot's airspeed command marker will be set on go speed—one hundred thirty-four knots," Griffin said, pointing toward the airspeed indicator in front of Sandi.

She nodded and tapped a long fingernail against a small window below the indicator. The number 134, which she had set earlier into the window, was visible. This setting would cause a white marker to center on her airspeed indicator when the C-141 reached go speed.

Griffin continued. "The pilot's airspeed command marker is set at rotation speed—one hundred forty-eight knots." He pointed toward the 148 in the small window below his airspeed indicator, then continued, "If any crew member notices a safety-of-flight malfunction prior to the copilot calling 'Go,' call out the one word 'Reject,' and I will discontinue the takeoff. If the malfunction occurs after the copilot calls 'Go,' describe the malfunction, but do not use the word 'Reject.' I'll handle it as an in-flight emergency."

The rest of the briefing covered the routine items—what would happen if everything went okay. Chisholm listened and was pleased that Griffin covered the difficult and the easy without a hitch. There was no confusion, no hesitation. The crew was ready and showing the calm professionalism that belied the dangers inherent in the takeoff.

When the Before Takeoff checklist was complete, Sandi called the tower for takeoff clearance. Chisholm watched a scene taking place at two armed jeeps parked in front of the aircraft. Finnegan was in an animated conversation with a Chilean colonel, who was the senior member of the security detail. From the amount of pointing both officers were doing, Chisholm assumed that they were arguing about sunrise.

The airfield was in the shadow of the Andes Mountains, but Chisholm could see sunlight creeping across the hills west of the airfield. In minutes the sunshine would reach the runway, technically ending the agreement permitting the C-141 to pass through Santiago.

Hearing the tower operator grant the clearance for takeoff, Griffin called for the Lineup checklist. As the final checks were completed, Griffin was watching the jeeps. "They're going to have to move."

Chisholm said, "Flash the taxi lights."

Griffin reached up and cycled the switch on and off several times.

Finnegan pointed at the lights and kept talking. The Chilean colonel was shaking his head.

"He's not going to let us go," Sandi said.

Finnegan looked toward the cockpit and stared for a couple of seconds. When he spoke again to the colonel, Finnegan cupped both hands over his own ears as if representing a headset. Then he pointed toward the cockpit, shook his head, and shrugged with an animated gesture of both palms up.

Griffin asked, "Does he want us to put out the scanner?" The scanner often went outside the aircraft when there was a need to talk with someone who did not have an aircraft radio.

"Negative!" Chisholm doubted that the Chilean colonel had understood Finnegan's signals, but Chisholm had—without a radio from the jeep to the airplane, there was no way short of gunfire to get the pilots to stop. "Give us seventy-five percent on one and four, but hold the brakes."

Griffin hesitated, then advanced the two outboard throttles. The RPM indicators rose to 75 percent and the roar of the engines increased dramatically.

Finnegan talked quickly and pointed toward the mountains that were blocking the sun. The colonel looked uncertain.

"Edge forward a couple of feet," Chisholm said, "but don't get us shot."

Griffin released the brakes, and the C-141 lumbered forward.

The colonel looked excited. Finnegan vaulted into the backseat beside the gunner and started pointing frantically toward the taxiway that led to the parking area. The colonel grabbed his hat and yelled at his driver. The jeep lurched away to the side and was followed by the other jeep.

"Remind me to send a thank you to Colonel Finnegan," Chisholm said as Griffin guided the C-141 onto the runway.

Sandi turned to Chisholm and shook her head slowly, "If you can't be good, be lucky, Colonel."

"Roger that," Chisholm said as he winked at her.

Griffin stopped the C-141 as close to the end of the runway as possible. When he signaled he was ready, Sandi moved the throttles for number one and four to full takeoff power. Held by the brakes, the aircraft shuddered noticeably. The noise would have drowned out normal conversations in the cockpit, but everyone was concentrating too much to talk.

Griffin kept control of the number two throttle and slowly advanced it. Because there was no balancing thrust from the inoperative number three engine, he could not bring number two immediately to full power. He had to wait until the C-141 was going fast enough for the rudder to keep the aircraft aligned with the runway.

When he released the brakes, the C-141 slowly began to accelerate its one-third of a million pounds.

Chisholm tried not to think about how slowly the aircraft was gaining speed. Instead he concentrated on the RPM indicators, watching for number three to reach 15 percent. At first there was little movement, but the windmilling RPM slowly increased as the airspeed built up. He leaned forward and looked more directly at the indicator. The lower angle made the reading seem higher, so he rationalized that the engine's RPM had reached 15 percent. He moved the Fuel and Start Ignition switch to Airstart and held it there. This sprayed fuel into the combustion chamber and provided a continuous spark to set the fuel-air mixture ablaze.

As he waited for indications that the engine had lit off, he looked ahead. Little more than half the runway remained in front of the C-141.

The temperature indicator for number three showed a sudden

increase, signaling that a fire had roared to life in the combustion chamber. The temperature rise was a good sign as long as the reading peaked out well below the upper limits. Chisholm looked toward Sergeant Jacobs, who nodded and mouthed the words "oil pressure." Lubricating oil was pumping through number three.

The RPM indicator rose to idle, indicating a successful light-off. Chisholm reached forward to the copilot's set of throttles and grabbed number three. He moved it toward takeoff power while removing the rudder trim Griffin had set to help control the aircraft with number three inoperative. The C-141 accelerated faster in response to having full power on all four engines.

As Chisholm positioned the throttle, his hand moved in beneath Sandi's. One of her responsibilities during takeoff was to make sure the throttles stayed at the takeoff setting. She lifted her hand slightly to let him move the number three throttle into place. Then she held her hand on his, making it difficult for him to withdraw his. If they were going to die, it would be hand in hand.

"Go," she announced crisply as the airspeed passed 134 knots.

They were committed, Chisholm thought, but now the airspeed was building more rapidly than before.

In a few more seconds the airspeed reached 148 knots. Sandi announced, "Rotate!" She squeezed Chisholm's hand, then released it.

Griffin pulled on the yoke. The nose wheels came off the runway, but the heavy aircraft seemed hesitant to leave the ground. Moments later the C-141 became airborne with almost a thousand feet of runway to spare. Cheering erupted among the crew members who had no immediate responsibilities.

"Never a doubt," Chisholm said.

"Gear up," Griffin said, then smiled for the first time in a long while. "After Takeoff, Climb checklist."

After the checklist items were completed and Sandi had made the necessary radio calls, the crew members began sharing thoughts on the intercom.

"Good job, crew," Chisholm said.

Griffin seemed more relaxed. "That was a takeoff I'll tell my grand-kids about someday when I have some."

"That was one of those million-dollar takeoffs, sir," Oliverio said. "You wouldn't sign up for one for a million dollars, and now I wouldn't give up the experience for a million."

Griffin asked, "Weren't you worried at all, Colonel?"

Chisholm shook his head but winked toward Griffin. "Like Major Turner said, 'If you can't be good, be lucky.' "

Sandi shook her head in mock disbelief. Chisholm sensed her reaction was one of admiration tempered by memories of their earlier frustrations. She pushed aside her headset and spoke to Chisholm. "You haven't changed a bit, have you?"

"I've changed in some ways," Chisholm said with a pleasant look she had seen many times years before. Then he added, "But not where the mission's concerned."

"It's nice—or maybe *interesting* is a better word—to be flying with you again, Colonel."

"Likewise, Major."

"Colonel Chisholm," Rick McClain said as he referred to the display on his laptop computer, "if we can cover twenty-eight hundred miles in the next six and a half hours, we've got a good target that comes in range at seventeen-forty-five Zulu."

"East or west of here?" Chisholm wondered if the ARIA, which would be flying in from the northwest, would be able to make the same rendezvous.

"That target will be fifteen degrees west."

Chisholm considered the answer as he looked toward the coast and the Pacific Ocean beyond. "That'll work. Get us a copy of the exact coordinates." Chisholm paused, then added with a smile, "Now that we've got the easy stuff out of the way, we can start concentrating on the tricky part."

35

Kaliningrad, USSR
Friday, 2 April, 1443 local (1143 GMT)

Novikov was meeting with his engineers in the *Borzoi* control center when a call from Minister Levchenko came in on a secure line.

"Petruk's men have failed," Levchenko said. He told of the C-141's escape within the last hour from Santiago. "What should my orders be to the pilots of the MiGs?"

Novikov hesitated. He had been concentrating on the satellites, not on aircraft. "Are the MiGs close enough to catch the American plane before it reaches Antarctica?"

"I don't know," Levchenko said.

Novikov heard another voice, obviously one of Levchenko's advisers on another telephone at the minister's end of the line. "No. They must refuel once more."

"Let me have a moment to check some data, Comrade Minister," Novikov said, quickly deciding that the MiGs would be of little immediate help. He grabbed the atlas and a computer printout, which listed the times and longitudes of each *Borzoi* perigee within the next twenty-four hours. Checking the atlas and now knowing when the C-141 had started south from Santiago, Novikov estimated that the Americans would be at eighty degrees south in about six hours. It took him only a moment's study of the perigee times and locations to identify the most likely first target—*Borzoi IX* would be almost due south of Chile in six hours and one minute. Novikov asked, "How soon can the MiGs reach eighty degrees south latitude?"

Hearing the sounds of muffled discussions at Levchenko's end,

Novikov realized that he was asking the right questions, but to the wrong people. He added, "That's about twenty-seven hundred nautical miles south of Santiago."

Moments later, the adviser answered, "The MiGs will require about seven more hours, plus whatever time is used on the ground for refueling in Argentina."

"And right now, Petr," Levchenko said, "I need to tell General Diakanov in Buenos Aires what to tell the pilots of the MiGs."

"One moment, Comrade Minister," Novikov said as he swiftly scanned his listing. Obviously *Borzoi IX* would have come and gone—or have been destroyed—by the time the MiGs could attack the C-141. Two hours later *Borzoi VII* would pass over Antarctica on the side closest to South America. "I can give you coordinates and times where I expect the Americans to be. Using GLONASS, the MiG pilots should have no trouble finding the airplane."

He knew that GLONASS, the Soviet's satellite-based navigational system, would solve the difficult problem of navigating in a polar region.

"No GLONASS," the adviser said to Levchenko, but loud enough for Novikov to hear.

"These MiGs are not equipped with satellite receivers," Levchenko said, referring to antennas that would receive data from the Soviet constellation of navigational satellites. "I will tell the pilots that your radar will guide them using the long-range radios. Now I must give that information to Diakanov."

"Wait, sir," Novikov said, wishing Levchenko understood the limits of the technologies. "*Zashchitnik I*'s radar will not give data on aircraft that are flying that far south of the equator."

"Then what can be done?" Levchenko sounded more irritated.

Do I have to do everyone's job? Novikov wondered, as he fought to keep his frustration from showing in his voice. His knowledge of cosmonautics had predicted the enemy's location eight hours in advance, and that miracle seemed totally unappreciated. "I can provide the locations and the times to the pilots, Comrade Minister. I cannot place the C-141 in front of their missiles."

Guam is west of the international date line, so it was early Saturday morning when Paul Edwards of NASA arrived at Andersen Air Force Base. Traveling under the alias of an Air Force major, Edwards had flown on a C-141 from McGuire Air Force Base, New Jersey, through

Elmendorf Air Force Base, Alaska, to Yokota Air Base in Japan. From there he had ridden to Guam in an Air Force C-21 Learjet. His aircraft was towed into a large hangar and parked beside Colonel Stuart's C-141 before Edwards deplaned.

Dr. Turnhill was waiting nearby, unsure why he had been brought out in the middle of the night. When he saw Edwards, Turnhill asked, "What are you doing in Guam, Paul?" Before Edwards could answer, Turnhill continued, "Something strange is going on here, because nothing's going on here. I've just been wasting my time."

"I understand," Edwards said as they were joined by Colonel Newton, the base commander.

"Doctor Edwards," Newton said, "I hope you won't mind, but for the security of the operation, we're going to use a closed van instead of a staff car to take you to the radar site."

"Fine," Edwards said.

Turnhill asked, "What's he talking about?"

"Explaining that is part of why I've spent the last umpteen hours on an airplane," Edwards said. Turning to the colonel, he added, "I'd like to have a couple of minutes to speak privately with Doctor Turnhill."

Once they were alone in the van, Edwards explained to Turnhill that his Prospector spacecraft had been launched from the moon and now was speeding toward a devastating rendezvous with Cosmos 3220.

At first Turnhill seemed stunned that so much could have happened on his project since he had left Washington little more than two days earlier. Then his face reddened with anger as he blurted out, "Why didn't anyone have the decency to tell me?"

"The reason no one told you, Bill," Edwards said, "was that we were afraid you'd go right to the *Post* or to one of the networks with—"

"Right," Turnhill said defiantly, "and that's exactly what should have been done! The American people should decide whether or not the military should be permitted to interfere with scientific space programs."

"President Grigoriev already made that decision," Edwards said firmly, "and you could have destroyed any possibility of our breaking the Soviet blockade." Then sounding conciliatory, Edwards added, "I also wanted to keep you from forcing the administrator to fire you. We need your talents on Moon Base—"

"I'd have been fired for speaking the truth?"

"You'd have been fired for the unauthorized disclosure of classified information," Edwards said.

"Sometimes a man has to take a stand for what he believes in," Turnhill said, as if delivering a lecture, "no matter what the consequences."

"My father taught me the same thing," Edwards said, "but he also told me to take a look around. Sometimes when you notice who's standing on your side of the dividing line, you discover that maybe your principled stand has put you on the wrong team."

"A lot of good people believe our threat is what forced the Russians to react," Turnhill said.

"But you don't, Bill," Edwards said, "because you're smart enough to know the Soviets couldn't build their space weapons in the last couple of weeks."

Turnhill crossed his arms in front of him but did not answer.

"Think it over, Bill," Edwards said. "I'd be pleased to have your help, but with or without it, I have to go do a job."

It was still Friday in Argentina when the three MiG-25s reached Río Gallegos after an uneventful flight from Lima. As Berezin taxied to a parking spot, all the people he saw were wearing Argentinean uniforms.

Stepping from the ladder in a steady breeze, he tried to stretch out the stiffness that came from spending eight of the last ten hours in the cramped cockpit. For a moment he savored the crisp, clean smell of autumn that was in marked contrast to the oppressive heat and stench of Managua. Too tired even to think about more flying, he wished he could stay for a few days.

The three pilots were greeted by a captain who spoke no Russian. Berezin's Spanish was good enough to learn that the MiGs were to be serviced immediately. Another aircraft, which was flying someone important from Buenos Aires, would arrive in twenty minutes. The captain also explained that food was available in a nearby building.

The flying had left Berezin very dry, so he retrieved his travel bag, which included the bottle of vodka he had added in Managua.

Inside the building he was shocked at the variety and quantity of food that had been set out on two large tables. The Argentineans had provided fresh fruits and vegetables and more beef than he had ever seen at one time. "Perhaps," he said in Russian, "we should volunteer to help this air force instead of the Sandinistas." Kapitan Kovalev and Leytenant Yashin agreed enthusiastically.

Berezin had been so preoccupied with the mission and with Pokrovskiy's death that he had not noticed how hungry he was. He and his wing men ate voraciously. During the meal he agreed that each man could have one shot of vodka, but no more until he knew when they had to fly again. Fifteen minutes later he was considering authorizing another round when he heard the sound of an aircraft landing. Wolfing down the rest of his third sandwich, Berezin stuffed four apples into his pockets then walked outside.

The Argentinean captain was accompanying a tall man in a business suit from the aircraft that had parked near the three MiGs.

"I am General Diakanov," the man said in Russian as he turned toward his aircraft. "Come with me. There is little time." He said nothing else until he had the three pilots enclosed in the privacy of the aircraft's cabin. Gesturing toward four large garbage bags, Diakanov continued, "Find clothing in there that fits. You must change while we talk."

Berezin dumped the contents of the nearest bag. He was surprised to find arctic gear similar to what he had worn while assigned to a base near Vladivostok. As he picked through the outer garments, he noticed that none had military insignias. He suddenly realized that there were no labels, no identification of any kind.

Diakanov unfolded a map of Antarctica. Several dots were on the circle of latitude at eighty degrees south. Each dot had a number beside it. "These dots represent the locations where Moscow expects your target to be at the Greenwich times indicated. You will take off as soon as your MiGs are refueled, then destroy the American C-141 as quickly as you can intercept it."

Fascinated by the map, Berezin stopped selecting clothing. The main geographic feature was a huge white blob with irregular edges, making him think of a serving of ice cream that had dropped a few minutes earlier onto a warm floor. And, he quickly decided, the map was about as useful for navigation as melting ice cream. There was less detail throughout the huge land mass than he had seen on aeronautical charts of the most remote regions of Siberia. He was feeling less confident with each new discovery he made about the mission he had been assigned.

Diakanov seemed to notice Berezin's dismay. The general rotated the map so that some islands along the edge were closest to Berezin and said, "We are located here at the southern end of Argentina."

That helped, but it seemed to Berezin that the small part of South America was a great distance from the dots that indicated the C-141's locations. "How long should it take us to reach the closest target area, Comrade General?" As Berezin started undressing, he tried to listen and to study the map at the same time.

"You can't squander fuel flying supersonic," Diakanov said, "so I was told that you will need about four hours to intercept. If you don't waste time, you should intercept the Americans about here." Diakanov pointed at a dot with the number 1944 beside it.

All three pilots looked, but Berezin's mind barely registered what he was seeing. Instead he was thinking that four hours of flying would leave little fuel for the rest of the mission. Even counting the fuel carried in the external tanks, his MiGs obviously would be unable to return to Argentina.

Before Berezin could ask where the MiGs would go after the attack, Diakanov pulled three packets from a briefcase. His tone was matter-of-fact as he continued, "Here are new identity papers. Give me your old papers and any personal effects you brought along."

Accepting his new documents, Berezin asked, "Where does Moscow want us to take the MiGs after we destroy the C-141, Comrade General?"

"The closest Russian base is Druzhnaya," Diakanov said. He studied the map of Antarctica for a moment, then pointed toward a small square on the coast, at the edge of an ice shelf. "The base's navigational beacon will transmit for the next twelve hours."

That would help find the base, Berezin thought, but he was more interested in knowing about the airfield. "How long is the landing field at Druzhnaya, Comrade General?"

"We have little time for questions," Diakanov said, as he began stuffing the pilots' personal effects into his briefcase. "There is no landing field. You will fly over the sea five miles north of Druzhnaya, then parachute from your aircraft. The ice fields will keep you out of the water but should allow your MiGs to sink and never be found."

Berezin glanced at Kovalev and Yashin, who had stopped dressing and appeared unwilling to believe what they had heard. "Will—"

"Even though you will arrive in darkness, do not overfly Druzhnaya," Diakanov continued. "The Americans now have a base that's less than ten miles away, and we want them to see and hear nothing that indicates military aircraft were in the area. Teams from Druzhnaya will deploy on the ice once you contact the base. If you encounter any Americans when you're on the ice, say that you are lost and that you recently arrived as part of a meteorology study team." Diakanov closed the briefcase as if signaling that it was time for the discussion to come to an end. "Do you have any questions about how you are to destroy the American aircraft?"

"It is unclear, Comrade General, how we will navigate to the place where the American aircraft should be," Berezin said, avoiding the question he wanted to ask—Did Diakanov or anyone in Moscow believe that the MiG-25s would have enough fuel to reach Druzhnaya? Knowing that asking such a question would do no good, he continued, "The magnetic compasses will be unreliable, and this map doesn't have enough detail to—"

In a degrading tone Diakanov interrupted, "Have you never flown over ice and snow before, Podpolkovnik? I cannot solve all your problems. I can only give you the information and order you to destroy the aircraft." He looked at his watch, then said, "If the refueling is completed, be airborne within twenty minutes."

36

The Pentagon, Washington, D.C.
Friday, 2 April, 1147 local (1647 GMT)

General Ramsey was at his desk having a salad for lunch when he received a call from the senior officer on duty in the Operations Center.

"General," the caller said, "the three Nicaraguan MiGs aren't on the airfield at Río Gallegos anymore."

"How long have they been gone?"

"Unknown, sir. Perhaps as long as an hour."

"Any chance we can locate the MiGs again?" Ramsey was almost certain the answer was no. The MiGs were in a part of the world with few radars and almost no American or allied observers.

"No, sir," the duty officer said. "Even if we had a space-based radar, General, we wouldn't have regular coverage that far south."

Ramsey looked at his watch as he opened a notebook, which had top secret markings on the cover. Checking the schedule that had been computed after the takeoff from Santiago, Ramsey confirmed that the C-141's first launch was an hour away. At worst, he decided, the MiGs were at least nine hundred miles behind. Although the fighters would get closer during that hour, Chisholm's aircraft was safe from the MiGs until after attacking the first satellite.

Ramsey decided that the showdown could come two hours later at the second target. The C-141 would move three hundred miles in those two hours while the MiGs would cover more than a thousand. With great concern Ramsey closed the notebook. If the Soviets knew where to send the MiGs, they could be waiting when the C-141 arrived for the second attack.

Using the call sign for Chisholm's aircraft, Ramsey asked, "Is Southern Star still in secure-comm range?"

"We should be able to reach it in a few more minutes through our comsats at GEO, sir."

"Tell them I'm concerned about MiGs at target two," Ramsey said, "and that I'm trying to get their air cover to them."

Ramsey used a secure telephone to call his counterpart in the office of the chief of naval operations. When the admiral answered, Ramsey said, "We're running out of time, Jim. Can you provide fighter cover at point Delta Two in three hours?"

"Stand by." Moments later the admiral responded, "Virtually impossible. The *Nimitz* is just moving into range, but she's fighting twenty-foot seas."

"Can you get some F-14s to Delta Two using tankers?"

"Doubtful, Frank. We were already counting on aerial refueling when I said they were about into range. The fighters would have almost no loiter time for coverage after the rendezvous."

"I'd say the C-141 needs its hand held for about an hour at the most," Ramsey said. "I can't see how the MiGs will be operating on more than fumes if they do get to Delta Two."

"The *Nimitz* and its group have just steamed through four days of mean seas, Frank," the admiral said. "After all that, we'll do our damnedest not to show up late."

Fifteen minutes later and seventy-five hundred miles away, the USS *Nimitz* started coming around into the wind in stormy seas near the Antarctic Circle. The sky above the ninety-one-thousand-ton aircraft carrier was sullen with portents of winter, and the wind was ripping white foam from the tops of breaking waves. In the distance the bow of the nearest destroyer periodically disappeared in geyser-like eruptions as the ship plunged forward.

U.S. Navy Captain Richard Walsh watched with experienced eyes. He stood quietly in the primary flight deck control room, which bulged out from the port side of the island that towered over the flight deck. As the primary air controller, or air boss, Walsh was in charge of launching and recovering the *Nimitz*'s aircraft. Spread out magnificently below him, the huge deck of the carrier was wet from thirty-six hours of rain. Scores of crewmen, wearing outfits color-coded to indicate their particular duties, were preparing to launch four F-14 Tomcats and two KA-6Ds, the aerial tanker version of the

A-6 Intruder. Most activity was near the catapults on the forward end of the flight deck. Across from the control room where Walsh stood, rotors were already turning on an SH-3 Sea King helicopter. In a few minutes Walsh would clear the helicopter for takeoff so that the SH-3 would be available immediately for rescue if one of the jets crashed during launch.

Lieutenant Commander Todd Mason was among the men with Walsh. Mason moved from one window to another as the *Nimitz* finished the turn. "I can't believe those guys who are steering the desks in Washington," Mason said. "Don't they understand that forcing a launch in these conditions can cost us airplanes and crews?"

"They understand, Todd," Walsh said patiently. "That's what assures me that we must be doing something pretty important."

For the last hour Chisholm had sat behind the pilot's seat, peering out the side window. Watching the spectacular Antarctic coastline and icebergs, Chisholm had felt more like a tourist than a military officer about to attack the forces of the Soviet Union.

The route to the first target brought the C-141 beside Palmer Land, an Antarctic peninsula that extended more than a thousand jagged, icy miles toward South America. Palmer Land and the Palmer Archipelago were the most populated segments of the ice-covered continent. From thirty-seven thousand feet, however, Chisholm had seen few signs of life. Instead the rugged mountains and narrow coastline reminded him of the Kamchatka Peninsula, stretching white and forbidding along the aerial route from Japan to Alaska.

Moments earlier the C-141 had left behind the pack ice of the Bellingshausen Sea and now was beyond the Bryan Coast. As near as Chisholm could figure, it was almost noon—about four hours after local sunrise; about four hours until local sunset. Most of the mission would be flown in the sixteen-hour darkness of the Antarctic night, so he wanted to see as much as possible. Now, however, there was little to see below except for varying shades of white. In some places the sun seemed to cast shadows, but he had trouble distinguishing shadows and ice fields from low clouds.

Chisholm decided that he might have felt overwhelmed if this were his first trip to Antarctica. Years earlier he had flown three resupply missions to McMurdo Station, on the Australian side of the continent. In each case he had landed his C-141 on McMurdo's runway of ice instead of heading inland.

On this mission he felt more like a veteran, ready to deal with the land of ice on its own terms. Still, he was glad that the C-141 was equipped to receive signals from satellites of the Global Positioning System (GPS). A decade earlier this mission would have required two navigators. They would have worked almost full time to locate each target area among the meridians of longitude that converged to a single point at the geographic south pole. Now, however, onboard computers were automatically processing signals from a constellation of NAVSTARs and updating the geographical position continuously. He had no doubts about Griffin being able to fly directly to the targets.

However, Chisholm had a new problem to worry about: the warning just received from the Pentagon about the possibility of MiGs at the second target. He had no doubt that Novikov knew exactly where to send the MiGs. The real question was whether the pursuing pilots could navigate to the coordinates Novikov would provide.

Certainly magnetic compasses would be of little help to the MiG pilots. Since the magnetic south pole was hundreds of miles from the geographic south pole, the C-141's magnetic compasses were already off by more than thirty degrees. At target two the magnetic variation would be nearly seventy degrees.

He imagined being a MiG pilot crossing this same coastline in an hour and a half. Looking across the vast, uncharted land below, Chisholm decided that he would much rather be in the C-141.

His thoughts were interrupted when Griffin announced on interphone, "Engineer and Load, it's time to wake everyone to start prebreathing."

Chisholm checked his watch: less than an hour remained before the scheduled launch of the first missile. He moved back to the navigator's seat and picked up his oxygen mask. He was not enthusiastic about donning the mask, but that was one of the necessary evils. Breathing 100 percent oxygen for thirty minutes before depressurizing the aircraft made it less likely that anyone would experience decompression sicknesses, such as the bends.

As the flight engineer and loadmaster acknowledged Griffin's directive, Chisholm connected his oxygen mask to a small portable cylinder of oxygen. By using one of the walk-around bottles, he could stay on oxygen yet move freely around the aircraft to observe the procedures for launching the first missile. If there were going to be any problems in getting the missiles out of the C-141, he wanted to observe those problems firsthand.

Fitting his mask onto his face, he was reminded of one reason he had never enjoyed high-altitude airdrops. For the next hour the mask would be pressed uncomfortably tight across his nose, the sides of his cheeks, and under his chin.

He hooked his headset up to a long interphone cord so that he could communicate and listen to the radios as he roamed throughout the C-141. With his oxygen and radios finally set, he went into the cargo compartment and joined the others, who were putting on winter flight suits, parkas, face masks, arctic mittens, mukluks, and parachutes.

When Chisholm had all his cold-weather gear on except for his gloves, Blake handed him a parachute and said, "Rules are rules, Colonel."

"You're making me think I should've monitored this mission from the Pentagon," Chisholm said as he accepted the parachute. The only part of Blake that was visible was the area around the sergeant's eyes, but Chisholm assumed there was a frustrated smile hidden there somewhere. Fitting the parachute over the other gear, Chisholm assumed that he and Blake were sharing the same thought— parachutes were a useless precaution on this particular mission.

Regulations required the loadmasters to make sure that everyone in the cargo compartment was either strapped in or wearing a parachute whenever the outer doors were open in flight. In this case Chisholm doubted that his parachute would matter in the long run if he were so unlucky as to fall from the aircraft at nearly twenty-five thousand feet over Antarctica. First, he would need to be lucky enough to keep hold of his oxygen bottle as he tumbled into the frigid blast of air rushing by the aircraft. Otherwise the metal cylinder was likely to yank away his mask or batter him into unconsciousness. In any case his parachute would not be attached to a static line, so he would have to activate the barometric release. Even if he survived the descent, he likely would die of exposure on some nameless ice field, since the security of this mission had prevented the positioning of any rescue forces.

He pushed such grim thoughts from his mind. Looking around, he found that everyone reminded him of oversized children bundled up by protective mothers for a few minutes out in the snow.

The C-141 was descending to the scheduled drop altitude of twenty-four thousand feet as Chisholm stepped into the doorway of the command-and-control module. McClain was similarly dressed except for the parachute. The young engineer would remain strapped to a chair while the cargo doors were open, so he did not have to wear a parachute. His computers were already linked electronically with those on the ARIA, which was 175 miles to the west in a race-track-shaped holding pattern at thirty-seven thousand feet.

After satisfying himself that McClain was ready, Chisholm moved toward the tail and looked over Blake's careful preparations for the first airdrop. The upper section of the shipping container had been removed from the middle missile in the last row. Most of the missile was covered from view by corrugated packing material that helped support the olive-drab packs of the cargo parachutes that now were on the container. A thick electrical cable snaked forward from the missile to the command-and-control module. As the Soviet satellite entered the coverage of the ARIA's radar, updated information on the satellite's orbit would be sent to the missile through the cable.

Other straps of olive drab stretched back to the extraction para-chute, which was suspended beneath a holder on the ceiling. The parachute was positioned to drop free behind the aircraft once the tail doors were opened and the pilot moved a switch on his panel that controlled the aerial-delivery system (ADS).

Finally the thirty minutes of prebreathing had passed, and the flight engineer announced that he was starting to depressurize. De-pressurizing was the first step in the coordinated series of actions necessary to drop cargo from a pressurized aircraft. Chisholm noticed the decrease in temperature as heated air from the engines stopped entering the cargo compartment.

When the pressure within the cabin matched that outside the aircraft, Griffin said, "Loadmaster, the doors are armed. You're cleared to open the pressure door."

"Roger," Blake said in response to Griffin's command, "we're dis-connecting the latches."

Chisholm had brought along a stopwatch, and he clicked the start-ing mechanism so that he could measure the time required to open the cargo doors: the pressure door, ramp, and petal doors.

Blake then joined Sergeant Claremont kneeling at the base of the large rectangular door that formed the pressure bulkhead at the back of the cargo compartment. Through the years a number of extra latches had been added to keep the door closed in spite of more than a hundred thousand pounds of pressure that pushed against it during pressurized flight. While these additions had reduced the number of rapid decompressions caused by the door being torn open, each latch had to be removed individually, thereby delaying the loadmasters.

Chisholm watched impatiently. There was still plenty of time, but he was uncertain how rushed things might get during later drops. He would hate to lose a shot at one of the *Borzoi* because the crew was unable to get the cargo doors open in time.

Finally Blake stood and announced on interphone, "Aux latches, cam jacks, and safety pins are removed." Reaching a panel that included controls for the doors and ramp, he added, "Opening the pressure door."

He moved a switch to Open and the lower edge of the door slowly swung back. The door, which was hinged at the top, rotated toward the ceiling to be out of the way for cargo loading and offloading— and airdrop. The pressure door was moving into the empty area above the two outer doors, called the petal doors. An observer outside the aircraft would be unable to tell whether the pressure door had been opened since its position did not affect the outward configuration of the C-141.

Chisholm now could see the inside of the two huge petal doors that tapered to a point at the aft end of the C-141's fuselage. At the moment the outer skin of the petal doors still provided a smooth, aerodynamic shape beneath the towering tail of the C-141. Once they opened, however, there would be a gaping hole across the end of the cargo compartment.

When the pressure door clanked against the ceiling, Blake had done all he could from his panel. The only remaining impediments to an airdrop were the ramp and petal doors. In flight the ramp and petal doors were controlled by the pilots since the aircraft could be damaged if these were opened at too high an airspeed.

"Pressure door's open, sir," Blake said.

Chisholm clicked his stopwatch, then struggled for a moment to uncover his wristwatch. He found that fewer than fifteen minutes remained until the scheduled airdrop.

In the pilot's seat in the cockpit Griffin had no view of what was happening in the cargo compartment, so he asked, "Are the doors clear?"

"Clear, sir," Blake answered.

"Ramp and petal doors coming open," Griffin announced as he moved the All Doors switch to Open on his ADS panel.

The ramp, which formed the last section of the floor in the cargo compartment, had been angled up from the floor like the head of a hospital bed. In response to Griffin's action, the back of the ramp lowered until the ramp was level with the floor. Then Chisholm saw the petal doors shudder for a moment and start slowly swinging down and out. As the doors separated, he gradually saw the sky and clouds and the vast whiteness of Antarctica nearly five miles below. At the same time the noise and turbulence increased noticeably. He slipped on his arctic mittens as he felt the temperature plummeting. The skin of the aircraft no longer formed a protective barrier against the air that was rushing by at minus fifty-seven degrees.

When the petal doors reached their limits, the view beyond the missile container was unobstructed except for straps that angled up to the extraction parachute.

We're over the first hurdle, Chisholm thought. He was surprised to discover that a part of him seemed astonished that he had really gotten this far with his scheme that had seemed so improbable days earlier.

"Three minutes to green light," Griffin announced, referring to the signal lights he would turn on to indicate that he was releasing the extraction chute.

"Confirmed," McClain answered from the command-and-control module. "The ARIA also confirms acquisition of the target."

Great, Chisholm thought, as he felt a shivery chill that was not caused by the frigid temperatures that now were painting flakes of frost on his eyebrows. He linked one arm through straps on a pallet of cargo near the middle of the aircraft. There was nothing left for him to do but wait and pray and try to ignore the intense cold.

"Thirty seconds remaining," McClain said.

Claremont removed the electrical cable from the missile and let the cover slide into place over the connector. Once that task was finished, he rushed toward the front of the cargo compartment.

At five seconds remaining, Sandi began a countdown. When she reached zero, Griffin pushed the chute-release switch to REL and turned on the green light.

As Chisholm watched through eyes blurred by the cold, the extraction chute dropped from the ceiling and fell into the slipstream behind the aircraft. The parachute had been rigged with nylon cords to keep it from opening fully and ripping apart in the airspeeds necessary to keep the C-141 flying in the less dense air at the higher altitudes. So the olive-drab cone of nylon blossomed only partially and seemed to stall momentarily as the lines pulled taut between the parachute and the container.

For one frightening instant Chisholm was jolted by the feeling that it wasn't going to work! He began to think about ways to rig up additional extraction chutes for the next try, even if this first opportunity for an attack was lost. As he was grasping for better answers, the drag caused by the parachute overwhelmed the friction that was holding the payload in the C-141. Suddenly the container rushed backward and dropped over the edge of the ramp. Chisholm hurried toward the doors, trying to get a look at the missile.

"All clear," Blake called into the interphone.

"Doors coming closed," Griffin said. Moments later the big petal doors started shuddering toward each other.

The partially opened chute had been trailing straight out behind the C-141 almost like a brake chute used to slow an airplane on landing. However, once the missile and its container left the ramp, gravity became the dominant force. The missile swung downward with the chute, causing the aft end of the container to point skyward. Twelve seconds after dropping from the ceiling, a timer in the extraction chute activated mechanical cutters, which snipped the nylon cords that were restricting the parachute. Other cutters released the shipping container about the same time that three cargo parachutes began deploying. The diameter of each parachute was about four times the length of the missile, so as the canopies billowed open, they immediately slowed the falling missile. The cluster of three parachutes looked similar to the clusters used on the capsules containing the returning Apollo astronauts as they completed their journeys to the moon and back. In this case the missile was now suspended like a pendulum in its cradle and pointed toward the center of the cluster of parachutes.

The missile was almost stabilized beneath the parachutes when the closing doors cut off Chisholm's view. From now on, he thought, the rest of the attack would be visible to him only in his imagination.

As Blake and Claremont hurried to replace the latches on the pressure door, Chisholm went to the command-and-control module.

Fifteen seconds after the main parachutes were fully deployed, the solid-rocket motor on the modified SRAM-II missile ignited. The thrust buildup was almost instantaneous. On a blinding plume of yellow-white fire, the missile leaped from the cradle and rocketed through the gap between the three parachutes. Accelerating rapidly to supersonic speeds, the missile quickly left the C-141 and Antarctica many miles below.

"We have indications of light-off on the missile," McClain announced on the intercom.

Chisholm entered the command module and raised a clenched fist to show his approval. "That's about step number 999,996 out of a million," he said on intercom.

McClain nodded as he continued listening to the reports coming into his headset. Moments later, he added, "Missile performance appears nominal. ARIA reports acquisition of the missile. Guidance appears nominal."

"Step 999,997," Chisholm said. He tried to sound relaxed, but the oxygen mask concealed the nearly constant movement of his teeth across his lower lip as he concentrated on the scene he could not see. He tried to visualize the missile racing above most of the atmosphere and slowly pitching over to turn downrange. He thought of the photographs of the *Borzoi* and tried to picture the satellite that was several hundred miles away—but racing toward the missile at nearly five miles a second. He wondered if any kind of electronic alarms had been triggered within the satellite, or at Kaliningrad, to warn that the first *Borzoi* was under attack. No, he tried to assure himself. He was confident that his missile was rising outside the cone-of-coverage of the sensors that were on watching the area below the satellite.

"First-stage cutoff," McClain said. "ARIA reports the velocity is near perfect at second-stage ignition."

"Nine-ninety-eight," Chisholm said. He pictured the SRAM-II. Now looking more like an empty pipe with tail fins than like the multimillion dollar piece of technology it had been, the first stage would be tumbling away as the modified Altair-III second stage accelerated the payload to hypersonic speeds.

Quiet seconds seemed to pass agonizingly slow as Chisholm waited for the next report. He rocked slowly from side to side, trying to force the chill back out through his boots and their coverings.

"ARIA reports second-stage cutoff and separation," McClain said. "We *are* in the window, and the on-board seeker has taken over the warhead."

"Step 999,999," Chisholm said as he slapped his two arctic mittens together. The impact made more of a swooshing sound than the sharp crack of enthusiasm that registered in his mind. He studied the time-to-run display as it decreased second by second.

"ARIA reports that the missile and target are converging," McClain said, his voice showing high-pitched excitement for the first time.

Chisholm pictured the tiny warhead streaking almost horizontally at three hundred miles above the earth. The on-board electronics now were tracking the *Borzoi*, which was converging head-on at a closure rate of well over twenty thousand miles per hour. He imagined momentary flashes on one side of the warhead, then another, as axial thrusters ignited, altering the flight path by pushing the warhead sideways—more directly into the way of the onrushing satellite.

As the number on the time-to-run display decreased from five seconds to four, McClain looked toward Chisholm and said, "Here we go." At the same time he moved a switch so that the signal coming from the missile could be heard within the module.

The alternating tone repeated itself each second, reminding Chisholm of a squeaky ceiling fan that needed oil. He stopped breathing as all his concentration was on the signal and the time-to-run display. The big mittens prevented him from retrieving a pen for his ritual tapping during a countdown, so he slowly tapped one mitten on the back of the other as each second passed.

Three hundred miles above Antarctica the heavens were in black contrast to vivid blues and whites of the sunlit clouds and earth that stretched from horizon to horizon. One moment the Soviet satellite and the American warhead were hurtling in opposite directions, nearly ten miles apart. In the next instant the two technological wonders collided in a dazzling flash that vaporized the satellite killer and destroyed the killer satellite.

Inside the control module on the C-141 the tone stopped abruptly just as the time-to-run display showed zero.

McClain let out a whoop, then shouted into the intercom, "Loss of signal!"

"One million," Chisholm yelled and grabbed McClain in a bear hug. With the parkas and heavy clothing, there was little sensation of human contact, but that did not diminish the excitement over what they had just accomplished.

Since the results were much less obvious in the cockpit of the C-141, Griffin asked, "What does that mean? Did the missile fail?"

"Negative," Chisholm said excitedly. "We hit something, and there was only one other object in that part of the sky."

Chisholm heard cheering from the flight station.

Oliverio sounded a little mystified as he asked, "Is that all there is, Colonel C.? I mean, well—" His voice trailed off as he seemed uncertain how to phrase his question.

McClain interrupted before Chisholm could answer. "ARIA reports loss of signal and loss of radar contact with the warhead. The first look at the data estimates that Cosmos 3225 passed within the seeker's window of coverage. ARIA believes that there is some change to the radar return from Cosmos 3225. ARIA estimates a probable kill of the target at seventeen-forty-four-forty-seven Zulu."

There was more cheering. When the yelling subsided, Oliverio sounded disappointed as he asked on intercom, "So we just thumped the Soviets good, and all we get to show for it is a radio report about changes in electronic signals? I've seen more exciting explosions on the arcade games at the NCO club."

"If you'd like to impersonate Slim Pickens and ride a missile up to three hundred miles," Chisholm said, referring to a memorable scene in the movie *Dr. Strangelove*, "you could get a better look. Otherwise, all you'll see on this trip is what you just saw, hopefully seven more times."

"I'll pass on the ride, thank you, Colonel C.," Oliverio said. "I guess I prefer something face to face and noisy, like with Matt Dillon or Wyatt Earp on the dusty streets of Dodge City."

"Or at least like how dogfights used to be," Griffin added, "where you could see the other birds and know right away if you won or lost."

Chisholm shook his head and exchanged amused glances with McClain. In one way Chisholm was disappointed that everyone wasn't in awe of their accomplishment rather than concerned that the experience seemed so analytical. "Spectacular or not, I think you've just gotten a preview of one form of twenty-first-century warfare."

"At least," Sandi said softly, "we just attacked the other superpower, and we didn't have to witness the flash of a nuclear weapon. We ought to be thankful for that."

"Agreed," Chisholm said.

For the last six hours Novikov had been preoccupied with two questions: Would *Borzoi IX* be the Americans' first target, and could they destroy it? This time, as the satellite had raced south across the equator thousands of miles west of Ecuador, he had forbidden all electronic contacts with the satellite until one minute after perigee passage. If the Americans were carrying some type of ASAT on the C-141, he did not want transmissions from *Borzoi IX* providing targeting information that would help guide the enemy missile.

Tapping his cane gently on the floor, Novikov sat watching the clock on the front wall of the *Borzoi* control center. The time for perigee passage had just come and gone. Now he waited with growing impatience for the second hand to move through the additional minute of radio silence he had ordered. He felt the sense of helplessness that he had expected to inflict on those who dared oppose *Krasnaya Molniya*. It was not supposed to happen this way—at least not this soon. He had believed that it would be months, maybe years, before the Americans could mount any kind of counterattack.

He found this aspect of space warfare, which permitted no real-time view of the conflict, to be disturbingly different from the tank-to-tank battles that Marshal Murashev had talked of so often and in such boring detail. Novikov envied Murashev's having had the instant feedback that occurred in such face-to-face confrontations. There you either destroyed the enemy or the enemy destroyed you—but you did not have to wait to find out what had happened.

Worrying doesn't help! Novikov chastised himself with words that had been like a personal mantra each time he had sat atop a *Soyuz* booster waiting to be rocketed into space. In those last few seconds before each launch, he had kept telling himself that worrying wouldn't change things. He was either going to survive for his journey through the cosmos or be blasted into tiny pieces—and *Borzoi IX* had either survived or had been blasted into tiny pieces, no matter how much or how little he worried.

He tried to remain optimistic as the second hand completed one rotation from the time of perigee passage. The controller looked over, and Novikov nodded his concurrence that it was time to contact the satellite.

As the controller began pressing keys on a computer keyboard, Novikov studied the inlays on the handle of his cane as if he were totally unconcerned. When five seconds passed without the controller reacting enthusiastically, Novikov knew that his constellation of *Borzoi* was in serious danger. He slapped the decorative handle against the palm of his other hand, knowing there was no possibility that his suspicions would be proved wrong. He had grossly underestimated Chisholm.

Less than thirty minutes after the launch against Cosmos 3225, a call came over the radio that linked the C-141 through a communications satellite to the Pentagon. "Southern Star, this is Sunglass."

Sitting in the jump seat, Chisholm recognized the voice—this time General Ramsey was on the radio. "Roger, Sunglass. Go ahead."

"Reports we're receiving from the radar at Ascension tell me that Cosmos 3225 is coming over in a greatly perturbed orbit," Ramsey said. "When I had them translate that into Okie, they said you messed up the first one somethin' good."

Another round of cheering filled the C-141's flight station.

37

Nearly four hours had passed since Podpolkovnik Gennadi Berezin had left Argentina. During the flight he had tried to be optimistic, hoping somehow to locate the American aircraft, destroy it, and still reach the safety of the Soviet research station. Yet as the man with his gloved hands on the stick and throttles, he could not dismiss the difficulties as cavalierly as General Tatlin had. Berezin finally had focused his hopes on spotting contrails, telltale white lines in the sky that might betray the American aircraft at distances well beyond the coverage of his radar.

Now, scanning from white horizon to white horizon, he saw no contrails, no signs of any kind that other men shared his space and time. Each minute that passed increased the feeling of hopelessness that gripped him. He had not imagined that Antarctica could be so unlike Siberia—no trees, no rivers, no settlements, no radar controller on the radio, nothing on the surface but cloud-trimmed mountains casting tentative shadows across glistening valleys of ice. He sensed that his very presence somehow was violating this pristine world of white earth and unblemished cobalt skies.

He shifted in the ejection seat of the MiG-25 and strained for a moment against his shoulder straps. Nothing seemed to affect the numbness in his hips that came from spending most of the last fifteen hours in the cramped cockpit.

The surge of confidence he had experienced upon finding the coast of South America now seemed as remote as if it had occurred in another lifetime. For a moment he tried to remember when he had ventured across the dark ocean trying to find Talara—this morning or yesterday. He was so exhausted that all sense of time seemed incomprehensible. Perhaps, he thought, he was becoming hypoxic. A glance at the blinker on his oxygen regulator confirmed the normal operation of the system. He was not hypoxic—he just felt as if he were.

More than an hour earlier Berezin had spread the MiGs into a very shallow echelon formation. With Leytenant Yashin's MiG forty-seven miles to the right and slightly ahead and Kapitan Kovalev flying at the same interval beyond, the combined radars of the three MiGs were searching a band of sky nearly two hundred miles wide. Berezin's tactic was risky. If the three MiGs got separated for only a few minutes beyond radar range, he would never get them back together. The magnetic compass, which he normally relied upon, was virtually useless, indicating that south was somewhere ahead instead of toward the south pole, which was several hundred miles beyond his left wingtip. The scarcity of recognizable landmarks robbed him of another form of reference that could be used in rejoining a scattered flight.

He glanced at his radar, taking a measure of comfort that there was still a blip near the right edge of the scope. A check of the fuel gauges told that it was almost time to give up the hunt. He figured that the Soviet base at Druzhnaya had to be behind them, somewhere to the east. By reversing course and putting the noontime sun just behind his left wingtip, he hoped to get within range of the locator beacon that would guide him to the base. Perhaps, he rationalized, he would still find the Americans, since, as lost as he was, one direction seemed as good another. Just as he started to relay his decision to reverse course in fifteen minutes, an electrifying voice blasted through his headset.

"Contact, contact!" Kovalev's voice was almost too high-pitched to be recognized. "Jaguar Two has a target, bearing one to two o'clock at fifty-five miles."

Berezin jammed the throttles forward and rolled his MiG to the right even before responding. "Hold your position on the target. Yashin, turn and close on Kovalev, but not so fast that I cannot keep you on radar."

"Yes, Commander," Yashin acknowledged.

"The target is at thirty-four thousand feet," Kovalev continued, "heading toward us."

Berezin felt a rush of excitement. He could not imagine why any aircraft other than the American C-141 would be at that altitude over Antarctica.

"Maintain contact, but hold your fire," Berezin said. "Acknowledge."

"Jaguar Two, holding fire."

"Jaguar Four, holding fire."

As the flight leader, Berezin rationalized, he was responsible for verifying the target. He also had a more personal motive. He was determined to report that at least one of his own missiles had hit the enemy aircraft. He switched to his long-range radio. "Pine Tree control, Jaguar has contact."

Tapping a pen on the edge of the navigator's table, Chisholm sat wondering if they had been lucky or if the warning about MiGs at the second target area had been a nerve-jangling mistake. Nearly thirty minutes earlier the second attack against a Soviet satellite had been a perfect duplication of the first. There had been no sign of enemy aircraft or of the Navy fighters that had been promised. Now the C-141 was flying east toward the third launch point as Griffin awaited his turn to refuel. Somewhere back nearly a hundred miles in trail a KC-10 tanker was refueling the ARIA.

Chisholm was waiting to call the control center in the Pentagon to ask what was happening. However, the C-141 was just moving within line-of-sight of a relay satellite. In the meantime he grabbed a copy of the master schedule, which forecast the times and locations of the refuelings and the missile launches. The next *Borzoi* they could attack would pass over Antarctica in two hours and two minutes. He was just starting to make his call when an excited voice came over the radio link to the Pentagon.

"Southern Star, Southern Star, this is Sunglass. You've got bogeys at your one o'clock. Come left immediately one hundred thirty-five degrees and contact War Paint three-zero-one on secure VHF, one thirty-five decimal two."

Griffin asked on intercom, "How in the hell can the Pentagon be giving us radar vectors?"

"Give him the turn while we're finding out," Chisholm said.

Griffin acknowledged with a nod and rolled the C-141 into a thirty-five-degree bank to the left.

From the copilot's seat, Sandi looked questioningly toward Chisholm. At the same time, she reached across and set the new frequency into one VHF radio as she acknowledged the call on another radio, "Southern Star's going one thirty-five decimal two, secure."

Chisholm's mind was racing as he moved to the jump seat. There were no ground-based radars within a thousand miles, so he assumed that the recommendation for a heading change had come from Navy fighters.

"V-One, crew, V-One," Sandi said to let the crew know which VHF communications radio had become primary.

"You're turning away from the next intercept point," McClain called from his control center in the cargo compartment. Obviously he had not been monitoring the Pentagon frequency.

"We may lose this intercept, Rick. Call Star Tracker and advise them we may have run into the MiGs," Chisholm said on intercom, then turned the wafer switch on his controller to VHF-1 and pressed his mike button. "War Paint 301, this is Southern Star. Do you copy?"

"Roger, Star, come left immediately heading three-four-five degrees." The voice was calm but insistent. "You've got three bogeys closing and not much time."

Griffin increased the bank to hasten the turn.

Chisholm asked, "Who are you, and what's your position, War Paint?"

"Paint's a flight of four Fox-fourteens. We'll be at your two o'clock at one hundred seven miles when you roll out. Start your counter-measures, if you have any."

"We've got to get the doors open so we can dump the chaff and flares," Chisholm shouted on the intercom. To protect the crew from physiological dangers, the aircraft needed to be much lower before depressurizing, so Chisholm grabbed Griffin's shoulder and said, "Depressurize and get her down to about twenty. Everybody awake and on oxygen!" He flipped up the guarded cover from the bailout alarm and moved the switch momentarily to its On position. Throughout the aircraft the warning horn blared a bone-chilling screech that would awaken any sleeping crew members.

"Engineer, Pilot," Griffin said, "you're cleared for emergency de-pressurization. Loadmaster, check that everyone in the back is on oxygen and get hooked up to open the cargo doors. Scanners, break out the chaff and flares!"

"You got it, sir," Blake answered.

Sergeant Jacobs, the engineer at the panel, grabbed his oxygen mask with one hand. With the other he flipped up the protective cover over his Emergency Depressurization switch and moved the switch to EMER DEPRESS. The cabin altitude began increasing from seven thousand toward the aircraft's actual altitude of thirty-four thousand feet.

In less than ninety seconds, Chisholm thought, the aircraft would be unpressurized, and the doors could be opened. He wondered if they had that much time.

Within seconds Griffin had his quick-donning oxygen mask in place and had disengaged the autopilot. He pulled the throttles to idle and let the nose fall below the horizon. Yanking the spoiler handle down to the flight limit, he deployed the speed brakes to steepen the dive while keeping the airspeed within limits.

As Chisholm watched the altimeter reading decreasing toward thirty thousand feet, he frantically grasped for ideas of how to hold off the MiGs until the F-14s arrived. The fighters now in trail had to be the Nicaraguan MiGs, but how well were they equipped? He hoped that his deceptive routing had kept the Soviets from having enough warning to organize a high-tech attack force. He knew that his makeshift use of chaff and flares would be overwhelmed easily by MiGs that were equipped with the most advanced counter-countermeasures. The uncertainty that now drove his heart at an accelerated rate would remain unresolved until the MiGs fired their first missiles.

The leader of the flight of F-14s made another call. "Green 'em up, War Paint flight. Break. Southern Star, you've got one MiG closing to within thirty-five miles. You'll be within range of his missiles in a couple of miles or so."

"Roger," Chisholm answered, his voice now distorted through his oxygen mask. He switched to intercom and said to Griffin, "The depressurization can't wait!"

Chisholm knew that there was a quicker, more dangerous way of dumping the cabin pressure. Griffin could release the latches on an overhead escape hatch in the top of the aircraft about fifteen feet aft of the cockpit. All the pressurized air in the aircraft—and anything loose within a few feet of the number two escape hatch—would disappear in a ten-second, potentially ear-popping, decompression.

Griffin nodded and gave Chisholm a determined look. "Load-master, Pilot. Is the area clear around the number two hatch?"

"Give us a second, sir," Blake answered. "Everyone get a grip on something." He hesitated a couple of seconds, then added, "Clear, sir!"

Chisholm grabbed the seat belt that would hold him to the jump seat and fastened the latch. As his eyes darted to Sandi's altimeter, he knew he was not going to like what he saw. The C-141 was approaching twenty-nine thousand feet, nearly a mile above the normal Air Force limit for unpressurized flight. However, his concerns about potential physiological consequences to the crew were pushed aside by the specter of the C-141 being blown apart within the next few minutes. In the background he heard War Paint 301 giving target assignments to the other F-14s.

"Hang onto your papers," Griffin said, then pulled the emergency depressurization handle on the overhead panel.

Straining against his seat belt, Chisholm lunged sideways toward the panel above the navigator's station. He barely got his hand onto his small American flag before the latches on the aft edge of the number two escape hatch released. Pressure within the aircraft forced the hatch open, and thousands of cubic feet of air surged through to the freedom of the Antarctic skies.

The air in the cockpit fogged briefly and became noticeably colder. Empty coffee cups, aeronautical charts, discarded food wrappers, and other miscellaneous pieces of paper whooshed toward the door leading to the cargo compartment. The door slammed partway closed, slowing the flow from the cockpit.

Chisholm looked at the differential pressure indicator on the panel above Sandi's knee. The cabin pressure had fallen almost to that outside the aircraft, so he knew that it was safe to start the lengthy procedure for opening the doors. "Loads, you're cleared to disconnect the latches on the pressure door."

Seconds later Sergeant Jacobs reported, "We're depressurized."

Griffin reached to the ADS panel near his left knee and moved the Door Arming switch to ARM. "Load, Pilot. The doors are armed. Tell me when we're clear to open."

"We need a few more seconds on all these damned latches," Blake said.

"Pumps are on," the engineer added, indicating that the pumps for the number three hydraulic system would supply pressure to open the doors.

Chisholm unlatched his seatbelt and moved to the doorway, where he could see part of the activity at the aft end of the aircraft. Blake and Claremont were kneeling by the base of the pressure door. Oliverio and Ingalls were preparing the chaff and flares.

"Be ready to throw open the right troop door," Chisholm said, referring to a door near the aft end of the cargo compartment, which was used whenever paratroopers jumped from the C-141. "We may not have time to wait for the pressure door and petal doors."

"If that's what it takes, Colonel," Blake said. "You make the call."

Safety rules dictated that the paratroop doors remain closed whenever the cargo doors were open since air rushing into a paratroop door could push someone off the ramp and out of the airplane. However, the smaller doors could be opened in a couple of seconds if flares and chaff had to be thrown out immediately.

Moments later, Blake said, "Aux latches, cam jacks, and safety pins are removed."

"You're cleared to open the pressure door, Load."

"Opening," Blake responded, then began operating switches on the panel for the cargo doors and ramp.

Chisholm saw the pressure door begin to open.

As the C-141 plunged through twenty-five thousand feet, Griffin eased back the yoke and reduced the rate of descent. Raising the nose also slowed the aircraft. He had to slow the airspeed below two hundred knots before he could open the outer doors.

"Pressure door's open," Blake said, indicating he had done everything he could do from the control panel in the cargo compartment.

The radio added a new level of urgency.

"Cleared to fire, War Paint flight. Cleared to fire!" The tranquil tone had disappeared from the voice of War Paint 301 as he ordered his flight to launch missiles at the MiGs. "Southern Star, the MiGs just began painting you with fire-control!"

"The Navy's engaged," Chisholm said, realizing immediately that he sounded much more analytic than he felt. He knew that longstanding rules of engagement prohibited American pilots from firing until the enemy threat was overwhelmingly clear. Obviously, he decided, the War Paint 301 had concluded that the change in radar signals from the MiGs indicated that time was running out.

As the airspeed marker passed through two hundred knots, Griffin moved the All Doors switch on his ADS Panel to Open and said, "Petal doors coming open!"

"They definitely are running," Kovalev said. "The aircraft is heading away at twenty thousand feet."

But they have nowhere to run, Berezin thought as he looked at the three blips on his radar screen. Kashin was less than two miles ahead, with Kovalev four miles farther in the lead. Those MiGs now were within range of the unidentified aircraft, but it was just beyond the reach of Berezin's missiles. His cutoff angle looked good. The others had to be patient for a few moments more, then all three MiGs would be able to fire.

"You aren't cleared to fire," Berezin said.

"Understand, cleared to fire," Kovalev answered, as he squeezed the trigger. "Missile one is off from Jaguar Two."

"Wait," Berezin shouted.

"—sile one is off from Jaguar Four."

Berezin realized that Yashin also had launched a missile at the unidentified aircraft.

As the large petal doors spread wider apart, Chisholm could see the light of a sunny Antarctic afternoon through the opening in the tail. His thoughts were interrupted by a rapid call on the radio.

"War Paint's got launch lights!"

"Get chaff and flares out now!" Chisholm shouted on intercom in a voice higher than usual. "We've got missiles coming our way."

He saw the four men on the ramp become more frantic in spite of the restraint harnesses and oxygen equipment that impeded their movements. Oliverio and Ingalls began throwing chaff over the end of the ramp and into the slipstream. The chaff separated into millions of individual pieces, creating a blizzard of swirling silver in the currents of air that lapped crazily around the open tail of the C-141.

At the same time, Blake yanked the lanyard on a parachute flare and heaved the cylindrical canister out past Oliverio. In assembly-line fashion, Claremont was ready to pass the next flare to Blake. Seconds after the flare fell clear of the C-141's ramp, a small parachute was yanked open and filled with air. The timer on the end of the flare had been set to ignite the flare almost immediately.

Frightened, Chisholm stood helplessly in the doorway overlooking the cargo compartment. His breathing—the sound of which was amplified by the tight-fitting oxygen mask—was coming in gasps.

"Incoming missiles!" Sandi and Blake shouted identical messages at almost the same time.

The frenzied words were doubly startling. She was up front and Blake was looking out the back, so Chisholm realized that their warnings could not be about the same missiles.

Sandi added, "They passed aft and above the right wing."

"Holy shit," Blake shouted, "Break right and pull up! It's coming in fast!"

The four men on the ramp grabbed the sides of the aircraft and held on.

Not much chance to evade, Chisholm thought as he heard the engines wind up and felt the aircraft sway sideways. With the doors open, Griffin could do very little.

Oliverio dropped onto the ramp as he shouted, "It's locked onto a flare!" He scrambled to the edge as the missile slammed into the flare and exploded an instant later. "Got it. It's no threat."

"But it's not their only missile," Chisholm said. "Keep on the flares and chaff."

Berezin was rapidly overtaking the other MiGs, so he yanked his throttles to idle. He was angry at the other two pilots for firing too quickly. Now he was concerned that there would be no target for his missiles as he moved into position to fire.

"Hold your headings," Berezin said on the radio. "I'm coming up at your seven o'clo—"

Yashin's MiG-25 disintegrated in a grinding explosion as the first Phoenix missile from the F-14s reached the MiGs.

For an instant Berezin was frozen in that limbolike sensation in which the brain denies what the eyes are seeing. Watching chunks of the airplane swirl away from the explosion, he wanted to speak but could not form any words.

Oliverio had gotten to his knees and was reaching for the next bundle of chaff when he froze in midmotion. "Brace yourselves! The next one's coming straight in."

Undeterred by the chaff, a radar-guided AA-6 was steering toward radar signals being reflected from the C-141. However, the source of the radar energy had been transmitters in the wingtips of Yashin's MiG. An instant after those radar transmitters became part of the tumbling wreckage, the guidance signal ceased, and the AA-6 missile detonated automatically.

"Jesus," Oliverio shouted in response to the bright flash and shower of shrapnel two hundred yards aft of the C-141. "I don't think I can take much more of this sober, Colonel C."

Berezin sensed that a streaking image of someone else's missile had just led a contrail into Kovalev's MiG. Before the image could register in Berezin's consciousness, the second MiG exploded, breaking apart aft of the cockpit.

"Holy Mother of God." Berezin mouthed a phrase that had not passed his lips in more than three decades. Instinctively he pushed the throttles forward even though he had no idea how to escape the unseen attackers.

As his MiG lurched toward the two clouds of debris and ugly black smoke, he saw the aft two-thirds of Kovalev's MiG tumbling wildly, spewing flaming fuel from ruptured tanks. Almost mesmerized, he watched the spectacle until another huge explosion ripped the MiG. For an instant he thought the main fuel tanks had exploded. Then he realized that fragments had arced toward him as if driven by the impact of another missile—a missile meant for his MiG.

Berezin was terrified. He shoved the stick left, forcing his MiG into a barrel roll, spiraling below the falling debris. His eyes went voraciously to his radar screen. One target—the C-141—was ahead at less than fifteen miles, near a large cloud of chaff. Four new blips were at two o'clock, less than fifty miles away. If the enemy fighters had fired only three missiles, he decided, he could still kill the C-141 before the next flurry of enemy missiles reached him.

Adjusting his radar to minimize the problems caused by the chaff, he locked onto the return from the single aircraft. The chaff convinced him to select a heat-seeking missile for his first shot. As he moved the switch, he raised his head to look beyond the MiG's sleek nose. Four bright spots of light shimmered below the dark form of the large enemy aircraft.

Now he was less certain of completing his mission. Could he defeat both chaff and flares before the other fighters got his MiG? And what if he did? His sense of duty clashed with a more basic instinct of survival. He searched frantically for a way to escape, but the vast, empty skies had become an aerial battlefield with no place to hide. Suddenly he realized that there was one place to hide—safe from the deadly missiles of his unseen adversaries. If he could reach that sanctuary, he might yet complete his mission *and* survive.

With a new sense of urgency, Berezin jammed the throttles into afterburner. As the MiG-25 accelerated, he selected his long-range radio and broadcast, "Jaguar has been engaged by a superior force of enemy fighters. I am pressing forward."

"We've splashed two, Southern Star," the Navy flight leader said, "but there's one more running right up your ass, and we don't have a clear shot at him."

Sandi responded, "What do you suggest, War Paint?"

"Keep dumping your flares and chaff. We'll be on top of you shortly."

"Traffic, two-thirty high," Sandi called out on intercom. "Looks like the four F-14s."

"We've got another miss—. Negative," Blake continued, "we've got a MiG coming at us like a missile."

Blake's words sent a shudder through Chisholm's chest and the feeling seemed to rise and jam in his throat. Had the Soviet pilot chosen to beat the flares and chaff by ramming his MiG into the missile-laden American aircraft?

Griffin asked the question on intercom, "Is he going to ram us?"

"Looks that way, sir," Oliverio said, spitting out the words almost too fast to be recognized.

"That's suicidal," Sandi said.

"Flying a MiG to Antarctica with no place to refuel is already suicidal," Chisholm said as he got a firm grip on the doorway and suddenly felt exhausted.

The image of the huge aircraft beyond the windscreen of Berezin's MiG was growing to frightening proportions. He stiffened both legs against the rudder pedals and leaned back against his ejection seat in a subconscious attempt to keep a safe distance between his body and the C-141. His survival depended upon catching the big American transport before the enemy fighters got another shot at him, but the visual cues on this join-up were much different than those when a fighter was the lead aircraft. Now he realized that he had misjudged the overtake rate—he was closing much too fast.

Yanking the throttles to idle, Berezin extended the airbrake beneath the tail of the MiG. He began a series of counterclockwise barrel rolls—forward spirals as if his canopy were gliding along the outside of a huge barrel of invisible air. He hoped that the increased wing loading and drag would keep him from overrunning the C-141 until he had slowed enough to extend the MiG's flaps to help match the larger aircraft's speed.

The C-141 seemed awfully slow for such a large aircraft, he thought as he made a quick check of the position of the enemy fighters. The larger aircraft blocked any clear shot by them, but. . . . Berezin was beginning to think offensively again, and he suddenly realized that he was not nearly as restricted as the F-14s, which now were within his range. He could slip out from behind his cover, fire a shot, then tuck back in before the enemy fighters could shoot at him.

He locked his radar onto the lead fighter and selected a radar-guided AA-8 missile. As his MiG swung up into the first part of the next roll, Berezin pressed the firing button while in ninety degrees of bank with his left wing pointing toward the ice of Antarctica.

"He's shooting agai—" Oliverio yelled. "Missed us."

"Break left, War Paint! Full jammers and flares!" War Paint 301's words came out in rapid fire, like bullets from a Gatling gun.

Chisholm could not see the F-14s from where he stood, but he looked at the radar scope near Griffin's right knee. The display suddenly had became an incomprehensible mixture of jagged and broken lines. Chisholm hoped that the F-14s' jammers were being as effective on the MiG's radar, which obviously was trying to guide the missile into the flight of Navy fighters.

Sandi pressed to get a better look out the side window. "He's scattered the Tomcats," she said, then added, "There's the missile. It's guiding away from—. It just detonated well clear."

"Keep coming around wide, War Paint," the leader called out. "We'll join up when we get around to six o'clock on this gaggle."

As the MiG overran the C-141, Berezin centered his roll on the big plane, engulfing it inside his invisible barrel of air. The strange paint scheme of greens and browns made the C-141 seem like an angrier airplane than he had imagined. He was inverted over the big transport when the MiG's speed decreased enough to deploy the flaps. As he moved the flap handle, it occurred to him that this was the first time he had ever extended the flaps when his aircraft was upside down.

Blake pressed his face and oxygen mask against the window on the left troop door. He could see into the top of the MiG-25's cockpit as the fighter arced down in its barrel roll a few feet beyond the C-141's wingtip. "Can you believe that? The son of a bitch is doing victory rolls around us."

Oliverio was stretched out on the ramp, trying to keep the MiG in sight. "His little airshow is beginning to piss me off."

Griffin asked from the pilot's seat, "Where is he?"

"You may not believe this, sir," Blake answered, "but he's tucking in next to us as if he were going to refuel."

"We've got other company," Oliverio added. "I can see two of the F-14s scissoring back and forth, trying to stay behind us."

Chisholm asked, "Can you get a shot at him, War Paint?"

"We should be able to take him with guns," the flight leader responded, acknowledging that the dogfight had transitioned into the close-in phase where air-to-air missiles were almost useless. "But unless we can get more separation between your bird and his, we've got a standoff on our hands."

"Give us a minute to work on that, Colonel C.," Oliverio said.

Chisholm asked, "Can you wait him out, War Paint?"

"We've got to head for the carrier in about fifteen minutes, Star," the leader answered.

"Two's going to be bingo fuel in ten minutes," his wing man added.

"Star, we don't have much time to move this into the end game."

"Understand," Chisholm answered, trying to think of a tactic to separate the C-141 from the MiG.

Berezin had moved beyond the point of being frightened. He would not pretend even to himself that he could beat the firepower and maneuverability of four U.S. Navy F-14s. His only chance was to outsmart them and outfly them for the next few minutes. Their aircraft carrier had to be somewhere beyond the huge ice floes that surrounded Antarctica, and that meant the F-14s had to fly a great distance to return to base. Since he had no plans to fly beyond the ice, he had an advantage—in a manner of speaking. He had one other advantage of which the Americans were unaware. In his day Gennadi Berezin had been one of the best pilots in the Soviet Air Force in close-formation flying. And, he thought with less enthusiasm, he was prepared to ram the big aircraft if somehow the F-14s stayed too long.

He also was close enough to see the men in their green flight suits and parkas near the open tail of the C-141. They must be very cold, he thought as he glanced around at the two fighters that were weaving back and forth a few hundred yards behind. He saw a third F-14 that was higher, gracefully swooping from side to side in much more exaggerated turns.

As Berezin returned his attention to the cargo plane, he noticed two of the men raising some tannish-colored objects over their heads. Suddenly the men threw the objects directly toward his MiG.

Berezin whipped the stick left and forward for an instant, causing the MiG to dip left as two large chunks of wood tumbled by. Immediately the MiG was buffeted wildly by the exhaust of the C-141's left inboard engine and by the airflow over the massive left wing.

Fighting the unseen currents of air, Berezin also fought his instincts that shouted one message: break away from the huge aircraft. He held in close, however, trying to find more stable air. His alternative was to drop back and become immediate prey to the guns of the American fighters.

The turbulence threw his MiG toward the enormous pointed door that hung open on his side of the C-141. In panic Berezin leaned away as he used rudder and aileron to try to stop the rapid drift. He yanked the throttles to idle and eased back on the stick, letting his MiG climb beside the C-141. The sudden reduction of thrust let the MiG slide back a couple of feet. The pointed tip on the aft end of the cargo door sliced down, seemingly inches in front of the MiG's swept-back wing. If he had had time to savor the excitement, Berezin would have marveled at how the door had missed both the missile on the outboard launching rail and the wingtip antenna—each of which extended nearly six feet ahead of the wing.

Unfortunately, he had more immediate problems: keeping his wingtip from smashing into the C-141's vertical stabilizer and stopping the climb before his MiG slammed into the horizontal stabilizer, which extended like another wing at the top of the tail.

Now that his MiG had risen above the turbulent air trailing behind the huge wing, Berezin had better control. He popped the stick forward momentarily to stop the climb. For an instant, his wingtip almost touched the American flag that was painted on the side of the C-141's tail. Then the MiG started sliding down and back.

Though his gut feelings screamed "No!" Berezin jammed the throttles forward. It appeared to be too early to add power, especially with the C-141 so close that he could see rivet heads under the dark camouflage paint. However, Berezin knew that in formation flying, if you delayed adding power until it looked like more power was needed, you had waited too long. The C-141 was already inching away from his MiG as the increased thrust from the big Tumanski engines took effect. If his MiG fell more than a few feet behind, his cloak of protection would slip away.

Moments after he stabilized his MiG-25 just behind and to the left of the tail, a shadowy image swooped by not far behind. Glancing back, he saw an F-14 pulling out of a steep dive, which obviously had been an aborted gunnery pass. Berezin felt a shudder through his arms and shoulders, then became more determined to fly the tightest formation he had ever flown.

With firm control of the stick and throttles, he eased the MiG down along the C-141's tail, passing behind the open door. This time he was prepared for the buffeting. In a few moments he found an area of relatively smooth air, in the edge of the exhaust from the C-141's left inboard engine.

Oliverio still was holding a piece of a shipping crate, which he had been ready to throw before the MiG had started its wild gyrations. As the MiG settled into tight formation just below and to the left of the cargo compartment, Oliverio turned to Blake and said, "Shit, I don't think we ought to try that again."

Blake nodded enthusiastically.

By then Chisholm had hooked into a long intercom cord, connected his oxygen mask to a walk-around bottle, and joined them in the back of the airplane.

"The MiG's right out there," Blake said, making an exaggerated pointing motion with his finger.

Chisholm pressed his face against the window on the left troop door and looked at the MiG and its Nicaraguan markings. "We lucked out, guys. MiG-25s don't carry a gun."

"If you think he's close now, Colonel C.," Oliverio said, "you should have seen him a minute ago."

"He's just right," Chisholm said. "He's too close for his missiles to arm if he decides to shoot at us, but close enough for us to shoot at him."

Oliverio looked confused. "The only weapons we brought along are M-sixteens."

Blake said, "I'd expect those little slugs to bounce right off a MiG."

"You don't have to shoot him down," Chisholm said as he left the window and stepped toward the ramp. "We just need to create a distraction."

Blake took hold of Chisholm's arm and said, "If you want to go any farther, Colonel, I need to equip you with either a safety harness, a parachute, or a prayer book."

"Just looking," Chisholm said as he knelt on one knee. Since the ramp had been lowered earlier, there was a narrow wedge-shaped opening between the side of the aircraft and the side of the ramp. Chisholm dropped to his hands and knees, putting his face near the floor. He could see part of the MiG. The view from nearer the edge of the ramp would be better, but more dangerous. "I suppose," Chisholm began in an accentuated drawl, "if a man were to flop down near the edge of the ramp, he'd have a pretty good field-of-fire."

Blake nodded. "And I suppose that man's going to be wearing seven stripes instead of eagles."

"Seems like a good idea to me, Sarge. Break out an M-sixteen and some ammo. I'll need to work some strategy with the Navy." Passing Oliverio, Chisholm said, "You make damned sure Big Tony doesn't fall out."

As soon as Blake was ready, Griffin said, "You're cleared to lock and load."

Pointing the rifle toward the empty sky behind the aircraft, Blake pushed the clip into the M-16 and chambered the first round. He had already removed his oxygen mask and unclipped the walk-around bottle from his parka. Oliverio now held those, pressing the mask against Blake's face so Blake could breathe the oxygen without being entangled in the equipment.

Once the rifle was loaded, Blake walked carefully to within one step of the edge of the ramp. Oliverio followed with the oxygen. Claremont took up the remaining slack in the tether to Blake's restraint harness, hoping to make it impossible for Blake to fall out in the maneuvering that would follow. Part of the MiG was visible from where Blake stood. Only his feet would be noticeable from the cockpit of the MiG, if indeed the pilot had time to notice.

"We're doing a little handoff with the oxygen bottle, Colonel," Blake said, "so how about giving us a countdown from five seconds?"

"Roger," Chisholm said. "You'll fire on zero. Major Griffin will begin his maneuvers one second later."

"Roger that," Griffin said.

Chisholm nodded, then asked, "You ready, pilot?"

"Pilot's ready," Griffin said.

"Okay, crew, the count will be on V-One," Chisholm said, then switched from intercom to the radio. "War Paint, Southern Star's about ready to do a countdown from five. Are your birds in position?"

"We're ready to get the show on the road on your count, Star."

Chisholm stood in the doorway and got a firm grip on the support for the upper bunk. "On my count. Starting five . . ."

Blake held the oxygen mask against his face for a deep breath, then let Oliverio take the mask away.

"Four . . ."

As Oliverio moved a few steps toward the front of the aircraft, Blake set his M-16 for automatic fire and touched the safety. In the cockpit Griffin reached over and lifted the spoiler handle, arming the spoilers for immediate deployment.

"Three . . ."

Blake knelt on his right knee. Chisholm glanced toward Sandi, and she nodded slightly in response.

"Two . . ."

No one moved.

"One . . ."

Blake dropped forward, landing prone with his forearms absorbing most of the fall. He extended the M-16, aimed it through the opening above the side of the ramp, and released the safety.

"Zero!"

Blake squeezed the trigger and fired the entire clip at the MiG.

Berezin heard the impacting bullets even before he noticed the jittering flashes from the tail of the C-141. The slugs glanced off the canopy or splattered against the steel skin of the MiG like hailstones during a thunderstorm. Though none penetrated the aircraft, their impact on his concentration was more devastating. He flinched, then looked instinctively toward the flashes, which had stopped almost as soon as they had started.

When he looked forward beyond the needlelike nose of his MiG, he saw that the C-141's wing had grown thicker. The American pilot, Berezin decided, had deployed his speed brakes, which extended in panels like solid barriers to the air above and below the wing. Berezin extended his airbrake and yanked his throttles to idle, but his cockpit was rushing toward the left inboard engine of the C-141.

A second after Chisholm's count had reached zero, Griffin had moved the spoiler handle to the flight limit. In response the spoilers had rotated out from the wings, becoming the barriers that Berezin had noticed. Griffin waited one more second, then rolled the C-141 hard to the right, away from the MiG.

The deceleration caused by the spoilers had helped Blake crawl forward, away from the nothingness beyond the end of the ramp. When the aircraft maneuvered so violently, however, he slid toward the opening between the ramp and the right side of the airplane. He had already exhaled his last gulp of oxygen and now took gasping breaths, trying to inhale enough of the rarefied air to stay conscious. Blake wedged his body against part of the side of the aircraft and fought to keep his leg from slipping into the air rushing by just beyond. Crawling across the cold floor, Oliverio grasped Blake's outstretched hand, then pushed the extra oxygen mask against Blake's face.

Griffin kept the C-141's nose level until the airspeed dropped below 185 knots, then called, "Flaps, landing."

"Flaps, landing," Sandi responded, moving the flap handle to the most extreme setting.

The C-141 decelerated noticeably as the huge flaps slid down, becoming like barn doors facing into the wind. Griffin let the nose fall as he continued a spiraling turn away from the MiG that he had not yet seen from the pilot's seat.

Berezin had flinched and raised his hand instinctively as he thought his cockpit was going to slam into the inboard engine of the C-141. Instead the big wing lifted as the nose of his aircraft passed under. The top of the MiG's right vertical stabilizer sliced through the drain mast beneath the C-141's inboard engine, causing superficial damage to both aircraft.

In the moments it took Berezin to recover mentally, the C-141 had continued slowing and tightening its turn away from his MiG. He jammed the right rudder to the firewall, trying to "bend it around" in a desperate attempt to catch the big airplane. His MiG-25—which had been built for speed and not for tight maneuvering—began to shudder as it entered a high-G, low-speed stall. The shuddering told Gennadi Berezin that he had lost.

Shoving the throttles against the stops, he rolled the wings level and pushed the stick forward to fend off the impending stall. Before he could reach the flap handle, the cockpit disintegrated in a hail of nearly four hundred slugs out of a four-second burst from the Vulcan cannon on War Paint 301.

"Splash three," War Paint 301 called out as his F-14 roared through the narrow corridor between the C-141 and the burning pieces of the MiG. Passing Griffin's side, the Navy pilot lit his afterburners and spiraled through five quick aileron rolls as his F-14 accelerated out ahead of the C-141.

"You know those Navy guys," Chisholm said on intercom as he looked toward Sandi, "always ready to show off when they think a pretty woman's watching."

She looked at him but did not respond. Her eyes suggested that there was a smile behind her oxygen mask.

"Great job, War Paint flight," Chisholm called on the radio as he watched the other three F-14s join up on their leader.

"Glad we could help. Now comes the fun part." He paused, then added, "First a refueling and then a landing in fifteen-foot seas."

"Good luck," Chisholm said.

"Happy hunting, Star, whatever the hell it is that you're hunting for down here."

38

Minutes after the Ministry of Defense had lost radio contact with Berezin's MiGs, Novikov was summoned to the Kremlin. By the time he arrived, Minister of Defense Levchenko and Chairman Petruk were already in President Grigoriev's office.

Even before Novikov reached a chair at the conference table, Grigoriev asked, "How many of your satellites have been destroyed, General Novikov?"

"We have lost contact with two, Comrade President," Novikov said.

"What can we do to save *Krasnaya Molniya?*"

"As long as *Zashchitnik I* is operational," Novikov said, "the Americans have an almost insurmountable problem. I recommend—"

"The Americans don't seem to share your confidence in your unbeatable blockade," Petruk interrupted sarcastically. "Agents in Florida say the Defender may be launched within a few hours."

"The Americans are bluffing, Comrade Chairman," Novikov said. "If they're stupid enough to launch while *Zashchitnik I* is working so perfectly, they will experience failure before reaching GEO."

"Can you guarantee," Petruk said, "that *Zashchitnik I* is safe from the Americans? Some sources believe that the ongoing American attack includes an action against *Zashchitnik.*"

Novikov felt a tinge of dread as he asked, "What kind of action, Comrade Chairman?" He was not surprised that the Americans would want to destroy *Zashchitnik I*, but this was the first indication that something might already be in progress.

"Since the Ministry of Defense has assured us that there are no vulnerabilities," Petruk said without looking at either Novikov or Levchenko, "it is difficult for me to predict the method of attack. I have learned that a noted NASA scientist named Turnhill was secretly taken to Guam this week for some important purpose."

But we've already decided that Guam was the deception, Novikov thought to himself, knowing better than to contradict the chairman. As he opened a notebook to write Turnhill's name, he said, "I'll be pleased to hear of any potential threats your sources uncover, Comrade Chairman, and I'll investigate what the NASA expert might do from Guam."

Petruk was not satisfied. "And what if all satellites of *Krasnaya Molniya* are destroyed while you are investigating?" Turning to Grigoriev, Petruk spoke with great intensity. "We must use those that remain to immediately destroy all American satellites that our lasers can reach!"

The suggestion took everyone else by surprise, and for a few moments, no one responded. Novikov knew that he could destroy all satellites that were orbiting below GEO, but he expected that that would be considered only as a prelude to war.

Petruk continued, "The opportunity of the century is slipping like sand through our fingers. Navigation, communications, weather, spying—they depend on satellites for everything. The Americans would need years to recover."

"But," Novikov said, starting to point out that the chairman was overstating the case and understating the risks.

Grigoriev interrupted, "The Americans would have to retaliate, and they would not have the choice of attacking in space. The purpose of *Krasnaya Molniya* was to intimidate, not drive us into a war that no one will win."

Actually, Novikov thought, Defender I might be able to do the same thing to Soviet constellations in a few days. However, that depended on Petruk's scenario of losing all *Borzoi* and *Zashchitnik I*, a disaster that Novikov was not ready to concede.

"But, Comrade President," Petruk said, "tomorrow may be too late to wish that you had taken my suggestion."

"That's preferable," Grigoriev said, fixing his blue eyes fiercely upon Petruk, "to wishing I hadn't."

Petruk sighed and turned his gaze toward the ornate decorations on the far wall.

After waiting long enough to be sure that Grigoriev was not going to continue, Novikov said, "*Zashchitnik I* is well above the American threat and remains in position to block any American launches. However, I have two more *Borzoi* loaded on their boosters at Plesetsk, and we should move them to the launchpads immediately. We can launch them into orbits that will stay above the American missiles and get reasonably good coverage over the northern hemisphere."

Grigoriev seemed to consider the idea for a moment, then asked, "How much higher would the satellites have to be, Petr?"

Novikov shrugged. "We have so little information at this point on the American missiles. Perhaps five hundred miles would be high enough."

"But you are uncertain if even that would be beyond the range of the American weapons?"

"Yes, Comrade President. But—"

"No," Grigoriev said, shaking his head slowly. "I can picture President Anderson instructing his secretary of state and the clique from the Pentagon. He's saying, 'Tell them to send more chickens. I have more foxes.' Are there no other ways to protect our satellites?"

"The Ministry of Defense speaks as if its exalted space machines are helpless," Petruk said with disdain. "Why not fire the lasers at the aircraft?"

"It's not that simple, Comrade Chairman," Levchenko growled. Then appearing to have reached the limit of his knowledge, he nodded toward Novikov and said, "Tell him, Petr."

"The Americans have chosen to attack from the most difficult location for our sensors," Novikov said. "*Zashchitnik I*'s radar is of little help that far from the equator. Each *Borzoi* will be at the lowest and fastest part of its orbit, so the spacecraft's cone of coverage is very narrow at such short ranges. The aircraft would be within the coverage of the sensors and in the laser's kill zone for only a minute or so."

"I thought lasers needed only seconds," Petruk said. Making a gesture of deference toward Grigoriev, he asked, "Has the Ministry of Defense misled us all about the capabilities of the machines used in *Krasnaya Molniya?*"

"Of course not," Levchenko said.

Grigoriev sat silently, not offering to enter the exchange.

"Comrade Chairman," Novikov said, trying to sound respectful, "the fire-control systems were designed to fire on spacecraft from well above the earth. The sensors require time to scan for targets, then discriminate the targets from the background, and then pass that information to the aiming mechanisms. Besides, laser beams do not work so well in the atmosphere."

"If that is true," Petruk said to Levchenko, "then why have we spent billions of rubles on your ground-based laser projects you're trying to develop to attack American satellites? Must we expect the Americans to dip their satellites low so your lasers can work in the atmosphere?"

Levchenko glared back. "Those lasers have many megawatts of power to keep the beam focused in spite of atmospheric disfusion!"

For an embattled bureaucrat, you got that pretty close, Novikov thought, recognizing the increasing frustration in Levchenko's voice. To be effective the laser's beam had to remain coherent—all waves of the beam of electromagnetic radiation precisely matched, crest to crest and trough to trough—until reaching the target. Within the atmosphere the beam was affected by atmospheric turbulence, thermal blooming, scattering, and absorption in cloudy weather. Such problems, Novikov understood to his regret, were more easily dealt with within a huge facility on the ground than in a package of electronics that could fit on top of a booster.

"The atmosphere gives aircraft some protection from . . ." Novikov stopped, having just mentally refuted the argument he was about to make.

Grigoriev asked, "What is it, Petr?"

"The troposphere," Novikov said, his thought rushing ahead of his words. "It's much thinner in the dense cold of the polar regions than anywhere else."

"Of course," Levchenko said, sounding as if the concept were as simple as day and night. "But what does that mean as far as the Americans are concerned?"

"The troposphere contains eighty percent of the atmosphere's mass, and it's only eight kilometers thick at the poles." Novikov paused, then added triumphantly, "The American aircraft are flying above most of the particles in the atmosphere. A shot from the cosmos might work."

Grigoriev looked more interested. "But you said the *Borzoi* couldn't aim their lasers in time at such a low altitude."

"They can't, but we can," Novikov said. He rose quickly from his chair, causing looks of surprise on the faces of the others. "I must get to a telephone and call the launch center at Plesetsk."

Grigoriev asked, "What can they do?"

"We must launch one of the tactical reconnaissance satellites that are sitting on alert," Novikov said excitedly. "With no other aircraft near the *Borzoi*'s perigee, the reconnaissance sensors should be able to locate the aircraft we need to destroy. That information will tell the *Borzoi* where to look!"

Petruk appeared dubious. "But will this new scheme be just wasting more rubles and another satellite?"

Grigoriev's piercing blue eyes flashed toward Petruk. "Do you have a better scheme, Viktor?"

Petruk shrugged. "Only if the Americans fly close to one of our bases."

"The sooner we launch, Comrade Chairman," Novikov said, "the quicker we stop the American attacks."

Grigoriev nodded. "Go ahead."

Novikov hurried toward the door wondering how many of the *Borzoi* he could save. Even as fast as his crews were, getting a booster onto a pad, fueled, and launched in less than eight to ten hours would be difficult. No time could be wasted on mistakes. In addition, the launch time would have to be coordinated with the orbit of one of the remaining *Borzoi* so that both satellites would pass over the same area at eighty degrees south at approximately the same time. He wished he knew more about the strategy of the American aircrew. In two and a half hours Chisholm had destroyed two Soviet satellites. In eight more hours, Novikov wondered, would he have any *Borzoi* left to save?

When Novikov returned to the *Borzoi* control center at Kaliningrad, he concentrated on planning the mission of the reconnaissance satellite that was to be launched from Plesetsk. Potential launch azimuths and times were matched with information on the *Borzoi* orbits and on the most likely locations of the American attacks.

He wished that he could park the reconnaissance satellite over the south pole just as *Zashchitnik I* stayed over a spot on the equator. A stationary orbit at ninety degrees south would provide coverage as each *Borzoi* reached perigee. Unfortunately, such orbits were physically impossible, and Novikov was glad that Murashev was not present to be wasting time with questions about why a satellite could not be parked over the pole.

Novikov's best choice was a low-altitude orbit that would pass over Antarctica about every ninety minutes. By selecting the right launch time and azimuth, the reconnaissance satellite could locate the American aircraft just before one of the *Borzoi* zoomed by overhead. He was working to identify the best possibilities when he received another piece of bad news: At 0114 controllers had been unable to reestablish contact with *Borzoi V* shortly after it had passed below the tip of South America. Three gone in four and a half hours. At that rate, he thought with some despair, by the time the reconnaissance satellite was in its first orbit, the cosmos over Antarctica would have no *Borzoi* satellites still capable of firing at the American aircraft.

An hour later he decided that little more could be done until the prelaunch procedures were farther along at Plesetsk. Now, he thought, it was a matter of waiting to see how soon the booster could be launched.

Exhausted, Novikov slumped into a cushioned chair in the back of the room and looked at his listing of when each *Borzoi* would reach perigee. Using a red pen, he lined out *Borzoi V* in the same manner he had done to *Borzoi IX* and *Borzoi VIII* earlier in the evening. Looking over the listing, he estimated that *Borzoi III* was less than an hour away from an attack by the Americans.

He closed his eyes for what seemed like only a few seconds. When he awakened, Polkovnik Nasedkin was standing before him.

"When you returned from Moscow, sir," Nasedkin said, "you asked me to find out about the American named Turnhill. Here's the information, Comrade General."

"Thank you," Novikov said, having trouble clearing the deep sleep that had overtaken him.

Nasedkin waited for a few moments to see if Novikov had any questions. When the general did not show strong interest in the information, Nasedkin excused himself and returned to Flight Control.

As Novikov looked at the information, he tried to remember why he had made the request. He found that the papers were a copy of an intelligence dossier maintained by the KGB. It included information taken from American biographical summaries, from government press releases, and from agent reports at international scientific conferences that Doctor Turnhill had attended. The NASA biographical sketch, which announced the scientist's appointment as the program manager for Moon Base 2010, reminded Novikov where he had learned Turnhill's name.

Novikov put the papers aside and checked the clock. Turnhill and the American diversion at Guam seemed of little importance considering that the losses in his *Borzoi* constellation probably would reach 50 percent within the next few minutes.

He leaned back and closed his eyes, trying to think of ways the Americans might succeed in launching the Defender satellite. Their countdown on the Defender had to be a bluff—there was no way to get Defender past *Zashchitnik I*, even if all the *Borzoi* were gone. Chisholm had to understand that he was wasting his time over Antarctica if he ignored *Zashchitnik I*. That thought brought Novikov's eyes open and made him sit upright in the chair—maybe Petruk was right. Maybe something really was going on at Guam.

Novikov asked himself how he would use an American expert on the island of Guam to attack *Zashchitnik I*. Nothing came to mind. Guam had tracking radars that looked out into the cosmos, but the island was nearly two thousand miles too far west to see *Zashchitnik*. When he picked up the papers on Turnhill, his eyes immediately fixed on the word *moon*. A shuddering feeling shocked the exhaustion from Novikov as he realized that Guam's antennas were perfectly positioned to track a returning moon probe and relay final corrections for an attack against a target nearly a third of the world farther east.

Novikov leaped from his chair and rushed to Flight Control. Hurrying down the hall, he thought about a return orbit from the moon. If he could determine when the spacecraft would pass through geostationary altitude, he possibly could move *Zashchitnik I* laterally faster than the spacecraft could change its trajectory. He recalled from studies—back when he had hoped he someday would walk on the moon—that a flight between the moon and the earth would take between fifty-five and sixty hours, depending on the orbit selected. How many of those hours, he wondered, were still left before Turnhill's probe would come streaking through GEO, if indeed it were already on its way? If—if—if. If he did not locate that American spacecraft quickly, *Krasnaya Molniya* was lost, and Kalinen's sacrifice would be in vain.

It was just after three in the morning, so only a few people were on duty in the large control room. Kapitan Voznoy was the only person in the section that monitored interplanetary and moon missions.

Novikov called Nasedkin and the others over to Voznoy's console and said, "Our radars must search immediately for a spacecraft on a trajectory from the moon!"

Everyone looked confused.

"Yes, Comrade General," Voznoy said, flustered by the general's sudden approach in the middle of the night. "Is there any information on where to start the search?"

"If I knew where to look, Kapitan, I wouldn't need a search!" The frightened look on Voznoy's face convinced Novikov that he was letting his own weariness get in the way of finding the answer. "Tell the radar operators to look at transfer orbits leaving the moon within the last couple of days and passing through geostationary altitude at about one hundred degrees west."

Voznoy looked uncertain as he started to write what Novikov had said.

Novikov grabbed a tablet and drew a circle representing the earth and a smaller circle for the moon. "If the earth and moon weren't moving, the transfer orbit would look something like this." Novikov put his pencil on the moon and drew half of an ellipse, which almost touched the earth on the opposite side from the moon. He added an arrow to the moon showing its direction of movement. "Since launch, the moon will have moved up to two and a half days in this direction, and the earth will be rotating. But we know that the space-craft will be moving toward perigee here nearly opposite from the moon," Novikov said, stabbing the pencil into the paper where the transfer orbit nearly touched the earth.

Watching Voznoy hurriedly write the words, Novikov realized how insignificantly the guidance would narrow the search area, even if Voznoy got everything straight. Novikov said to the assembled group, "Start computing possible trajectories from the moon. Comrade Na-sedkin, call in everyone who understands interplanetary trajectories."

Nasedkin rushed away to a telephone while the others hurried back to their computers. In the minutes that followed, however, Novikov did not observe anyone who appeared to have any real idea of how to attack the problem. Several men had experience in com-puting ICBM trajectories between the missile bases in central Russia and targets in the United States; few knew how to account for the effects of both the moon and the earth on a spacecraft's orbit. Without providing the start time or the characteristics of the rocket that would propel the probe away from the moon, Novikov knew he had given them a nearly impossible task.

As he continued to watch, he saw nothing encouraging. Radar sites were responding throughout the Soviet Union, but all had a common demand—give more guidance on where to focus the search within the 384,000 kilometers separating the moon from the earth.

Novikov paced, tapping his cane noisily on the floor with each step. If he could determine the launch time from the moon, the search could be narrowed quickly. Perhaps a call to Petruk. Yet Novikov doubted that there was enough time to get instructions to KGB agents in America, find out when the probe was launched, and get the information back to the men controlling the radars.

He was about to call Levchenko to explain the potential new threat when the answer flashed into his mind. "Seismic data!" Novikov yelled out the words. "We have scientific sensors on the moon that study the hazards of meteors to potential moon bases."

"Yes, Comrade General," Voznoy said. "Once a day we receive signals that report any jarring of a meteor impact exceeding a threshold value of—"

"I need to see the data that came in over the last two . . . no, three days," Novikov said. Voznoy looked confused, so Novikov added, "Do I have to press the keys for you, Kapitan? I want to know if the sensors detected the launch of an American spacecraft from the moon."

"Yes, Comrade General," Voznoy said excitedly as he began retrieving computerized files of data. In less than a minute, he said, "There are no reports available from the last eighteen hours, since the next report is scheduled to be trans—"

"Before that! Check what is available."

"Yes, sir," Voznoy said, calling up earlier files. "There usually isn't much on any particular day, Comrade General, except for the monthly moonquakes that occur when the moon is closest to the earth."

"I'm not interested in routine moonquakes," Novikov said as the data reached the screen.

The last report that had been sent from the sensors showed no activity in its twenty-four hours. Good, Novikov thought. If the American spacecraft had been launched in the last eighteen hours that were yet to be reported, he would have more time to counter the attack.

"Here's something strange, sir," Voznoy said as he displayed the previous report. "Let me switch to the seismographic type of display."

As Novikov waited for the data to reappear in its new form, he asked, "When was that signal?"

"It was at 0145 international time on Thursday, the first of April."

Novikov quickly made the conversion—this particular report of a seismic event on the moon had been recorded approximately forty-seven hours earlier.

The display screen blanked out, then repainted in lines that looked like the jagged lines from the pens on a seismograph. The signal diverged back and forth across the centerline in a sequence of increasing spikes, then dampened abruptly back to the centerline.

"What's the time scale?" Novikov asked.

"The entire perturbation occurred in about four to five seconds, Comrade General," Voznoy said. "This signal is very strange. It does not look like a meteorite strike."

Novikov knew little of the seismic sciences, so he was uncertain what to expect. "What does a normal meteorite strike look like?"

Voznoy called up data from another file. The display showed that the pointer had spiked abruptly to each side of the center, then settled back on the centerline with little additional disturbance. "This is typical, sir. A strong strike, then nothing."

"Not like the building up of thrust on a rocket motor," Novikov said as he pictured the previous display of increasing spikes. The Americans had a forty-seven-hour head start, he concluded, but now he could solve the equations. "Until we can compute the most likely trajectories, concentrate the radars' searches about a sixth of the way to the moon."

39

Over the Ronne Ice Shelf, Antarctica
Saturday, 3 April, 0120 local (0620 GMT)

Chisholm was in the copilot's seat, having been there since before the successful attack on the sixth satellite. Sitting in the left seat, Sandi had turned the C-141 toward the coordinates for the seventh attack as the crew waited for the KC-10 to finish refueling the ARIA.

As soon as the cabin altitude decreased to below ten thousand feet, Chisholm pulled off his oxygen mask. He massaged the bridge of his nose, trying to relieve the ache caused by wearing the tight mask for the last hour. Moments later Sandi started an almost identical routine on the pilot's side. She appeared to be as tired as he felt, but her eyes still had the spirited look he had gotten used to whenever the subject had been airplanes and flying.

Just behind the pilots' seats and the jump seat, a pair of blackout curtains stretched from one side of the cockpit to the other. Their purpose was to improve the night vision of the pilots by shutting out light from the rest of the flight station. Someone could push through between the curtains at any time, but everyone else besides one flight engineer was resting. So, for the first time since leaving Hawaii, Chisholm felt that he and Sandi had a small degree of privacy.

Normally the setting would have been far from romantic, but a solar storm was producing a dazzling display of southern lights in the darkness beyond the windshields. The night sky was illuminated by dancing flashes of reds and oranges, punctuated by occasional bursts of greens and violets.

Trying to look serious, Chisholm said without using the intercom,

"Arranging this light show cost plenty, but I've always believed that making a good impression on the first date is important."

She responded with a suspicious smile and said, "You didn't even know I was going to be along, Colonel." She teasingly emphasized the last word.

"While you were sleeping, I got a phone patch on HF," Chisholm said, referring to the ability to make telephone calls through ground stations monitoring the long-range radios. "They put me through on Mother Nature's one-eight-hundred number, and I charged it on my Visa."

Sandi laughed and shook her head slowly. "Thank you. I've never been more impressed." She paused, then added, "By everything. You're going to pull this off, aren't you?"

"The odds seem better now than when we'd scored only two hits and had a flight of MiGs on our tail." Exhaustion made the dogfight seem days ago, even though the MiG attack had been fewer than ten hours earlier.

"I always admired how you could take on tough jobs and make them look simple."

"If you can't be good, be lucky," he said with his customary wink.

"You're not here because of luck, Mike. You're here because you were the best man—probably the only man—in the Air Force who could break the Soviet blockade."

Chisholm appreciated her compliment and her sincerity. However, over the past two days he had been thinking about how he had ended up on this improbable mission. "You really want to know why I'm here, Sandi?"

"Why?"

"Because my brother died a quarter of a century ago."

"What?"

Chisholm laughed at her confused expression. "From the moment I saw you at Hickam, I've been coming to terms with why I do what I do."

Sandi looked at him seriously. "I didn't think you'd ever had any doubts. You were determined to be a general." She paused, then added, "Even if that didn't include being married to a captain or a major or whatever."

"Truce, remember," he said, but not too seriously. "From the time I was sixteen, I never had any doubts about my motivations. I was just dead wrong about what my motivations were." When she responded only with a look of fascination, he continued, "The last thing Brett ever said to me was, 'Kid, you're doing great. Now go out there and enjoy the life I'll never have.'"

She looked as if she wanted to reach across to console him, but the distance was too great. "I can imagine how painful it was to see your hero die. He was so much a part of you that his death was also yours."

He nodded. "I took his words as a decree to live out his life instead of enjoying mine."

"But surely you've enjoyed life, Mike. You've been successful beyond most people's imaginations."

"Oh, I've enjoyed most of it, except for the friggin' paperwork that swamps my desk every day. But it's been for him, not for me." He paused thoughtfully, then continued, "My apartment has this cozy little room with a fireplace. I've always thought of it as my inspiration room."

"I can imagine," Sandi said, raising an eyebrow slightly with a hint of suppressed jealousy.

"No conquests to brag about," he said, noticing the slight change in her mood, "though a visit from you could be inspiring. While you were sleeping earlier, I was realizing that the room's not an inspiration room. It's a what-might-have-been room—what might have been with Christie, with Brett, with me . . . and with you."

"I'm not sure I understand," she said in the supportive tone to which he had always responded warmly.

"Above my fireplace are Christie's picture, Brett's medals, my Yankees' baseball, and the picture of us on the beach the day we got engaged—things that might have been but didn't work out at all."

"Brett's life may be over, but yours isn't, Mike."

"Right," he said as he turned to face her. "I can't keep thinking of Christie as my little girl who hasn't grown up. I can't give Brett his career, and I'm never going to be a Yankee, but I could change how I reacted to you and your career. When this is all over, I want to get us back to the closeness we had Waikiki."

She did not respond immediately. Finally she said, "I keep my copy of that picture on my dressing table." She smiled mischievously and added, "If you keep being so nice, I'll have to remove the red horns, tail, and pitchfork that I drew on your side of the picture."

"As sassy as ever," he said with a grin.

Before she could react, a pilot on the tanker called and said they would be ready to refuel in twenty minutes.

"If you can keep us out of trouble for three minutes," she said, "I'll get Major Griffin." Griffin and Sandi had to be in the pilots' seats during refuelings.

"Copilot's aircraft," Chisholm said, acknowledging that he had accepted responsibility.

Sandi unstrapped from the pilot's seat and handed her equipment across to Chisholm for when she returned to get into the copilot's seat. Before stepping through the curtains, she leaned down and sensuously kissed him.

"Nice," he said when she stepped back.

"I just wanted to do that," she said, then added before disappearing, "That's the first time I kissed a colonel on the flight station."

And probably the last time, too, he thought with a smile. He pulled out a handkerchief to ensure there would be no comments from Oliverio or Blake about the attractive new shade of lip balm he was wearing.

A few minutes passed before Major Griffin stepped through the curtains and stood by the jump seat, stretching and yawning. "I don't think my body was made for a twenty-four-hour mission on a cold airplane," he said, rubbing his hands over his opposite shoulders.

"We'll all be lucky if we don't catch pneumonia," Chisholm said.

Griffin coughed as if on cue. "The dry air in one of these birds is bad enough on a normal mission."

Griffin settled into the pilot's seat, and Sandi moved through the curtains and waited for Chisholm to vacate the copilot's seat.

"Star Tracker should be coming off the tanker, King Zero-three, in about three minutes," Chisholm said. "We're due to hook up in about fifteen."

"Pilot's aircraft," Griffin said, so that Sandi could change places with Chisholm. Massaging his legs, Griffin added, "I hope I can get awake by then."

"Roger that," Chisholm said before disconnecting his headset and seatbelt. He understood that for the rest of the mission, fatigue would be as much of an enemy as anything the Soviets could send against them.

As he moved by Sandi, he took hold of her hand, gave a gentle squeeze, then allowed his fingertips to graze lightly across her palm as he let go. "Until later," he whispered in her ear.

She gave him a smile and nodded.

Chisholm checked the time—nearly three hours remained until the next satellite would return. He decided that he would take Sandi's place to let her get some sleep on one of the crew bunks. However, that exchange of places could not happen until she had finished assisting with the refueling, so he went downstairs for coffee and a sandwich and to check with McClain in his little control center. By the time Chisholm returned to the flight deck, the aerial refueling had started. As he pushed through the blackout curtains and settled into the jump seat, he sensed something unsettling—something more than the tension of trying to hold the C-141 steady a few feet below the huge tanker.

Griffin and Sandy were concentrating on small panels, which had the aerial refueling lights, and on the massive image that blocked out the night sky ahead. Chisholm noticed that Griffin seemed to be in constant motion—head, arms, legs, and body never quite still at the same time. Each pilot reacted differently to the stresses of aerial refueling, but Chisholm did not remember so much movement by Griffin during the two previous refuelings. However, Chisholm rationalized, those refuelings during daylight had been less stressful.

Griffin's left hand dropped quickly from the control yoke and pressed against his knee. As his leg tensed, he pressed the rudder enough to cause the C-141 to yaw slightly. Sandi glanced over, then looked toward the KC-10.

"Sorry," Griffin said as he grabbed the yoke. His voice sounded dry and scratchy.

Chisholm asked, "Are you okay?"

Griffin made an exaggerated shrug of his shoulders and moved his head around as if trying to ease a stiff neck. "I'm not sure, sir." Suddenly he released the yoke and grabbed at his right shoulder. At the same time, his right arm stiffened, and his hand pushed the throttles forward.

Sandi's left hand was resting lightly on her set of throttles, and she immediately fought the forward pressure Griffin had added. In the moments it took her to wrest control, the C-141 lurched forward, overrunning into the narrow distance separating the two aircraft.

The boom operator on the KC-10 broadcast a chilling warning. "Breakaway! Breakaway! Breakaway!"

Chisholm grabbed Griffin's arm, pulling his hand from the throttles.

"Copilot's aircraft," Sandi shouted as she pressed the aerial refueling disconnect switch and pulled her throttles to idle. Then she yanked down on the spoiler handle, forcing the spoilers abruptly into the air that had been rushing smoothly above and below the wings. She eased the nose forward, trying to descend without gaining enough speed for the C-141's tall tail to strike the tanker.

The pilot on the KC-10 responded to the warning by adding power to accelerate away from the C-141. The boom operator moved the long refueling boom clear of the receptacle on top of the C-141.

Chisholm felt the helplessness of seeing what was happening and being unable to do anything—Sandi had already done everything he would have done. He watched the tail of the KC-10 loom larger, then almost immediately the C-141 began falling away. Chisholm knew that the immediate crisis was over but another had started—Griffin was suffering from depressurization sickness.

Chisholm assumed that tiny bubbles of nitrogen gas had been evolved into Griffin's blood during the rapid decompression before the MiG attack. The pain in the larger joints signaled that more and more bubbles were being trapped in capillaries that were too small to allow the bubbles to pass. Chisholm decided that additional cabin pressure could help redissolve the nitrogen bubbles back into the blood, so he called on intercom, "Engineer, give us maximum cabin pressure and get me someone to help with Major Griffin."

"Yes, sir."

"And awaken everyone," Chisholm continued. "Find out if anyone else has symptoms of decompression sickness."

Chisholm chastised himself for not recognizing the signals earlier. Suddenly he was faced with a difficult dilemma—abandon the mission or continue, but at great risk to Griffin. The blockage of tiny blood vessels in the joints had already been painful; similar blockages in the brain or other critical organs could prove fatal. The best treatment was to put Griffin into a recompression chamber for a few hours so the extra pressure would eliminate the bubbles as quickly and as thoroughly as possible. Unfortunately, there were no recompression chambers within thousands of miles.

Helping Sergeant Jacobs move Griffin to the lower bunk, Chisholm searched for options. Completing the air refueling was one of his concerns. Returning to the jump seat, he called the KC-10. "King

Zero-three, Southern Star. We've got a problem. How long can you stay with us?"

"King can give you maybe an extra hour, Southern Star, depending on how far east we go, but we may not be able to give you a full load."

"Stand by one, King, while we talk things over," Chisholm said, unsure what options he had. Changing to intercom, he asked McClain, "Rick, verify the time to the next target."

"With only two left, sir," McClain said, "we're having to wait almost a full orbit for Cosmos 3208 to return, so we have about two and a half hours."

"Distance to our next launch point?"

"A little over two hundred miles from here, sir."

Good, Chisholm thought. He could spend nearly two hours solving the medical problem and still have the C-141 in position for the next attack.

"Colonel, Loadmaster," Blake said. "The chief seems to be abnormally cantankerous, even for him. I think he's hurting more than he's admitting."

"Damn," Chisholm said, but not on intercom. At least two people out of eight were affected. "Anyone else?"

No one responded.

Sandi asked, "Is it allowable under these circumstances to make an emergency landing at McMurdo to get Major Griffin and the chief to a doctor?"

Chisholm considered her question, although he knew that the answer had to be no. "McMurdo's at least eleven hundred miles away."

"That's half as far as Chile or the Falklands," she said.

"But if we land in Antarctica, we take on a whole host of political problems that would probably prevent us from continuing the mission."

She whirled and looked at him questioningly. "We were getting shot at by MiGs a few hours ago and now we have people's lives on the line, and you're worried about politics?"

Chisholm shrugged, unwilling to take the time to educate her on what he had learned in three tough years of dealing with story-hungry reporters and image-conscious politicians. "That's how America fights its wars. Ask any Vietnam vet. Anyway, the airfield at McMurdo isn't open except in the Antarctic summer."

Diverting to McMurdo would mess up the timing too much to resume the attacks, he thought, even if the president ordered him to disregard the treaty. However, leaving Griffin and Oliverio in Antarctica might be the compromise he needed. He pulled out a map and checked locations of the American research stations that were manned this time of year. Almost immediately he found the answer he was looking for.

After setting new coordinates into the INS, he said to Sandi, m"Here's our next destination. Descend to nineteen thousand, so we can bring the cabin altitude to sea level."

"Yes, sir."

After giving a set of coordinates to the crew on the KC-10, Chisholm explained his plan to Griffin, who seemed to be feeling better.

Griffin asked, "Do we get any vote on this, sir?"

Chisholm shook his head. "I would appreciate it if you'd keep an eye on the chief. He's not in the best shape in the world."

"I'll do my best, sir."

In the cargo compartment Chisholm found that Blake had Oliverio covered with blankets and stretched out on several red canvas seats. As Chisholm approached, Blake gave him an encouraging nod.

Chisholm knelt beside Oliverio and said, "You should have mentioned earlier that you were having problems, Chief."

"When I felt the stiffness," Oliverio said with his lop-sided grin, "I figured my joints were complaining about no lubrication for the last couple of weeks."

"I'm afraid that's not it, Chief," Chisholm said. "We're going to take you and Major Griffin to an American research station on one of the ice shelves."

"I thought we couldn't land in Antarctica on this mission."

"The C-141 can't." Chisholm paused, then added, "In this medical emergency, you and the major can."

Oliverio's grin faded. "You talking about a nylon letdown, Colonel C.?"

Chisholm nodded.

Oliverio sighed and rubbed his hand across his mouth. "I've been feeling better in the last few minutes, sir. Really."

"We've descended and increased the cabin pressure," Chisholm said, "so some of your nitrogen bubbles should be going away. Unfortunately, we have to return to altitude for two more shots. The depressurizations could kill you."

Oliverio shrugged. "You always knew how to make a persuasive argument, Colonel C. I suppose parachuting beats dying," Oliverio said, sounding philosophical. Then he grinned and added, "But not by much."

"You'll do fine, Chief. I'll need to count on you to take care of Major Griffin."

"I been looking after pilots for most of my career, sir," Oliverio said with a wink, "so once more shouldn't be any problem."

Chisholm stood to return to the flight station.

"Uh, Colonel C.," Oliverio said, seemingly serious, "there was one item on your Sun Prairie list that I've been meaning to ask about."

What a strange time for a question about the equipment lists, Chisholm thought. "Is there a problem?"

"Not really, sir," Oliverio said. "There was a line of garbled letters after the last item. It might have been a screwup by our teletype machine, but . . ." Oliverio paused for effect, "it looked like you might have ordered me to include three cases of beer."

"I can assure you—" Chisholm stopped, then shook his head. "Where's the beer?"

"It's packed away, of course. In the bottom of that big container," Oliverio said, gesturing toward one of the crates. "I knew that if you put it on the list, it was for a postflight victory celebration."

"Right," Chisholm said with a slight grin. "I'm sure that's exactly what you thought, Chief. And that's what we might do with it."

"The real question I have, Colonel C.," Oliverio said, attempting unsuccessfully to look serious, "is, do you suppose it's possible for a guy to keep hold of a case of beer during the parachute's opening shock?"

"I doubt it, Chief," Chisholm said, shaking his head as if he were exasperated. He glanced toward Blake. "But if the case were tossed out the door with its own chute . . ."

"I could rig something, sir," Blake said with a smile.

"I'm thinking mainly of something for the guys down there," Oliverio said. "I mean if they're going to take care of us, I'd like to be able to show our appreciation."

"Right, Chief," Blake said drolly.

"I need to finish the coordination," Chisholm said. Then he put a hand on Oliverio's shoulder and added, "We couldn't have gotten this far without you. Little Nick would have been proud."

Oliverio nodded. "Yes, sir, I suppose he would have. Thanks for giving me another chance at something he could've been proud of, Colonel C."

40

Druzhnaya Research Station, Antarctica
Saturday, 3 April, 0356 local (0656 GMT)

Seven hundred twenty-five nautical miles from the South Pole, Sergei Iakukhin was dozing in a chair in the radio room at Druzhnaya when he awakened abruptly. Had he just heard a woman speaking in English on one of the radios, or was the silky voice part of a dream? Probably the latter, he thought, but he clicked on a tape recorder used to record American communications—just in case.

After a moment an American radio operator responded from a scientific station on the ice about ten miles away, "Aircraft calling Filchner Station, say again your identification."

She hadn't been in a dream, Iakukhin thought enthusiastically, as he rolled his chair over to his desk and opened a log book. He wondered if the Americans at Filchner were about to have visitors. And, he thought, the good fortune was his to be the only one at Druzhnaya aware that at least one female visitor might be coming onto the ice. He started thinking of excuses that could justify a trek over to the American station in the morning. Otherwise, he had not expected to even see a woman again until the resupply ship returned to the Weddell Sea sometime in November.

"Roger, Filchner," Sandi Turner answered from the C-141. "We're a MAC Charlie one-forty-one with a medical emergency on board. Do you have a doctor at your station?"

As Iakukhin wrote C-141 in his log, his interest in the conversation abruptly took a new direction. He found a piece of paper with instructions he had scribbled a few hours earlier—a C-141 was the kind of aircraft he had been told to be alert for.

The American radio operator answered, "Filchner Station has a doctor but as much as I hate to say it, we have no landing strip for an aircraft of your type, ma'am."

Now fully awake, Iakukhin picked up a telephone to call Fedor Sakov, the political officer assigned to Druzhnaya.

"We're considering parachuting the injured men," Sandi said. "Say your winds and weather."

While the radio operator at Filchner Station was giving the information, Sakov sleepily answered the call from Iakukhin. Three minutes later Sakov was in the radio room.

Iakukhin spoke quickly to the political officer. "The airplane asked permission to drop two paratroopers in about thirty minutes, Comrade Sakov."

"You're sure of the aircraft type?"

"Yes, Comrade."

Sakov could not believe his luck. The instructions received a few hours earlier supposedly had come from Chairman Petruk himself. If the C-141 appeared, it was to be destroyed in any way possible. "Get Gushkov and Utkin here immediately!"

Sakov went to one of the large supply cabinets and removed several boxes from a lower shelf. Then he pulled out a long case, which was marked on the outside as wind-measuring equipment. His hands were shaking with excitement as he removed a chain with several keys from around his neck. Moments later he unlocked the case and opened it, revealing a *Strela* surface-to-air missile launcher and two missiles.

For nearly one hundred miles the C-141 had flown north across the Filchner Ice Shelf, a solid sea of ice that never melted. Leaning forward in the copilot's seat, Chisholm used his hands to block the cockpit lighting from diminishing his view of the Antarctic night. Now that Sandi had guided the C-141 down to fifteen hundred feet and slowed for the upcoming airdrop, he had a view that was spectacular in a peculiar sort of way.

The black sky was clear, bright with stars whose brilliance was diminished only by the thickness of the windshield. There was none of the pollution Chisholm had taken for granted at night above Washington, D.C. The moon was low in the northwest sky, casting a glimmering, yellowish trail across the frigid surface that glistened a dark bluish-white in the reflected starlight. In the distance the ice looked so smooth that Chisholm thought of a giant rink, quietly awaiting a horizon-to-horizon game of hockey. When he looked downward, however, he discovered that the majestic setting was not all that it seemed. He saw dark, jagged lines—deep crevasses torn by the crush of ice that had been disgorged for centuries from glaciers along the rim of the Filchner inlet. He saw more than one chasm massive enough to consume a C-141 without a trace.

In this part of Antarctica there also were signs of man's presence. Ahead Chisholm saw four irregular clusters of lights, marking the locations of scientific stations. Each was near the pseudo-coastline where the iceberg-choked Weddell Sea bordered the permanent ice shelf. About twenty miles off to each side of the C-141's flight path, the two most distant sets of lights were those of Argentinean stations. The lights about ten miles to the right came from the Soviet scientific station at Druzhnaya. The conglomeration of lights straight ahead matched the coordinates Chisholm had put into the navigational computer for the American settlement known as Filchner Station.

Chisholm's thoughts were interrupted by a call from the radio operator at the American station. "MAC, Filchner has you in sight, due south of the drop zone."

"Roger, Filchner, we're about two minutes out," Chisholm answered, pleased to have someone on the ground confirm that the C-141 was headed for the right spot. He had taken over the radios now that Sandi was concentrating on keeping the C-141 on a very precise course and altitude. Earlier she had made the initial contacts with Filchner, carrying on an unofficial tradition in MAC. Long ago it had been recognized that just hearing a woman's voice could be a much-bragged-about morale booster for Americans serving long tours at remote locations. Chisholm had that in mind as he smiled toward Sandi, then added on the radio, "We're still planning to just fly over and drop our paratroopers unless you've managed to clear a runway for us by now."

"If you could give us twenty-four hours, MAC," the radio operator said, "I'm sure every man here would be out there smoothing out the ice."

"Maybe next time, Filchner," Sandi said in a more playful tone than characterized most of her conversations on the radio.

"You might be even more of a showstopper down there than you were that night in the Drifter's Reef," Chisholm called across the cockpit without activating the intercom.

"I doubt that," she answered, giving him a very knowing and confident smile.

Chisholm still remembered vividly a night years earlier on Wake Island. By the 1980s the population on the strategic island in the mid-Pacific had become all male, contract employees who managed the airfield and aeronautical facilities. The Drifter's Reef was the only bar on the island, and just the presence of a woman there could be the social highlight of the week—or month. The first time Chisholm had taken Sandi into the Reef, she had been wearing a soft, summery dress. Her arrival had stopped every conversation in the room, and the experience had been one that she and Chisholm had laughed about for years afterward.

Once again he pushed aside happier memories to focus on the present mission. Pressing the upper switch on his yoke, he asked on the intercom, "Everybody ready and eager in the back, Load?"

"We've got them ready, Colonel," Blake said, standing near the open paratroop door, "though they're not particularly eager."

Since the cargo doors remained closed for personnel drops, Blake's preparations had been much easier than for the airdrop of the missiles. Once Sandi had slowed the aircraft, he had opened the right paratroop door. Then he had deployed the jump platform and the air-deflector door—a heavy piece of metal with a pattern of holes that let some air through. With these two pieces of equipment extended, a parachutist could stand outside the C-141 with some protection from the frigid air rushing past at 150 miles an hour.

Dressed in their heavy arctic gear, Griffin and Oliverio sat on red canvas seats forward of the paratroop door. Both men felt better. With the C-141 now just fifteen hundred feet above sea level, the ambient pressure had dissolved the bubbles of nitrogen that had formed during the rapid decompression.

"The closest lights you see a few miles to the right belong to the Russians," Chisholm said to Blake, "so keep an eye in their direction."

"Roger, sir," Blake answered. During his career he had flown on several resupply missions that had landed on the ice at McMurdo Station on the other side of Antarctica. He knew that international agreements prohibited military armaments at the stations, but he glanced subconsciously at a parachute flare that had remained near the door since the MiG attack.

In the cockpit the computers, autopilot, and inertial navigational systems were guiding the C-141 toward the Computed Air Release

Point, where the first paratrooper should jump from the aircraft. These systems were sophisticated enough to airdrop men or equipment without the aircrew ever seeing the drop zone, but Sandi and Chisholm carefully cross-checked each step.

He watched the ALERT light on the INS panel. When the light started blinking, he announced, "One minute to green light."

"One minute," Blake shouted over the sound of the engines and the air roaring by the open door.

Griffin and Oliverio stood, then moved toward the open door. They pulled along their static lines, which linked the ripcord on their parachutes to an overhead cable. Blake grabbed the parachute that enclosed a case of beer and moved it to the seat closest to the door.

The noise, the parkas, and the arctic facemasks made conversation difficult, but Oliverio motioned for Blake to get close, then said, "If I ever try to stow away on one of your airplanes again, Tony, I expect you to call the security police and have my ass thrown into the can, right then and there."

"And miss all this fun? Not a chance, Chief."

"Screw you, Tony," Oliverio said, then embraced the taller sergeant. When he stepped back, he added, "I'm only shaking, you understand, because it's so friggin' cold."

"I understand," Blake said as they tried to interlock their arctic mittens in a makeshift handshake. "Happy landings, Chief."

In the cockpit the ALERT light stopped blinking, and Chisholm announced, "Ten seconds." He placed his face against the windshield, trying to look below. Most of the lights of the makeshift drop zone and the station had disappeared beneath the nose of the C-141.

In back Blake relayed Chisholm's message, and Griffin stepped out onto the small jump platform. He held tightly to the frame of the paratroop door with his back to the air rushing through and around the air-deflector door. Blake kept a firm grip on Griffin's shoulder as they both watched the signal lights beside the paratroop door. The red lights glowed brightly. The green lights were dark.

At five seconds remaining, Chisholm started a countdown on the intercom.

At zero the ALERT light on the center console came on steady, indicating that the C-141 had reached the Computed Air Release Point.

"Green light," Sandi said, raising the Jump Lights switch on her ADS panel.

In back the green lights flashed on, and the red lights extinguished. "Go!" As Blake shouted, he shoved lightly on Griffin's shoulder. Griffin hesitated an instant, then stepped off the platform.

Oliverio shuffled onto the platform and stepped off two seconds later as Blake shouted, "Go!"

As soon as both men were clear, Blake picked up the parachute with the beer, knelt, and threw it out beyond the jump platform. He crawled to the edge and looked behind the aircraft. He saw that two large parachutes already had deployed and the third was streaming from its pack.

As Blake started to pull the jump platform back inside, he saw a brilliant flash well behind the wing, about four miles beyond the lights of Filchner Station. Immediately the solitary light rose on a tail of flame and smoke, accelerating on a curved path toward the C-141.

"SAM! From the right!" As Blake screamed into the intercom, he lunged toward the flare that was stowed near the door. Flinging off his heavy mittens, he twisted the timer setting to minimum delay, yanked the lanyard as he stepped into the doorway, and hurled the flare into the darkness. As soon as his fingers found his intercom button, he shouted, "Get me more flares!"

Sergeants Jacobs and Claremont hurried to a crate, which was strapped down nearer the front of the aircraft.

At the same time an excited voice at Filchner Station came over the radio, "Someone just shot a missile at you, MAC!"

Chisholm strained to see what Blake had seen, but the wing and engines blocked his view. At the same time he shoved the yoke and throttles forward and said, "Let's speed up to two hundred knots." The C-141 was limited to that speed with the doors open and the flaps extended.

"Roger," Sandi responded, "Flaps approach."

"Approach," Chisholm responded, moving the handle without giving it any conscious thought. Instead he was grasping for ideas that might save the C-141 if a flare did not divert the missile. For an instant he thought about rolling the big transport into a steep bank, turning toward the missile and trying to mask the hot exhausts of the engines. That maneuver sometimes saved jet fighters, he thought, but a C-141 wasn't going to outturn the missile. He decided that trying to outrun the missile made more sense, since it probably was a shoulder-fired SAM with a limited range. Diving toward the ice would increase the airspeed more quickly and would increase the chances of a survivable crash landing if the SAM exploded in one of the engines. He jabbed a finger down toward the ice and shouted to Sandi, "Take us down to three hundred feet! There's no terrain ahead of us."

She nodded and maneuvered the C-141 lower.

Blake looked back into the cargo compartment and shouted, "Where the hell are the rest of those flares?" He saw that the scanner and loadmaster were frantically trying to loosen the tiedown straps that held the crate closed. Yelling wouldn't help, he thought. Closing one eye to protect its night vision, Blake knelt in the doorway trying to pick out the SAM before the flare ignited. Seconds later the flare flashed momentarily, then sparkled into a blinding yellowish-white light. Shimmering ghostlike across the ice floes of the Weddell Sea, the flare drifted lazily beneath a small parachute.

Blake watched breathlessly, now unable to see the SAM since its rocket motor already had burned out. He braced himself, fearing that at any moment the SAM would slam into one of the engines just a few feet beyond his reach.

Suddenly the flare seemed to leap sideways, jolted in a grinding collision with the SAM. Even before Blake recognized what had happened, the missile exploded, extinguishing the flare and sending fiery pieces of shrapnel arcing forward, then down toward the ice.

Blake exhaled for the first time in several seconds, then said on the intercom, "The SAM's no threat. It hit—"

The words seemed to jam in his throat as another flash caught his attention. Dropping flat onto the floor and lunging until his head was beyond the edge of the door, he saw a second SAM arcing up on a fiery tail, trailing a shadowy ribbon of exhaust from where the first had been fired. "They've launched another one!"

He heard the radio operator at Filchner broadcast a similar warning.

Instead of being as much to the side of the C-141 as the earlier missile had been, this SAM was chasing from farther behind. Blake watched the rapidly accelerating missile for a few seconds then looked toward the other two men. "Hurry!" In spite of his shout of encouragement, Blake recognized that they were not going to get another flare to him in time.

He stretched out into the swirling air, which at two hundred knots was buffeting the deflector door more strongly than before. The

SAM's motor had already burned out, so Blake had trouble spotting the missile, even using the night vision he had protected earlier by keeping one eye closed. He used the smoke trail from the launch site to help locate the warhead, now a dark mass streaking supersonically toward him. Almost mesmerized, he tried to keep the object in sight against the moonlit surface of the Filchner Ice Shelf. Thoughts of Millie and Little Tony flashed through his mind along with a silent plea for help.

As seconds passed, Blake had trouble focusing his eyes, which were blurred by the wind and cold. Yet he realized that the dark object he was watching was sinking toward the frozen sea. Two seconds later he saw an explosion that cartwheeled flame, smoke, and debris across the flat expanse of ice a quarter of a mile behind. The C-141 had flown beyond the range of the shoulder-fired missile.

Cold and exhausted, Blake rolled onto his back and pressed his mike button with fingers now painfully stiff. "It detonated well clear, crew, but let's get the hell away from the guys with the missiles."

"Roger that," Chisholm said. "Get her buttoned up. We've got to find our tanker."

Minutes later the airdrop equipment had been retrieved and the paratroop door was closed.

As the C-141 was in a climbing turn, well to the west of Druzhnaya, the radio operator at Filchner Station called, "Your sergeant asked that I report that all three jumps were completely successful. He said you'd understand."

"Understand," Chisholm said, sharing a smile with Sandi.

41

Paul Edwards was surprised to learn that Dr. Turnhill had requested entry. Watching the scientist walk through the door, Edwards saw that while the regular scowl remained, Turnhill had the look of a defeated man. Edwards realized his impression might be biased—Turnhill was still wearing a bow tie and business suit, now rumpled and sagging from two days of Guamanian heat and humidity.

Without even saying hello, Turnhill said, "You didn't dump the samples, did you, Paul?" Edwards looked confused, Turnhill added, "The moon rocks? By last week Prospector had collected four hundred seventy pounds."

"I don't think we unloaded," Edwards said. "That subject wasn't mentioned, and we didn't have much time to waste on nonessentials."

"Your schedule wouldn't have been so compressed, Paul, if you'd sent me off to this God-forsaken steam bath a couple of days earlier."

Turnhill almost looked serious, but Edwards recognized that the expression was as close as Turnhill ever came to smiling. "If we're successful, I could let you stay here an extra day or two to celebrate."

Turnhill shrugged. "If you're successful, I just want to get home and start rebuilding my program."

"Do you have some ideas—about Cosmos 3220, I mean?"

Nodding, Turnhill asked, "How long until you'll be making the final corrections to the trajectory?"

"About four hours. What do you have in mind?"

"Think shotguns and skeet shooting, Paul. You have a better probability of hitting the clay pigeon with lots of little pellets than with one big slug."

Edwards began nodding thoughtfully. Any rock that was separated from the spacecraft would follow the same general trajectory and have the same lethal velocity. "So we start spreading out the rocks once we're on the final trajectory?"

"According to my calculations," Turnhill said, "you should increase the chances of a collision by more than five hundred percent. At the worst, you'll create an unforecast meteor shower above the equator."

During the last four days, the countdown for Defender I had gone through numerous stops and restarts as problems were encountered and resolved. At 0438 hours on Saturday at Cape Canaveral, the count finally reached the planned hold at T minus fifteen minutes. The president had ordered that the countdown go no further as long as the armed satellites of the Soviet Union were still operational.

A few minutes later and more than five thousand miles away, Cosmos 3239 roared away from a launchpad at Plesetsk. The launch azimuth of this high-resolution reconnaissance satellite was almost due north. Within the following hour Cosmos 3239 would pass near both poles before its scheduled rendezvous with *Borzoi IV*—and the team of American aircraft that had destroyed the other seven *Borzoi*.

Novikov was nearly exhausted—physically and mentally. During the hour following the launch, a combination of coffee and nervous energy had kept him awake. He tried to be optimistic, telling himself that at last he had a plan that would defeat both American attacks. By saving only one *Borzoi* and *Zashchitnik I*, he could maintain the blockade until he convinced Grigoriev to launch the two *Borzoi* that remained concealed beneath the forests of Plesetsk.

Watching the minutes slowly clicking off on the time-to-perigee counter, Novikov grew increasingly impatient with the waiting. Finally he crumpled a piece of paper into a tight ball and dropped it on the floor. Flipping his cane, he grabbed the opposite end as if it were a short hockey stick, then extended the handle downward. With three deft moves he centered the ball of paper between two rows of consoles then used a modified slap shot to drive the paper between the legs of Nasedkin's chair.

"Novikov's shot at the buzzer ties the score," Novikov said as a mock announcer, then extended both arms above his head.

Nasedkin looked around and smiled.

Novikov asked, "Did you ever play hockey, Nicolai?"

"No, Comrade General. I could barely stay standing on skates."

"Then you've never waited to start an overtime period?" Nasedkin shook his head. Novikov gazed with tired eyes at the displays on the front wall and added, "My last game with the national team was like this. We'd played our guts out and barely achieved a tie in the last few seconds. Then we had to sit around bone-tired, waiting for the clock to say it was time to start again." Novikov slumped into a chair at one of the control consoles, cradled his cane across his chest, and said, "It's called sudden death—the first one to score wins it all."

"Who won?"

Novikov flashed a confident but weary smile. "Do you have any doubt, Comrade?"

Nasedkin shook his head. "Not where you're concerned, Comrade General."

Novikov turned back to the displays and wished he were as confident about the showdown coming within the next half hour. He was nostalgic for those earlier times when he could ensure victory through the sheer force of his personal determination. Now as the last of his *Borzoi* plunged silently through the cosmos above the South Pacific, victory depended upon two satellites accomplishing a mission neither was designed for.

Cosmos 3239's specialty was locating enemy fleets on distant oceans. Although the sensors could pinpoint ships within a few hundred meters, inaccuracies of a few miles did not matter when the objective simply was to find the ships. Unfortunately, from Novikov's point of view, such inaccuracies were too imprecise for fire-control against an aircraft with a wingspan of fifty meters. Nevertheless, the sensors could detect the hot exhaust from high-flying aircraft, and Novikov hoped that would give him the edge he needed.

The *Borzoi*'s sensors could accurately aim the lasers anywhere within the sensor's cone of coverage that spread out below the satellite. However, the sensors could focus with that kind of accuracy only upon a small part of that cone at any time. This limitation was of little consequence when the target was a satellite, since its orbit would be known for hours, if not months, in advance. And when the *Borzoi* had been thousands of miles above the northern hemisphere, a target satellite could spend several minutes with the cone of coverage. Thus Novikov had been pleased with the design of the *Borzoi* for the killer-satellite role.

Now he faced the harsh reality that with *Borzoi IV* near perigee, the cone of coverage of its sensors would sweep across the aircraft in only a few seconds. Unless the sensors already were focused toward the aircraft's predetermined location, Novikov had decided, the sensors had maybe one chance in a thousand of finding the aircraft in time. However, if the reconnaissance satellite had already pinpointed the jets' hot exhausts within a few hundred meters, the *Borzoi's* sensors would know almost exactly where to look. Novikov wasn't sure his improvised scheme would work, but his gut feelings convinced him that he'd rather be in the *Borzoi* control center than in the American aircraft.

Finally *Borzoi IV* was racing almost due eastward, fewer than ninety seconds from perigee. Several hundred miles ahead, Cosmos 3239 had already passed almost over the south pole and was racing northward crossing nearly two hundred miles below the *Borzoi's* path. The displays on the front wall of the *Borzoi* control center showed that Cosmos 3239 was locked onto infrared images from two airborne targets and was feeding that data directly to *Borzoi IV*. Novikov assumed that one was Chisholm's aircraft and the other was the ARIA that had disappeared after taking off from American Samoa.

"No sensor lock yet on the primaries, General," Nasedkin said, referring to the *Borzoi's* onboard sensors, "but *Borzoi Four* has a firing angle on target one."

Borzoi IV's lasers were gimballed enough to aim beyond the cone of coverage of its sensors. Thus the lasers could fire ahead into part of the region covered by Cosmos 3239.

"Commence firing, maximum power," Novikov said, since firing ahead of the aircraft's exhaust trail might score a lucky hit.

Moments later a blinking light on the fire-control panel confirmed that the armed satellite was pumping pulses of laser light into the upper atmosphere above Antarctica. There was no direct display of the sensor data from the *Borzoi*, so Novikov studied the display from Cosmos 3239, hoping to see a sudden change in the IR image of the first target.

For the last couple of minutes, Chisholm had felt elated. He had never imagined that the airdrops would go so smoothly. The eighth missile had disappeared into the void behind the C-141, then lit up the predawn darkness. As it streaked upward toward the final intercept, the doors were being closed for the last time.

Now Chisholm's main concern was fuel. The delay caused by the diversion to Filchner Station had reduced the amount of fuel the KC-10 had been able to transfer, so Chisholm was unsure enough remained to reach the next tanker. He started considering options.

"We're being fired on from above!" The ARIA's frantic message came through the radio as a shout, jolting Chisholm almost as if it had been an electric shock.

As he squeezed the transmit switch on his yoke, he leaned toward the windshield, trying to see into the darkness beyond the dim lights of his flight instruments. "Take her down, Star Tracker. Put as much atmosphere above you as you can." Chisholm knew that the laser's beam would become less effective as it passed into the denser atmosphere of the lower altitudes. Unfortunately, he thought, the ARIA was almost completely above the atmosphere's protection.

"It's a red beam, flashing down all around."

"Evade," Chisholm said, straining to see the laser in spite of the miles that separated the two aircraft.

Sandi asked, "If the ARIA stops tracking, what happens to our missile?"

"At this point the ARIA's just making minor refinements. The warhead's either in the window or it isn't."

"*Borzoi*'s about four seconds from primary sensor lock, Comrade General," Nasedkin said.

Novikov nodded and checked the second hand on the clock on the front wall. Sweeping across the skies above Antarctica, the cone of coverage of the *Borzoi*'s own sensors was about to reach the first American aircraft. Returning his attention to the display from the Cosmos 3239's sensors, he tapped his cane against his palm, marking the passage of each second.

"Star Tracker's out of thirty-seven thousand," a pilot on the ARIA said, indicating that the aircraft was descending.

"We're well clear," Chisholm said, realizing as soon as he had spoken that it was a superfluous call, since the two aircraft were more than a hundred miles apart. Pressing the switch for the intercom, he asked, "How are we coming with the doors, load?"

"Just a few more seconds on the petal doors, sir," Blake said.

"We need some maneuverability," Chisholm said, "so let us know when the ramp closes." Sandi could not accelerate the C-141 to normal flying speeds until the petal doors and ramp were closed.

"Star Tracker's going to descend to about—" The transmission ceased cleanly.

Chisholm pressed his forehead against the cold inner pane of the windshield. He saw a dim flash near the horizon, like lightning deep within a large storm cloud.

"You were broken, Star Tracker," Sandi said on the radio. "Say again your last transmission."

As the image of light faded, Chisholm tried vainly to make out any clouds. Then he remembered—the area had been clear of clouds when he had flown through on the way from the last target.

"I'll try a call on guard," Sandi said, her voice now hollow with the realization that there was little chance of receiving a response on the emergency frequency.

Novikov watched the thermal image of the first target grow momentarily, suggesting a change in the heat source detected by Cosmos 3239's infrared sensors. Then the image dimmed, becoming more diffuse as the seconds passed. Was that really what it looked like, he wondered, when a spacecraft shot down an aircraft?

Nasedkin turned toward Novikov and said, "The sensors are losing the image on tar—"

"We hit the target!" Novikov sprang to his feet and raised his cane above his head.

As everyone else in the room joined in a noisy celebration, Novikov let out a rousing growl. Immediately his thoughts returned to the second aircraft.

"Target number two," Novikov shouted to Nasedkin. "Switch the *Borzoi* immediately!"

Destroying both aircraft should set back the Americans twice as far, Novikov thought as he watched for the displays to change. The light on the fire-control panel stopped blinking as the laser was shut down while Nasedkin altered the targeting priorities for *Borzoi IV*.

"Comrade General, the second aircraft is twenty-three seconds ahead of the coverage of the sensors on *Borzoi Four*."

"Ramp and petal doors are closed," Blake said.
Sandi pushed the throttles forward and said, "Flaps up."

As Chisholm started to move the flap handle, a pencil-thin streak of red flashed by about a quarter of a mile ahead.

"Jesus," Sandi said.

"Hang on!" Chisholm yanked the throttles to idle, then grabbed the flap handle. "Flaps coming to landing!"

Another flash of red passed somewhere behind the left wing.

Chisholm shoved the yoke forward. Although he was uncertain whether changing altitude could save them, he knew that with the flaps fully extended, a C-141 descended like a runaway elevator.

"But we'll hardly be moving," Sandi said as she tried to push her set of throttles.

Chisholm overrode her pressure, keeping his set of throttles firmly in idle. "A few knots one way or the other doesn't matter," Chisholm said, "not when you're evading a laser traveling at the speed of light."

Red blazed for an instant just beyond the right wingtip.

"Rick," Chisholm called on the intercom, "how much time remaining on the missile."

"Six seconds!"

"Hang on and pray," Chisholm said, rolling the aircraft as much as he dared at the low speed.

"Two seconds to primary sensor lock, Comrade General," Nasedkin said.

Novikov nodded, his confidence increasing markedly with each blink of the light on the fire-control panel. One, two, he said quietly to himself.

"Target acquisition by the primary sensors," Nasedkin said. "Fire-control is switching to the primaries."

Novikov watched as the light on the fire-control panel stopped blinking during the momentary switchover. He leaned forward, his head nodding in anticipation of the next blink of the light, but it did not illuminate. Novikov looked to see what Nasedkin was doing—and discovered that he was doing nothing. The switchover was to have been automatic but had not occurred.

"We seem to have a loss of signal," Nasedkin said with a sigh.

"Loss of signal on missile number eight," McClain shouted into his microphone. "On time! On schedule!"

"Thank you, Lord," Chisholm said, then asked, "Any doubt?"

"Negative, sir. We scored a hit."

"Proshchai, Borzoi," Chisholm said quietly.

Sandi looked toward him and asked, "What was that?"

"Goodbye, Wolfhounds," he said as he pushed the throttles forward, then eased the flaps up, and began leveling off. In the dimly lit cockpit he clamped his fist as hard as possible on the throttles. He was trying to conceal the trembling caused by thoughts of the people on the ARIA nearing the end of their seven-mile plunge to the ice below.

The stirring deep beneath his seatbelt suggested that if he did not keep busy, he might even get sick. He selected the radio that was linked by satellite to the command post in the Pentagon. After taking a drink of water to clear the dryness from his mouth, he pressed the transmit button and said, "Sunglass, this is Southern Star. We've had a problem."

Novikov sat back in his chair, drained of the energy that had carried him through the last few hours. Cosmos 3239 was streaking northward over the South Georgia Islands, leaving behind the single image of an aircraft beneath the orbit of *Borzoi IV.*

Nasedkin pushed back from his console and removed his headset. "It's not the communication links, sir."

"I know," Novikov said with a tired sigh. He looked at his marked-up printout that showed the projected perigee passages for the eight *Borzoi.* Pulling a red pen from his pocket, he drew a line through the data for *Borzoi IV.*

Novikov checked his watch. It was time to return to the main control room, where he would maneuver the big satellite out of the way of the American probe that was returning from the moon. He stood, trying to reassure himself that his chances of saving *Zashchitnik I* were in no way affected by the defeat he had just experienced. And, he thought as he slowly walked toward the door, even if *Zashchitnik I* were the only satellite still operational during the launch from Florida, the Americans still would lose Defender I.

When Novikov entered the main control room, he was surprised to see Marshal Murashev, especially on a Saturday afternoon. The old man, his expression grim, stood behind one of the control consoles. Its operator, a dependable young kapitan—whose face was pale, almost ashen—looked with wide-eyed shock toward Novikov.

Sensing that something had happened, Novikov whirled to check the status indicators on the front wall. The only operating display showed less than thirty minutes remaining until the American probe would strike. All displays representing *Zashchitnik I* were either in alarm or exhibiting no data at all. He stood frozen for a few moments, unable to comprehend why there would have been an unexpected loss of signal from all sources on the huge satellite.

"*Zashchitnik I*'s tumbling out of control," the operator said in a voice weak with fright.

"Why?" Novikov roared the question. "What happened?"

"Fix it, General," Murashev said. His words were firm but at a higher pitch than Novikov had ever heard from the older officer.

Novikov's mind raced but failed to produce an answer that would solve the nightmare proclaimed by the displays. If he were going to save *Zashchitnik I* from the American attack, he needed to send the maneuver commands immediately. Unfortunately, those commands—and any from Kaliningrad that might stabilize *Zashchitnik I*—had to be received by uplink antennas that now were revolving uncontrollably along with the spacecraft.

"Fix it," Murashev repeated.

"It will have to fix itself, Comrade Marshal," Novikov said, "and that may take hours." He assumed that sensors aboard *Zashchitnik I* already were taking readings, trying to locate the sun and earth, but the process would be slow if recovery was possible at all.

"But you required only minutes to stabilize the craft when it first reached orbit." Murashev's tone returned to that of a marshal who had been giving commands for nearly fifty years.

"Then, Comrade Kalinen was alive!" Novikov was angry at having to deal with Murashev's inane meddling instead of being able to concentrate. Turning to the console operator, Novikov asked, "What caused the loss of stabilization?"

The operator looked terrified. "I . . . I . . . We tried to turn the lasers toward the attacker, Comrade General."

"You know that they won't point away from the—" Novikov suddenly realized what the young kapitan was saying. "You tried to reorient the entire spacecraft?"

The operator tried to say words but could only nod.

Novikov grabbed the front of the man's tunic and yanked him from his chair. The cord on the operator's headset snapped taut, wrenching the apparatus from the kapitan's head. "Why?" Novikov's face was flushed with rage. "Why would you do something so stupid?"

"I . . . I was ordered to." The operator gasped out the words in spite of the choking grip Novikov had on the uniform.

"What?" Novikov relented slightly.

"I tried to tell him, but he wouldn't listen, sir."

Novikov released the man, then pivoted to face Murashev. "You meddling old fool," Novikov said as he raised his cane like a club. In the instant before the cane slashed downward, he thought he was going to crush Murashev's skull. Instead Novikov angled the blow sideways, barely missing the old man's shoulder. The cane exploded into jagged splinters as it smashed into the top of a control console in the row behind Murashev. "Your incompetence has killed us!"

Murashev's knees were shaking so badly that he had to grab onto the console to remain standing.

Novikov paused for a moment, looking at the remains of the cane, his prized possession now shattered, as were his career and his life. Turning to the kapitan—who remained unmoving, sprawled across his chair—Novikov handed him the teak and ivory handle and said, "Sorry."

Novikov turned, then limped toward the door, knowing that there was nothing left to be done in Flight Control.

42

At GEO above the Pacific Ocean
Saturday, 3 April, 0414 local (1114 GMT)

Zashchitnik I tumbled slowly as it continued eastward at nearly seven thousand miles per hour. The fragile structure of one section of solar panels had snapped during the initial roll that was commanded from Kaliningrad. Those panels now were bent back toward the body of the satellite.

From fewer than fifty miles above in the darkness of space, the Prospector raced downward within a disorganized formation of greenish-gray moon rocks. The cross hairs of Prospector's rendezvous sensor were locked onto *Zashchitnik I*. For the last two minutes, the on-board radar had warned continuously that the overtake rate was excessive for a normal rendezvous. The on-board computers had been generating commands to fire the retro-rockets on Prospector, but those commands were being overridden by the control center on Guam. Prospector remained on a collision course, streaking toward an invisible crossroad where neither craft had the right of way.

Moments later pieces of the moon smashed through solar panels, communications antennas, and the phased-array radar. Prospector struck a glancing blow, breaking open *Zashchitnik I* just aft of the airlock. The parts of both spacecraft, which were not vaporized by the intensity of the impact, hurtled away as sparkling shrapnel, reflecting sunlight into the darkness of the heavens.

Fewer than ten minutes later American sensors had confirmed that *Zashchitnik I* no longer existed as an operational satellite. Since the radars at Ascension Island already had verified the destruction of the last *Borzoi*, President Anderson ordered the launch of Defender I from Cape Canaveral.

Thirty-seven minutes after sunrise, low clouds offshore still blocked the sun as it moved higher above the horizon far out across the Atlantic Ocean. When the countdown reached its final seconds, suddenly it seemed as if the sun were about to make its appearance from beneath Defender I.

Clouds of angry gray-white smoke billowed upward, dwarfing the huge booster and its launch tower. As the thunderous roar resounded for miles around, thousands of birds took to the air before Defender I moved. Finally the booster lifted from the pad, slowly accelerating past the tower on a tail of yellow-white flame that grew even longer than the booster. The fiery plume, reflecting from the Banana River and hundreds of tidal pools, seemed brighter than the sun at noon.

Vice President Hatcher watched the spectacle from a viewing area several miles away. After Defender I pitched over and started downrange, Hatcher turned to an aide and said, "Well, this swings the balance of power in the other direction. I hope the Lord gives us the good sense to know how far to take it."

About three hours later Sandi was sleeping in the pilot's seat. Chisholm was guiding the C-141 toward the Falkland Islands, the destination he had selected because of fuel, when General Ramsey called from the Pentagon.

"The British weren't crazy about getting involved," Ramsey said, "but they've agreed to let you land at Mount Pleasant."

Blake was listening at the navigator's station and said on intercom, "Maybe they'd be more enthusiastic, Colonel, if General Ramsey told them we were bringing the beer."

Chisholm glanced over his shoulder and said, "I don't think so." Switching back to the radio, he said, "It's a little late for them to change their minds, because our fuel gauges say that one way or the other we're ending up in the Falklands."

"It's all taken care of, Mike. General Gillette sends his congratulations and wants to know how his bird is?"

"We've got to replace a starter shaft," Chisholm said, "and we'll need a few hours of crew rest, sir, but we'll be glad to get out of there ASAP. Are you hearing anything out of the Soviets yet?"

"Within the last hour," Ramsey said, "Tass broke into regular television programming in Moscow. They didn't seem pleased that we'd launched Defender I. They're complaining that in spite of Ambassador Galkin's gentlemanly attempt to keep weapons out of space, we've responded rudely."

Chisholm was surprised. "What about their loss of nine satellites in the last twenty-four hours?"

"Not a peep about that," Ramsey said. "There was something earlier about their new solar observatory being damaged in what appeared to be a collision with an old communications satellite."

"But, General, they've got to know exactly what happened," Chisholm said.

"It's not a matter of what they know, Mike," Ramsey said. "It's what they're willing to 'fess up to. You gathered in all their million-ruble chips, so I think they decided to throw in their cards and sneak out through the swinging doors."

"It would've been better if they'd never challenged us to the game," Chisholm said, thinking of the casualties: the cosmonaut, the fighter pilots, and the crew on the ARIA. He also thought about a memorial service for those on the ARIA and about facing the new widows and the children who would grow up without the nurturing of their fathers. He repeated the haunting question that he already had been asking himself: Could he have broken the blockade in any other way?

A few minutes later Chisholm loosened his seatbelt so that he could reach Sandi in the pilot's seat. She was sleeping so peacefully that he hated to waken her. Thinking of a couple of more intimate times when he had awakened her, he placed his hand lightly on her arm.

Her eyes flashed open, instinctively scanning the instrument panels before she seemed aware of his hand. Then she looked at him and smiled. Stretching, she said, "I guess it's time for you to get a nap."

He shook his head. "We're twenty minutes from descent."

She looked surprised. "You shouldn't have let me sleep the whole time."

"Why not? You're the pilot who's going to land this machine. I'm just an unqualified passenger."

She smiled but did not answer.

At 205 miles south of the Falkland Islands, two Harrier fighters of the Royal Air Force intercepted the C-141 to verify that it was an American aircraft. A few minutes later Chisholm established contact with a radar controller, who gave a heading for the airfield at Mount Pleasant.

"Our landing conditions this morning are not very pleasant," the controller said. "The rain continues in a downpour, and the winds are erratic, varying from one-eighty to two-forty degrees at twelve gust twenty. The peak gust in the last hour was twenty-four knots. Runway two-three is closed."

"Stand by a moment, please," Chisholm said as he looked at the airfield diagram.

"That's no big factor," Sandi said. "Two-three's thirty-five hundred feet shorter and only half as wide as the main runway. See if holding will do any good."

Chisholm asked on the radio, "Any chance of your weather improving if we hold?"

"It usually improves a little in the spring," the controller said, "but down here that means September."

"I was thinking more in terms of an hour," Chisholm said.

"Sorry, sir, but we can only forecast based on what we see out the window and on the radar. Looks like we've got several more hours of the same, maybe a little better, maybe a little worse."

Chisholm looked toward Sandi for her response.

She made some fine adjustments to the picture on the radarscope.

If the erratic winds were caused by thunderstorms moving through the area, the C-141's weather radar would show the storm cells. None appeared on the scope. After making her own weather check, she said, "I'd rather try an approach now while we still have enough fuel to go around if the first try doesn't look good."

"We're ready for approach," Chisholm said on the radio.

For the next few minutes the controller directed descents and heading changes that positioned the C-141 east of the airfield for a long final approach. Chisholm handled the radios and the other co-pilot duties, while Sandi piloted the aircraft. During her briefing she paid particular attention to the dangerous crosswinds and the wet runway.

"I'll plan on an approach-flap landing," she said, "and I'll be adding the current gust increment to final approach, threshold, and touchdown speeds. Even with the extra speed and the wet runway, we have more than twice as much runway as the book says we need."

Good, Chisholm thought. By choosing not to extend the flaps fully, she reduced the chance of losing control if the C-141 was hit by a sudden gust of crosswind. The higher airspeed until touchdown covered the possibility of a gust suddenly dying off and leaving the C-141 with less airspeed than needed.

Getting closer to the ocean, the big airplane started shuddering and bouncing through the shifting currents of air. While they still were in the clouds, Chisholm periodically checked the wind readout on the navigational computer. The direction and speed kept changing, almost as if the machine were malfunctioning. Chisholm was getting thrown against his lapbelt and shoulder straps enough to be convinced that the readout was reflecting the real conditions.

As the altitude decreased to a thousand feet, Chisholm watched the heavy rain and the clouds beyond the windshield. Concentrating on her flight instruments and the radar controller's instructions, Sandi kept the C-141 aligned on the precision approach path for runway two-eight.

Finally Chisholm saw the first flickering of brightness through the blur of water on the windshield. "I've got lights." He reached to the overhead panel and turned the selector switch to Both for Rain Removal, which would blow hot air across the windshields. "Rain removal's coming on."

As he waited for the air to pass through the long tubing leading to windshields, he strained to identify the rain-blurred lights. They looked to be so far to the right that he was unsure if they were at the airfield. His quick check of the heading indicator verified that Sandi had the C-141 pointed well left of the runway heading. The maneuver, often referred to as "crabbing into the wind," had the big aircraft moving like a crab in a different direction than it was pointed. Chisholm always found the sensation to be like skidding straight along an icy street in an automobile pointed toward the curb a half of a block ahead. However, the combination of wind and heading were moving the C-141 straight toward the runway.

After a couple of seconds, air at a temperature of 230 degrees centigrade blasted from the rain-removal nozzles at the base of the pilots' windshields. With most of the rain being blown or vaporized from the windshield, Chisholm announced, "Runway's in sight," as he got his first view of the dreary scene below the overcast.

He saw treeless hills that were gently sloped. The island looked like ominous shadows connected to brooding clouds by sheets of rain. The lights of the airfield and the nearby settlements were the only hints of life in the near darkness of late morning. Yet, Chisholm thought, as remote as this haven was, the small islands had not been spared twentieth-century warfare. Somewhere ahead in the channel to the left, the downpour was splashing on the watery grave of RFA *Sir Galahad*, the last ship of the Royal Navy sunk during the Falklands War in 1982.

For a few moments Chisholm watched, verifying that the C-141 still was flying directly toward the runway. He could also see the precision-approach path-indicator lights beside the runway. Though blurred by the rain, the lights provided additional confirmation of the radar controller's continuing assessments—Sandi was keeping the C-141 on course, on glide slope.

Chisholm held his left hand lightly on his set of throttles. He had tried to keep his right hand on his control yoke. However, Sandi was rotating the yoke so abruptly in response to the rapidly changing winds, he was afraid his touch might cause problems. So he held his hand barely away, ready to grab hold if necessary.

Despite not having any real rest in the last forty-five hours, Sandi was flying a near-perfect approach. By the time the C-141 descended below three hundred feet, Chisholm was remembering how much he loved being at the controls during a good crosswind landing—and how much he disliked crosswind landings when anyone else was at the controls.

"Land," Chisholm said, indicating that the C-141 had reached the minimum altitude for the instrument approach and that the aircraft was in position to land.

Sandi eased back the throttles to let the airspeed decrease as the C-141 approached the runway threshold. Although she was still fighting the shifting winds, she had to change her method of crosswind control because the aircraft had to be headed down the runway at touchdown. She pushed the right rudder to align the nose with the runway while she banked the aircraft slightly to the left. By using bank and opposite rudder, she had the nose pointed straight down the runway as the C-141 crossed the threshold at 130 knots.

She pulled the throttles to idle, then eased the nose up slightly to break the glide. Moments later the C-141 touched down firmly on the left main gear and settled onto the right.

After touchdown, everything happened very quickly.

Sandi lifted her throttles and pulled them back to the first stop. This began moving the thrust-reverser doors into place behind each of the four jet engines. "Spoilers," she called as she pushed the yoke forward to get the nosewheels on the ground.

Chisholm raised the spoiler handle, and the automatic deployment mechanism moved the spoilers to the ground limit. The C-141's big wings still had flying speed, so extending the spoilers helped kill the lift and get the weight of the aircraft on the main gear—and brakes.

He glanced once out the windshield, but it was blurred again with rain—the rain-removal system got its hot air from the engines, and there was not enough air whenever the throttles were in idle. He also grabbed his yoke and helped Sandi fight the gusty winds that were trying to raise the wing on her side of the aircraft as the C-141 streaked down the runway.

"Brakes aren't testing well," Sandi said with an edge to her voice that showed her concern.

Hydroplaning, Chisholm thought. There was too much rain on the runway, and the C-141 was floating on the water. "Four greens," he said as the fourth THRUST REV EXTENDED light illuminated, indicating that all four engines were ready to help slow the aircraft.

Sandi yanked the throttles toward full reverse, revving the engines almost to full power. Now the exhaust, which was slamming against the reversers, was being deflected forward.

Even before the reverse thrust took effect, Chisholm felt the C-141's nose coming left as the aircraft started to skid into a ground loop—like a car spinning out of control on a sheet of ice.

Sandi said in a commanding voice, "Copilot's yoke! Keep the wing down!"

"Copilot's yoke," Chisholm said, already holding full aileron into the wind.

As soon as he responded, Sandi grabbed the nosewheel steering wheel near her left knee and tried to turn the nose back toward the far end of the runway.

As the engines wound up, hot air fed into the rain-removal ducts, and Chisholm could see outside clearly again. What he saw was terrifying—his windshield no longer offered a view of the rest of the runway but showed instead the area beyond the side.

Carried by its momentum, the C-141 hurtled along the runway on a thick sheet of water as gusty winds slammed into the huge vertical stabilizer. Lacking the normal friction between the tires and the runway, the C-141 was weathervaning into the wind.

"I've got no nosewheel steering," Sandi shouted as she realized that turning the nosewheels was having no effect on the rain-covered runway.

The landing-gear warning horn blared its chilling shriek as the C-141 skidded sideways. For an instant Chisholm assumed the landing gear was collapsing from the side loads, but there was no sinking or scrapping. He decided that the horn was a false warning, caused by microswitches that no longer were making contact as the gear strained sideways.

By the time the main gust of crosswind died away, the nose had swung through ninety degrees. With less wind now than necessary to stop the rotation and keep the nose pointed into the wind, the spin continued on the slick runway. The C-141 was skidding almost tail first, drifting toward the opposite edge of the runway when the spinning stopped.

During long, boring hours of flying over the oceans, Chisholm often had thought about how to respond in a C-141 that was sliding off a runway. In all those scenarios, however, the aircraft was moving forward, not backward, and he could see where he was going. Now he had no idea whether they were skidding toward drainage ditches, buildings, revetments, or parked aircraft. In addition, the thrust reversers were accelerating the aircraft backward instead of slowing its forward motion.

Chisholm jammed the throttles forward, cutting the power to all four engines and starting to close the thrust reversers. Nevertheless, swirling exhaust gases already were being deflected forward and re-ingested into the big fan-jet engines. As the turbulent air was sucked into the compressors, compressor stalls shook the aircraft with frightening booms. Streaks of fire shot forward from the engines, adding eerie flashes to the gloomy scene beyond the windows.

Chisholm kept forward pressure on the throttles, and as soon as the thrust reversers closed, he pushed the engines toward takeoff thrust. The left main landing gear was sliding off into the mud as the engines took effect. The aircraft was at about half its original takeoff weight, so after skidding a few feet farther into the mud, it leaped forward. Moments later the wheels were back on the runway, and Chisholm pulled the throttles to idle.

"Pilot's aircraft," he said, touching his forehead as if tipping his hat, then extending his hand toward Sandi.

She gave him a wide-eyed look, then said, "Pilot's aircraft." As she caught her breath, she smiled and added, "Not bad for an unqualified passenger."

Sandi taxied the C-141 to a parking spot.

A few minutes later Sandi, Chisholm, and Blake stood together on the flight deck with most of their gear gathered into helmet bags and briefcases. Chisholm noticed the small American flag that still was attached to the panel above the navigator's station. Removing the flag, he started to put it into his briefcase, then changed his mind.

"I think you've earned this, Major," he said, offering the flag to Sandi.

She hesitated, then said, "It was a team effort. Everyone—"

"But our team would've ended up one pilot short if you hadn't insisted on staying with the mission."

He persisted and she finally accepted the small flag. Before she said anything else, a rain-soaked major of the Royal Air Force climbed up from the C-141's cargo compartment.

After brief but proper introductions, he said in a thoughtful tone, "We don't see very many landings like that, Colonel. I thought for a frightful moment that I was going to have to call out the chaplain."

Chisholm slipped his arm around Sandi and pulled her against him, "Keep his number handy. If this bird needs any lengthy maintenance, we may want to use his services anyway."

The British major looked confused.

Blake smiled broadly. "You know what they say, Colonel. If you can't be good—" He paused.

"Be lucky," Sandi said as she nestled against Chisholm, looked up, and flashed the smile that had been his favorite.